The Fall Out

D J ARTHUR

First published in Great Britain in 2021 by
The Book Guild Ltd
9 Priory Business Park
Wistow Road, Kibworth
Leicestershire, LE8 0RX
Freephone: 0800 999 2982
www.bookguild.co.uk
Email: info@bookguild.co.uk
Twitter: @bookguild

Typeset in 12pt Adobe Jenson Pro

Printed and bound by CPI Group (UK) Ltd, Croydon, CR0 4YY

ISBN 978 1913551 766

British Library Cataloguing in Publication Data.
A catalogue record for this book is available from the British Library.

Prologue

In July of 1981, Jane O'Brien gave birth to what proved to be her only child, Marilyn, in a London maternity hospital, after a prolonged and difficult labour. Just over three years later, she was pushing her daughter along the high street when she met the local Catholic priest, Father Delany.

'Let me see the little one, Jane,' he said. 'My, that's a fine-looking wee girl. They aren't babies for long, are they? And how's Mother these days? Feeling happier?'

'Tired, Father, and a bit lonely. Patrick's away again, in Saudi, on those oilfields.'

'Well then, my dear,' he said, taking hold of her hand, 'why don't you come along next Tuesday to our young mothers' group? Get you out of the house, and your low mood, if I may say so, Jane.'

'I'm not—'

'Och, nonsense. See you on Tuesday. Two o'clock sharp now!'

In spite of feeling disinclined to go, Jane got Marilyn ready and strolled along to the church hall. Inside, she was taken aback by the noise of twenty or so babies and toddlers making themselves heard. Marilyn, also surprised by the hubbub, looked up at her mother, holding out her arms, but before she had loosened the buggy strap, a bright, auburn-haired girl, about three, tall, and confident-looking, ran towards them.

'What's your name?' she said to Marilyn in a loud, demanding voice. 'Mine's Anita, and I'll let you be my best friend. Is that your mummy?'

Jane lifted an apprehensive Marilyn out of the buggy, and no sooner had she deposited her on the floor than Anita firmly took hold of her hand, and looking directly up into Jane's eyes with a triumphant expression said,

'It's OK, you can go now. Marilyn's my new forever best friend now. Bye!'

Jane watched as the two girls walked away hand in hand, with Anita talking eagerly to her daughter, thinking that Marilyn, a quiet, reserved child much like herself, would benefit from having a bright, outgoing friend.

As the years passed, the two girls grew closer, going to the same schools all the way through to university. Both entered the hallowed portals of Oxford, Marilyn reading English, Anita modern languages, until, in their final year, an incident occurred which ended their friendship.

Marilyn had started a relationship, platonic, with a fellow student, Gareth, from Wales, who seemed very fond of her, and on a sunny warm evening in June 2002, she decided, their finals being over, to surprise him with a bottle of wine. Her intention had been to consummate the relationship, with the alcohol hopefully giving her Dutch courage, and climbing the stairs to his rooms she imagined, not for the first time, a lasting relationship leading to marriage.

Nervously ringing the doorbell, she thought she could hear the sound of muffled voices, one of them female. After a few moments Gareth opened the door, looking startled.

'Just a minute, Marilyn. I can explain—'

'No need, Gary,' said a half-dressed, flushed-looking Anita, emerging slowly from the bedroom. 'Sorry, Marilyn, don't know what came over me. Still, no harm done. He obviously loves you, and this was only fun. Didn't mean anything.'

Marilyn turned and left the flat, stunned at the action of someone she looked on as a sister. They wouldn't see or speak to each other for the next six years.

*

Two boys, destined to become part of Anita and Marilyn's lives, had come into the world within three days of each other in May 1979 – John Duncan, the older, in Leeds, and David Murray in nearby Bradford. When he was two, David's father was relocated to Headingley, and the boisterous toddler enrolled in a local nursery, which is where they first met. The nursery staff were struck by the immediate rapport between them. Later, they went to the adjoining primary school, and their friendship developed to the extent that, on the regular parents' evenings, their teachers remarked on the closeness of the two – 'like brothers,' one very impressed classroom assistant told John's mother.

It is often said that opposites attract; John was quiet, reserved, with an occasionally sardonic frame of mind, rarely smiling, while David loved, craved, attention and being at the centre of things. Over time the two boys became inseparable, going around to each other's houses after school and on most weekends. David took up cricket, his father being a member of Yorkshire County Cricket Club. He took John one Saturday to see his hero, Geoffrey Boycott, and from that day onwards the friends became avid followers of the game, becoming junior members, attending many first-class games, including test matches at Headingley, on occasion bunking off school to watch their heroes.

Their friendship survived the parting of educational ways; David passed and John failed the eleven plus, and they went off to different schools, but remained close all the way to university.

Chapter One

John and David went along together to the open day at Leeds University, and, both of them happy with the facilities, signed up. After graduating, John joined a firm of brokers in the city, and rapidly made himself very affluent through his uncanny abilities with hedge funds, but left abruptly six years later after a furious row with his boss over the sacking of a junior trader. He took to financial journalism, where he made good use of his many contacts. David, having less of a head for business than his friend, was apprenticed to a firm of family solicitors in central London, near the Inns of Court.

Their days as boys about town were curtailed five years later when David fell head over heels for Anita Wilson, a civil servant in the Foreign Office. The two men saw much less of each other; David's previous interests were relegated as his relationship with Anita ate up virtually all of his free time. John, although disappointed at not seeing his friend as often, could see, on the few occasions they met, that the guy was besotted.

On a frosty March morning in 2008, John took a call from a nervous-sounding David.

'Hi, John, can we meet up for a drink?'

Noticing his friend's anxious-sounding voice, John said,

'Yeah, of course. I was thinking we haven't had a catch-up for quite a while. How about tonight at six, in the White Hart, you know, the one where you tried to pull—'

'Can you make it there in half an hour?'

'It's only ten-thirty, Dave.'

'I know. See you in there at eleven.'

The phone was put down. John was concerned by the urgency of the request; David was among the most confident – to the point of arrogance – individuals he'd ever come across. As he picked up his jacket and walked briskly along to the pub, he became increasingly worried. In the public bar, empty at five to eleven, he strode up to order. A large, thick-set barman sauntered over.

'Two pints of bitter,' John said.

'Right you are, squire. Bad day at the office, is it?'

'Just the two drinks if you don't mind.'

'OK.'

Just as he was paying for the drinks, in walked David. Turning to face him, he said,

'I got your usual, Dave. What's up? Been struck off, have you? Told you not to—'

'Anita's up the duff.'

'Charming way to describe your beloved. I believe "congratulations are in order" is the correct response—'

'You don't understand, mate. It wasn't planned, and neither of us is in a position to—'

'What? I thought you said you were going to propose to her, followed – you seemed set on it – by asking her father for her hand – and the rest of her too of course.'

'Don't you see, John,' said his friend, obviously nervous, 'this could change everything. We'd made plans to get married in a couple of years, saving up and all that, but now...'

'How does Anita feel about this?'

'Oh, she's thrilled. Fate, she calls it. Told me I've finally risen to the occasion. She's good with words.'

'Listen, Dave, stop fussing. Go and ask her father. He might not be best pleased, and you're not exactly Robert Redford, but you've got a good steady source of income. Who's ever met a poor solicitor? Then push on and marry the girl. Before you ask, I'll be your best man.'

*

A month later David and Anita got married in her parents' church. Devout Catholics, they'd insisted on the full service with all the trimmings. Anita being pregnant turned out not to be a problem for them, and as best man, John was a big hit at the reception, giving a humorous, not to say risqué speech. Later, he spotted a tall, strikingly attractive, dark-haired young woman, sitting alone at the bar, wearing a downcast expression.

'Hello,' John said as he walked toward her, 'can I venture to buy you a drink?'

The woman looked at him with large brown, but, so it struck John, sad eyes.

'Thank you. Can I have a tomato juice?'

'No problem. My name's John, John Duncan. Oh, of course you probably know that already.'

She looked directly at him. *Those eyes*, John thought.

'You made a really good speech. You didn't have to come over to—'

'Yes, I did, and I'd really like to know your name.'

'Marilyn. I've known Anita all my life, until we... lost

touch. I was surprised to get her invitation. We haven't spoken since we left university.'

'Well, I'm glad she invited you. Would you care to dance? Compared to my clodhopping friend, I'm a veritable Gene Kelly.'

*

Returned from honeymoon, David called John at work.

'How did you get on with young Marilyn? Anita spotted the two of you deep in conversation at the reception.'

'OK, I think. She's very quiet. We're going to the theatre tomorrow. *Othello* at the National.'

'Listen, John,' David said apprehensively, 'has she mentioned—'

'Mentioned? Mentioned what?'

'Anita told me all about it while we were in Greece.'

John, slightly irritated, said,

'What is it, Dave? I'm in something of a hurry.'

'That's the reason Anita invited her. She felt a certain empathy for the poor girl. They hadn't spoken in years. Funny thing about girls, don't you think, John? One minute they're best friends, the next they aren't talking. Anyway, when I asked her why not, she shut me down, but I got the distinct impression the two of them—'

'What reason, Dave?'

'She was engaged to a guy in the Met, based at Hammersmith nick, I think. They were due to get married a couple of years ago after she discovered she was pregnant, and then, a few days later, the fiancé was murdered, by person or persons unknown. It was very strange—'

'Oh God! What happened to—'

'She collapsed when her head teacher broke the news, and miscarried shortly afterwards.'

John, shocked, said,

'I knew there was something odd, no that's the wrong word, I mean, she's really quiet. We spoke for most of the evening at the reception, but throughout it I can't recall her smiling. Now I know why, but we made a—'

'You're seeing her again then?'

'Yes. Wait, I've just told you, Dave. Still half asleep after your fortnight of debauchery?'

'What are you doing for lunch?'

'Sandwich and orange juice.'

'Come on over to the Admiral Benbow, you know, from the old days. I want a few words of advice re—'

'OK, but I can't be there until two.'

'Lunch is on me.'

John arrived at the pub just after two. He spotted his friend standing at the bar, seemingly engaged in serious conversation with a tall, buxom blonde woman, who looked no older than twenty.

'Hi, Dave, oh sorry, I didn't mean to interr—'

David wheeled round, momentarily embarrassed, going crimson.

'Err… No problem, John. This is Sarah, a colleague from work. She was asking how the wedding went off. This is the dashing best man, Sarah.'

The girl held out her hand and, taking it, John was struck by its clammy feel. She appeared to be embarrassed.

'He's not talking shop, is he?' said John, aware, despite his attempts to hide it, of his friend's discomfort.

'Shop?' replied Sarah, with a puzzled expression. 'Oh no, I work in Dave's other office, in Birmingham.'

'She's down here on a course.'

'He's not laying down the law, is he?'

'No, I'm in the accounts department.'

'Well, Sarah, thanks for the advice on the expense issue. Maybe you'd better get back before you're missed. See you later.'

Sarah, taken aback by his abruptness, said,

'Err... Oh, right. Nice to have met you, Jim.'

She left the pub.

David wiped his forehead.

'I was thinking, John, maybe I shouldn't have put you on the spot.'

'What do you mean?'

'Telling you about Marilyn's background. It was unfair on her really. Anita says she was always the "go to", sensible girl back in their schooldays, although she was a bit of a loner. Anita was her only real friend and—'

'Dave, I'm only going out on a simple date, I haven't proposed to her. Nothing like that's on the cards.'

'OK, OK, John, forget I said anything. What do you want to eat? I fancy some genuine British grub for a change. Anita's very catholic when it comes to food, as well as religion, but you know me, John, nothing beats the old jellied eels.'

*

Although John discounted David's coded – so he thought – message about Marilyn, he mulled over the words more than once prior to meeting her. They'd arranged to go for a meal before *Othello*, and during the three courses John listened intently as she spoke quietly, apparently very relaxed and at ease, even telling him a couple of anecdotes about Anita's less than discreet adventures at university. As the evening progressed, he found himself getting more attracted to her, and, after the play, while discussing Shakespeare in general terms, John knew he would be asking her out again.

'Can I give you a lift back to your place?'

'That's very thoughtful of you, but I can make my own way home.'

'Where do you live?'

'Clapham. Twenty minutes on the Tube.'

'It's very late, and I'm aware the subway can be pretty rowdy, so, please, let me escort you.'

Then he said, immediately regretting it,

'My intentions are strictly honourable.'

Marilyn's eyes narrowed.

'Did you really say that? You can't be so naïve as to think I'd risk going out with someone who wasn't, as you quaintly put it, honourable. I'm going for the Tube. Goodnight.'

She walked out of the pub, looking distinctly unimpressed, bumping past two men trying to get to the bar.

'Wasn't she up for it then, mate?' said one of them, leering at John as he made his way to the exit.

'Piss off.'

Feeling deeply embarrassed, and annoyed at his verbal clumsiness, John went home, thinking that a potential relationship had been torpedoed.

Chapter Two

For the next few days John, despite being extremely busy completing an investigative piece for his paper, mulled over the wisdom, or otherwise, of attempting to speak to Marilyn, but unusually for a man used to making potentially risky decisions, found himself in two minds; if he spoke to her, would she rebuff him? She'd looked angry that night in the pub. On the other hand, he suspected that his continuing thoughts of her meant he wanted to see her again; that there was a connection, certainly on his part.

The article completed, John emailed it off to the paper, closed the laptop and stared blankly at his mobile lying next to the computer on his desk. He picked it up and scrolled through the contacts list, but couldn't see her number. Unsettled, he speed-dialled David.

'Dave the Rave isn't available at the—'

John stopped the call and made for the kitchen, intending to make a coffee. Halfway there, he turned, picked up the mobile again and called Anita.

'Oh, hello there, John, I've been wondering how your date went. I called Marilyn. She said she'd call me back, but so far she hasn't. Always the quiet, deep one.'

'That's why I'm calling, Anita. Can you give me her number? I've lost it somehow and—'

'You sound agitated, John,' she replied, laughing, 'unlike mister calm and collected.'

'Very funny. Even I can lose things on occasion, so, if you could—'

'Yes.'

He dialled Marilyn's number.

'Hello,' she said, 'who am I speaking to?'

'It's John Duncan,' he replied tentatively. 'I was wondering if you'd like to go out again?'

'Were you?'

'Err… Yes, I was, I mean, am. I'd like to see you. How about a trip to Stratford? *Henry V* is on, perhaps the matinee, and then a meal…'

'Yes.'

'You mean—'

'I said yes. I'd like to… see the play. You sound apprehensive. Are you sure you want to see me? I'm not a charity case.'

Emboldened by her response, John regained his customary self-confidence and said,

'Marilyn, I don't do charity cases, or much charity to speak of. Most of them are sinecures for inadequate academic types in my experience.'

'You sound like a journalist.'

'And you're very perceptive, for an English teacher.'

She laughed.

'I knew Anita was wrong.'

'Wrong? What do you mean, John?'

'She assured me you're a serious type, like me, she said.'

'Anita was never diplomatic. Being in the Foreign Office hasn't changed her.'

'So, it's a date then, the Saturday matinee? You can advise me whether Henry's marriage with that French princess was a romance, or merely a diplomatic one.'

Half an hour later, John, his mood considerably improved, decided to try David's number again. At a loose end after completing the article, with nothing on the cards for the rest of the working week, he felt, as someone famous – he couldn't recall who – had described it, 'unbuttoned'. The man himself answered. It was twelve-thirty.

'Hi, John, it's OK, no need to tell me, Anita said you'd asked for mysterious Marilyn's number so—'

'Mysterious? We're going to Stratford on Saturday, but that's not why I called. Fancy a pint? You can meet me at the Benbow... What do you mean, mysterious?'

'No reason. An in-joke with me and Anita. OK, give me twenty minutes. As it's you, I'll make time in my frantic day poring through title deeds...'

'Come on, Dave, let me into the joke. Why mysterious?'

'Anita calls her that, probably from university, but... No, you probably haven't sussed—'

'If she means the woman is quiet, reserved, well, yes, I can see... But it's not a hanging offence, and besides, she seems a capable person. Must be, teaching nowadays... Anyway, how's the pregnancy going?'

'Anita's got me into attending the next scan, the day after tomorrow. All OK so far, but while we're on the subject of procreation, John, I wouldn't bring up... You know, with Marilyn—'

'Yes, Dave, I know, I won't raise the subject with her. I'm not stupid.'

'Of course you're not. Giving up the megabucks in the City to be a scribbler, brilliant I call that. Perhaps Marilyn's the girl to land you. Don't see why you should be the one to escape.'

'Escape? You can't mean that, Dave. You're about to be a parent and—'

'Joke,' said David, slapping his friend on the back.

*

The outing to Stratford turned out to be a great success. They both enjoyed the holiday-like atmosphere of the Bard's home town, and Marilyn seemed relaxed in John's company, so much so that she agreed to a third date.

For the next two months John began increasingly to look forward to seeing her, and they became close relatively quickly. Normally sceptical about personal entanglements, possibly because of his parents' antagonistic divorce and the machinations of several of his erstwhile colleagues in their love lives, he sensed that she was becoming important to him. On a couple of occasions when she'd had to bail on evenings out, he felt almost cheated.

Marilyn was unlike any other female he'd encountered; a notably conservative dresser, tall, with raven-black hair and dark, piercing brown eyes, he thought there was a definite, though understated, charisma about her. He recalled Anita's comment about her being the 'go to' girl, and could understand the reasoning behind the epithet. Marilyn seemed very level-headed, to the point of being almost too serious in John's eyes, but he regarded that as a positive trait. Since leaving university and entering the often frenetic, highly charged world of finance, he'd come across several women whom he might have taken up with – one-night stands in most cases after drink and drug-fuelled gatherings. He'd never really had what could be termed a serious relationship, apart from a girl in his squash club which had petered out because of his fourteen-hour days.

He began to think that his burgeoning feelings for her might be reciprocated; she always greeted him warmly, and the unfortunate first date was a distant memory. Because of his relative inexperience in relationships, John, at the age of twenty-nine, was unsure about taking things with her to a more physical, intimate stage; casual sex with inebriated girls was one thing, but a serious commitment would be a novelty. He was also concerned about Marilyn's possible reaction should he make a false move; how would she respond? John pondered over this, to the extent that on some nights after being out with her he found he couldn't get to sleep. He decided, at the risk of being the butt of David's schoolboyish wit, to ask his advice.

'Are you being serious, John? I've seen you at more than one function with some dazzling bird on your arm, and in your bed later no doubt. What's the problem?'

'The problem is me. Believe it or not, Dave, until now I haven't – no, listen, don't give me that gormless look – I haven't felt anything more than the basic physical drive for anyone, but Marilyn, well, I—'

'John, you know she was engaged before, that she was pregnant until that miscarriage—'

'Your point being?'

'I know you said she's quiet, reserved, as Anita described her, but she's not a nun. In fact, *entre nous*, as the cognoscenti put it—'

John sighed, shaking his head.

'Sorry, mate. I hear she's very fond of you.'

'Who told you that? Anita?'

'No, Santa Claus! Of course it was Anita. I know this because two weeks ago she called Marilyn to see if she wanted to go to some college do in Oxford… their old college, I think, but Marilyn said she couldn't make it because she had an "important" meeting. Turned out the important meeting was with you.'

'Right,' said John, going crimson. 'I'm seeing her tonight.'

'Better stay sober then, Don Juan,' David said, with a wink and a nudge.

*

Later that evening, exiting the cinema, Marilyn said,

'Fancy coming back to the flat for a nightcap, or a coffee?'

'OK, that sounds like a plan,' he replied nervously. 'Can we get a taxi? This rain'll soak us before we get to the Tube, so—'

'Yes, hail that one. He's free.'

And so, the affair began, on the sofa.

Chapter Three

John proposed to Marilyn three months later, during the interval on a night out at the theatre. In the bar, he took out a jeweller's box and put it on the table, much to her surprise.

'John, is this—'

'Yes, it is. Marilyn, the past few months have been… Well, I want to ask—'

'Yes, I will, if you're crazy enough to take the risk—'

'Risk?' John said, more comfortable now that she'd agreed. 'The only risk I could think of was you turning me down. Go on, open it.'

The single diamond sparkled as she examined it before slipping it onto her finger.

From nowhere, tears began to run down her face. She wiped her cheeks with a tissue and said, sounding nervous,

'You know, John, my background is somewhat… I… I've not been completely honest with you, and now I'm—'

'If you're going to tell me about what happened to your fiancé, don't fret, I know all about it, and the mis—'

Marilyn stood, turned away from him and rushed to the

washroom. Ten minutes later, just after the interval bell had rung, she returned, very pale, but apparently composed.

'John,' she said later, when they were having a drink at a nearby hostelry, 'I should have been clear from the start. I hate the fact that… that you might think I was hiding things from you.

'I'd known Grant from primary school, and we only bumped into each other when he brought his niece to school to discuss a problem she was having with another of the English teachers… We started going out, and six months or so later we decided to get engaged, partly because I was pregnant… He was always so thoughtful and caring toward me but, well… Grant was in the Fraud Squad. He'd moved up the ladder very quickly, I suppose because of his expertise in those matters – financial, I mean, and was going to interview a businessman down by Canary Wharf. It's been assumed he'd just finished parking his car when he was struck by another vehicle which didn't stop. He died at the scene…'

'I really don't know what to say, Marilyn, I'm lost for words.'

She carried on, still very nervous, after finishing her drink.

'The headmaster called me to his office the next morning. I was already in a foul mood because Grant hadn't turned up to give me a lift home after a parents' evening. As soon as I went into the head's office I knew, don't know why, just knew, before he managed to give me the news. Next morning, I woke in a private room at the London Hospital, and in came a po-faced doctor to give me the second hammer blow: no fiancé, and no baby either.

'It's taken me two years to get over it. Since it happened, I've put all my waking hours into the job. Having a social life was off the agenda, and it was only when Anita and David sent me the invitation, very much out of the blue, that I ventured out of my self-imposed comfort blanket. I'm glad I did.'

She leant forward and kissed him.

'Thank you, John.'

'What for?'

'Anita joked that you were a bit of a lad, a playboy is how she put it, but I think it's a face you like to put on for public consumption. Just now, when I was regaling you with my sad tale, I could see it in your face—'

'See what?'

'That there's more to you. I think you're a kind, caring person.'

'You sound like my mother.'

'Well, she's right.'

'She has to think it, being my mother—'

'I think it too. When do you want to tie the knot?'

'Anytime you want, Marilyn, and anywhere. I suppose we'll have to plan it around your school commitments. Perhaps in October, during half-term?'

'Yes, that's probably best. It gives us, what, a good month and a half or so to arrange things.'

In his state of exuberance, John blurted out,

'Should we move in together? My place has the advantage of convenience for my work, being near City types, but I think your flat is much—'

'No, John, I'd be uncomfortable doing that. Blame my Catholic upbringing, but I'm not sure it's essential. It's only six weeks or so, and to be honest, I've been thinking of going for a new place. That's maybe something else we could pencil in – a new house for a new couple.'

Taken aback, John said,

'OK, if you want. My flat's worth a fair amount. I've no mortgage, so we could pool our resources and actually get a house, near your school preferably.'

'Yes, I think that's a good idea.'

'It's getting late, and I've got some notes to write up before I send off a piece to the *News*, so how about coming back to my place for the night?'

'Don't laugh, but I prefer to sleep in my own bed. Makes me feel comfortable, emotionally, I mean.'

*

On a very hot, humid late August morning, John was immersed in a project, analysing the prospects for a mooted takeover bid, when his mobile rang out loudly in the quiet of his study: Marilyn.

'Oh, hi there, thought you'd be busy with prep work for the new term, but this is a pleasant surprise. I know, you're taking me for lunch. Maybe that trattoria where we finally—'

'John,' she said, her tone betraying anxiety, 'let's just get married. Now. We can get a special licence and do the deed, then honeymoon in Rome. No point in hanging around, all the fuss and palaver doesn't do it for me…'

She paused, as though catching her breath. John thought he could hear a muffled sob.

'Marilyn,' he said, feeling apprehensive, 'there's no rush, but, if that's what you'd prefer, well, yes, why not? We can discuss this tonight.'

'It is definitely what I want, John. Talk later.'

This was the first time he'd encountered this side of her character. He was convinced, or had been until now, that she was, as Anita had described it, a calm, rational person. Her sudden, unexpected desire to get married quickly unnerved him momentarily. He sat pondering the new situation, and after a few moments, he closed his spreadsheets, turned off the desktop, grabbed his keys and left the flat. He decided to take a stroll around the expanse of Canary Wharf, the streets beginning to fill with City workers making their various ways to grab lunch. It was just after twelve. As he walked along, John thought of why she'd insisted on a quick ceremony; she wasn't pregnant, as far as he knew. Marilyn had sounded anxious, and that noise… was it a sob? If so, why? Never having been romantically involved before, he was, like most men in a similar position, bereft of ideas.

Passing a noisy hostelry, he walked in, strode listlessly up to the bar and ordered a pint of Guinness. He took the glass, sat down at a table near the window and stared out at the now busy concourse. His mobile rang out, the tone insistent.

'Going to answer that, mate?' said a dark-haired, middle-aged man clad in stained overalls. 'Might be your lucky day.'

John stared blankly at the man, and extracted the phone from his jacket pocket, but before he'd managed to open the flap on it, the ringing ceased.

'Don't worry, squire, if it's the trouble and strife she's sure to call you back.'

'Right,' said John, trying hard not to show his irritation, 'probably a cold call anyway.'

'Check the number,' continued the telephony expert, 'if it's withheld you can—'

'Thanks,' said John, as he scrolled the calls list. Marilyn. He quaffed the Guinness swiftly and left the pub.

'Have a nice day now, squire,' bellowed telephony man.

'Prick,' muttered John as he pressed Marilyn's number.

'Hello, John. Sorry for earlier. I've been thinking for the last couple of days we should just go ahead. You said there's no rush, and that made me worry you might be cooling—'

'Marilyn, you shouldn't try to overanalyse my every last word. We'll get married, asap, wherever you want, and then jet off to Italy. I've not been there as it happens. Shall I pick up a few brochures and look at the options? Rome will be hot at this time of year, but who cares?'

'That sounds like a plan. Oh God, I hate that phrase, but yes, we can make arrangements tonight. I've made an appointment to speak with Father McCann this afternoon to get a date and time for the ceremony—'

'In church?'

'Yes, my mother asked me the other day. When I tell her we're getting hitched quickly I can picture her face, and what she'll suspect, but, anyway, I've always imagined getting married, the veil, the sacrament... It was going to be how...'

John, hearing the nervousness in her voice, said,

'No problem, Marilyn, in fact, can I come along with you and talk to the priest? From what you've said, he sounds an interesting character.'

'Four-thirty, at St Patrick's in Hackney. He's keen to meet you too.'

'OK, I'll be there. I'd better get back and finish what I'd started early on this morning. I had something like writer's block, so I took myself out for a walk. Feeling much more lucid now. Bye.'

Chapter Four

The clock on the living room wall chimed: one, two, three. John, startled, raised himself from the sofa, moved quickly into the bathroom, tidied himself up, got dressed and left the flat. On the Tube, he mulled over, again, his fiancée's anxiety over the nuptials. Until their conversation earlier in the day, Marilyn had always displayed a calmness which impressed him. As head of the English department in her school, a position she'd held since she was twenty-five, he knew she had the intellect to weigh up the pros and cons of any issue, so her rush to get married was something he couldn't fathom. She had implied that he might be having second thoughts; did that indicate a needy personality?

John arrived at the church at four-twenty. He walked tentatively down the grave-lined path and into the vestibule, then on into the main building, looked around the empty church and sat on a pew at the back. Five minutes passed. A door creaked behind him. He turned around to see a white-haired, rotund man, dressed in a full-length cassock.

'Good afternoon, my son. You must be Marilyn's young man.'

'Err... Yes, hello,' muttered a nervous John, 'and I take it you're Father McCann. Pleased to meet you.'

'The feeling is mutual, my boy. You look nervous, or should that be terrified? Don't worry, I'm harmless. Come through now to the vestry. Marilyn's in there. She looks nearly as worried as you.'

The two men made their way through the old wooden door, along a dim corridor and turned into a small room. Inside, sitting bolt upright on a very uncomfortable-looking chair, was Marilyn, fidgeting and drumming her fingers on her handbag. When the priest shut the door behind him, she started, turned around, stood and kissed John on his cheek.

'You made it. I was... Well, Father, this is John. He's not a Catholic, but I know—'

'It's not important, my dear,' said the priest, smiling benignly at her and winking at John. 'You know, my boy, Marilyn's always been a serious, thoughtful person, and I wasn't surprised when she asked me to marry you two youngsters. Now then, let's get down to business. My earliest vacancy is Tuesday the ninth, of October that is.'

When the chat with Father McCann had finished, Marilyn said she would go into the church to light a candle. The priest took hold of John's arm and said, making sure she heard,

'Got a minute, my boy? I hear you're an expert on cricket. Some of the boys here are thinking... Oh, go ahead, Marilyn, I'm just picking this young man's brains.'

When she'd left the room, the priest, closing the door behind her, said,

'John, you know something of Marilyn's recent history?'

'Yes, Father. I presume you're referring to her first fiancé?'

'Indeed I am. After the poor man was killed, between you and I, he wasn't really her type, but she was besotted with him, and suffered greatly with depression for a considerable time, and of course the loss of the child tore her world apart. That said, she's come back from the abyss. It's taken a fair amount of time, two years, and, thank the Lord, the last few times she's been to Mass I've noticed a marked improvement in her. Down to you, I'd say.

'Well, John, I'm glad I've had the chance to have this little chat with you. I could see the concern, the love, in your eyes when I was—'

'What was that, Father?' asked Marilyn, as she came back into the room.

Father McCann, flustered, said,

'We were discussing that Botham fella's antics in the Ashes. John here was telling me he—'

'Yes, Marilyn,' John broke in, 'I don't know what you've been telling him about me. I love watching the game, but I'm useless with a bat in my hand. Dave could tell you more than one anecdote—'

'That reminds me, Marilyn,' said the priest, 'I've not seen or heard from either of those two since the wedding, a good few months ago now. I was a tad put out when she chose St Mark's over this place, but hey ho, that's youngsters for you. Is David your best man, John?'

'Oh… I'd better get a move on with that. Listen, Marilyn, if we're finished here, let's pop over to their place after we've eaten. I'll give the joker a call now.'

'Sounds like your husband-to-be is getting in a state. John, Marilyn here told me you were a very focused individual, but then, you aren't the first terrified groom to be standing here. Yes, we are settled then, the ninth of October, two-thirty, and then you can drive off to your reception and honeymoon. Can I ask where you're going? My lips will be sealed, confession-like naturally.'

'Rome, Father. John's booked a small *pensione* near the Vatican.'

'You'll love it. I encountered the Holy City when I attended a seminary there in my youth. The city is magnificent, awe-inspiring, whether you're a believer or not. Well, my dears, if that's all, I'll bid you good day.'

He shook both their hands, made the sign of the cross over their heads and walked back into the church.

After leaving the building, John called David.

'Hello, mate, how's it hanging?'

'Same as usual, John, a bit tired of late though. Overworked, if you—'

'Dave, do you fancy popping out with Marilyn and me tonight, say seven? With Anita too.'

'OK, we're both free. Come to think of it, we've not met up for a while. Been busy, have you? Keeping Marilyn happy, if you know what I mean—'

'Only too well. We need to ask you something, a favour if you like. Marilyn's keen to—'

'Keen eh? You lucky git… Joke, Johnny boy.'

'As subtle as ever, Dave.'

'Try my best. Give me a clue. What kind of favour? Some legal advice about your dodgy mates in the City?'

'Not exactly, but we can go through it tonight.'

'That was a funny conversation, John. Do you think he knows why we want to meet up? He's normally fast on the uptake.'

'Yes, he is,' said John, looking puzzled, 'but no matter. If he hasn't guessed, he'll know soon enough. Come on, let's get some food inside us. I'm famished now. Didn't manage to eat anything for lunch. To be honest, I was dreading meeting up with Father McC… Jeez, I've forgotten his name already.'

'McCann.'

'Right… Yes. I'm relieved now, having survived the Inquisition. He's not so—'

'What was he droning on about while I was—'

'Oh, he took the opportunity to regale me with his views on how cricket, and sport in general, is being compromised by the big bucks.'

Marilyn, her eyes narrowing, said,

'Yes, of course he was, and I believe you. Was it a fierce lecture on the sanctity of marriage?'

'Something like that. The man loves to talk,' John said, relieved she hadn't pressed him, and more relaxed, continued, 'He's certainly quite fond of you.'

'Before he got the senior job there, he was in charge of the choir. The place has always had a strong musical background. I joined the children's choir at five and he encouraged me to take my singing further. "It's a gift from the Almighty," he often told me. When I was older, I joined the Gilbert and Sullivan group in Hackney. Did a few lead roles, but when I went to university, my studies took over.'

'There you are. I've discovered something new about my fiancée! Not only is she a gifted teacher, she's a budding Maria Callas.'

'Nothing like. I'm – or was – a contralto. I used to be a regular attendee at the South Bank, mostly for orchestral, you know, classical. I've not asked, what's your taste in music?'

'Oh, this and that, mainly—'

His mobile rang.

'John, make it eight, in the White Hart, you know it. I've cleared it with Her Majesty. She's very curious. Anything to tell me? A clue? You haven't got her—'

'See you, Dave, at eight.'

Chapter Five

The White Hart, an old-fashioned, traditional pub set in a quiet residential area less than ten minutes from John's pad, was crowded and noisy when Marilyn and John entered the lounge bar. Casting his eyes round, he didn't spot the Murrays, who were sitting behind a pillar at a large table.

'Hi, you two!' shouted David as he stood and walked over. 'Busy tonight. What are you drinking?'

'A Guinness and a vodka and tonic thanks, Dave. Where's Anita?'

'Back there. You go on over, Marilyn. John and me'll bring over the bevys.'

Marilyn nodded and walked away toward Anita.

Standing at the bar waiting for the drinks, David piped up, 'So, what's the great secret? You've got Anita dreaming up all kind of possibilities.'

'Don't be so melodramatic. I'm not surprised that you haven't been able to work it out, but I was sure that your wife would have, within ten seconds.'

David's brow furrowed. He stroked his chin, looking curiously at his friend. The penny dropped.

'You haven't—'

'Yes, Dave, I proposed and she said yes. That's why we wanted to speak with the two of you tonight. Will you return the favour?'

'What?'

'Best man duties…'

'Well, John boy, you're aware of my very crowded schedule over the next few months—'

'The ninth of October, in St Patrick's, Hackney.'

'Christ, John, you're planning well ahead, aren't you? That's, what, thirteen months away.'

'No, Dave, this October.'

'Are you telling me she's—'

'Don't go there, Dave, but no, she's not.'

'Then why the rush? I understood Marilyn's a serious, cautious type.'

'She is, but as she said, there's no point in hanging around. Marilyn insists that what she calls the flummery of a big do isn't a priority for her.'

'Like it is for you, John. Still, even without the "flummery" I know it's always the man who compromises.'

'Strange observation for a man married less than a year himself.'

'Taking me seriously, are you? Come on, the girls will be thinking we've eloped. Probably thirsty by now too.'

Walking over to the table, John was puzzled at his friend's flippant, not to say cynical, attitude. David had always been light-hearted, the type of person who didn't appear to take life seriously, but since he'd met Anita, he had shown a more thoughtful approach. Now, his remarks seemed to point to a man still imbued with a bachelor ethos, or perhaps it was Dave being, well, Dave.

'Hi, John,' said Anita, her eyes sparkling with anticipation. 'Come on now, don't be shy.'

'Shy?' said John. 'How are things going with you?'

'Never mind me, do you have something to tell us? I've already asked Marilyn here. All she did was blush.'

John exchanged glances with Marilyn, who nodded her head.

'We're getting married, on the ninth of next month. I've explained to Dave. We see no reason to hang about... And before you say anything, Anita, Dave's agreed to be my best man.'

'Of course he has, but what's my role going to be?' said Anita, looking at David, who began to fidget.

'My maid of honour. I'd like that.'

'Oh, would you now?' said Anita, suddenly looking stony-faced. 'Well, OK. That's cutting it fine, three weeks. I'll need to liaise with you re the outfits. Who will you be having for bridesmaids?'

Marilyn, as taken aback as John at her abrupt change of mood, said,

'It'll be a quiet ceremony, so, just the four of us with Father McCann. He—'

'Why the secrecy? A wedding is a big thing, a celebration and—'

'No secrecy, Anita, I just want an intimate affair, with no fuss.'

Anita gulped down her vodka, and tapped her fingers on the table. Lifting the glass, she barked at David,

'I'd like, really like, another one of these, Dave. Go and get it please... Shake yourself!'

A depressed-looking David excused himself and walked off to the bar. Anita looked directly at Marilyn and said, trying to ease the tension,

'Sorry, Marilyn, I didn't mean to be short. It's just that I love weddings, the bigger the better, but hey, we all have our views on such matters. I'd be glad to be your maid of honour, especially as I'm certain you must have dozens of friends and acquaintances closer to you than I am—'

'Yes, Anita, I'm sure you'll do a great job,' said a clearly irritated John, having picked up the ambivalent remark, and moving the strained conversation away from the wedding, he asked,

'How's the pregnancy going?'

'My last scan was normal. David wanted to know the sex, but I'm old-fashioned, he'll have to wait. You know, he's got names and schools lined up for his "little buddy". It's bound to be a boy, he says, as if he'd know. He'll have to take what he's given and—'

'Did I hear my name being taken in vain?' said David, arriving at the table with two drinks, his and Anita's.

'No, you didn't, Dave.'

John and Marilyn looked furtively at each other.

'Anything else to tell us about you two?' said Anita, picking up her glass.

'No that's it, I'm afraid,' said John.

'There's no vodka in this glass, Dave.'

'No, that's right,' he replied, 'it's time for you to abstain. Not good for the bambino.'

'He's getting to be my prison guard.'

'Better hope John doesn't develop similar tendencies, Marilyn. They can't help it. We have to control them. It's like house-training a puppy.'

'No,' said a nervous-sounding Marilyn, 'he won't. Wouldn't have said yes to him otherwise.'

'Oh, they all start out full of empathy, but once—'

'Let's call it a night, guys,' said David, his face displaying irritation. 'I think all this is getting a bit too emotional. So, you'll let us know the arrangements in due course?'

'Don't be stupid, Dave, it's called planning,' Anita said, rolling her eyes at Marilyn. 'And you want him as your best man, John? Very brave of you.'

'Yes, we'd better be making a move too,' said an increasingly nervous John. He picked up Marilyn's jacket, and they left the lounge, with their companions still talking somewhat heatedly about Anita ordering a second drink.

Chapter Six

As the day of the wedding drew near, both John and Marilyn felt the tension rising. In spite of the fact that they had wished for a small, intimate ceremony, the ordering of the various aspects common to any nuptials had turned out to be more fraught than either of them could have imagined, primarily because of Anita's involvement. She took the maid of honour role very seriously, to the point where Marilyn had expressed to John that she wished she'd never asked.

'My mother would have been less trouble,' she advised him more than once in the remaining time leading up to the big day.

Seeing the effect Anita was having on a nervous Marilyn, he decided to have a quiet word with his friend.

'What's wrong with her, John?' asked Dave, puzzled. 'I can't see the problem. Anyone would think she didn't want to get married at this rate. It's just pre-wedding nerves. Anita wanted the whole world and his wife to know about us getting hitched, took control of every little detail. Who can understand the female of the species?'

'Marilyn sees it differently. She hates flashiness in anything and—'

'So, you're telling me my wife's—'

'No, Dave, I'm not having a go at Anita. We both understand she's enthusiastic. Maybe I shouldn't have mentioned it. In any case we're only just over a week away.'

'That's right,' said David, more relaxed now that his friend had rowed back. 'Are you fit for the stag night? I've booked a table at the tandoori place along the road from our favourite watering hole.'

'Yes, Friday night. Who've you invited?'

'Your cousin Andy, plus some of your old mukkas from the money factory.'

'Right. Well, Dave, I'm glad we've had this little *tête à tête*. Don't mention it to Anita.'

'I'm not stupid, John,' David replied, with a wry smile.

*

The wedding and reception went off very well. Marilyn's nerves, which had given John no end of worry, evaporated once she'd got to the altar, and they jetted off to Rome, arriving there on a warm, sultry evening. They spent the next four days traipsing around as many of the tourist traps as their legs would allow. On their first excursion, John, in spite of his innate scepticism toward organised religion, was nonetheless awestruck by the Vatican, St Peter's in particular, and as the two of them stood, watching believers with devoted expressions file past the statue of the founder of Catholicism, he felt a lump in his throat. Later, as they climbed the seemingly endless staircase to the top of the cathedral, he said, breathlessly, to Marilyn,

'Will you be going to the Mass at four o'clock?'

'I think I will, John. You can have a wander round the museum while—'

'I'll join you, at Mass, I mean.'

'Oh, really? You don't—'

'I know, I don't, but…'

She smiled at him and said,

'It's an overwhelming place, isn't it? The atmosphere startled me too. I used to think my Catholicism was tepid to say the least, but being here's brought back the power of the message for me.'

While they sat in a small restaurant that evening, John's thoughts kept returning to the unexpected, emotional reaction he'd experienced earlier. It troubled him, and the following day, while standing in the Sistine Chapel, looking up at Michelangelo's handiwork, he ruminated on the Mass he'd attended with Marilyn. The majesty of the ceremony, with its air of unworldly mystery, and the grandeur of the cathedral itself, combined to give John an inkling of the power which the Catholic Church had wielded over the peoples of Europe and beyond. His own background in matters religious had been attendance at Sunday school in a Methodist chapel in Leeds. Once he'd reached his teenage years, John left organised religion behind; indeed, his only steps inside any church before his marriage had been accompanying his widowed mother to Christmas Eve carol services.

'Where will we go tomorrow, John… John, are you listening?'

'Sorry, I was miles away. You know, Marilyn, I'm really glad we came here. My first idea for the honeymoon was Venice. You and me, drifting along the Grand Canal, with the gondolier serenading us with—'

'"O Sole Mio"?' said Marilyn with a quiet chuckle.

He looked at her smiling face, the eyes glittering.

'Well, husband?'

'Well what?'

'Tomorrow's itinerary.'

'Let's change the emphasis. The Colosseum, Forum, and maybe the baths, what are they called? You know, the ones where those three opera guys sang during the World Cup…'

'Caracalla.'

'Yes, that's it.'

'John,' whispered Marilyn, her eyes dancing, 'pay the *maître d'*, and then back to our room.'

*

They checked in at the airport, leg-weary, on another hot, sticky day. Marilyn wandered over to one of the many tourist shops, telling John she'd like to get a small gift for her mother.

'She always wanted to come here with my father, but now that he's gone, and with her arthritis, she doesn't feel able to—'

'Go on, I'll be right with you. I'm going to pick up an English paper over there.'

John, having bought the paper, walked back toward the shops where Marilyn had gone. He couldn't spot her at first, and cast his eyes around the large concourse. Then he saw her, standing, a shopping bag in her hand, hesitantly conversing with a tall, swarthy man, well-dressed, who was jabbing his finger at her. She looked upset. Annoyed, and worried, John moved forward briskly, nearly breaking into a run.

'Marilyn!'

The man, hearing John's angry-sounding voice, looked round briefly, then turned and marched away quickly. Marilyn stood, fumbling with the bag, as though searching for something in it.

'Who's that guy? He seemed to be hectoring you. Tell me. You look upset.'

'Oh... I...'

'What on earth's the matter, Marilyn? You are upset. What did that man want? Does he know you?'

'He gave me a shock, John,' she said, slowly recovering some composure. 'He was asking for Anita's phone number, told me he needed to settle something with her.'

'What made him think you—'

'He said he recognised me from a photo Anita showed him.'

'Did you—'

'No, but he got quite agitated. Maybe she had some kind of liaison with him before. Never mind him, do you think my mother will like this?'

She took out a small but expensive-looking replica of St Peter's from the bag.

'What do you think? OK, it's a bit tacky, but she likes this kind of gift. When we used to go away on holiday, Mum was forever searching around the shops for them. Drove my father mad.'

'Yes, her house does resemble...'

He stopped, having eyeballed the man who'd harassed Marilyn, standing next to a photobooth.

He was staring back at the two of them with a distinctly unfriendly expression.

'Wait here. I'll go over and put the guy straight, accosting you like that.'

'No... No, John,' she said, taking hold of his arm, 'please, don't, just forget it!'

'OK, if you insist,' he said, but the incident unsettled him for the rest of their journey back to London. He recalled her anxious face as the guy was, so it appeared, haranguing her, and he wondered why he'd been so anxious for Anita's contact details. Very well and expensively dressed, in a three-piece suit complete with collar and tie, he wouldn't have looked out of place in the City, John mused.

Going through to the arrivals lounge, they were surprised to see their surname being held aloft by a uniformed man with a peaked cap.

'Oh, look, John! Did you organise this?'

'No, I didn't,' he said, perplexed, 'we can ask the guy about it.'

'Hello, Mr and Mrs Duncan. Where to?'

'Hackney, Eggleston Road, number 28.'

'Right you are, sir, and madam. Was Rome up to expectations?'

'Err... Yes, but can I ask who's organised this? We were looking forward to a pleasant hour on the Tube.'

'Sorry, sir, and madam, I only take orders, don't give 'em. Here's the card for Merton Limousines.'

John took the offered card and examined it. The text included both landline and mobile numbers, an email address, but he was wrong-footed by the absence of a postal one.

'Where are you based... Err...'

'Jack. Sorry, I work from home. This car's on personal contract. They get hold of me when I'm required... Then they send my money direct to the bank. All very easy. Good business for me, and that's before any tips... Oh, I didn't—'

'John, do you think one of your work colleagues might have organised—'

'No, I left the City ages ago, and I've had no contact with them since... since we fell out, big time. They'd more likely—'

'Oh yes, of course, John. I'm not close enough to anyone who'd dream this up. Who could it be?'

'A real mystery, but I'll make enquiries with these… these Merton Limousines people.'

Overhearing this, the driver said,

'Good luck with that, sir. When they first came to me, the boss – no, I don't know his name – emphasised the confidentiality aspect. Most of the celebs I've picked up insist on it, or so he told me.'

'We'll see about that,' whispered John, irritated in spite of the favour a person unknown had done. He hated surprises, especially ones which were shrouded in mystery, and he thought anyone springing this kind of stunt would certainly make themselves known. Taking out his wallet, John put the card carefully into it, and resolved to contact 'Merton Limousines' one way or another.

Chapter Seven

Marilyn took off for work early the following morning. Extremely conscientious, she'd indicated to John her desire to meet and greet the four new recruits to her department.

'I know what it's like, going to your first post as a new teacher,' she told an impressed John. He, after a disturbed night, checked his laptop for messages; seventy-four popped up. He sighed as he scrolled down the list, deleting the overwhelming majority, until he came across one from Merton Limousines. The message read simply, 'Mr Duncan, please see attached the invoice for your recent order. We hope you enjoyed our service, and should you have any comments on it, or our chauffeur, please don't hesitate to contact us. Regards, Merton Limousines.'

Gobsmacked, he opened the attachment: an invoice for £250.

'This is way beyond a fucking joke,' he said aloud, and angrily. 'I'll get to the bottom of this!'

He drafted a very acid response, recommending, in graphic terms, what they could do with their invoice, and was about to send it off when his mobile rang: Marilyn.

'Hello, John, I didn't wake you, did I? Listen, my colleagues here have given me, us, a really lovely gift—'

'Oh? What?' John said, as he stood and moved into the lounge.

She picked up on his tone.

'Are you OK?'

He decided not to mention the invoice.

'Sorry, just a bit jet-lagged. What have they given you?'

'Us, John, us.'

'Yes, sorry.'

'Two tickets for *Les Misérables*, in the Grand Circle, and, get this, a table for dinner at the Ritz.'

'They must think an awful lot of you, Marilyn. Not as much as me, obviously, but, well, you deserve it.'

'What are you doing today?'

'Nothing in the diary, but I'm thinking of dropping in on Fred McTaggart. I think I've mentioned him before. He dropped me an email asking if I'd like to do an extended piece on the likely consequences on the City, in financial terms, money markets and so on, of the country's possible exit from—'

'I'm falling asleep over here, John.'

'OK, OK. He's emailed me again, suggesting we meet up, so I'm going to respond. He likes big lunches. One of the declining tribe of journos and City types who enjoy a midday gorge.'

'Right, well I'll be finished by four today, so if you like, I could do a quick dash round the local Tesco on my way home, unless you don't want to have—'

'No, I won't be overindulging.'

'OK, John. When can I expect you?'

'If I manage to get hold of Fred, we'll likely be meeting up at twelve, so I'll probably be home before you. It's only twenty or so minutes back from Canary Wharf. Old Fred used to love the set-up back in what he likes to call the "golden age" before the Wharf changed everything.'

'Talking shop, are we? I'd better go back to my new recruits. They all look so young and, if I didn't know better, terrified.'

'Young? Thus spake the ancient twenty-nine-year-old.'

'Very funny, John. Bye for now.'

John smiled, closed the call and walked back to his desk in the study. He scrolled down the emails, clicked on McTaggart's, and sent a reply suggesting a meet for twelve in the Hangman's Rest, near Canary Wharf. Within thirty seconds came the reply.

'Thanks for getting back, Johnny boy. No problem, I'll have your tipple on the bar by the stroke of twelve sharp. Unfortunately, your favourite barmaid, you remember, Jolene, got the boot a few weeks back. Gave a feisty customer a lager shower! Oh, Christ, what am I saying! You've been hooked, line and sinker too. Sorry, old man. Looking forward to any sleaze you've got on… oh, I don't care, anyone!'

John smiled at the screen as he read, with some amusement, Fred's characteristically florid way of communicating. The man could be mistaken, in appearance if not in accent, for Les Patterson, the famous Australian diplomat. Tall, ruddy-complexioned, with a perpetually scruffy mass of white hair and less than perfect teeth, he was a regular, valued patron at more than one hostelry.

After quitting his lucrative, frenetic job as a trader, John had briefly worked for Fred, then editor of a small, politics-focused publication. The magazine was his pride and joy, full of rumour and gossip on political and, occasionally, City matters, which, because of Fred's cavalier attitude to checking facts, had led to not infrequent apologies, couched in language which was usually ambiguous.

'He actually bought me a drink, Johnny boy, didn't spot the irony in the piece,' Fred told him after one politico had come to the magazine to thank him in person for his 'apology'. 'What a prick. Bound to make it to the top of the greasy pole. He's devious enough to climb it, a future PM.'

*

John walked through the glass doors of the Hangman's Rest, an odd name for a pub nestled amongst the gleaming tower blocks, John had always thought when he'd been a regular. He spotted his old colleague, sitting on a stool, shamelessly flirting with a tall, blonde barmaid. He tapped Fred on the shoulder.

'Well, if it ain't the ex-City slicker himself? Long time no see, you crafty bugger!'

'Hello to you too, you old reprobate,' John said, shaking Fred's hand. 'Still on the sauce then?'

'Johnny boy, I never touch sauce, gives you bad breath. Doesn't impress the ladies, you see. That's right isn't it, Brenda?'

'I'm Belinda,' said the barmaid, faintly amused at Fred's verbal gymnastics.

'That one's yours, old boy. You don't have to ask the missus for permission, do you? You know, Brenda—'

'Belinda.'

'You know, Belinda, my ex-wife was forever scolding me about my refreshment strategy. When I told her how it was, the strategy, I mean, she couldn't understand it, so she left. Unlike you of course, Brenda, some women can't comprehend such—'

'I shouldn't have to ask, Fred, do you want another of those?'

'No, you shouldn't, and, Brenda, sorry, Belinda, bring over a little chaser to keep the bitter company.'

Belinda walked off, smiling.

'Only a joke, old boy, about the missus. A teacher, I hear.'

'Yes, but listen, Fred, you asked about my availability for an extended—'

'I asked… Oh, yes, how would you like… that is, would you be interested in researching, and then writing, a piece on the possibilities, likely outcomes if you will, for the services sector, of the UK exiting the prison camp they call the Single Market?'

'If you want, Fred. I've nothing specific on at the moment. I had considered venturing into fiction, maybe some kind of thriller, but what with getting hitched, the idea melted away—'

'Fiction, you say. Isn't that what most journos, the political guys, the pundits, write these days?'

'Are you including yourself in that put-down, Fred? I seem to recall, let me see now, some of your scoops got you into scalding water.'

'Ah, you're wrong there, my young friend. I always considered my "scoops", as you describe them, to be genuine. These days digging out chicanery is *passé*. Coming across an honest politico, now, that would be a headliner. Well then, are you up for it? The article, I mean. Usual rate, naturally.'

John looked at his old colleague, and said,

'Can I get back to you, Fred, tomorrow if that's OK? I'll admit, the idea appeals. No, what the hell, I'll do it. Can I ask you something though?'

'Shoot.'

'Why a piece about the EU now? I'm well aware of rumblings about our membership of the EU, but we've not tied ourselves to the Euro—'

'Johnny boy, I'm convinced there's an undercurrent of antipathy to the project in the country, away from the "establishment" types. All I'm looking for is a forensic piece on what would happen if—'

'OK. I'll do some preliminary work. When do you want the finished piece?'

'No rush, but before Christmas. Yes, you can stand me another one, as you're insisting.'

*

On the Tube going back to Hackney, John found himself eager to start. As he'd indicated to his old friend, he had been making some notes regarding a novel, but since meeting Marilyn the project had fallen into abeyance. Now he had a specific task to get his teeth into.

Turning the corner into his street, he saw Marilyn, lugging two heavy-looking shopping bags. He called out. She looked back, then stopped while he rushed forward to greet her.

'Hi. Is this what you call picking up a few things?'

'I thought I might as well stock up, that corner shop is expensive. We need to be more rational when it comes to food shopping.'

'Rational, is it?' John said, with a sly look. 'A novel way to describe being thrifty.'

'Are you trying to be funny?'

'No. Sorry, but you should have called me. These bags weigh a ton.'

'Yes, they do. Can you take hold of them? I'll get the key.'

He took the bags and they climbed the half dozen stairs to the front door. John moved through to the kitchen, deposited the bags on the floor and said,

'Fancy a coffee? Thirsty work talking to Fred McTaggart. He asked—'

'Yes, leave the bags for the moment. What did he want?'

'He's lined me up for an investigative piece, a big one. Probably keep me occupied for a month or two.'

'So, you've agreed to do it then?'

'Provisionally, yes. It'll mean a lot of digging and talking to quite a lot of people. Old Fred, the devious git, he knows I've still got many contacts in the City.'

Marilyn frowned.

'Do you hanker after your days there?'

'No, I'd never go back. Being self-employed's much more rewarding, if you discount the financial side of it.'

Chapter Eight

A week later John was sitting at his desk, busily typing up notes from his initial enquiries when his email pinged. He finished the sentence and clicked on his email box. A solitary unopened message, from Merton Limousines. The text read:

'Mr Duncan, this is a gentle reminder; the attached invoice is overdue for payment.'

He sat back, scratched his head, becoming angry at the intrusion. Perhaps they hadn't received his answer, or else it had been ignored. Determined to settle the mystery, he called the mobile number listed at the foot of the invoice. Ten rings later, a young woman answered.

'Good afternoon, my name's Elsie. How can I help?'

'Hello... err, Elsie. Your company has sent me an invoice—'

'What's the number?'

John read it out and said,

'I think there's been a mistake. I didn't order the limousine.'

'Your name is Mr J. Duncan?'

'Yes.'

'Well, if you can hold for a minute, I'll check.'

Nearly ten minutes went by until Elsie could be heard sitting down on a decidedly squeaky chair.

'Mr Duncan, according to the order book, we took a call from your office on October the seventh and booked the car for the fourteenth, for a journey from Heathrow terminal five, to—'

'Wait, I don't know who called from my "office" simply because I don't have one, so it follows,' John said, adopting the pompous tone he fell into when agitated, 'that you're mistaken.'

Silence on the other end of the line until John said,

'Was it you who took the order?'

'Yes, it was.'

'Did this person leave his name, as a contact?'

'No, but—'

'Then, no buts about it, I did not require a limo.'

'Oh... Yes... I remember now, it was a woman's voice. She was quite rude when I asked for her name, you know, as a reference. Sorry.'

'Is that all you can remember?'

'The office was crowded with people that day, we had a big wedding and—'

Getting very angry, John barked,

'Tell me your address, and the name of your boss. I want this matter cleared up.'

She read out the details, sounding nervous.

'I'll be there in an hour. Let Mr Jarvis know.'

Realising he'd not told Marilyn about the invoice, he decided to find out the identity of the person who'd made the order before telling her, and, just as importantly, why the practical joke had been instigated. He arrived at Merton Limousines' shabby-looking, two-storey building; it consisted of a garage on the ground floor, with a metal door leading to the office upstairs. When he rang the bell, he noticed a rat trap parked next to the door.

'Yes, what do you want?' said an irritated male voice with a strong West Country accent.

'Hello, it's John Duncan.'

'Bully for you. What is it?'

'I've come to sort a problem and—'

'We don't do problems here, mate, try the Samaritans.'

'I spoke to Elsie a couple of hours ago, about a duff invoice, and I'm not leaving until I speak to someone in authority here,' said John, lapsing again into his pompous mode.

'Duff invoice? Oh, right, you're the geezer who ordered the Heathrow job.'

'No, I'm not the "geezer", some joker's played a trick on both of us.'

The door buzzed open. John clambered up the fifteen stairs and pushed through the wooden door into a small, untidy room. A tall unshaven man, about fifty, with greying, longish hair, was fumbling through official-looking papers. A young, blonde woman, probably about twenty-five, whom John presumed to be Elsie, was staring at a desktop screen.

'OK, squire, what's the story?'

'Hasn't your assistant told you?' John said, and looking toward her, he went on,

'Now then, Elsie, can you divulge the name of the person who called?'

'Err... No, she didn't give me her name, I told you that. Sorry, Mr Jarvis, she sounded, well, very official. Scary too.'

'What? Scary? So, there you have it, Mr... Mr Jarvis, you've sent the invoice to the wrong person. I can't help you regarding payment, though I have to say, it's surprising—'

'What's surprising?'

'That a new customer places an order and yet you didn't want payment up front.'

Mr Jarvis was getting redder by the minute. He looked daggers at Elsie, who leant forward and locked her eyes onto the screen.

'Did this woman give you any details, Elsie?' he barked, clearly wrong-footed.

She passed him a docket. Jarvis looked at it, then handed it to John, who examined it carefully.

'That is my email, but there's no postal address. Very odd, particularly as the limo was booked to take us home. I would have thought you'd require the destination details to establish a price. Anyway, you can take it as a fact that I won't be coughing up for the hire.'

'But you ordered the job. The email address, that says you did.'

'You think so? This piece of paper, what you'd likely use as a purchase order, isn't signed, which renders the thing worthless, as far as a contract goes. Sorry.'

John turned around and walked out of the office. On the Tube, he wondered about the mystery individual who'd taken it upon herself to play such a crude, unfunny prank. The fact that no address had been given to the firm might indicate that the woman didn't know where John lived; alternatively, it could mean that the person was attempting to maintain anonymity. But why?

Turning the key of their front door, he was greeted by Marilyn, who shouted from the kitchen,

'Where've you been? I was expecting to see you glued to that screen in the study. Dinner's been ready for the last ten minutes.'

'Sorry, I had to see a man about a dog—'

'I hate, hate, that expression, John,' she said as she put two plates on the dining table. 'It's so slovenly, lazy. You're a journalist, not a wide boy.'

'Speaking of wide boys, I discovered the address of the limo company, that's why I'm late. The boss, a guy by the name of Jarvis, showed me the order. It had my email, but not our address, and the thing was unsigned. His assistant said a woman called them from my "office" and placed the order. Very mysterious, and anyway, I haven't got an—'

'Should you tell the police, John? It's a very odd, bizarre thing to have happened. Worrying.'

'No crime's been committed, Marilyn, unless you look at it from Jarvis's viewpoint. He's lost out on a job worth 250 smackers. He was less than pleased.'

'I can't think of any criminal, sinister motive for it though. Tell you what, I'll get in touch with an outfit I used to patronise occasionally back in my City days for digging up background information on individuals I suspected of... Yes, I'll give old Graham a bell tomorrow.'

Marilyn seemed uncomfortable as she said,

'Do you think that's wise? On second thoughts, maybe we should just ignore it. We can put it down as a schoolboy "joke". You've told me often enough about the excesses, fuelled by drink or drugs, which went on, maybe still do—'

'I think your assessment might well be on the mark, but Graham's an old pal, and he's also very good at digging.'

Standing up and taking hold of the dinner plates, Marilyn said, in a more light-hearted tone,

'By the way, Anita phoned me today, at school. She can certainly pick her moments. I was in conference with the head about changes to the timetables. I've got to take over a class of year sevens from the start of next term, not what I was expecting and—'

'What was she after?'

'Nothing. She's invited us to dinner at the weekend. You know how she loves to show off her culinary talents. I asked her what was the occasion. She advised me, in that special tone of hers, that it was merely a polite invitation to see old friends. "We haven't seen you two in ages," she said. "Dave's been away in Manchester on cases, and it's time for a catch-up.'"

'I see,' said an amused John. 'Saturday or—'

'Sunday, two o'clock.'

'Are we going? You don't sound keen.'

'Oh, yes, I don't see why not. Anita told me the baby's due in two weeks now, but she's taking it all in her stride. "A piece of cake" is how she described being pregnant. Typical of her. Everything in life's either a piece of cake or—'

John stood, walked over to his wife and kissed her.

'It's… I'm OK, John. Water under the bridge. *Que sera…*'

'Listen, Marilyn, fancy popping along to that quaint, old-fashioned pub down the road for a couple of drinks—'

'We've got a bottle of red from—

'No, come on, let's move. We've both had somewhat trying days. I think they have quiz nights on Thursdays, and we make a good team.'

Half an hour later John and Marilyn were sitting at a table in the public bar. As John had mentioned, the pub, the Red Lion, a traditional East London hostelry, held weekly quiz nights, and the two joined in eagerly, winning the first prize after five rounds of fiercely contested questions, with Marilyn correctly answering the final one, a quote from Oscar Wilde, 'the heart is made to be broken'.

'I knew you'd nail that one, Marilyn.'

'Why did you say that? I teach English. Don't care for Wilde, but that line is truth spoken in jest. Unlike many of his witticisms, I think he believed it.'

On the way home John, slightly tipsy after five pints of bitter, not his usual drink, stopped, put his arms around Marilyn, kissed her and said,

'I'm glad you agreed to marry me, really glad.'

'I'm so happy you're glad,' she replied. 'You sound under the influence.'

'Yes, I am, but still, I meant what I said. Listen, don't bother about Anita's moods, it's just her way. Dave told me she can be a handful.'

'So can he, I'd guess. Anita said he's away a lot on business, trying to ingratiate himself with the partners, I'll bet.'

Chapter Nine

They arrived at Anita and David's bright, terraced house in Barnes by taxi at precisely two o'clock. As John was paying the cabbie, their front door opened and David shouted,

'Well done, guys, you're just in time for the starter. Anita's been slaving away all morning, sent me off to the White Hart. I'm only back five minutes ago. Come on. Hurry up.'

He looked flustered. John could smell his telltale breath when he was ushered into the dining room.

'Hi, Anita!' said John. 'Something smells good.'

'It's the taste that counts,' said the serious-looking cook. 'Sit down, both of you.'

They sat down dutifully, Marilyn opposite her husband. David, moving somewhat erratically around the small table to his seat, asked,

'Who's for a spot of liquid grapes? This one here, it's Australian, but then, you can't have everything, and I—'

'For Christ's sake, Dave, get to your place,' barked Anita, 'I'll do the wine. None for you after your excursion to spittoon city.'

John exchanged furtive glances with Marilyn. Anita said, while pouring the wine for them,

'He's such a plonker at times, Marilyn. I don't know how he'll cope with a small person in the house. Did I tell you the names he fancies for the boy?'

'You know the sex of the child? I thought you didn't want—'

'Gender, Marilyn, gender. Get the terminology right, dear. Anyway, he was droning on about how advantageous it would be. No, Marilyn, I can't see how either. He was desperate to find out, so in a weak moment I concurred. Yes, it's a boy.'

'Come on, Dave, give us all a laugh,' said John playfully, 'we can take it. Peregrine? Jocelyn? Algernon?'

David winced, and replied,

'Well, since you ask, I've always considered my own moniker pretty good, but—'

'He asked me if I thought Joseph or Declan might pass muster,' said Anita, with a hint of sarcasm. 'They don't, so now he's racking his brain for one I might like.'

'Choosing names is a tricky exercise,' said Marilyn. 'My father overruled my mother's preferred name for me, Valerie, for Marilyn. Mum told me once, after a few sherries, that he'd always lusted after the actress. I told her I like my Christian name. It suits me, John says.'

'Marilyn, he's got to say that—'

'No, Anita, I don't.'

Anita smiled knowingly and left the room for the kitchen.

'You must be getting excited, David,' said Marilyn. 'Not long now.'

'Oh, he's very excited now, Marilyn,' said Anita as she put down her guests' dessert bowls, 'telling all and sundry he's going to be a dad. Once the child pops and comes into the house, we'll see how excited he is then.'

Getting uncomfortable, Marilyn said,

'When do you stop work, Anita?'

'Stop work? No, I'm going back as soon as the maternity whatsit period ends. We've been discussing childcare arrangements. Dave's been checking local nurseries.'

'Yes, guys,' piped up David, who'd been sitting quietly, 'Anita's determined to climb the corporate ladder, sorry, the Foreign Office one, and well, I'm making slow but steady progress to being made a partner. Having a kid, so early on, I'm not saying it's inconvenient, but we have to be realistic, for the kid's sake, obviously. School fees are sky high, and if our incomes can't cope, he'll suffer.'

John, trying to steer the conversation to safer territory, said,

'Are you still involved with your church choir, Anita? I hear it's going to be on the radio at Christmas. *The Messiah*, isn't it?'

'No, John. What with the bloody morning sickness and Dave being away so often I had to resign, temporarily. That's another thing this pregnancy's affected: my voice. I'm halfway to being an alto. Not over fond of *The Messiah* anyway. We always did Gilbert and Sullivan every speech day, remember, Marilyn?'

'Could I ever forget old Simpson in full flow, conducting the school orchestra? John, he was the senior music teacher, and we all thought he considered himself an overlooked genius. Some of those rehearsals, Anita, so funny, watching his antics, lurching into Italian phrases for an English piece! I'd guess he put a lot of students off music for a lifetime.'

'You were never short of acerbic descriptions of teachers if I recall correctly, Marilyn,' said Anita, 'and yet here you are, head of the English department.'

'I don't recognise the irony. I love the subject, so it was a natural avenue for me. You can't talk, sounding off in class about the elites, and how they hang on to power through their old school tie networks, and where do you end up? Working in the natural home of the status quo, the Foreign Office. All you're missing is the bowler and the umbrella.'

'*Touché*, Marilyn,' said Anita, clearly stung by the retort, 'but very funny. Five for effort, out of ten.'

'Marilyn, let's you and me do our bit, the washing up—'

'No, John, it's fine. One of Dave's rare good ideas. He forked out on a dishwasher, to help me out, he said. More like a cute way of avoiding getting his hands dirty.'

Disturbed by the undercurrent of hostility, John, knowing his friend's passion for the Premier League, said,

'Isn't there a game on this afternoon, Dave?'

'Yeah, I was thinking of watching it in the pub, but Anita frog-marched me out of the house earlier, so I can't really go back—'

'Oh hell, take him down there, John. Marilyn and I can exchange horror stories about marriage, and men in general. If he gets legless, don't bring him back.'

The two men got their jackets and wandered off, John winking at Marilyn as he closed the front door behind him.

'I didn't know David was interested in football,' said Marilyn. 'John told me they were both cricket fanatics growing up.'

Anita's face creased into a wry smile. She said,

'Yes, he took up watching football, even going to games – did you know they're very expensive days out? – when he joined that cabal of shysters. I suspect all the men there are so constricted, threatened, by the presence of equally able women at work. The firm trumpets its "equality and diversity" policy, which is fine, but that means the guys need, or think they need, an outlet, somewhere they can go to vent their frustrations. Do you know what'd be a good laugh? If any of the women decided to tag along with them to the football.'

'Enough of football talk, Anita. Can I be blunt?'

Anita looked at her.

'Blunt? What can you possibly mean?'

'Well, you've come across today as someone who's… who's…'

'Someone who is… I know what you're trying to say… Yes, Marilyn, you've hit the nail on the head. I am unhappy…Very fucking unhappy!'

She slumped onto the sofa beside Marilyn, covered her face and began sobbing.

Marilyn, very agitated at her oldest friend's obvious distress, put her arm around her shoulder and said quietly,

'Tell me if I'm wrong, but this is more than a hormone-related issue. David looked on edge too earlier and—'

'He's so thoughtless! I know people assumed we got married in haste, because I was pregnant, but I love him, Marilyn, honestly, I do. I wasn't a silly, naïve girl marrying someone whilst wearing rose-tinted glasses—'

'David thinks the world of you, Anita. Most men, and John's no exception, are clueless when it comes to dealing with pregnant wives or girlfriends.'

'What did you say?' Anita said sharply, her face red. 'Are you pregnant too?'

'No, I meant that they're incapable of understanding how it can affect women. You said you're unhappy. If we set aside the pregnancy, is there something else?'

Anita gazed at Marilyn with what was almost a pleading expression, wiped her eyes and said, slowly,

'Last week, Dave and me had been invited to his firm's anniversary do. It was unexpected, but he was over the moon to get it. We got a taxi to the restaurant, near Green Park. The place was full of people whom you could recognise as legal types. Dave told me all the partners would be there and eventually, after standing around like lemons, a bald, supercilious character strolled over to Dave and me at the bar and introduced himself. "Glad you could make it, young Murray, and this must be your good lady." Who talks like that in the twenty-first century, Marilyn?! He had a limp, and an effeminate handshake too.'

'He didn't impress you then, Anita.'

'During the course of the evening, the other partners came over, like Hopalong Cassidy, for a cursory hello and a handshake, obviously doing "the right thing". Dave's moaned at me more than once how he feels like a leper sometimes in the office. Those guys hardly ever acknowledge him at work, and yet, there they were, coming over all polite. Don't know why he puts up with it, and all these away days they lumber him with! I tell you, Marilyn, I wouldn't tolerate the arrogance. Half of them looked incapable of tying their shoelaces unaided… What? It's true!'

'You were never afraid to say what you think, were you? In any situation.'

Ignoring Marilyn's comment, she went on, running her fingers through her hair,

'And then, there's his fling with that empty-headed tart! He calls her his "personal assistant"! A couple of times, when he's been away on his trips, I've called the office, you know, to check on her—'

'Check on—'

'The last time he was out of the office, I phoned to leave a message for him, a pretext. When the receptionist said he was out, I asked for her – Jane, she's called – to be told she wasn't in either. Two and two usually add up to four.'

Marilyn, very uneasy at her friend's seeming paranoia, said,

'Not always, Anita. David's crazy about you. I'd agree that he can be impulsive, childish even, but I can't see him being devious, or—'

'Marilyn, you always were naïve when it came to men. Their brains aren't located above the waist. I've seen them in the office, sober-looking guys you'd never suspect of having primal urges, falling victim to their loins, and...'

She stopped. Marilyn consulted her watch and said,

'Maybe we should get out of here for some fresh air. The boys won't be back for another hour or so. Is that trendy coffee shop you took me to before our wedding still on the go?'

Anita looked blankly at her, then replied,

'OK, you're always the calm one. Yeah, let's go. I need to do something to lift this constant feeling of being... being trapped. No doubt you think I'm off the wall... Sorry about before, Marilyn, embarrassing you and John, but did you notice how Dave just didn't take it in? Brushed it aside. Everything's a joke to him... Why can't he understand how I feel?'

They left the house and walked along to the coffee shop, where a few weeks before the two women had discussed the arrangements for Marilyn's big day. Staring across the small table at her friend's tormented face, her thoughts went back to when she'd complained to John about Anita's frenetic behaviour in the run-up to their wedding, and a feeling of guilt made her feel uncomfortable.

'You said earlier you'd be taking the minimum time off after junior arrives.'

'And?' came the surly reply.

'I was thinking, perhaps you and Dave should take a short break before the baby, a weekend away, just the two of you. It might—'

'No, Marilyn, it wouldn't. We're married, not a pair of love-struck teenagers, star-crossed more like. My problem boils down to this: I love him, but I've discovered recently, I don't like him. He annoys me at times, but he doesn't cotton on to that fact. Let's get back. I'm feeling tired. The doctor told me I should… Come on, Marilyn.'

*

Drinking a late-night cup of tea, Marilyn said,

'John, what did you and David talk about?'

'Football. The guy's now a fully paid-up member of the José Mourinho fan club.'

'Very interesting, I'm sure. I meant—'

'I know what you meant: their marriage.'

'God, they've only been hitched for five minutes, and yet here we are talking about—'

'He told me what, in his words "a great girl" Anita is. She's unhappy, isn't she? Dave made a joke of it in the pub. "It's all hormones, women's stuff," was his considered diagnosis.'

'While the two of you were watching football, we had a long chat, or, to be accurate, Anita let rip: the pregnancy, her job, and, at great length, her dissatisfaction with David. Not just her impression that he's not fully signed up with the baby, no, she actually suspects him of carrying on with… with someone at work. She even called his office, after he'd told her he'd be away for a couple of days on business, with the specific purpose of checking if his secretary, or personal assistant, was in the office. Ostensibly – that's the word Anita used – the girl was on holiday, but she's got it into her head that David's playing away with this person. She hasn't any concrete evidence, but the suspicion's eating away at her. Her blood pressure must be sky high.'

'Dave's always been very candid about women. He could always, as he liked to describe it, "pull the talent", but I have to say, Marilyn, since he first met Anita, all he could talk about was how great she was. Same in the pub. Two girls were sitting near us, obviously eyeing us up, and one of them offered to buy us drinks—'

'Both of you?'

'Yes, but I think Dave was the one they were interested in. Anyway, he declined the offer and cheekily held up his left hand, displaying the wedding ring.'

'The girl said, "Doesn't bother me, handsome."'

'"Well, it bothers me, I'm spoken for," Dave told her. Sounds to me like Anita needs to see her doctor. All this needless worry can't be doing her, or worse, the child, any favours. You should have suggested—'

'I did, but she ignored it. Better tell David, the sooner the better. Spying on him, it's not healthy.'

'I'm not sure if… We're meeting next Saturday. He's got hold of a couple of comps for the Chelsea game, at Stamford Bridge. If the mood's right, I'll mention it in passing.'

Marilyn frowned.

'What's the matter?'

'Perhaps I should pop around… Yes… I'll pick up a little something for the baby and have another chat.'

'If you think that will help… But aren't you just a tad concerned about us getting too involved in someone else's marriage?'

'John, I know she and I have only gotten close again recently, but Anita needs someone right now.'

Chapter Ten

For the next few days John attempted to put his friend's marital situation to the back of his mind, but David's seeming ignorance of his wife's emotional condition bothered him.

On the Thursday before the Stamford Bridge outing, John was poring over statistics on EU farm subsidies when he heard the landline ringing in the lounge. Before he'd managed to get there, the call ended.

'Damn,' he said aloud as he walked back to the study. Then his mobile rang.

'Did I catch you out, Johnny boy?'

Fred.

'Why ring the landline, Fred?'

'First number on the list. Anyway, how are you getting on with my little assignment?'

'Sorry, Fred, just started on it. I was looking at aspects of the Common Agric—'

'What? Stuff that! I'm not concerned about farmers, I told you. It's the financial services sector I'm interested in. With an election due by 2010, and the big two avoiding the European issue, we want to have a dispassionate analysis of—'

'Yes, Fred, I understand what you're after, a debunking of the probable scare story of how catastrophic leaving would be for the City.'

'Scare story? No, you're wrong. I've got this feeling in my water, that there'll be a hung parliament, possibly a coalition, which would lead to a new attitude toward the EU.'

'Don't follow you, Fred.'

'John, you know as well as me, there's an *animus*, a resentment of the EU across a swathe of the voters, ignored by our betters up to now. I'll be less than shocked if some of those Lib Dem opportunists in the Commons suggest a referendum. Mark my words, Johnny boy.'

'Listen though, I'm meeting up for a few refreshments in the Hangman's Rest tonight. Fancy joining us? Should be fun. Two of our esteemed friends from the City are going too. I think you've crossed swords with them. They told me you're a ruthless, devious bastard. Naturally, I had to disagree, but I know the truth…'

John heard the familiar booming laughter.

'What's the occasion, Fred?'

'Come along and you'll find out, but promise me this: don't make any reference to this little exercise you're carrying out for me. We'll be there from seven till late.'

'OK, Fred,' said John, mystified, not for the first time, by his old colleague's cryptic tone.

Marilyn came in just after six, to encounter John, hastily getting ready for his night out. Realising he'd omitted to tell her, he said, apologetically,

'Sorry, I should have let you know, I've got a meeting re this job I'm doing for Fred, and—'

'Don't be drinking too much,' said Marilyn, fully aware of Fred's fully justified reputation. 'I suppose you'll be late home?'

'Expect so.'

'My turn to spill. Anita called today, asking me round to theirs. David's away until tomorrow night, so perhaps this evening could be put to good use. I'll grab a quick bite and get a cab.'

'She called you?' said John, surprised.

'Yes, she sounded much calmer than Sunday. Good timing though. I went out at lunchtime and acquired a few items of clothing for the baby. I hope she'll like them.'

'Right, must be off. Do you want me to swing round to Anita's later? We'll probably be in the Hangman's until chucking-out time, so I could be with you by eleven-thirty or so.'

'Oh, no, John. Anita said she's tucked up by ten nowadays.'

'See you later then,' he said, kissing her on the cheek.

Sitting in the overcrowded carriage on his way to the pub, John wondered how his wife's visit to Anita would go. He couldn't put his finger on it, but he felt a vague concern. Marilyn's description, 'she sounded calmer,' stayed with him throughout the evening; it worried him.

*

At seven the following morning, a hungover John walked gingerly down the stairs and into the kitchen. He'd arrived home shortly after midnight and had avoided waking Marilyn by crashing in the spare bedroom.

'Morning, John, what time did you get in? I was tucked up by eleven. Anita wanted me to stay over, but I've got an early start this morning, a team meeting. I felt ever so slightly guilty about not… Gosh, you look rough. That Fred, he must be well over sixty, in age if not in maturity. What was he after? He wasn't chasing you for that report? You told me he gave you Christmas as a deadline.'

John, smiling at Marilyn's understated, but accurate, description of his old mentor, said,

'He's getting all worked up concerning what he calls inside gossip of a snap general election. He confirmed that was his reason in asking me to do that piece on—'

'You're saying he wants you to get into politics?'

'No, but he introduced me to two men who made no secret of their intention to start things rolling—'

'Which party?'

'No party, just two guys who share Fred's view—'

'View? What view?'

'That the UK should leave the EU. They'll have their work cut out. All the potential government parties are in favour of the status quo.'

'So, Fred's a modern-day Don Quixote? From the stories you've told me about him, he's a dreamer straight from cloud cuckoo land.'

'From the way he was talking last night, I think he's—'

'Well, John, can you sort yourself out for breakfast, though by the look of you, I'm not sure you want anything. See you tonight. I'll probably be home by five.'

She leant over and kissed him, but as she started to move away, John held her and said,

'How did it go with Anita last night? You haven't said.'

'Superficially, she was much more calm, rational you could say, but as I've told you, there's something fundamental troubling her, something—'

'Dave, you mean?'

'We were chatting away, mundane stuff, me with a glass of vino, Anita with a soft drink, when she came out with a strange comment, given her background.'

'Well, tell me, Marilyn, I'm curious now.'

'She asked me if my faith has ever been shaken.'

'What? Your Catholic faith? I thought she was the more devout one.'

'Yes, that's right, Mass every Sunday. Her question took me by surprise. When I replied in the negative, she sighed, shook her head and commented that despite all the troubles which afflict mankind – war, disease, natural, inexplicable events – her own faith had remained untouched – until now.'

'I asked what had brought this on. She said, "I don't know. What if it's all one big cruel joke, Marilyn?"'

'Oh dear, is it her paranoia about Dave, do you think?'

'She didn't bring that particular issue up, but I'm confident it's at the core of her depression. That's what it is, John, depression. I asked her if she'd been to confession recently. She ignored me and changed the subject, very abruptly. The rest of the evening passed normally, and she was pleased with the baby things. I'm concerned. We spent a good three hours with small talk, but that interlude, and the way she shut me off when she picked up on my anxiety, well...'

'Yes, I can understand you being worried, although I think you have to allow that some of her condition, her emotional state, could be due to the pregnancy. Once the boy arrives, that'll be when you'll get a better take on her.'

'John, I'm convinced it's more than that. She's more than angry with David. I think you—'

'Raise the subject with him? Dangerous territory, Marilyn... But you're obviously agitated, so I'll try to find out, but knowing the guy, well—'

'I know we can't interfere, but honestly, John, Anita needs support... Urgently, judging by her condition last night... Those extreme mood swings, it's just not natural.'

Chapter Eleven

John, while ordering drinks in a noisy bar near Stamford Bridge, asked his friend, in a casual, matter-of-fact tone,

'Not long to go now, Dave. You must be getting excited, or more likely, nervous.'

'Oh, Anita's got it all in hand, mate, as usual. My old man used to say, "Leave women's things to the experts, women."'

Suppressing a chuckle at David's naive, offhand remark, he said,

'Dave, tell me, have you been to the ante-natal classes with your wife?'

'Christ, John, no! All those gruesome videos, and then the lectures from know-alls, most of them dry old spinsters I'd wager—'

'Didn't it cross your mind that Anita might like you to go, for support, as a couple?'

'Well, John, as a matter of fact, when I drove her to the first session, I asked if she wanted me to go in with her, but she barked at me, saying I'd be better off at work.'

'And what did you say?'

David, beginning to suspect his friend was trying to tell him something, said,

'Listen, John, it's OK for you, what with your pile of cash, to preach, but just now is a sensitive time in my career. I can't afford to be absent from the office too much. Anita knows that.'

'So, when you made the suggestion, she told you to head off to work... rather than...'

Realising he was getting into very tricky territory, John changed the subject.

'Never mind this girlie stuff, how do you think the game'll pan out?'

'A walkover, John,' said David, seemingly more relaxed, glad to be on safer ground. 'Two of the partners are here, in those corporate boxes. That'll be me one day. If you're lucky, I'll invite you to join me. The champers is top drawer, I'm told.'

As the game progressed, with Chelsea making short work of the opposition, John eyed up David, excited by his team's performance, shouting, and on a couple of occasions, chanting along with the home crowd. He thought back to their carefree days, and how they'd shared the ups and downs of Yorkshire's cricket team. David was in his element, amongst a mass of like-minded men, with nothing in their heads bar the spectacle in front of them. How many of them had wives, girlfriends, sweethearts, waiting for them to come home?

John puzzled over how David, having been bowled over by Anita, endlessly telling him how much he loved her, on one drunken occasion saying that he couldn't imagine life without her, could be blind to her current emotional state. He felt torn; if he spoke frankly, he risked fracturing a long-standing camaraderie. On the other hand, Marilyn's stark description of Anita's condition cried out for... for resolution, but how?

The two made their way back to the pub for 'a quick snifter', in David's words. Jostling to the bar, John ordered two pints, paid and handed David his glass.

'I've only got time for this one drink and then I have to be off. Marilyn's invited her mother for dinner. Seven o'clock sharp, she advised me. Our single days are history now, Dave.'

'Speak for yourself, John. Being married, well, obviously, I love Anita, but I don't see any—'

'Hear that, lads?' shouted an overenthusiastic, scruffy guy with a Chelsea scarf around his neck to the assembled drinkers crowded around. 'This muppet's brought his marriage guidance counsellor!'

Roars of laughter.

'Keep your wit to yourself, mate,' said David, stung by the barb.

'Come on, Dave, let's piss off before you get involved.'

As John pulled the door open, the comedian shouted over the hubbub,

'See you next week, mate, the missus permitting.'

Ignoring this, the two marched off to Fulham Broadway station.

'Fancy coming over to ours for dinner next week, Dave? Marilyn's a great cook, and it'll do Anita good, to get out of the house for a spell—'

'She gets out every day, John, down to the high street, and that little coffee bar to meet her friends from the ante-natal, hates being mollycoddled, but yeah, I'll ask her. Talking of ante-natal, meant to ask, did Marilyn ever say that Anita invited her to go to the classes a while ago?'

'No, she didn't, must have slipped her mind,' said John, and wondering why his wife hadn't told him said, 'Frankly, I'm a bit surprised Anita would have asked, Dave, after the miscarriage thing back when her—'

'Yeah, I told her asking Marilyn was a bit off, but she insisted Marilyn was fully on board.'

'See you later then, Dave,' said John when they got to the station entrance. 'I'm going for the bus, and remember, give us a bell once you've spoken to Anita.'

'OK, tell Marilyn I was asking after her.'

*

John got off the bus an hour later, walked the quarter of a mile to their street and opened the front door. His wife came running in from the kitchen, looking very upset.

'Oh, thank God you're home! We have to get to the London!'

Seeing the tears in her eyes, John took hold of her and said,

'The London? What's happened? Is it your mother?'

'Anita phoned not ten minutes ago. She's in an ambulance on her way there now. The baby's coming, but, John, she sounded, well… strange, distant, like the other night.'

'Better call Dave. He'll want—'

'She doesn't want him there, John—'

'What?'

'She begged me, us, not to tell him, and I—'

'That sounds like she's hysterical, not rational… I'll call him. He can at least go to the hospital, to be there should she, I mean when, she calms down.'

After calling for a cab, John left a message on David's mobile, and the two made their way to the hospital. As they sat in the taxi, Marilyn gripped his arm tightly. She was weeping, silently, making him very uneasy.

They arrived shortly after six-thirty, and, getting hastily out of the taxi Marilyn said,

'God, I haven't... John, ring my mother, she'll be leaving anytime now. I'll go in and check on Anita's condition.'

When he'd made the call to his very confused mother-in-law, he went to casualty, to be advised that Mrs Murray was in labour and had been installed in the emergency room because of 'distress to the foetus'.

'Is Mrs Duncan in there with her?'

'Mrs Duncan?' said the vacant-looking receptionist. 'Oh, you mean her sister, yes.'

'Sister? Err... Yes, Marilyn's her first name,' said John, losing his customary calm demeanour.

'Don't worry yourself, Mr Murray, your wife's in good—'

'I'm not Mr Murray. He's on his way, I think...'

John turned away from the receptionist, wondering what she made of his enquiries, and rang David's number again. No reply. He sat on a very uncomfortable chair opposite the entrance. Half an hour went by, with no sign of David or Marilyn.

'Where the hell is he?' John asked himself.

'Mr Murray?' asked a white-coated, anxious-looking young man.

'Err... What?' said John, whose thoughts were miles away from the hospital. 'No, he's on his way... I think. What's the matter?'

'Oh, I see. This is difficult. Is he far away? The consultant wants to speak with him – urgently.'

'I'll tell Mr Murray as soon as he arrives. You look worried, if you don't mind me saying. How is Mrs Murray doing? Your receptionist mentioned something about distress.'

The young doctor turned crimson, and could only mutter,

'Well, I'm sure the consultant can enlighten Mr Murray when he arrives.'

He scurried off, through a set of double doors. John sat back down and checked his mobile for the umpteenth time. It was now seven-thirty, and no sign of David. Speculating wildly as to where the man could have got to, he tried to think. When they'd parted at the Tube station, he understood him to have been making for home, twenty minutes away, so he should have been there by now, unless he had been diverted, gone to the shops or... the pub... John shuddered at the thought, mindful that his friend could be unpredictable.

He was disturbed out of his reverie by the sound of the double doors being thrust open; Marilyn emerged, obviously distraught. She rushed over to John, threw her arms round him and sobbed,

'She's lost it, John. Stillborn. Anita's hysterical! Where's David? Have you called him?'

'Yes, Marilyn,' he said quietly, and taking her by the hand went on, 'I can only presume he's been delayed somewhere en route. Christ, this is beyond terrible! Why? They were both so looking forward to being parents. Dave was only saying at the game, that he—'

'Saying what exactly?' said Marilyn, pulling her hand away from him, her face taking on an intense, terrifying expression, one John hadn't seen before. 'Why isn't the thoughtless idiot here, now?'

'He gave me the impression he was going straight back home, and when—'

Marilyn, still with a venomous look, barked,

'Oh, really? At the most important moment for any woman, when she expects her husband to be with her... But he's failed, let her down. Good old Dave, a great guy! Wait till I see him. Anita says he thinks me a calm, rational person. Well, he's in for a rude shock when I—'

She stopped, having seen David, grinning, walk casually through the main entrance.

'Has she popped junior yet? I must have missed her by a couple of minutes, but—'

Marilyn was about to launch into a tirade, but was prevented by the almost simultaneous appearance of the consultant, a man with a lugubrious expression, more suited to an undertaker than a medic. Approaching a disconsolate-looking John, he said,

'Mr Murray, can you follow me into—'

'This is Mr Murray,' said John, pointing to his friend.

'Ah, I see. Mr Murray, please follow me. This way please.'

David, with an excited look, walked past John and a very angry Marilyn saying,

'Don't look so worried, guys, sounds as though the boy's made his appearance early.'

He walked briskly behind the consultant, and, with a broad, childish smile, turned around briefly at the double doors and waved back at them.

The young doctor emerged. Marilyn rushed over and said,

'Excuse me, doctor, will we be able to visit Mrs Murray after her husband?'

'Not until tomorrow, I'm afraid. She's been medicated, and will be out of it until morning.'

'I think we should wait here for David,' said John. 'He'll need support when he comes out of there.'

'OK. I think I've made my opinion known about his attitude, but, well, yes, he should stay with us tonight, if, or rather when, he comes out. It'll be a terrible shock to him, bearing in mind his childlike optimism. Maybe if he'd been more... paid more attention... Oh, who knows why these afflictions come about! It might sound harsh, even cruel to him, but, honestly, I'm more concerned for Anita. Men can usually brush off this type of... But women...'

Chapter Twelve

A week later Anita was discharged. David had stayed at John and Marilyn's while his wife recuperated; she had lost a considerable amount of blood during the birth process. David spent most of his time at the hospital, overcome with grief and, possibly, remorse.

'I'll never get over this,' he confessed to John late one evening after returning from seeing his wife. 'Why didn't she tell me there were complications while she was expecting? You know me, John, I like to see the upside of things, but... Why... Why?'

Anita surprised everyone by her demeanour once she got home. The day following her release, she went into work, telling David she wanted to get back to normal – 'We must move on, it was just one of those things.' On a night out two weeks later with Marilyn and a few old friends and colleagues from Anita's office to celebrate a thirtieth birthday, she unnerved her by saying quietly,

'I'm the only one of us, Marilyn, who hasn't produced, hasn't done her "female duty"... But hey ho, I don't care. Just listen to the smugness of them, talking about sick and nappies.

I had a lucky escape, and anyway, I've got a good career in prospect at the FO, and take it as gospel, I'll be moving up the ladder. No smart-arse man's going to stop me.'

Marilyn bit her tongue at Anita's unfeeling, thoughtless remarks. Back at home, she told John,

'Anita's not right, John. I think she should be talking seriously to someone, a professional, or maybe Father Delany, about what happened—'

'Dave tells me she's on top of things, very controlled, taking care of everything. She's applied for a promoted post in the FO, and is likely to get it, a big step up, with potential postings abroad, which—'

'That's odd, she didn't mention... Anita's always very talkative about herself, especially if she had something positive to report... How would it affect him, given his own career ambitions?'

'I assume she must have discussed the possibilities with him, but he didn't raise the subject. I think it could be a problem though—'

'Well, he'd better brace himself for a change. She's decided to push on, "up the ladder", which could take her – them – anywhere. It might be one of those marriages where the wife is more successful than the husband.' Marilyn let out a sly chuckle. 'Do you think he'll cope with it?'

'Marilyn, in case you're wondering, no, I'm not going to raise the subject with him, but I think you might be less than fair to the guy. You saw how he was that week he was here, he barely ate the whole time... No, don't look at me like that, he loves her, "lost without her" as he said, so—'

'I hope he supports her, because if he doesn't, well, who knows what the outcome for their marriage will be.'

*

John's investigation for Fred McTaggart's article took him to Brussels the week after this conversation, and on his return, he was sitting in his office working up some notes when his mobile rang out: David.

'Morning, John. How's the job going? Marilyn told Anita you were hiding away in bandit country for a while, but... Well, can we meet up for a session? I've got some news might interest a hack like yourself, and if—'

'Hi, Dave. How's Anita doing?'

'Oh, stop worrying! Everybody keeps asking me. She's fine. Never ceases to amaze me, and I expect you've heard about her new job in Whitehall. Just fantastic. She's some girl, John, in every way if you—'

John, uncomfortable at the comment, said,

'Can't afford the time really, Dave, but I might be able to squeeze in a couple of pints, say tomorrow lunchtime, the usual place. Marilyn told me Anita was in line for a big promotion, with overseas possibilities—'

'What are you on about, John?'

John, thinking he'd put his foot in it said,

'Perhaps I misheard and—'

'Overseas possibilities? You should stop sniffing that stuff. OK, see you at the Hangman's tomorrow... Overseas! Ha ha.'

John, concerned, found he was unable to give due attention to McTaggart's project. David's dismissal of Anita's possible move abroad for work pointed to a lack of communication, or alternatively... Maybe she hadn't thought it necessary to discuss the matter with him. Worried, he phoned Marilyn.

'Hello, St Mary's Grammar.'

'Morning, this is John Duncan. Is my wife available? She should be on her break at the moment.'

'Just a moment please.' The line went quiet.

'What is it, John? We're not supposed to have personal calls during—'

'In a weak moment I let slip to Dave about Anita's—'

'Oh, for God's sake, John! What were you thinking?'

'Yes, OK, but this is the thing, he obviously isn't aware, told me I must be mistaken, but we're meeting up tomorrow lunchtime, so if he tells Anita—'

'What's done... as the saying goes, so we'll be... He was bound to find out in any case.'

Thinking he was off the hook, John said,

'Funny thing though, Marilyn, he instigated the call, sounding as hyped up as usual. It seems he's got "something exciting" to tell me. At least I know it won't concern Anita's prospects.'

'You don't think it might be in connection with his own situation, career-wise, that is?'

'No idea, but whatever it is, Anita's promotion isn't it.'

'I think I'll call Anita, for an update. She'd said I'd be "kept informed"... That's another thing, John, she's normally frank in nature, and open, but since she came out of hospital, well, I can't really fathom her. When we were at that thirtieth night, I got the impression her colleagues were just that, co-workers, not friends, the way she and I are, or perhaps were. Listen, John, I have to get back, the bell's rung. Let's talk tonight about whether it's appropriate, or more accurately, wise, that we should get involved.'

'Right, Marilyn. You'll be home before me, I expect. I've got an appointment with the dentist at four, a check-up, so I should make it back by six.'

'OK. I'll probably have spoken with her by then. I need to know what's going on, but I'll call on the pretext of enquiring about the children's service Anita's helping to organise at the church. Last time we spoke, she seemed very fired up with it.'

*

Marilyn duly contacted Anita, but noting her cold, offhand tone, ducked out of asking about her job situation, sticking to what she considered 'safe' subjects.

'Do you want any help with the children's service? I could suggest a few approp—'

'No thank you very much. I'm quite capable of organising a do for a dozen or so snotty-nosed kids.'

Taken aback, Marilyn replied,

'Oh, sorry, Anita. I had the impression the service was a big event.'

'No idea how you got that into your head, are you feeling well? I know teaching is a stressful gig these days. Perhaps you should consider a career change, Marilyn. Ask John what he thinks. He's never backward at putting his fourpence worth in.'

Staggered, Marilyn decided discretion was definitely preferable to valour.

'Well, it was nice to hear your voice,' she said, and eager to end the conversation on a light note, 'See you soon, I hope.'

'Not if I see you first,' came the frosty response, followed by, 'Joke, dear. Bye.'

John got home at five; the dentist had called him to defer his appointment due to illness.

'Marilyn,' he called out after walking through the ground floor rooms. He went into the hallway, and, making for the stairs, he stopped; he could hear faint sobs. He took the stairs two at a time, and went into the master bedroom to encounter Marilyn, lying face down on their bed, weeping.

'What the hell's the matter?'

No answer.

'Marilyn,' he said as he sat next to her on the bed.

Slowly, she raised herself up, and turning to face him she said,

'I shouldn't have phoned her... A bad idea, but I—'

'Yes, you tried to help the woman, and this is the state she puts you in. I think we have to leave them to work out their relationship. Don't get involved with them from now on—'

'I didn't raise the job thing with her, John, but no, she jumped down my throat, then tried to make out she was being light-hearted.'

John, inwardly angry, said, trying to stay calm,

'Get yourself sorted, Marilyn, we're going out for dinner. Where do you fancy? That Indian's got a good reputation, let's try it out.'

'Alright.'

*

'That jalfrezi was excellent, don't you think, Marilyn?' John said as they walked the half-mile from the restaurant two hours later.

'Yes, I suppose so.'

During the meal Marilyn had been less than talkative, despite John's efforts to get her to engage, asking her about the new members of staff she'd been discussing animatedly over the past week. He was angry at Anita's seeming callousness; had she forgotten his wife's own tragedy? Marilyn's overt concern for her old friend highlighted her natural kindness to others. Tempted as he was to confront Anita, John determined to keep his counsel. Any intervention would only exacerbate the situation, and he knew Marilyn hated confrontation of any sort.

'Fancy a cup of tea, Marilyn?' he said as they went into their house. 'Or perhaps something stronger?'

'Tea will be fine, John,' she replied, 'and by the way, thank you.'

'For what? I haven't made it yet.'

'I could see in your face earlier, that you were annoyed—'

'More than annoyed, angry, very angry by her—'

'She was always too quick with that uncontrolled, or rather uncontrollable tongue.'

'Typical. You're making excuses for her. Marilyn, as a teacher, would you tolerate that kind of cruelty? That's what it is, mental cruelty. It's too easy to dismiss people's actions, words, by saying what you're saying, that she can't help it. Uncontrollable tongue? No, she lashed out because of her own mood. She was upset, bored, angry, but that's no excuse, no excuse at all.'

'Well, you may be right, John, but please don't, for my sake if not for theirs, remonstrate with her.'

'No, I wasn't intending to, but promise me one thing—'

'Yes, we won't be having any form of socialising with either of them for the time being.'

'And definitely not in the next two weeks.'

'It's half term.'

'Yes, I know,' he said, and casually went on, 'We're off to America, a fly-drive on the West Coast – LA, Vegas and San Francisco. Remember when we first met, at their wedding? You said you always imagined driving along the wide highways, under the big sky. Well, now we're doing it. I told Fred I'd finish his piece after we get back. I've got all the required data, so it's merely a question of writing the thing. Twenty thousand words will do it, he said.'

Marilyn, clearly taken aback, said,

'You took a risk, not telling me, but… yes, that's great!'

She put her arms around him, kissed him on the lips and said,

'Forget the tea.'

Chapter Thirteen

John had decided to take Marilyn away for a break, almost on the spur of the moment, after learning of Anita's unfeeling comments on their night out. He'd known since David had introduced him to her that she was prone to making remarks without considering their potential effect on her listeners. He also knew that Marilyn, contrary to her public persona, was a very emotional individual, and the double loss she had suffered was never far away, possibly influencing her outlook and actions.

Ten minutes out from Los Angeles, Marilyn leant over and whispered,

'John, you don't think Anita – I know it'd never occur to David – might think we've gone off in a strop?'

'Why should we care?' said John. 'No, I don't think our being away will cause her any problem. She's most likely salivating at the prospect of a lucrative, exciting posting with the FO,' he continued, and laughing at the thought, 'like North Korea. Great cuisine there, I believe.'

'Do you think David knows about it yet?'

'You mean the job? He must do, but listen, Marilyn, stop

talking about them. Oh God, I hate this part of flying. There go my ears.'

*

They picked up the hire car an hour later and drove off east toward Las Vegas. John looked forward to hearing his sometimes strait-laced wife's opinion on the gambler's paradise. It was her first trip to the States, having told John shortly after they'd met that she thought it both frightening and exciting.

As they left the metropolis and headed into the desert, the road became less crowded, and it wasn't long before they had it virtually to themselves. John switched on the car radio, and attempted to locate a decent station, but there seemed to be only a choice between country music and religious outlets.

'I thought these kind of radio stations were a feature of the mid-western and southern states,' said Marilyn.

'Been doing some research, have we?'

'When I was a teenager and, I suppose, into my early twenties, America fascinated me, the music especially. So much variety, no doubt because of the waves of immigrants during the last 200 years, and—'

'Whoa! Sounds like you're still in teacher mode. You'll be giving me a lesson on American literature soon.'

'Why do you say that? The first time you took me back to your flat I spotted quite a number of books in that spare room, nestled amongst all those textbooks on finance and economics. I suspect, my dear husband, that you've dipped into more fiction than you'll admit.'

'You think?' said John, happy that his wife's positive side was reappearing. 'You're right, I did go through a phase of reading for pleasure, distraction if you will. I suspect you're going to ask who my favourite writer is, well... Guess.'

'Now, let me think... Not Dickens—'

'American writers, Marilyn... Think.'

'Hemingway?'

'Try again. Look around you.'

'Oh! I've got it. Kerouac, *On the Road*.'

'No, someone way better, come on, you're the English teacher.'

Marilyn's brow furrowed. John saw her face, concentrating, from the corner of his eye.

'Of course! Steinbeck!'

'At last! *East of Eden*. I've read it four times. "Frailty, thy name is woman!"'

'That's not from—'

'I know, but Kathy, wouldn't like to have come across her. We've been driving for two hours now. Three more until we get to the den of iniquity. I think we should make a pit stop soon, check that map. When's the next roadside diner? Oh, look, what does that sign... "Jerry's all you can eat restaurant." Sounds very inviting, don't you think?'

They pulled into the car park. Two pick-up trucks were parked side by side in front of the diner, a small, square building, with its full-length windows reflecting the strong early evening desert sunlight. They got out of the car, stretched their weary limbs and walked slowly into the diner.

'Afternoon, folks,' shouted a cheery, uniformed woman, presumably a waitress. 'Take a seat. You guys look shot. Long journey?'

'Just got in from London,' said John, as they sat down in a booth at the massive window with a view of the barren, flat landscape. 'Can we have coffee please?'

'Coming right up. You folks want something to eat? Today's special is, uh, whatever you want really.'

She poured out the coffee.

'Can we have… two steaks please… Well done for both of us?'

'You got it.'

Putting the coffee mug to his lips, John looked around. Two men, dressed in checked shirts and overalls, probably the drivers of the trucks, stood up and began walking to the door. Hearing Marilyn asking John how long it would be before they reached Las Vegas, one of them said,

'You guys from England?'

'Yes,' said John.

'My old man spent four years there, air force, somewhere called… Norfolk, I think, and—'

'Really, how did he like it? Norfolk's very rural, but much greener than—'

'Yeah, he thought he was on to a real good thing, till he got shipped out to Iraq. Came back without his legs.'

'Oh, sorry to hear that,' said Marilyn. 'War's a terrible thing.'

'You're right there, ma'am. He ain't the same guy now. Never leaves the VA hospital.'

He smiled wanly, tipped his hat and left the diner, followed by his silent friend, both of them making their way to the pick-up trucks.

'Those two guys come in here regular,' said the waitress as she poured two more coffees. 'Benny, that's the quiet one, never talks. We used to think he was, you know, backward, but a year or so back, when Harry came in by himself, he told us Benny saw his folks being shot by a couple of hoods from Vegas. Couldn't pay off their debts. The poor bastard. Oh sorry, ma'am. He just follows Harry everywhere.

'You folks better get moving, it'll be dark soon, and the desert's cold at night.'

'Thanks. How much do we owe you for the coffees?'

'On the house. We don't get hardly any English folks. My pleasure. Have a nice day now.'

Marilyn, looking anxious, said,

'Was she warning us?'

'No, but she's right, these roads are best traversed in daylight. If we broke down, well, she said it, the temperature drops very quickly.'

They got in the car, drove off, sped along the empty highway and into Las Vegas.

Chapter Fourteen

A week later John, now in San Francisco, got a phone call from a very agitated-sounding Fred McTaggart. Marilyn answered the mobile as John was showering when its urgent-sounding ring disturbed the quiet of their hotel room.

'Is Johnny boy there?'

'Who's calling? Oh, yes, it's you, Fred. Hold on, I'll get him for you.'

John, hearing the ring tone, had put on a dressing gown, and walked into the room.

'It's Fred for you.'

'Hello there, what's the occasion? Do you need bailing out again?' John said, winking at his wife.

'Change of plan.'

'Come again?'

'Scrap that article I—'

'Fred, I've nearly—'

'Never mind. I've got it on good authority that a referendum's on the cards. Cameron and Clegg have come to an understanding, I hear. They're working on the presumption that no party will get a majority in the election.'

'And?'

'When do you get back from the land of the free? Or have you emigrated?'

'We're booked to fly back tomorrow night.'

'Can we meet up the day after tomorrow? I've got a new proposition for you. A big one.'

'Sounds intriguing, but let's say Friday, at noon.'

'What did he want, John, as if I didn't know?'

'Well, to be honest, I suspect he's… The rumour is there's going to be a referendum on the EU, so my piece on the financial aspects of our membership has been spiked even before I've finished it. This is just typical Fred. No wonder I demurred at the prospect of working full-time for him again. You'd think that he might have mellowed by now, but no, always looking for the next journalistic scoop. It's getting to be old hat these days, what with the rise of social media.'

'You say that, John, but you are going to meet with him, aren't you?'

'Yes, I am. If nothing else I'll need to be recompensed for the aborted article. If I know the old reprobate, he'll huff and puff, then toss me a bone. I have to admit, though, his mentioning the prospect of a public vote, well, yes, it is intriguing and could be a really big story, and a controversial one at that.'

'It's certainly controversial, and potentially very divisive, John,' Marilyn said, with a concerned look, something which her husband picked up.

'When I was in the City, and then working in journalism, I did detect misgivings surrounding the direction the EU was taking, although most City types would be very nervous about our leaving, given the potential ramifications, and—'

'This "proposition" Fred referred to, it might drag you into some—'

'Marilyn, he'll probably be wanting me to write pieces

on the overall economic and financial aspects. I may have opinions, but I'll be studiously impartial, and in any case, people don't usually shoot the messenger.'

Looking unconvinced, she replied,

'Be careful, John.'

*

They arrived, weary, at their flat to be greeted by an 'urgent' message from David.

'Hi, you two vagabonds! Need to rendezvous asap. Got some big news that'll surprise you both. Call me on this number to set up a meet.'

'I can guess what that refers to,' said Marilyn. 'Anita's finally given him her news. He sounded chipper though. Intriguing. Call him back to arrange, John. Suggest, oh, I don't know, tomorrow lunchtime.'

'I'm seeing Fred then, Marilyn,' he said, while dialling David's number. 'Let's see when they're available. Sounds like he'll be flexible. Hi, Dave, what's up?'

John was silent for over a minute. Marilyn came in from the kitchen with two mugs of coffee, putting them down on the small table as she parked herself on the sofa. She took a sip from her mug and looked up at her husband, who began to smile, and he gave her a thumbs-up.

'Tomorrow evening at seven then, Dave. It'd be a lot cheaper if you just spilled now, I'm very hungry these days… No, Dave, not for that… OK then, we'll see you both in the Venetian at six-thirty.'

'I'm guessing he didn't enlighten you, John.'

'No, he's very excited about something though. You don't think she's pregnant again? Didn't you say her doctor had advised against it for the time being?'

'Well, not exactly, but she gave me the impression he was cool about trying for a baby so soon. She got a bit teary at the time.'

John picked up his coffee and was about to ask if Marilyn would consider going out for dinner when his mobile rang.

'No rest for the wicked,' he said, as he replaced the mug. 'This better not be Fred again.'

He picked up the mobile.

'Hello? Oh, it's you again.'

David.

'OK, I'll let her know.'

John ended the call, turned to Marilyn and said,

'That was Dave again. He asked if you could give Anita a bell tomorrow at work. She wants to speak with you urgently. Odd, why couldn't she talk to you now?'

'Annoying. She knows I'm not back at work until next week, so she thinks… I was going to pop over to my mother's with that gift, but… I'll speak to her in the morning. John, let's go out for something to eat. I can't be bothered slaving away in that kitchen. We can end our break with a quiet meal, just you and me.'

Leaving the flat, the elderly spinster who lived in the flat below accosted them, saying,

'Did your friend manage to get hold of you? She was very anxious, I think.'

Marilyn said,

'Who was this?'

The woman, now apprehensive, said,

'Oh, err… I heard a banging on the door, and when I peeked out, she saw me and rushed down the stairs. She looked frightened—'

Marilyn, looking concerned, said,

'Was she a tall, fair-haired woman?'

'Err, yes, I think so.'

'What did she say?'

'Oh, she asked me if I knew when you'd be back, but before I could answer she rushed off.'

'Thank you, Mrs...'

'Miss Harris.'

'Right,' said Marilyn, momentarily embarrassed. 'Perhaps you'd like to pop in for a cup of tea sometime?'

'Why, yes, that would be nice. Maybe after I'm back from church on Sunday evening. Goodbye.'

'That was awkward, Marilyn, but funny too.'

'You told me there was an old widow woman downstairs, and naturally, I assumed—'

'OK, OK, but your face. Back to business. What are we going to do concerning our two friends? Do you think it was Anita that woman encountered? I'll bet she was mistaken. Only one way of finding out. Are you going to speak to her now, before we go out?'

'No, I'll contact her in the morning.'

Chapter Fifteen

After John had left the flat the following morning, on his way to the library, telling Marilyn he would be ensconced there for the day apart from his lunch with Fred, she picked up the phone and called Anita. There was no answer, so she went over to her mother's, an hour-long Tube trip across to Chiswick, to give her the present from their trip. Being a widow who'd lost her husband when her only child was four, Marilyn's childhood and youth had been heavily influenced by her sense of duty to her parent, who wasn't given to displays of affection. She seldom invited her school friends home, after an unfortunate visit by a fellow pupil at primary school who'd inadvertently spilt milk on the kitchen table, prompting an explosion of anger.

As the train rattled noisily along, Marilyn's mind wandered back to her schooldays, and her only close and lasting friendship, with Anita, a fact which many of their contemporaries and teachers found puzzling, almost strange. They were very different personalities, but had developed a strong bond, despite Anita's frequent brushes with authority figures; she was the archetypal rebel, no matter how trivial or ephemeral the issue, and she appeared often to take a twisted pleasure in rubbing up people the wrong way. Her rejection of accepted norms in school culminated in near-expulsion, after she got drunk at the annual speech day and staggered into the theatre, demanding to know if the headmaster had really had sex with a young female gym teacher. Anita was only saved when Marilyn spoke on her behalf at a disciplinary hearing, telling the members of the panel tearfully that her friend had acted totally out of character, because of her frequent susceptibility to extreme hormonal problems. She recalled Anita's whispered comment after they left the hearing, 'I'll never forget what you said in there, Marilyn. Never, believe me.'

When she arrived at her mother's, the mobile rang. As she was fumbling for it in her handbag, her mother came to the door and said,

'What are you doing, girl? Come in out of the rain, you'll catch a death.'

Marilyn stumbled over the doorstep, and before she managed to locate the phone, it stopped ringing. She sighed and dropped her large handbag, making a loud bang as the thing hit the umbrella stand next to the door.

'Can't see the need for those stupid little contraptions,' said her irritated, unsmiling mother. 'What's so vital that someone needs to speak to you anyway? How's James?'

'It's John, Mother. He's fine, and sends his best wishes. He had—'

'Oh, I see, couldn't be bothered to come to see his widowed mother-in-law. Young people these days, no manners. I remember your father always used to say—'

'Actually, Mother,' said Marilyn, getting irritated, 'I've brought you a gift from California. John chose it for you.'

She took out a miniature of the *Queen Mary*, thinking it would remind her of a cruise her parents had made before she was born.

'What's this?' she said, peering at the box.

'A model of the ship you and Dad went on, remember?'

'Oh, I see. You've been off gallivanting, that's why you didn't answer the phone when I called you last week. I hope it wasn't expensive. You'll have to control your husband, dear. They all love spending money like there's no tomorrow. I know that from experience!'

The two women sat down to tea. As her mother told a long, detailed story about a neighbour who'd omitted to put her bins out, Marilyn surveyed the living room, thinking back to her childhood in the house; just the two of them in the large four-bedroomed property. A lonely existence, not helped by her introverted personality.

'Well, girl? Are you listening?'

Marilyn stirred. 'Yes, Mother… What were you saying?'

'Never mind. Have you got any news worth telling me? Are you still working at that terrible school?'

'Yes, and it's a good school, Mother. Have you any plans for today? We could pop along into town and see a film—'

'I'm going to the Women's Guild meeting with Father Delany at two o'clock. You could come along. Father is always asking me how you're getting along, he's such a nosy old crone. But I suppose you're too busy to spare the time.'

She stood, put the crockery onto a tray and walked off to the kitchen. Marilyn, following her, said, 'I'd love to, Mother,' prompting a surprised look.

Marilyn arrived home, weary, at five-thirty. John wasn't in, presumably still with his nose in some form of printed material, she surmised. Half an hour later, the sound of the front door opening startled her. She moved toward the hallway.

'Hi, Marilyn, had a good day? How's your mother?'

'Same as usual. She seemed to like the gift. We went along

to her Women's Guild thing at church. Father Delany was asking after you.'

'Did you summon up the nerve to contact Anita? I have to confess, I've not spoken with Dave, but no doubt he'll be in touch… Oh Christ, we're supposed to be eating with them in the Venetian. Seven, wasn't it? Should I call and cancel? It's nearly six.'

'Would you mind, John? I'm not in the mood. I've had a depressing day, and the prospect of—'

'Good,' said John, picking up on his wife's downbeat mood, 'I'll do it now.'

After letting a disappointed-sounding David know, he said,

'Fred called me this morning. Embarrassing, I forgot to put the mobile on silent. It woke up half of the punters in the reading room. He called off our meet, saying he'd get back to me by Friday. He sounded very… conspiratorial, but he was insistent he's on to something big. Shall we go along to the Italian?'

'OK, John, I don't fancy cooking. Funny, I said that last night too. Maybe we need a live-in cook/housekeeper.'

'How about your mother? I'd wager she'd love that, ordering both of us around!'

'That wasn't remotely funny, John. If you'd suffered her for twenty-odd years you wouldn't even make a joke of it.'

'Sorry, Marilyn.'

By ten, they had returned from the trattoria, and were staring at the television blankly when Marilyn's mobile rang, faintly. John stood, walked over to his wife's handbag, took out the phone and handed it to her.

'Hi, Anita, how are… Hold on now, calm down! John called David just after six this evening to cancel and… Yes, very irritating. Listen, yes, should we meet up for a chat, no, not tomorrow, but Friday? I'm not due back at school until Monday, so if that's—'

Marilyn shook her head in irritation, put the mobile on the coffee table and said,

'She says David didn't tell her we'd cancelled. She went to the restaurant, waited for him, and us, so you can probably guess her mood. What planet is he on? Wouldn't like to be in his shoes when she gets home. Oh, she agreed to my suggestion—'

'Suggestion?'

'Yes, she said originally we could meet up for a chat tomorrow. It might even have been interesting, but I'm seeing Mother again, so we agreed on Friday. Anita said she's definitely in line for a big step up, a new job, and she's convinced herself it's a done deal, a promotion. I hope she'll not be disappointed if it doesn't materialise. You haven't heard anything on the subject from David, I suppose?'

'No.'

'I hope for both their sakes things work out for her. Anita's got a good brain, and this may be the spark she needs to take her out of this depression.'

Chapter Sixteen

Neither John nor Marilyn saw their friends over the next week; Anita cancelled the date with Marilyn on Friday morning, saying casually, 'Too bad, Marilyn, see you later.' All seemed to have gone quiet.

Fred McTaggart phoned John, asking if he was free for a session in the Hangman's, 'anytime, anytime that suits you, Johnny boy,' so he arranged to meet him on the Friday before Christmas. It turned out to be a cold, damp afternoon as John got off the Tube and strolled the quarter mile to the pub. Inside, the place was heaving with revellers in various states of inebriation. John scanned the crowded bar; before he saw Fred, he heard the familiar bellowing laugh coming from the far side of the bar, then he spotted the white-haired, red-faced visage, with a hand lifting a half-empty pint glass to his lips. John moved, with some difficulty because of the closely packed crowd, toward him, in the midst of a small coterie of admirers, the majority of them less than sober. Spotting his old protégé, he said,

'And here, my disciples, is the one who got away! Johnny boy, if only you'd stayed with me, you might have earned a

Pulitzer by now, or maybe picked up a few libel suits. What's your poison? I haven't dropped that rumour about your misadventures at the Tory conference a few years back, before you got hitched and respectable of course.'

'A pint of bitter, any kind, thanks, Fred. Having a celebration, or is it just a Christmas piss-up?'

'Err… Well… Yes, Johnny boy, and no. I've got something, a really, really, mind-bendingly front-page story… behind—'

'Behind? Behind what?' John asked, bewildered.

Fred put down his empty glass, inclined his head to the nearby barman and said,

'Not here, my boy… These young cubs are… not to be trusted with… this particular subject—'

'If I'd known this was only a session, well, I wouldn't have wasted my—'

'Now, now be patient. Later, Johnny boy, later,' said Fred with a sly, knowing wink. 'Down that insipid-looking pint first and then, back to the coalface where I can give you more, as they say, intelligence. A poncey word to describe rumour, don't you think, but…'

John, from his two years of working, often chaotically, with his old mentor, knew that the man often became very animated with what usually turned out to be mere tittle-tattle, but he prided himself on being able to read his friend. Although full of drink, this was one of those occasions. Fred had stumbled across some information, perhaps significant, and probably of import. Standing at the bar, watching him holding forth to his young, adoring fan club, he thought back to editorial sessions where he would pressure his small team of budding journalists with stentorian instructions to 'skewer the lying bastards good and proper'. Fred considered politics to be the lowest form of human endeavour, practised by rogues, charlatans and criminals, and liked nothing more than exposing chicanery masquerading as public service. For him, democracy in Britain was an elaborate con trick, a sham perpetrated on the people.

'So, Fred, you don't think there'll be an election anytime soon?' said John, attempting to flush out what he thought was behind Fred's cryptic statement.

'How would I know? But there has to be one next year,' replied Fred with a wink. 'Brown no doubt has got his ear to the ground, but there's a mood I detect abroad, a vague feeling of dissatisfaction, which means he may go to the country sooner rather than later. Signing that treaty in Lisbon, sneaking in through the back door, with the cameras of our ever-vigilant news channels strangely absent... that tells you something, Johnny boy, tells you something about what the politicos think, and how they operate. And how Europe works too. Avoid telling the plebs what's really going on, what they're actually up to.'

He stopped, obviously – to John if not to the others – unwilling to continue, a fact which convinced him that his old friend did have, or had come across, something big. He finished his pint, and nodded to the barman, holding up his empty glass. Fred, looking around to check there were no 'spies' nearby, leaned forward to John and said in hushed tones, holding a hand over his mouth,

'Listen, John, can you spare a few moments of your precious time to talk, at the office? I know you consider me a politics nerd, but, as the old song goes, "There's something in the air."'

'Blowing in the wind maybe, Fred?'

'Can't stand the sanctimony in that song, John. No, I mean it. People just might be getting a chance to...'

'To what?'

'The chance of getting a say. Remember what I said about the two C's? And their cunning plan to get into office? Promising a phony referendum in their manifestos?'

'What's this, Fred, you aren't going soft, are you? When it comes to admiration of our democracy, I've always been as sceptical as you. Getting a say? Don't make me laugh. Who was it said, "If voting changed anything, they'd abolish it"?'

'OK, John, as I said, we can go through what I've learnt, and plan out what we can do to… Can you make it the day after Boxing Day, ten o'clock? Unless the missus has got other plans,' Fred winked, 'for your time. Christ, you must be thirsty! Another one over here, my good sir. This man over here's gagging!'

Having sunk seven pints, John decided to hail a cab to get home, not willing to risk the Tube late at night. He took out his key and tried clumsily to insert it into the lock, but before he'd managed the normally simple task Marilyn opened the door.

'My goodness, John, your breath! Steady there, I'll get you a coffee. A good session, by the look and smell of you. Thank goodness you don't associate with that man often.'

'Sorry, dear,' muttered John, only now beginning to realise he was under the influence as he staggered around the coffee table, and, trying to lessen his feeling of guilt, continued, 'Well, it's Christmas and… Marilyn, what are we doing for dinner on… Are we going to your mother's?'

He slumped into an armchair, reached over to the table for the remote and managed to switch on the television. Marilyn deposited two mugs of coffee and said,

'Yes, now, Christmas Day lunch. Now don't react, I'm thinking of asking Anita and David over. She told me they've no plans, but said she's worried David's parents will be expecting them at their place. His brother from Canada is coming over to spend the holidays with the parents, but Anita's not keen on being, as she described it, "a family trophy"…'

'Did she ashk what we were planning?'

'Not exactly. I got the distinct impression she was fishing for an invite. You know how charming she can be—'

'When she's after something. OK, Marilyn, go ahead. My mother'sh away on a cruise to the Northern Lights, so we're free. What will you do about your mother though?'

'I've already mentioned it. She said she'll let me know.'

'Oh good. I think I need to hit the hay. Busy night.'

He stood unsteadily, Marilyn assisting him.

'You really are drunk, aren't you? This is the first time I've seen you so helpless with alcohol. I always assumed David was teasing me, trying to make you out as a premier league boozer when the two of you were at college. Maybe—'

'No, he was trying to lead you on… Wait, that came out wrong—'

'Yes, it did, but changing the subject, didn't you say Fred had a matter of substance to discuss with you? Anything interesting?'

'Yesh, and no, or… Did I mean no and yesh… I'm certain he's got what used to be termed a "scoop", and he was dying to talk, all nudge, nudge, wink, wink, but he was just sober enough, I mean, aware of the surroundings, to be circum… circumspect—'

'You're none the wiser then?'

'Again, dear, yes and no. We've agreed to meet up after Christmas. Judging by his barely disguised enthusiasm, he'sh got information, which no doubt he'll want to discuss with me. The way he was talking generally, you know, all cynicism about politics – they're all either corrupt or stupid, and sometimes both – I'd guess he may be on to something. He was banging on about Europe. If he's told me once, he's told me a million times, he was one of the minority who voted no in 1975 and have since been proven to be right. He really hates the EU, with a passion. God, I'm feeling a bit rough now, Marilyn. Shorry to get into such a state, won't do it again.'

He sat back into the chair and fell asleep.

Chapter Seventeen

Christmas Day loomed. Marilyn duly invited Anita and David, together with her mother. In the week leading up to the big day she had spent a long day in the West End shopping with her old friend, both of them in good spirits, with Anita spending money like there was no tomorrow, buying presents for her work colleagues as well as her extended family, which surprised Marilyn, given Anita's dismissive comments about them in the past – 'bunch of two-faced snobs'.

While having lunch in a small trattoria, Anita eyeballed a tall, grey-haired man, dressed in an expensive-looking three-piece suit, and shouted across the room,

'Martin, over here!'

The man, initially startled by Anita's loud call, swivelled round and walked briskly over to their table.

'Playing truant again, Anita?' said Martin, with what struck Marilyn as a cynical grin. 'What's the excuse this time?'

'You know me too well, Martin! Oh, forgive me, I'm being rude, this is my best and oldest friend, confidante if you will. Marilyn O'Brien.'

'Marilyn Duncan,' she said, proffering her hand, noticing his handshake was limp, the palm cold.

'What? Oh of course, yes. She's donned the shackles of love too. Martin's my boss. Not too bad, despite being a man. What are you doing here?'

'Err... having lunch. Can I get you two a drink?'

'I'll have a brandy, Martin, the usual size of course. How about you, Marilyn?'

'Orange juice please.'

'She's always been the quiet, reserved one, Martin. Forever keeping me in my place, on the straight and narrow, you could say.'

Martin, beginning to look apprehensive, said,

'Well, nice to have met you, Marilyn. Must dash. See you at work next week, I mean after the holidays, Anita.'

He walked away quickly to his table.

'Is that your new boss, Anita, or your old one?'

'What? I don't... Oh, Marilyn. I've told you I'm sure. I'm in line now for a decent posting in the diplomatic section of the Foreign Office. You remember I said my application was put on hold pending... Well, whatever the reason, it's no longer an issue. I expect he'll be recommending me for somewhere exotic, by the middle of next year I've heard on the grapevine. What are you going to order?'

*

After opening their presents early on Christmas morning, John and Marilyn left the flat for a morning stroll. The fresh, crisp air was still frosty, with the sun blazing down. Half an hour into their walk, Marilyn's phone rang.

'Hello, Mother. Yes, and a Happy Christmas to you too. What? Is he a definite? I would have thought he'd be tied up, today of all days. No, I'm not suggesting… Fine, he'll be most welcome.'

'That was my mother. She says she's bringing—'

'Her new boyfriend?' said John, chuckling at the suggestion.

'Very droll. No, she says Father Delany's invitation to the bishop's do has been cancelled, don't know why, so she thought—'

'No problem, Marilyn. Didn't you say he can talk the hind legs off a donkey?'

She smiled and said, 'Yes, that's true, on religious matters but—'

'Don't stress. Anyway, three of the company at the table are Catholics. Wait, I know! We could have a Bible study session after the Queen, like Trivial Pursuit, only with theology questions. Does God exist? Or is he an invention by man? Dave'll love it.'

John burst out laughing, Marilyn eventually following suit, thinking back to how her mother would encourage her to take part in similar quiz games in Sunday school. A naturally assiduous person, Marilyn regularly excelled, a trait she carried through to university, only narrowly losing out on being picked for the *University Challenge* programme.

'Just as well I bought that turkey, and here I was thinking it was too big.'

'Did you tell them when you intend to serve up? Marilyn, did you—'

'I'd better call her back.'

On the stroke of two, Anita and David appeared, she in a bright green, low-cut number which exposed rather too much in Marilyn's opinion.

'Hi, guys!' shouted David, who seemed to have started early. 'Anita lost the toss, so it's chocks away, John. Hey, what's that smell, Marilyn? Hope it's not the meal! Who else is joining us? Anita said something about a priest…'

'My mother's invited her parish priest, Father Delany,' said Marilyn, adding a touch sarcastically, 'he's the one who married us, David, after old Father McCann cried off, so you might just recognise him.'

'You never know, babe. Anita here dragged me off to Mass this morning, the six o'clock service. Did you go, Marilyn? Or did John keep you in the kitchen? He likes his grub.'

'Less of the banter, Dave,' whispered a clearly annoyed Anita, and more audibly, 'he's only allowed one drink before the meal and then a toast for the Queen. You know, Marilyn, he likes to tell far-fetched anecdotes about his exploits at uni, but after a couple of libations he's as daft as a brush, and as useless in—'

Interrupting what was potentially an awkward situation, the doorbell rang.

'I'll get it, Marilyn,' said her husband.

'Thank you, John, I expect it's my mother and Father Delany. Dinner's in ten minutes, people. Can you pour the drinks please, Anita? Mother likes dry sherry, and I think Father prefers a whisky, and whatever you two are inclined to—'

'He's on a solitary glass of red, Marilyn, then the fizzy water.' David, affecting the hurt expression he'd developed as a teenager to soften up his mother, usually successfully, appealed to his friend,

'See what I have to put up with, John,' who, as he ushered in the final two guests, replied,

'Stop whingeing, Dave, it won't get you anywhere except into your wife's bad books.'

'True, John, true.'

The meal progressed uneventfully, with the conversation centring on family and social matters. Father Delany proved to be an urbane, surprisingly worldly guest, to the extent that his fellow diners forgot that he was a man of the cloth. When the clock on the wall struck three, Marilyn switched on the television, saying,

'Oh dear, we nearly forgot one of the more important rituals.'

'Good old Marilyn, Her Majesty's most loyal and devoted subject,' said Anita, with a hint of sarcasm. 'Even at school, she had this fetish for the royals – Diana, her brats and the rest. It used to make us laugh. Remind me, Marilyn, where were you the day of her funeral?'

Father Delany, sensing the latent tension between the two women, intervened.

'Yes, that was a very sad day, though one couldn't help but admire the dignity of the occasion.'

'Dignity?' said Anita raising her eyebrows. 'All those pathetic teenage girls throwing flowers. I was half expecting Elvis to appear and—'

'Shush!' said John. 'Let's just hear what Her Maj has to say.'

'Something anodyne as usual, I expect. Anyone else for a top-up? Not you, Dave. Make yourself useful for once and grab that bottle. No takers? OK. Well, I'll just have to finish it off myself, an onerous responsibility.'

As she poured the dregs of the bottle into her glass, the room fell silent while the Queen spoke.

'Call me old-fashioned,' said Father Delany, 'but I've always enjoyed listening to her homespun addresses. Her message was always heard respectfully in the seminary. She managed—'

'Oh no!' said Anita. 'Let's not drag religion into it—'

She began to laugh.

'Sorry, Father, I've had too much of God's water…'

'That's alright, my dear,' said the priest, smiling at her benignly, 'I'm not here to preach, merely to celebrate with two of my congregation and their lucky spouses, not forgetting one of the pillars of my parish, Mrs O'Brien. That was a wonderful meal, young Marilyn. Your mother's taught you well.'

'She didn't get her talent from me, Father,' said Marilyn's mother, 'or her liking for drink.'

'Now, now, Mrs O'Brien,' the priest chided her, again displaying his smile, 'if I may, as I'm amongst you worldly types, what do you think about this upcoming election? Does anyone think there may be a change in the wind? Thirteen years of, what's it called, oh yes, New Labour, have certainly moved things along.'

'At the risk of provoking controversy,' said David, looking solemn, 'I've made a decision.'

Everyone looked at him, most in curiosity, except Anita, who poured a drink as he continued, 'I've been accepted as a candidate for the Tories, in Benfleet.'

John rocked back in his chair, open-mouthed.

'Well, Dave, you certainly kept that under the radar!'

'Not with me he didn't,' said Anita, after gulping the drink, 'but I suppose he needs a hobby, now that we've discovered we can't—'

Marilyn interrupted, saying, 'Anita, could you give me a hand in the study please? I've… we've got a few gifts to hand out. Come on, we can't keep everyone in suspense.'

Puzzled, and clearly shaken, Anita followed her friend out of the room.

'Is Anita OK, Dave?' said John.

'What? Sure, just put out because I announced it off the cuff. She's OK with it really,' he concluded, glancing anxiously around the table. Unnoticed by the two men, Father Delany and Marilyn's mother exchanged knowing looks. John said,

'I wasn't aware you were keen on politics, Dave. In fact, every time the subject came up you were dismissive, if not abusive, about politicians. And now you want to join the club?'

'Times have changed, John. The crisis two years back shook the edifice. You must know that, being in finance, and it'll be years before things are sorted. Brown and his gang of cowboys will never be able to put the country back in good financial order. I'm not overly political in strict party terms, but it's only a party signed up to the merits of the free market that can do it. Cameron looks the part to me, so when I was approached, I—'

'He wasn't "approached", John,' said Anita coming into the room with two wrapped parcels, 'he sneaked off one evening a few weeks ago, to a selection committee in some shady backroom in Benfleet. He only told me after he'd been selected. Apparently, he's lucky. The place is what they call a "safe seat", so after the election, when it comes, I'll be an MP's sidekick. Can't wait for those socials. Talking to the blue rinse brigade, answering inane questions about my fam… I mean our private life. Great fun, wouldn't you agree, Father?'

'Now then, Anita,' replied the priest, patting her hand as she handed over a parcel, 'serving the wider community is a noble calling. I'm confident David, with his background in the law, will make a positive contribution.'

'He sells houses, Father. Conveyancing.'

John cut in, trying to suppress, unsuccessfully, a chuckle.

'That's right, Dave. A couple of years in and you could make the housing minister's job your own.'

David, initially annoyed, saw the joke and replied, 'Well, John, that's you off my list of special advisers now.'

'Never thought I'd make it, Dave. Wrong school.'

Marilyn's mother let out a shriek, making the others turn anxiously toward her.

'How did you guess, John? Marilyn wouldn't have, not in a million years.'

She had unwrapped her gift to discover a set of prints based on William Blake's drawings, complete with segments of his poetry.

'That'll have to be a secret, Mother-in-Law,' he said, 'but I can say, as a mere journalist, that the man certainly knew how to write, and draw, as we can see. But seriously, you're underestimating Marilyn. She teaches English after all.'

'I know that, you silly man, but she doesn't like Blake. No taste.'

Everyone laughed, and, eventually, the Blake admirer followed suit, holding up her arms to embrace first Marilyn and then her son-in-law. Marilyn took the remote and changed channels, announcing to her guests that, as usual, they would be watching *Mary Poppins*, a Christmas ritual, as she described it. Two hours later Anita and a strangely subdued David took their leave.

Marilyn's mother said after they exited the house,

'Those two didn't look comfortable, did they? What did she mean about not being able to… something or other? She's not happy. Marilyn, didn't you tell me Anita had—'

'She lost the baby, Mother… I've told you that already.'

'A great shame,' said Father Delany, shaking his head. 'It may be a trite phrase, but the Lord moves in mysterious – to humans anyway – ways. Very sad. But I hope and pray that one day they'll be blessed.'

John, concerned at this line of conversation, said, 'Yes, but Dave taking up politics, that was today's big surprise. I was gobsmacked. In all the time I've known him I can't recall him showing any interest, or opinions for that matter.'

'Would you consider helping him, John?' said Marilyn.

'Not sure, dear, but it's unlikely to happen. As a virgin candidate he'll most probably be spoon-fed his lines, and his campaign will be guided by Conservative Central Office. I must say, though, safe seats like Benfleet are normally in the gift of the party, not the local associations, which… which leads me to surmise that Dave's been practising some greasy pole skills. Funny that, he was very critical of fellow students canvassing support to be elected onto the union, and here he is now… Well, I suppose we all change over time.'

'You sound, well, vaguely disappointed, John,' said Father Delany.

'Do I? It's just that Dave, despite appearances, the bravado, the wisecracks, is rather an insecure person. He loves to be liked, admired. You saw the way he was with Anita today.'

'She likes to be liked too, John,' said Marilyn, 'and I'd be surprised if his being involved in politics will go down well, particularly in light of her new posting. What if it turns out to be a foreign one? Anita doesn't know the word compromise.'

'Yes, she was always a stubborn, pig-headed girl, bossing my Marilyn around. You were too tolerant with her whims, Marilyn. Her mother spoiled her rotten too. Anything that took her fancy, she got. Spare the rod and spoil the—'

'Yes, yes, Mother, you've never taken to her.'

Father Delany, obviously uncomfortable with the dialogue, said to Marilyn's mother, 'Come on now, my dear, I think it's time for us to make our exit, or is it exeunt? Believe it or not, my friends, I've got confession duty. Yes, even on Christmas Night! Some of our more devoted parishioners take it extremely seriously, thinking they have to beg the Almighty's forgiveness for overindulging. Once again, Marilyn and John, thank you for the splendid hospitality. God bless you both.'

After their final two guests left, Marilyn said,

'I could do with a stiff drink now, John. They say Christmas is a stressful time, and today was, well, very awkward at times. Thank goodness old Father Delany was here, to ensure a modicum of civility. What the hell is David playing at? He must be aware of Anita's potential move, more than likely abroad. I can see stormy waters ahead in their marriage.'

'What did she mean about discovering… No, forget—'

'Don't look so worried, John, the subject's not taboo.'

Marilyn came over to the sofa and sat beside him. He could see from her serious expression there was something on her mind.

Taking hold of his hands, she said, 'No need to tiptoe around the subject. I've been thinking recently… thinking, perhaps we should consider starting a family. We're fairly well placed financially, and my job is beginning to grate. It's less satisfying, and I seem to spend more time on administration than actual teaching.'

John stared at her.

'What do you think?'

'Err… Well, yes, if that's what you want.'

'It is, but are you sure? You don't look exactly—'

'Sorry, it's just that I was taken aback, especially after the circus this afternoon.'

'Yes, it was fraught at times. Oh, and Anita's reference about discovering… She's been told having children will be difficult.'

'Do you think that may explain her moodiness?'

'No, she's always been like that. You heard what my mother thinks about her.'

Recovering composure, but still pondering why his wife had chosen this time to raise the subject, he said,

'Can we have another drink? I don't know about you, but I think a whisky would go down a treat. It's been an exhausting day.'

As they supped the malt, John looked at his wife with a mixture of affection and trepidation.

Chapter Eighteen

Fred McTaggart called John two days later.

'Have a good Christmas, my friend? I said I'd be in touch, and I always keep my promises. My ex-wife was telling me at lunch the other day, "Fred," she said, "you're one of life's more reliable—"'

John, his mind still on his wife's unexpected declaration, cut him off.

'I've heard that one several times before, Fred. So she's talking to you again—'

'Yes, she can't resist the McTaggart charm. Invited me over for Christmas lunch, with all the trimmings, if you catch—'

John laughed, and said,

'I take it you're calling to remind me about meeting up to talk over this "scoop" you hinted at the other day. I'm going over to my mother's today with Marilyn, but I'm free up until New Year's Eve.'

'As it happens, I'm tied up today too, but let me think. Yes, how about the day after tomorrow?'

John looked at his diary and said,

'That suits me too, Fred. Where? Not the Hangman's, if we're going to be discussing—'

'Quite right, old boy. Come on round to Sylvia's. She was asking after you at lunch. Bring the missus too. Does six o'clock suit? She's a great cook, among her other talents.'

John, initially surprised by Fred's invitation to dine with him and his ex-wife, replied,

'OK, Fred, that sounds good. I take it you and Sylvia won't be exchanging insults over the meal?'

'Oh, we're way past that nonsense now. Tell Marion—'

'It's Marilyn, Fred.'

'I know, tell Marilyn Sylvia's dying to meet her. We can go through my proposition over a nice meal and a few aperitifs. I think you'll be amenable to my suggestion.'

'Can you give me a hint, Fred? I'm presuming here, but I expect you want—'

'You presume correctly, Johnny boy. I've a feeling in my water. The good times are going to roll once again. Six o'clock on the thirtieth then. Sylvia's moved, yet again, so I'll email you the address. Very impressive pad, close to Marylebone tube. Don't figure how she swung it. Last time we spoke the old girl was fending off the bailiffs. See you later, Bernstein!'

John smiled at the reference to his old nickname.

'Bye, Fred.'

He walked into the kitchen. Marilyn was emptying shopping bags.

'How's Fred? Has he sobered up yet?'

'He's invited us over for dinner.'

'Don't tell me, to a burger joint, with us paying.'

'Perhaps you'd better sit down before I tell you. He's asked us to join him and Sylvia, you remember, his ex-wife, at her place on the thirtieth. Yes, I was amazed too. They're on speaking terms now, he assured me. If nothing else, Marilyn, it should be entertaining. Sylvia's the only person I know who can match Fred for repartee. And he promised… the plates will stay on the table. They got through a lot of crockery when the marriage was folding.'

'Yes, OK, John, but will it be a purely social gathering? No mention of this scoop?'

'Yes, he said he'll be raising it. Should be a good evening. On that particular matter he wasn't forthcoming, but he's certainly buzzing. I heard from a normally reliable contact that the government, or to be precise, Brown and his advisers, are worried about the election. It has to be next year. June's the favourite month. I won't burst Fred's balloon though, I'll let him announce whatever it is, in his usual manner.'

'Is that other analysis job on the back burner now? It'd be a shame. You've spent a good deal of time and effort on the piece. I trust you'll be insisting on being paid!'

John smiled; he'd learnt very quickly Marilyn's built-in prudence in financial matters, a characteristic he admired. John, in spite of his financial acumen, which had brought him affluence, was curiously inept with his personal affairs.

'I expect we'll be discussing it, yes. Fred's got many failings, but he's not mean. One of the reasons his ventures failed in the past was because of his generosity to people who didn't merit it. Don't fret, we'll work something out. Anyway,' he continued, 'he knows you're as tight as a hangman's noose—'

'I suppose you'd categorise that remark as a joke. I don't think it's funny at all. A fool and his money are soon parted. Didn't our illustrious Prime Minister pride himself on being termed Mr Prudence?'

'That didn't last long. Old Fred used to say mention of Brown made him reach for the bottle, not that he needed an excuse. In all the time I've known and worked with him, I haven't been able to nail his politics. He loves to parade his cynicism, but you know what they say: scratch the surface of a cynic and you'll see a disappointed person—'

'John, you really have an extraordinary facility to talk gibberish. I'm not remotely political, hate even hearing the subject being mentioned, but if you ask me, Brown should have opted for 2007, before the crash.'

'I thought you said you weren't—'

'I'm not. Just saying though.'

*

On the morning of the thirtieth, Marilyn, working at home despite the holidays, had her concentration disrupted when, reviewing her department's timetable for the new term, her mobile, which she had forgotten to put on silent, rang out.

'Hello, Anita, how are the slopes? Plenty of snow, I expect—'

'We didn't go in the end, Marilyn. Dave had to cancel, at the last minute. I'm going to have trouble getting the money back. Can we pop out for dinner tonight? Just you and me, a girlie chat? He's had to go and ingratiate himself over at Benfleet. He asked me to go along with him, but the prospect of facing a bunch of nosy old bats—'

Marilyn bit her lip and said, her voice betraying anxiety, 'Oh that's annoying, Anita, I'm booked to go over to an old colleague of John's. Could we make it tomorrow? At lunchtime perhaps?'

She heard Anita's familiar sigh and asked,

'Are you OK? You sound depressed.'

'Why do you say that? I'm perfectly fine, thank you very much! No, I was only going to tell you about my new posting, but you're much too busy. Talk later.'

Marilyn put the mobile on her desk, wondering if Anita's invitation for chat was cover for a more substantive reason, a personal one, with the potential new job the ostensible excuse.

Had she and David crossed swords over the issue? Their body language on Christmas Day came back to Marilyn. The relationship was clearly an intense one; David's easy-going manner was in stark contrast to Anita's headstrong, sometimes overpowering personality. She was, in particular since the tragedy, focused on her career, so her husband's conversion to public life, with all its commitments for both of them, could be problematic, to put it mildly. Marilyn switched off her laptop, unable to give the unfinished task any meaningful attention, and went into the kitchen to make a hot drink. Abruptly, she turned off the kettle, walked into the lounge, having taken a wine glass, and poured a large measure of John's malt into it. The alcohol had an immediate effect on her; she started to feel guilt. From her brittle-sounding tone, Marilyn suspected Anita was in trouble, and she had turned her down because of a pre-existing commitment. Should she speak to John, maybe to postpone the meal, or even absent herself because of... Because of what? It was also possible that Anita merely required a sounding board for her real, or perceived, difficulties, in which case, she could dismiss the call as trivial.

She heard John's key in the front door.

'Hello, dear. Sorry I'm later than I expected. There I was, sitting minding my business in the library reading room, when who should tap me on the... Marilyn, are you alright? No, I can see something's up. Tell me.'

Marilyn said nothing, a shake of her head the only response.

He sat beside her, put his arm on her shoulder and said,

'What is it? Something noteworthy, judging by the fact that it required a drink.'

'Anita called earlier. She asked me over for a chat, to tell me something about her job, she said, but now I'm concerned she wanted to divulge something. When I told her about our date with Fred and…'

'Sylvia. How did you leave it with her then?'

'Oh, I'm not sure, but she put on her shield, affecting not to care whether I'd go over and see her or not. John, I can't shrug off this gut feeling they're in some kind of difficulty. What was David thinking, getting involved in politics? He must know how much importance Anita attaches to her job, particularly now she can't have children. I was surprised by the call, thinking they were in Austria for skiing, but apparently David cancelled because of an "urgent" appointment in Benfleet. He may well love her, I remember your saying he was besotted from the start, but… but, how can he be so bone-headed?'

'Do you want me to postpone the Fred and Sylvia show? It's not exactly a summit meeting. Fred won't mind.'

'Are you sure?'

'Yes,' said John, hitting his speed dial.

'Hi, Sylvia, would you mind postponing our date this evening? Something fairly important's come up.'

He was silent for about thirty seconds, then said,

'That's great, Sylvia, thanks a lot. Regards to the old reprobate. Tell him from me, a night off the booze will keep his head clear. See you.'

The call ended. John looked at Marilyn and said, 'Go on, call Anita back now. Maybe I'll get hold of Frank, Bill and a couple of others from my less than respectable past, then advise Dave to meet us in our favourite watering hole after his Benfleet thing. Dave never refuses a boys' night out, and from what you've told me he might be glad to get—'

'Thank you, John,' Marilyn said, 'I only hope her invitation's still open.'

She dialled Anita's number. David answered, sounding distant, and said, 'Hi, Marilyn, Anita's not here just now. She must have been in a rush, leaving her phone behind. What can I do you for?'

'She called a while ago, David, to ask if I was free for dinner this evening, but I thought at the time I had another engagement. That's been postponed, so I was wondering if her invitation is still open—'

'Oh, right,' he replied, 'well, I'll get her to call you when she gets back. See you, Mari... Wait, that's her now! I'll have to get a locksmith in to fix the—'

Marilyn could hear her friend's voice cursing at David, who said, 'It's Marilyn.'

'Hi, Marilyn, glad you called me again. I've been on cloud nine the last forty-eight hours. Great news! I'm in pole position for the job in Brussels, attached to the Commission. My linguistic skills seem to have nailed it for me. Oh God! Here's me blabbing to you before I've told Dave! He looks excited, I can tell you! Why did you call, Marilyn? Got news for us, have you?'

'No, I was curious as to whether your dinner idea was still on.'

'Dinner? What do you mean? No, Dave is just over the moon, judging by the look on his physog, and he can't wait to celebrate with me... In the accepted way of course. Isn't that so, darling? What? Can't you tell those old bores you've got a better offer, Dave? Why not? Oh, fuck off then, I don't care how long it will go on for... Anyhow, Marilyn, I'll be in touch for a gossip session soon. Bye.'

Marilyn looked at her husband and said, 'I think your boozy session is cancelled, John. David's got a big meeting in Benfleet, and... I don't think he should be going... That post Anita's been fretting about for weeks, if not months, has finally materialised.'

'That should make Dave's life easier. I mean, now that she can settle down—'

'Brussels, John. A long commute from Barnes.'

John gazed at his wife, open-mouthed.

'Really? I thought all her spouting about a lush foreign posting was hyperbole. Jeez, Dave's got a dilemma on his hands now. Still, a lot of marriages work on the basis of weekends at home and—'

'No, John, in some marriages it can work, but there's more to it in their case. I've got a strong feeling she wants the job to get away from something. Surely it can't be their marriage? They're newlyweds in the scheme of things. Remember their antics at our reception? Couldn't keep their hands off each other.'

John said, hesitantly, 'But since then, losing the baby, followed by that shattering prognosis? Yes, I can see… see how the prospect might…'

Marilyn, sensing her husband's trepidation at raising the subject, took his hand.

'That's a possibility, but, well, ever since I've known Anita, she's always been determined to make her own way, to be an individual. Anyone she deemed to be thwarting her became an enemy. I'll say this, John, David had better come to terms with this situation, and quickly, because if he cavils at her being a weekend wife, he'll be the loser.'

John said,

'Yes, you could be right, and Dave getting tied up with politics doesn't make for an easy resolution. Old Fred could tell you a host of anecdotes about married politicians living the high life while they were tied up in Westminster away from their partners. In Dave's case it'll be the opposite. Tricky one. That reminds me, I'd better contact the old dipso before long to rearrange.'

Chapter Nineteen

John and Marilyn saw in the year 2010 with her mother. They had originally intended to spend the New Year celebrations with Marilyn's head teacher and other colleagues, but her mother's comment when Marilyn mentioned the school event changed their minds.

'Don't worry about me, dear, I'll be having a quiet night in front of the television with Barney.'

'John, I think maybe we should see the New Year in with—'

'Of course, Marilyn,' said John, smiling at his mother-in-law's less than subtle piece of emotional blackmail. 'I expect Barney could do with the company too.'

Barney was her dog. Early on New Year's Eve they trundled over.

'I thought you'd made arrangements. You really didn't have to come and sit with me and listen to my gripes. I'm quite content in my own company.'

'Aren't you forgetting old Barney here?' said John as he took off his coat in the hall.

Ignoring him, she said to Marilyn, 'Have you spoken to Anita recently?'

'Yes, as a matter of fact, Mother, I have. She's very excited with her new job.'

'Do you mean that foreign job she was going on about to me at Christmas? Nonsense if you ask me. The girl's still as flighty as ever. Always dreaming. They hardly ever come true.'

By two o'clock, with both mother-in-law and Barney snoring away, John and Marilyn crept up the creaky stairs to her old room.

'How did you survive up here?' he said, shivering as he got undressed. 'So cold, a real passion-killer.'

They laughed, and despite the arctic conditions fell asleep quickly.

John managed to contact a hungover-sounding Fred two days after the New Year freezathon. 'Oh, it's you, Johnny boy. Have a good New Year? Who'd have guessed it?'

'Guessed what?' said John, anticipating, wrongly, one of his long-winded anecdotes.

'Sylvia wants to take me back.'

'How much laughing juice did you pour down her throat, Fred?'

John quickly moved the handset away from his ear.

'Oh, very fucking droll, you cheeky git! The woman just can't live without me.'

'Sorry, Fred. I hope you'll both be very happy. Listen, can we arrange a date and time? I've spent the holiday period in unbearable suspense, wondering—'

'Not for much longer, my friend. Tonight, at a local hostelry, near you in fact. The Pelican. Did you know that was the original name of Drake's—'

'Yes, Fred, see you there. Bye.'

John left Marilyn at home and walked the half-mile to the Pelican. The public bar (Fred never frequented what he termed 'louche lounges') was virtually empty, and walking to the bar he spotted his friend, sitting at a table, talking animatedly to a bemused-looking grey-haired man in overalls. Eyeballing John, he shouted,

'Very timely, Johnny boy! My interlocutor and I are very thirsty. Two pints! And don't forget to get one for yourself.'

John brought over the tray with three pint glasses and edged it carefully onto the table.

'This is one of my protégés, John Duncan. Taught him the ropes,' Fred drawled; the pint wasn't his first.

'Oh, John, this is... Err... Joe—'

'Joe Donovan,' said Fred's new drinking buddy, standing up to shake John's outstretched hand.

'Pleased to meet you,' replied John. 'Has this man been boring you with his sparkling repartee?'

Joe said, slightly embarrassed, 'What? No, he was asking about that new-build across the road. I'm on the crew outfitting the place, and—'

'That's right, I was advising Joe here to get into property. With all the financial chaos after the crash, there's nothing like bricks and mortar, or gold of course, to guard against penury.'

John smiled as he imagined what poor Joe was thinking; he'd most likely come in for a soothing pint after a day's toil amidst the dust, and then gets saddled with the pub bore.

'I used to work, if that's not stretching the word, with Fred. Can you guess why I don't anymore?'

Joe laughed, grabbed his glass and downed the pint.

'Thanks for the drink, John. Have to get back to the missus else I'll be in trouble.'

He stood, put on his donkey jacket and made for the door.

'Great conversing with you, my friend!' shouted Fred. Joe waved, without speaking, and left the bar.

'Another satisfied customer,' said John. 'You were a loss to the world of financial advisers.'

'Most of them are similar to fortune-tellers, taking hard-earned money off gullible punters. I didn't start that discussion. He was moaning that guys like him were paid farthings while the bosses breakfasted on champagne. Way of the world, old boy, way of the world.

'Never mind, let's get down to serious business—'

'Good idea, Fred. I expect you'll be needing another lubricant to assist you in—'

'A double malt. I've long since lost the ability to down more than six or seven pints these days, and now the old dear is laying down the law. She says my paunch is off-putting when we roll in the hay. In her inimitable words, "You'll need some block and tackle to move your bulk soon."'

'I must admit, Fred, I was gobsmacked when you told us Sylvia had taken you back—'

'No, John, you've got it wrong! I took her back, when she asked me about seeing off those fucking bloodhounds chasing her for rent.'

'OK, OK, Fred,' said John, shaking his head, 'now, what's this revelation you've been chuntering on about? And more to the point, why do you require my... my... Well—'

'You know there has to be an election this year, and I've heard, in spite of the usual crap-filled soundbites, that the Tories aren't convinced they'll get a majority—'

'So?' John said with a sigh, expecting yet another lecture on Fred's obsession.

'So, he says! Without that majority, there'll be a furious bout of horse-trading between them, the Tories that is, and the Lib Dems. Labour's shot its bolt, with my fellow Scotsman's undertaker's mug giving everyone a fucking headache – too much porridge when he was a boy. Which means there could be a big change in attitude toward the EU.'

'Fred, all the big parties are signed up to Britain's membership—'

'Oh yes, totally agree. All the politicos I speak to just love it, but for a while, a few years I'd say, there's been a growing undercurrent of antipathy toward it from the great unwashed.'

'That may be true, Fred, but come election time they still put their cross against the candidate picked by their tribal leaders, whatever the candidate says.'

'I'm not so sure, Johnny boy. That fella, Joe, I asked what he thought of the EU, just out of curiosity. His response? "Wankers." A very reasoned opinion, and I'd wager a fiver it's a widespread, and growing, view.'

'OK, yes, I've heard that kind of description before too, but how does that tie in with the election?'

'John, think. The Lib Dems have said they'd support a referendum on membership. If the Tories are correct about the election result, and they end up the largest party, they'll cobble together a coalition, probably informal, with them. Part of any agreement would entail a commitment to granting a vote on the EU issue.'

'Bit of a stretch, Fred. Where's the advantage? Can you actually see any government, of whatever colour, allowing a vote? I can't.'

'I didn't say any of the parties would actually risk submitting the issue to a vote, only that if it's in the manifesto, they could say, a year or so into government, hand on heart, that thanks to the government's tough stance, the EU is reforming along the lines the UK has always wanted, therefore, no need for a costly and potentially divisive campaign. Quite brilliant, in a way. Con the punters who hold unacceptable, luddite opinions with the prospect of having a voice in how their country is governed.'

Getting more animated, he went on, oblivious to John's bored expression.

'And, probably the most devious, cunning aspect: I'd bet at least half of the electorate likely to vote to get out of the EU are Labour voters. If enough of them transfer their allegiance on the prospect of a referendum, Labour will be stuffed.'

'All very interesting, Fred,' said John, frustrated now, and beginning to wonder why his friend was so anxious to speak with him, 'but why are you—'

'Are you serious, Johnny boy? Well, maybe... Get me another malt and I'll outline my idea.

'I'm planning a long-term strategy for the paper, with the specific object of delving into the relationship between Britain and the EU. You've been over there, in Brussels and Strasbourg, for me in the past doing sundry assignments on particular matters which we deemed of interest to our readers. You know, John, sometimes I did feel a drop of sympathy, not much I'll admit, for you, having to sit through those interminable talking shop sessions at the so-called parliament.'

John winced at the recollection.

'Yes, some might call it purgatory. So much talking, so many useless speeches without any meaningful outcome, apart from those fabulous lunches. Are you offering me a proper job, Fred? It'll cost you, really cost you, believe me.'

Fred smiled at him and responded coolly,

'How does fifty grand sound?'

John rocked back on his seat, visibly startled and said, 'Christ, Fred, are you serious? Last time I checked, your circulation was less than 15,000, so how—'

'We've secured a guarantor, my boy, a very important, but terribly shy donor, with a very deep pocket. Admittedly a devout sceptic concerning the EU, but nonetheless he, or should I say, he or she, has given us complete journalistic freedom to dig, and dig properly, into the depths of the cesspit if you will.'

John, still reeling, said, 'The figure you quoted—'

'Yes, fifty grand, on an annualised basis. You look puzzled, my boy.'

'Puzzled? Not the right word, Fred. Amazed is more accurate. Fucking amazed in fact. I was going to say, give me time to think it over... Done that... Fifty... OK, yes. I suppose you don't want me to complete that piece on... a pity, I spent a lot of time—'

'Keep it on the back burner. We may be able to incorporate it later as part of the findings. Get a couple more malts and we can seal the deal with a flourish.'

When John returned to the table with two malts, a double for his old friend and a single for himself, Fred surprised him.

'I hear on the grapevine your old university pal, David, can't remember the last name, is about to get access to the greasy pole. He got a safe seat too. Remarkable, a cynic might add, suspicious, how he managed it, but as I'm certain we'll discover, old boy, the next decade may well prove to be remarkable also.'

'Yes, Fred,' said John, 'we were wrong-footed when he told us over Christmas. Dave never showed the slightest interest in politics. He's – or was now, I suppose – your typical family solicitor.'

'The world is full of surprises, Johnny boy, though I'd bet he's got some influential people behind him. Have we got a deal then? For Christ's sake don't tell me you'll have to run it past the wife—'

'Yes and no, Fred. I am going to talk to Marilyn. She's been badgering me for a while to make myself useful, so... what the hell, yes!'

They stood, shook hands, and then to John's surprise, Fred embraced him and said, with a thick voice John hadn't heard before,

'Great, great! We can get to work, tomorrow. I'll email over our new premises' address. Bring your laptop and your brain.'

They parted at the pub entrance, Fred doubtless back to Sylvia's pad. John, perhaps because he'd had a couple more drinks than normal, reflected on his old friend's enthusiasm. He was over seventy – John didn't know by how much – but he was like a headstrong, reckless teenager when it came to a scoop, a revelation, an exposé. If Fred's premonition was correct, something John doubted, this could be a major story, and probably a long-running one. Walking home in the chilled night air, he felt a surge of anticipation and excitement, a sensation he hadn't experienced since he left the City.

The salary figure Fred had casually mentioned seemed excessive; John, having worked as a jobbing hack, was well aware of the market rate for the type of work he assumed Fred had in mind for him. His initial shock had, while talking with him, turned into scepticism, despite Fred's confident assurance that his publication was financially viable after years of scraping around for funds. He decided to ask for Marilyn's opinion when he got back to the flat. Yes, he told himself, she would definitely have a view.

Chapter Twenty

He turned the corner into the quiet, deserted street and walked quickly toward his building, beginning, despite the effects of the alcohol, to feel cold. As he strolled along, he was startled by a rustling noise from behind one of the large waste bins at the side of the steps leading to the flat. He stopped, suddenly very alert; he recalled the local rag's hyperbolic story about a series of muggings in the area.

'Who's there?' he shouted, trying to make his voice sound aggressive.

A moaning sound, and then,

'Is that you, John? It's me, can you help me up?'

David.

John went toward the bins, and after looking around in the darkness, eyed his friend. He grabbed hold of him, but in attempting to lift him up, David groaned,

'Oh fuck! My arm's on fire, John!'

John looked closely at David's left arm. He saw that the jacket had been torn, but more worryingly, noticed his head was oozing blood, from just above the eyebrows. John, with some difficulty, supported him and carefully struggled up the stairs to the flat entrance. Holding onto David, he couldn't get to his pocket for the key, so he pressed the intercom with his forehead.

'Hello, is that you, John? I told you not to forget your key, it's—'

'Marilyn, just open the fucking door! I've got Dave here. I think he's been—'

She opened the door.

'Oh my God!' Marilyn screeched when she saw David's dishevelled appearance. 'What on earth's happened to him?'

'Marilyn, I think... I think,' David said, sounding confused.

John took off David's coat, and assisted him onto the sofa.

'Call for an ambulance, Marilyn, now. He's got an obvious head wound, but there might be other injuries. Those marks on his coat suggest he got a kicking too.'

Ten minutes later, the sound of an ambulance's siren heralded the arrival of the paramedics. Marilyn opened the door to them. They rushed over to the prone David, lying semi-conscious on the sofa.

'Do you know what happened to him?' said the older medic to Marilyn.

'No,' she replied, her voice trembling, 'my husband discovered him outside and brought him in. Will he be OK?'

The two ambulancemen ignored the enquiry, busying themselves with checking David's vital signs. A second siren could be heard approaching, and seconds later the intercom was buzzed. Marilyn, dazed, pressed the button; two policemen entered.

'Sorry to disturb you folks... Oh right, this is probably why we got the—'

'Not probably, definitely,' said John.

'Yes, sorry, sir. We received an urgent call twenty minutes ago from a lady in the vicinity who claimed she saw four young men running along the street. She was worried because a few minutes before she'd seen a man, well dressed, she said, walking unsteadily, toward this building, and then she saw them running back. Very suspicious, she told us, because she advised us helpfully there've been a spate of incidents locally. Not often we're called out to this area—'

'What's going... Where am I?'

Marilyn rushed over to the semi-conscious David, who held up his arm, as if in recognition.

'It's OK, David, these men will be taking you off to casualty.'

He stared blankly at her.

'Why... What am I doing here... Oh Christ, my head hurts!'

He fell back on the sofa and closed his eyes.

'We'll get him to hospital, quickly. I think he may have internal injuries and—'

'What about that awful gash on his forehead?' said Marilyn. 'All that blood!'

'Probably superficial, Mrs...'

'Duncan.'

'Can you two hulking lads help us to lift him down the stairs to the ambulance,' said the lead paramedic, 'he's a big weight to carry.'

The policemen took hold of the stretcher and David was moved carefully down to the ambulance.

'I think we should let Anita know. She must be wondering where Dave's got to.'

'Can you do it, John? I'm not sure I can—'

He took her hand.

'Of course. Give me your mobile and I—'

The two policemen re-entered the flat. Taking out his notebook, the older, grey-haired one said, with a distinctly cool attitude,

'If you don't mind, we'd appreciate your answering a few questions. I believe the man our colleagues have taken to casualty is known to you, sir.'

John, taken aback by the assumption, said,

'Actually, officer, that's correct, he is, but what brought you to that conclusion?'

'Your wife referred to him by name, so—'

'Yes, you're right. Sorry, this has given both of us a shock. Dave's one of my closest friends, so you can imagine—'

'Of course I can, sir. Any idea why he was walking around here at this late hour? We understand he lives on the other side of town, but he was walking away from the Tube station. It would appear he was making his way here, to your place. Were you expecting him?'

'No, we weren't. Funnily enough, I was speaking with him this morning, and as a consequence he knew I would be out this evening, at a meeting, so I can't think why he'd be making his way—'

'Any ideas, Mrs...'

'Duncan. No, it's a mystery to me too, constable.'

The policeman wrote something in his notebook.

'Is that everything, officer?' said John.

'Just one more thing, sir. I understand you discovered him in the street.'

'No, behind the bins under the... I was about to go up the stairs when I heard his groans. He'd obviously been mugged. Dave's a big strapping bloke, as you know from carrying him down the... I'd say he must have been taken by surprise, so if I were you, I'd be looking out for those four hoodlums your informant mentioned.'

'We'll be making thorough enquiries, sir, don't worry about that,' he replied, looking at John with an air of indifference. 'Do you recall seeing anyone, or anything untoward when you were approaching—'

'No, I didn't notice anyone lurking around. I would have. It's deserted most evenings... But you said anything. For example?'

'Maybe a vehicle?'

'Again, no. Anything else?'

'Not for the moment, sir... Oh, one more thing, you're a close friend of the victim—'

'His name's David, David Murray.'

'Yes, sorry, do you have a number for his next of kin? His wife perhaps?'

'Yes, why?'

'We have to inform her.'

Marilyn took her mobile from John and gave them Anita's number.

'Thank you. Goodnight. If anything comes back, Mr Duncan, or you, Mrs—'

'We'll let you know.'

They left, slamming the door behind them.

'That was unnecessary,' said Marilyn, 'they were definitely a bit off with you, John. You'd think they suspect you battered poor David.'

'Yes, they were what you'd term offhand. Puzzling though. That woman told them four young men were running away from our place, and yet the plods come here. Can't fathom it.'

'They probably saw the ambulance parked outside. Should we call Anita now?' said Marilyn nervously, pacing up and down the room.

'I expect the police will be contacting her, but... They'll say he was injured near us, you found him and brought him up here… So… She'll most likely assume we should have called her as soon as—'

'Give me your phone, Marilyn. I'll speak to her now.'

She stood, silent, running her hand through her dark hair as John put the device to his ear and listened, without a response. After five minutes, he tried the number again, with a similar result.

'Give it another few minutes, John.'

The doorbell rang out, startling both of them. Marilyn said,

'Who can this be now? Not the police again surely!'

She pressed the intercom button.

'Marilyn, let me in for God's sake!'

'It's Anita,' she said, shocked.

'Of course it's Anita, Marilyn! Just open the fucking door! It's brass monkeys out here.'

'I'm finished with my so-called husband,' she said, out of breath after bounding up the stairs to the flat, 'he pissed off to yet another of his oh-so-vital meetings tonight. Told me he'd be home by ten, and when I get back home, I discover a message on the answerphone, to the effect – he sounded blotto – that he was making his way over here, not—'

'Anita, sit down please. I think you're going to need a drink. Dave—'

'I see he's not here. Been and gone, I suppose. Never mind the drink, John, I'll go home and wait for him to surface. If I didn't know better, I might suspect he's still having—'

'Anita, calm down and listen to me,' said John, holding her hand. 'Dave's been taken to hospital, casualty—'

She stood, as if to make for the door, burst into tears, putting her hands over her face and collapsed back onto the chair.

'Oh, Dave, you poor thing!' she screamed, and looking

pleadingly up at John said, 'What happened to him, John? How badly is he—'

She fell back, wordless, sobbing.

'He was found, I mean, I found him outside. He'd been assaulted, but, listen now, the paramedics don't consider his injuries serious. If you like we can all get a taxi to the hospital, though I expect the doctors will have sedated him by now. Marilyn, can you get hold of the cab company please.'

Anita began to compose herself. She wiped her face with a tissue Marilyn had given to her and said, now seemingly calmer,

'Thanks, John. How long will it take to get to the hospital?'

'With no traffic to speak of at this time of night, about ten minutes, I think.'

*

By the time the three of them reached the accident and emergency department, David had been assessed and taken to a side room for the head wound to be stitched up. The triage nurse assured Anita that his injuries were not too serious, but he would be kept in overnight for observation.

'When will he be released?' asked a tearful Anita. 'I'll have to arrange time off from work. Can you give me—'

'That's up to the doctors, Mrs Murray, but as I explained to you, he'll be kept in until—'

'Yes, yes, yes! I heard you the first time, dear.'

The nurse smiled, despite Anita's agitated response, and walked off.

'Anita, he'll be out for the count until the morning,' said Marilyn, taking her arm, 'so let's go back to our place. You shouldn't be by yourself at a time like this.'

'Leave it, Marilyn! I'm not a soppy child. I can look after myself, thank you. Let's get a taxi, and I can drop you and John off. God, this place is the pits, isn't it? Half of these losers could do with a good bath and a boot up the backside. Go on, call for a taxi then.'

'OK, if you're sure.'

'Of course I'm sure, Marilyn! For Christ's sake, drop your head girl act,' she said, rolling her eyes, and then, 'Sorry, I don't mean to sound... I've got a big meeting first thing in the morning and I have to review...' She stopped abruptly, her lips moving silently, and then, 'Oh... If they let Dave out in the morning, would either of you be able to see to him? It'd be a great help. I really can't afford to miss this thing tomorrow. Why did he have to go out tonight? He's already been adopted for that stupid constituency. He's getting to be over fond of his own voice. Do you know, I caught him talking to the mirror the other day, complete with hand gestures. A real Pericles, or so he thinks.'

Interrupting her monologue, John, returning from the entrance, said,

'The cab's outside, you two. Come on, it's very late.'

When the taxi drew up outside Anita's house, after a silent ten-minute drive, Marilyn, briefly glancing at John, said,

'Are you certain you don't want to come back to ours, Anita? We could sit and—'

'Don't go on at me! I've got work to do. I told you back at the hospital.'

She lurched forward and embraced Marilyn, and said, in a thick voice,

'Thank you, Marilyn. Goodnight.'

The taxi moved off toward their flat. John, seeing that his wife was upset, said,

'Don't let her tone bother you. She's had a terrible shock.'

'John, I'm concerned—'

'Listen, Marilyn, I've said it before, more than once: you can't live other people's existences for them, and particularly not their relationships. Whatever issues the two of them might have… are none of our affair. I've known Dave a lot longer than you, and take it from me, when he's confronted by something, anything, be it financial, physical, or, in this case emotional, he always backs off, compromises. Anita will soon work that out.'

Marilyn, wiping her eyes, said,

'Are you busy in the morning? I'd go to collect David, but—'

'Yes, I'll ring the hospital first thing and if he's discharged, I'll take him home… On second thoughts, should I bring him back to our place, since Anita's got that terribly vital meeting, or seminar tomorrow? Knowing Dave, he'll make the most of the situation. A real drama queen.'

'Good idea, John,' she replied, as the taxi drew up outside their building. 'No, I'll pay the driver.'

They entered the flat. As Marilyn was making coffees, John checked the answerphone – one message, timed at eleven-thirty, and from an unexpected source.

'Good evening, Mr Duncan. My apologies for calling you unexpectedly. You may be aware that an acquaintance, or rather a friend of yours, Mr Murray, has been selected as the Conservative candidate for Benfleet. As part of the party's standard vetting procedures, we take up references, and Mrs Murray has authorised us to approach several of his friends and employers. I'm sure, as a journalist, you can appreciate the necessity, in these days of social media. I'll leave my number for you to contact me, at your convenience naturally. Oh yes, my name is Streeter, Oliver Streeter. Thank you. Goodnight.'

Marilyn, having caught the last few words as she brought the two mugs of coffee in, said,

'That sounded official, John. Did I hear David's name being mentioned? It wasn't the hospital again was—'

'No, it wasn't, thank God. It was an officious-sounding guy by the name of Streeter, calling from a mobile, asking me if I'd like to endorse Dave as a suitable candidate. Odd, he said Anita had put my name forward. Mrs Murray, he said... Maybe a slip of the tongue. I thought Dave said he'd been adopted already. Most organisations do their vetting before they offer... But... I can imagine these committee types being less than professional in that respect. Some of those muppets in the H of C wouldn't get past the first interview with any decent outfit, but...'

'Are you going to return his call? He won't have learnt about David's incident. You must call him asap to let him know. Drink that coffee now and come to bed. We have an appointment.'

Chapter Twenty-One

John's mobile rang out, vibrating on the bedside table. He opened his eyes and looked around. Marilyn was lying diagonally across the bed, fast asleep, with her legs on top of his. He struggled up after gently dislodging himself and reached for the phone, which stopped ringing just before he managed to grab it. He looked, still half-asleep, at the missed calls list: Fred.

'Who was that, John?' said Marilyn, as she raised herself up. 'What time is it?'

John looked at the phone.

'Jeez! It's eight-thirty. We shouldn't have had those drinks last night after all that kerfuffle with Dave. Oh no, didn't we agree I'd call the hospital this morning?'

Marilyn got out of bed and went to the en-suite, saying as she moved,

'Yes, and I'm late for work! I'm due to take a class at ten. You call the hospital now and after I get myself presentable, I'll call school. Come on, John! Move!'

He took the phone, still puzzling why Fred had called at such an early – for Fred – hour, but picking it up, David had priority. He dialled the hospital.

'Hello, can you put me through to... Well, I'm not sure, but my friend was brought in last night—'

'Name?'

'John Duncan... Oh no, sorry, David Murray.'

He heard a sigh, followed by, 'Which is it?'

'David Murray, he was mugged.'

'Are you a relative?'

'Err... No, but I'm only asking if he's being released. His wife asked if I'd collect him as she's working today—'

A long silence, until,

'He left ten minutes ago. One of the porters took him to a taxi.'

'I see. Thank you for your help.'

He ended the call and shouted through to Marilyn, over the sound of the shower,

'Dave's already been released. Apparently he got a taxi home a quarter of an hour since.'

'Did I hear you correctly, John?' she said, as she emerged, putting on a jacket and grabbing her briefcase.

'Yes, he—'

'Well, that's one problem resolved. Maybe you should call him in half an hour or so, once he's settled in. It's almost nine now. Can you give Mike at the school a ring? I'll get a move on. By the time you get through to him I'll probably be halfway to the Tube. Thanks, John. See you later. Oh, and remember to contact that man from Benfleet. Bye.'

He got hold of Marilyn's head teacher and was about to return Fred's call when the intercom buzzed. He walked over, pressed the button and said,

'Hi there, who is this?'

'It's me, John, Dave.'

He released the outside door, walked to the front door

and opened it, to see his friend navigating the stairs with some difficulty.

'Hi, Dave, I was going to collect you this morning, but when I called—'

David looked at him, smiled ruefully and said,

'Anita rang the hospital and said she couldn't pick me up, so I got a cab over here. Wouldn't have bothered you, John, but my keys got lost somewhere between the pub and here last night and... What happened to me?'

'Come on in, Dave. You shouldn't be out and about, you're looking pretty weak.'

'No, I'm fine, just a bit sore. Funny, John, my ribs hurt, but not the head. Just a superficial gash, no concussion. But I can't remember a thing. The doc said you found me downstairs. For the life of me, John, I've no idea how I got there, or why I was... Were we supposed to be—'

'Sit down over there, I'll make a coffee.'

John helped his friend into a chair, went into the kitchen, returning with two mugs, and was surprised to find David asleep, his breathing laboured. Disturbed by this, he called Marilyn.

'Check his pulse and try to lie him down properly. Maybe you should call his doctor too.'

'OK,' he replied after confirming that the pulse was normal and regular. 'Do you think I should let Anita know?'

'Maybe later. If you're concerned, call an ambulance. Frankly, John, I'm surprised he was released, judging by how he is. Maybe—'

'He told me he discharged himself.'

'The man's a fool. Head injuries need to – have to – be taken very seriously. Really! How could he be so stupid?'

'Wait a minute, Marilyn, he's coming around.'

'Take him back to casualty, John, now. Better safe than

sorry. I'll call Anita, or at the very least leave an urgent message for her, given she's got that meeting. Keep me posted.'

'Yes, I think you're right. I'll call for a taxi. Speak later.'

'What… Is… Oh, my head hurts, it's throbbing.'

'I'm taking you back to the hospital, Dave. You shouldn't have left there. Just try to stay calm now.'

'Where's Anita? John, where's my wife? We're supposed to be going to Brussels today… I think… To look at apartments for her—'

'Never mind, Dave. Marilyn's going to contact her, so you'll see her soon, back at casualty.'

David nodded his head, and was about to say something when he staggered, fell back against the coffee table and collapsed onto the floor. John took his pulse again and shuddered at the ashen look on his friend's face. Terrified, and thinking his friend was at death's door, he dialled 999, then sat on the floor next to David and, for the first time since he was a child, prayed, willing the ambulance to arrive before it was too late.

Two hours later, John was sitting anxiously in casualty. He'd cancelled the ambulance and got David to hospital by taxi after he'd briefly come round, its driver chuntering throughout the ten-minute drive about his, doubtless genuine, experiences with drunks and casualty departments. The triage nurse, recognising the patient, pulled a cynical face, saying,

'Mr Murray, yes, he knew better than the professionals this morning. Some people have no idea how much extra work they cause the NHS.'

As he sat, impatiently waiting for news of David's condition, his mobile rang. He took the thing out of his jacket pocket, and saw it was Fred.

'Fred, what is it you want?'

'Good grief, old man, you sound hacked off. Have you got your orders from Mrs Duncan yet?'

'What? Are you trying to be—'

'Sounds as if you haven't. I was going to invite you for lunch, to meet a couple of fellow conspirators, but if you—'

Realising how he must have sounded to the old rogue, John replied,

'Sorry, Fred, but I'm in casualty at the moment. Dave was assaulted yesterday, discharged himself this morning, but collapsed at our place, so I brought him in. That was two hours ago, with no word so far.'

'Christ, John, that sounds bad. Was it just a mugging?'

'It appears so, yes. Dave had been at a constituency meeting in Benfleet, and after a few drinks had decided – this is only my theory, he hasn't been *compos mentis* enough to explain – to come over to ours. I found him at the bottom of our stairs, just lying…'

He felt a lump in his throat, unable to continue. Fred, knowing his friend well, said, quietly,

'I'm sure he'll be OK, Johnny boy. Can't damage these Tory boys by a bang on their heads. Never mind my question about lunch today. Give me a bell when you're ready. Oh, by the way, speaking of Tories, I have it, on great authority I might add, that Central Office are going over all the candidates for this year's circus with a fine toothcomb. They're paranoid, with some justification, after all those scandals, to ensure everyone standing is pure as the driven white stuff… err… snow.'

This off-the-cuff remark brought John round.

'That's peculiar, Fred, you saying that.'

'I don't say peculiar things, my boy,' said Fred, laughing, 'my reputation is that of a—'

John cut him off, laughing at his friend's affected pomposity.

'Last night someone called asking me to give Dave a reference, you know, now that he's been adopted for—'

'Benfleet, I know. Was it Streeter by any chance?'

John, despite knowing Fred's superhuman memory for names and faces, said,

'God, is there anything that escapes you? Do you actually, no, have you met the guy?'

'Let's just say, he and I have crossed swords before. In layman's terms, Johnny boy, he's a Jodrell banker, of the first order. Worked himself up to be chairman of Benfleet's Tory association. At one time he harboured the ambition to be its MP, but, well, his unfortunate weaknesses in the romance department were brought to the attention of influential people at Central Office. As if they're any better.'

'And here's me thinking, Fred, taking up references was a normal, run-of-the-mill procedure. Streeter didn't come across as a... well, to be honest, I thought he was ticking a box, going through the motions.'

'No, he'll have been poked in the back to ensure all's above board with young Dave. Now that his own attempt at worldly fame's been stymied, he'll be looking for a gong in future honours hand-outs, and as a loyal worker for the party – sorry, the public – he might just qualify for a meeting with Lizzie—'

'OK, Fred,' said John, feeling buoyed, for the umpteenth time, by his friend's gentle cynicism, 'enough of this. Assuming I get out of here sometime this week, tell me, when's good for you?'

'Tomorrow morning, nine sharp, at our new premises, just around the corner from St Paul's. My new apprentices are dying to meet you. They've had a very good reference concerning your experience and character—'

'Fred, what... Sorry, I mean yes, I'll be there, once you

email me the address. Oh, hang on, a nurse with a very serious face is making a beeline toward me, probably about Dave, so, OK, my friend, see you in the morning.'

'Mr Duncan, Mr Murray is asking for you.'

'Thanks, nurse. I expect he wants me to chauffeur him home. Nothing ever changes with—'

'Mr Murray is not going anywhere, not unless you include the theatre.'

John shivered at the word.

'Do you mean he's going to have an operation? Why?'

'It appears he's had a bleed in his brain, and the doctors have assessed that it needs to be relieved by surgery. He's going to be treated imminently, but as I said, Mr Murray wants to speak with you. This way please, Mr Duncan.'

'Have I got time to contact his wife?'

The nurse looked at him curiously and replied,

'If you wish, but Mr Murray specifically said, demanded if you will, to speak with you before he goes into theatre.'

'Can anybody give me an idea of just how serious the condition is?'

'Not until he's been assessed by the surgical team. As you aren't his next of kin, that's all I can tell you. I suggest you contact Mrs Murray.'

John, shocked at this, followed the nurse meekly through to the pre-op area, trying as he walked to convince himself that his friend must be disoriented; he knew David was besotted with Anita, seemingly immune to her sometimes acid remarks. His mood wasn't improved when he came across David, lying, helpless, strapped to some contraption or other, with two tubes attached to his arms. He got to the bedside and said, trying to be light-hearted,

'Told you to watch your drinking, buddy. You'll be teetotal for a good while.'

Dave, obviously drugged to his eyeballs, smiled wanly and said,

'Very funny. I don't remem—'

His eyes closed. The nurse standing next to the bed barked,

'Move aside please, sir, Mr Murray's off to theatre.'

John walked back, out to the reception area, knowing he'd have to get hold of Anita, but recalling Marilyn saying she would call her, he dialled her number.

'No, John, she wasn't available, but I left a message. How is he?'

Trying as best he could to sound calm, he said,

'Dave shouldn't have left the hospital, Marilyn. By the time I'd got him here he was beginning to hallucinate, and now... now...'

'What's the matter, John? You sound... tell me!'

'Apparently, he's suffered a bleed on the brain, and he's been taken into theatre to sort it. I think I should stay until they've finished doing what they have to. He looked terrible, Marilyn.'

'Is he in danger of... of... Did the doctors give you any idea about a prognosis?'

'No, they're tight-lipped, but by the grim looks on their faces, I'm worried, Marilyn, scared in fact. I don't know how long he'll be in theatre, and I think Anita has to be here. Do you know where she is today?'

'At the Foreign Office, I think, John. I can't be more specific... Oh wait, I'll get her office number. They must know her location. Anita's moaned more than once about how she has to account for her movements, something about security. She's so melodramatic. Hang on.'

John heard the clatter of her mobile as she put it down. A few seconds went by before she returned. The noise in the casualty reception erupted as an emergency vehicle roared up to its entrance and deposited three injured young men. John

walked out of the building. The cold damp air outside hit him
as he answered his wife's question.

'John, are you still there?'

'Yes, it was getting too loud inside. Did you get the
number?'

She read the number out, saying after she'd repeated it,

'Let me know after you've got hold of her, John. I'm coming
along to the hospital now. I want to be there before she arrives.
I take it you're staying until—'

'Yes, I am. I'll try to contact her now, so…'

'OK, let me know as soon as possible… on my mobile. I'm
leaving now, by taxi. Should be with you in half an hour or so,
and, John… John, are you listening?'

'Yes, you're coming here. I'll get on to Anita now. Bye.'

Beginning to feel chilled, he dialled the landline number.
It rang out for several seconds until, 'Good afternoon, Anita
Murray's PA speaking. Who's calling please?'

'Oh, hello, my name is John Duncan. I need to – have to –
speak with Mrs Murray urgently. It—'

'I'm sorry, Mr Duncan, I can't divulge where Mrs Murray
is at this moment. Her—'

John, increasingly concerned for his friend, quickly lost his
cool with the woman.

'Listen, I'm not interested in where Mata Hari might be.
I have to tell her something, something urgent, about her
husband—'

The bored-sounding woman said, 'Well, if, as you claim, it
is an urgent matter, I can pass any message you might have to
Mrs Murray, when I speak with her, though that may not be
until tomorrow.'

'For Christ's sake, you stupid woman! He's in hospital, the
London, in surgery to be exact, so if you can't, sorry, won't put
me through to her, perhaps you could find the time, between

doing the *Telegraph* crossword and gossiping, to let her know. Thanks for nothing!'

He ended the call, shaking with impotent rage. He'd experienced similar roadblocking before during his period working with Fred, and he suspected this was another example of the technique. Anita may have instructed her minions to fend off nuisance callers; screening was the official term. Despite his feeling of helpless anger, he hoped that the almost desperate tenor of his pleading with the woman, the receptionist he'd presumed, would prompt her to inform Anita.

Dejected, he walked back into the stuffy, crowded casualty reception, sat down and stared at the staff, some strolling, some rushing, around the room, going from cubicle to cubicle. He picked up a magazine, a two-year-old edition of a nondescript fashion publication, filled to the back page with glossy photographs of mainly skinny, anorexic-looking young women; some of them could benefit from coming in here for treatment, he mused.

'Hello, John…Wake up!'

He stirred, nearly falling off the chair; the magazine fell to the floor.

'Oh, hi, Marilyn. You got here then.'

'Are you alright?'

'Yes, I suppose so. I tried to tell Anita, but her guard dog said she wasn't available.'

'How's it going with David?'

John explained briefly the situation, with Marilyn looking at him, surveying his face as he recounted the sequence of events since he'd brought his friend in. In her eyes John was in a very emotional state, and when he'd finished, running his hand through his hair, she said,

'Try to stay calm, John. None of David's problems, I mean, his being in here, are down to you, he was assaulted by persons unknown... John, listen to me... It was a simple mugging, and could have occurred anywhere. The fact that he may... I said may, John, have been on his way to see you is pure coincidence—'

'Why would anybody pick on him? Big as he is, the guy's as soft as a blancmange.'

'He was unlucky. Wrong place, wrong time. You know our neighbourhood is one of the safest in London, making David doubly unfortunate. How long since he went in, for surgery, I mean, John?'

He looked at her with a distant expression.

'What?'

Before she could ask him a second time, a young man, dressed in surgical gear, walked diffidently toward them.

'Mr Duncan... and I presume you're Mrs Murray—'

'No, she hasn't arrived yet. This is my wife. Another friend of David's.'

'Oh, I see, I beg your pardon—'

'Don't waste time with the pleasantries, doctor,' barked John, 'just tell us... How is he? Bleed on the brain sounds very bad, dangerous.'

'As neither of you qualify as next of kin, I can't give you—'

'Is he going to die?'

'Mr Murray has undergone surgery, and is in a stable but serious condition.'

He walked off, obviously ill at ease at the confrontation.

'Well, Marilyn, that was a total farce.'

'At least we know he's come out of the surgery. He's a young man, John. I'm sure he'll be OK. When did you call Anita's office?'

'An hour or so ago, I think. Why?'

'I'll try on my mobile this time. Give me a minute. You sit here in case any more news comes out. That young medic obviously hasn't had doctor-to-patient dialogue training.'

She stood, bent over, kissed John's forehead, and walked out into the carpark, determined to contact Anita, thinking, *Unlike John, as a former journo, to allow himself to be batted away by a jobsworth.*

I'll get hold of her, one way or another, she thought, *John was too polite to press the issue with whomever it was he contacted.*

Chapter Twenty-Two

Anita, having succeeded in her long-held ambition to enter the diplomatic service, thanks in part to her fluency in three languages, had spent the previous few weeks in her induction training, attending a host of seminars. She revelled at the prospect of a foreign posting, and when she was told her first assignment was to Brussels, as part of the British delegation to the European Commission, she was ecstatic. Her first action on learning of this was to book tickets on the Eurostar, without telling her husband. 'He'll be happy to go along with it,' she'd informed her friends, including Marilyn. 'I need to check out the property market there, for rentals in the short term, that is.'

When John attempted to make contact from the hospital, Anita had been involved in a role-play session in a conference room not fifty yards down the corridor from the room where her PA was seated. Marilyn knew, from previous dialogues with her friend, that it was common practice for instructions to be given to secretaries, PAs and executive assistants to block any attempts by outside callers to contact staff, not only cold callers, a serious and recurring nuisance, but also personal calls. Senior management actively dissuaded contact by relatives during working hours, telling first responders to take a sceptical view when relatives demanded to speak with members of staff.

Marilyn dialled Anita's mobile ,which responded with the standard message, informing the caller that 'Mrs Murray is unavailable.' After a few seconds, Marilyn wandered back into the reception. 'John, any news?'

'No, but a nurse said, a while ago, I think, that Dave will be under sedation for a few hours, and we could go home, but maybe one of us should stay, in case—'

'Will you be OK sitting here for a bit?'

'Yes, probably, I've nothing on today. Why?'

'I couldn't get hold of Anita, so I thought I'd go to her place of work and demand to see her. They must have breaks for lunch, coffee.'

'OK, sounds like a plan. I'll be fine, Marilyn, the shock's wearing off now. I'll grab a sandwich from that cafeteria over there. Why didn't that PA pass on the message?'

He stood, embraced her, they kissed, and she called a taxi. Twenty minutes later, Marilyn stepped out of the cab in front of the forbidding-looking building and walked briskly up its steps. She approached the large desk, where two women in uniform were sitting, both of them staring at her with suspicious, disdainful countenances.

'Good afternoon, can I—'

'I have to search your bag, madam,' said a uniformed man from behind Marilyn.

'Yes, of course,' she replied, and handing over her small handbag, she started again. 'I have to speak to a Mrs Murray. I believe she works here.'

'What is your business with her?' asked the older-looking official, who continued to look down at a screen as she spoke in a monotone.

'It's a personal matter, and before you say anything else, it is extremely urgent. I've come from the London Hospital, not exactly around the corner I'm sure you'd agree, to let—"Sorry, madam, all I can do is speak with Mrs Murray's secretary, to ascertain whether she is available. Please sit... over there. I didn't catch your name.'

'I didn't throw it,' Marilyn shot back, her nerves fraying. 'Duncan, Marilyn Duncan. Please hurry.'

She wheeled around, seething at the insolent attitude, and sat on one of the deep chairs, more appropriate for a brothel than an office, she thought. As the minutes ticked by, with only the inaudible conversation of the two women at the reception desk breaking the silence, Marilyn became increasingly annoyed, and was about to lift herself from the uncomfortable chair when her mobile disturbed the funereal atmosphere.

'Hello? Oh, John, no, not yet. I'm waiting for her secretary to—'

'No calls allowed in here, miss. Please end the call now.'

'I have to go, John. Any news? Oh good, that's a relief. I'll speak to you—'

'Mrs Duncan?'

She walked over to the reception desk.

'Have you located her then?'

'She left here two hours ago.'

'Left? But my husband... Has she gone home? Let me speak with her secr—'

'Sorry, that's all I can tell you. I suggest you call her yourself.'

'Thanks, you've been very helpful.'

When she reached the door, the security man opened it and said,

'Have a nice day.'

'Oh, I will, once I leave here.'

She hailed a taxi, asking the driver to make for Anita and David's place. When she arrived outside the entrance, Marilyn noticed a large, executive-looking vehicle in the place where Anita's runabout normally parked. She paid the cabbie hurriedly, telling him to keep the change, ran up the stairs to the flat and rang the bell several times. A muffled sound of laughter stopped, and then a figure could be seen through the opaque glass. Anita opened the door, obviously very surprised to see Marilyn standing in front of her.

'Marilyn,' she said, running the back of her hand across her forehead, 'to what do we, I mean, I, owe the—'

'You need to come to the hospital. David's come out of surgery, but… The doctors want to advise you of his condition. It's serious, Anita… Really serious. You have to be there…'

'Calm down, Marilyn, I know all about it from the hospital. He'll be fine. Come on in. Graham and I were nearly finished anyway, but you look like you could do with a stiffener… Come on, Marilyn.'

She took her arm and guided her along the narrow corridor into the cosy, overheated sitting room and said,

'Graham, this is my best, and I might add, most discreet friend, Marilyn O'Brien… Oh, sorry, Marilyn, where's my memory! Marilyn Duncan. Graham's a colleague from the diplomat… Dear me, what did I say about being discreet, Marilyn! Anyway, he and I were scratching our heads over… well, a problem.'

Marilyn, thoroughly disoriented, said, while holding out her hand,

'Pleased to meet you. So, you've been given all… the details about David then, Anita?'

'Yes, and you can switch off the panic button now, Marilyn… Really, girl! Graham, Marilyn's husband is one to keep an eye on. He used to be a hot shot in the City, but gave it up, can you believe it, to be a journo, chasing after "scoops", as they call gossip. He's tied up with that old soak Fred McTaggart, you recall, the guy who got sued weekly back in the day. Thought you'd have talked him out of that, Marilyn.'

Graham, appearing ill at ease, said,

'Yes, I've come across Mr McTaggart before. I believe his imagination often takes control of his pen, or rather his keyboard. Sorry, Anita, I must be going, it's my turn to pick up the boy from school. His mother's got something on this afternoon. And thanks for the... advice. I'll take it on board. We can discuss the matter further when old Surtees gets back. He'll no doubt have an opinion. Very glad to have met you, Mrs O'Brien... I mean Mrs Duncan. Do forgive me.'

Anita ushered him out of the room, giving him his jacket as they walked to the front door. Marilyn, confused, sat on the large sofa. She heard a *sotto voce* conversation in the hall, then Anita's familiar laugh, and the door closing.

'Why did you feel the need to rush over here like a naïve schoolgirl?'

Taken by surprise at her friend's acerbic question, Marilyn responded,

'Neither John nor me could get hold of you, and the situation—'

'Talk about a pair of drama queens! I called the hospital, so I'm fully aware of how my husband is.'

'They didn't mention you'd called them... And anyway, why did the doctor ask John if he'd contacted you?'

'Oh, stop all this speculation. I'm going to see Dave tonight. Not for long though as he's under sedation. Turns out I'll be able to pop in for a few minutes, though he'll most likely not recognise me. Doing my wifely duty you'd call it, I suppose.'

Marilyn's brows furrowed.

'You mean to say David's been assaulted, had an operation to relieve a bleed on the brain, and you're—'

'Stop preaching, Marilyn. I suppose if John was in Dave's shoes you'd be the devoted wife, lying at his bedside holding his hand. For Christ's sake, Marilyn, grow up! He's in safe hands, and I'm not going to allow a distraction like this prevent me from… Oh, forget all this, is there anything else you want to lecture me about? I have to attend to several emails before I make my way over to the London. I expect, given his condition, I'll be able to see him before the official visiting time.'

Marilyn, successfully managing to hide her annoyance, said,

'Give me a minute while I call John. He's most likely waiting for news of your whereabouts… Hello, John, I'm at Anita's… Long story, but she's been informed of his condition. What? No, she called the hospital to check on David. I'm going home. Yes, I think we could see him later. Bye.'

'OK, Marilyn,' Anita said, 'thanks anyway. Pity it was a wasted journey for you. This new job's taking a great deal of my time and attention. I hope Dave can get his head around the fact, if not… Ignore that, Marilyn, he's bound to go along with it. I'll be in touch.'

Chapter Twenty-Three

By the time she got home, Marilyn's mood had darkened; Anita's character, her overt cynicism, had been evident to her old friend since they were young girls, but she was shocked by what she considered her friend's callousness toward David's hospitalisation. The man, in spite of his thoughtlessness on occasion, was devoted to her, in his own, naïve way. Since their marriage, Marilyn had listened, several times, to complaints about David's behaviour toward her; he was 'careless, untidy, never argued,' the last being the trait which annoyed Anita the most. She couldn't rid herself of a vague feeling of unease; outwardly, Anita behaved as she always had, but Marilyn began to consider, not for the first time, that the tragedy of the stillborn child had affected her. When the four friends met, the subject was never discussed, and Marilyn had picked up on Anita's doleful expression one day, when the two were out shopping and bumped into a woman shepherding four toddlers across a pedestrian crossing. The look was momentary, but it strengthened Marilyn's sense that the loss was raw, a festering wound, similar to what she'd gone through when she'd lost her unborn child.

It was dark by the time John made it back to the flat. Marilyn, despite having told him they were going to eat in, hadn't started dinner; the time since she'd got back from Anita's had been spent in reflection on how similar their fates had been.

'Have you been back long?' John asked. 'I called your mobile, but you didn't answer. Is it on silent?'

Marilyn grabbed her phone, lying on the coffee table beside her chair, and looked at it – three missed calls. She couldn't recall hearing any ring, or putting it on silent mode, and, confused, said,

'Sorry, John, I was miles away. Yes, I think I must have put it on silent… I don't recall—'

'It's not, dear,' he said, after checking her phone. 'Are you alright, Marilyn? You don't look too good. Was Anita suitably remorseful?'

'Remorseful? What do you mean?'

'About not going to the hospital.'

'What do you think? She was certainly surprised, a trifle rattled, to see me, now that I come to think of it, when I turned up. Yes, definitely wrong-footed, embarrassed, at least as close as she can be to being embarrassed. She was finishing a meeting with her colleague, Graham somebody, and ushered him out sharpish. Odd, I—'

His eyebrows raised, John said,

'Marilyn, you aren't sugg—'

'No, no, of course not, but it was strange, to witness Anita caught on the hop. The way she looked at me – almost funny.'

She started to laugh as she recalled Anita's face when she'd opened the door.

'Will we be able to see David tonight? Visiting time's seven till eight.'

'Yes, I think so. The doc said he'll be fully awake by then.'

'In that case, as it's nearly six, let's eat out and go see him afterwards. You never know, but Anita might show her face too.'

They parked in a side road near the hospital, its own car park being full, and walked briskly into reception. It was ten to eight; their meal, at a local curry house, had dragged on, and the roads around the hospital were busy, delaying their arrival. John asked where his friend was, and they took the lift to the second floor. Entering the ward, crowded with visitors, Marilyn spotted David, lying in the end bed, reading a newspaper. She took her husband's arm, and they marched over.

'Oh, hi, guys,' said a cheerful-looking David. 'I was expecting guests, but I suppose you'll have to do. How's it hanging, John? Still a gentleman of leisure?'

Marilyn attempted a smile and said,

'Never mind him, David, how are you?'

'Me? Top of the world, ma! Great film, isn't it? The doctor told me I'm under observation. Sounds like I'm a suspect for whatever, but I swear to you, Marilyn, I didn't do it!'

John shot back,

'Stop arsing around, Dave. When I was here earlier, you'd been taken in for an operation, and I expect they're keeping you in here to make sure everything's OK. You should—'

Marilyn tapped John's arm and said,

'David, we were all worried for you. The doctors told us you were lucky the injuries weren't more serious.'

'I know, but it's so dull in here. When I woke up, the room was silent. Thought for a moment I was in the mortuary, and then I saw Anita, buttonholing the doctors about keeping me in here until they're confident I'm fully recovered—'

'She said what?' Marilyn exclaimed, her face betraying her surprise. 'Did she really ask them to keep—'

'No worries, Dave,' John interposed, seeing his wife's annoyed expression. 'Anita was telling Marilyn this afternoon she'd make certain you'd be getting the five-star treatment. Good on her, I say.'

'She's the business alright,' David replied. 'When she called a few minutes ago to ask how I was doing, she suggested we go on a break, a short one, before her posting to Berlin, but I—'

'Brussels, I think, David,' said Marilyn. 'Has she been in to see you this evening? I thought we might have caught her.'

'No, but I was sure I… She was intending to dash in, I think they said, but it turns out her boss called late on, just as she was getting ready to pop over. Something about a problem, security or… Can't remember…'

His voice suddenly became hoarse. Marilyn, sensing a problem, stood and walked to the nurses' station. In the few seconds it took for a nurse to arrive at his bedside, David had lost consciousness.

'You have to leave, now. Please,' the nurse barked.

Stunned, Marilyn and John walked meekly out of the ward and down the stairs. She took out her mobile and called Anita, without a response.

'Well, John,' she said, her voice trembling, 'we've done all we can. I expect if it's serious, life-threatening, they'll call Anita. Why didn't she—'

'Who knows, but you're right, there's nothing more we… Try not to worry, he sounded happy enough, didn't he? Come on, let's go home. We'll find out soon enough.'

There were two messages on the answerphone: one from a very agitated-sounding Fred, asking when John would be available for a 'confidential chat, old boy', and another from Marilyn's mother, demanding her daughter's presence the following Sunday.

'What's that all about?'

'I completely forgot, John, what with… my mother's birthday. She always has people round, mostly her contemporaries, and they talk and eat the whole day. Shouldn't say it, but it's pretty boring.'

'What a shocking thing to say!' teased John, attempting to lift her mood.

'True, but I have to go, and if you come along, you'll see what I mean. On the positive side, the new priest, Father Murphy, I think he's called, will probably be there too. Mother will be pleased once she sees you walking through her front door. Are you going to call Fred back?'

'He can wait till the morning. He's got a point, though. I should have made contact before now, but thanks to Dave—'

'Now, now, he didn't ask to be mugged.'

His face took on a quizzical look.

'What are you thinking, John?'

'Don't you think it odd, that he was attacked just outside, at the bottom of our steps? Why would four yobs, obviously not from this neighbourhood, happen to be wandering around when Dave hove into view… You don't think he was being follow—'

'Are you… saying it wasn't random?'

'Perhaps it was, but doesn't it strike you as very strange? He'd been to a political meeting, a good distance away, in a less salubrious area, but… Oh, ignore me, I'm dissembling. Yes, he was just unlucky, I guess. If he's crafty enough he'll use the incident to his advantage—'

'How would … yes, I get you. "Brave candidate fights off his attackers. David Murray, your 'keep the streets safe' choice."'

'That's probably out of his hands, Marilyn. The local paper will doubtless give it a front-page spread, and his association will jump on it too. "The Labour government's feckless attitude to law and order, unsafe communities etc etc." Bound to play well.'

Marilyn frowned.

'Am I right in thinking Fred's eagerness to have you on board stems from the upcoming election and his antipathy toward Europe? You're more of a financial man, and I've never heard you intone about the subject. I don't even know how you vote—'

'With a pencil and a—'

'Very funny. It is about Westminster machinations though, isn't it? Fred is well-known there, as a trouble-maker, I'm told. Be careful, John.'

'Trouble-maker? Yes, he's certainly careless when it comes to writing about politicians. You know, he's been sued more often than he's had hot dinners, but he's never lost a case, priding himself on what he terms his "battle scars", but stop fretting about it. He wants me to analyse the party's upcoming manifestos from a financial viewpoint. I won't be uncovering any sexual or corruption stories, he's the master on those kinds of issues. As he puts it, they're great for his paper's circulation, but less so for the cardiovascular systems of the scoundrels he exposes. After thirteen years of the Blair/Brown circus, Fred's convinced there'll be a change. Fresh-faced Cameron, despite his toff background, seems more attractive than dour old Brown. I'm not a betting man, but the Tories should walk it.'

'Changing the subject,' Marilyn said, with a solemn expression which John had come to know well, 'I've been pondering on the child question. When I mooted the idea, I got the impression you... you acquiesced to please me. If you're at all doubtful—'

'No, Marilyn, I'm not doubtful. Having kids wasn't something I'd ever considered in the past but, now, yes, I'm happy with it, and I can see it's the top of your agenda right now. We're in a good situation financially and there aren't any health problems, so, yes, the sooner the better.'

They retired to the bedroom.

Chapter Twenty-Four

David's sudden, dramatic lapse into unconsciousness proved to be a false alarm, and by the end of the week he was discharged by the doctors. He informed John by phone that he'd been given the all-clear, asking him if he fancied going out for a 'few beers, nothing over the top, can't afford to annoy the missus'.

John declined the offer, and when he mentioned it to Marilyn, she replied frostily that 'David needs to grow up, he's nearly thirty now.'

'You've hit the nail on the head there, but it does show he's back on form, ready for the challenge—'

'He doesn't know the meaning of the word. I tell you, John, if he's serious about getting into the House of Commons, he'll have to behave like a grown man. Anything other than propriety will bring hacks like Fred McTaggart down on his head. After the expenses shenanigans, politicians of all stripes... Oh you know what I'm getting at, John. By the way, you haven't said, did you manage to speak with that constituency guy?'

'Yes, sorry, I should have said.'

'What did he want?'

'Not much really. They – the committee – were very taken with Dave according to Streeter, who's the local party chairman. He didn't ask any penetrating or searching questions, just the usual "Would you consider him trustworthy?" type of thing. That was easy to confirm. Dave has his faults, but... Well, I'd trust him with my life, that's the rub. I'd be more concerned that he might not be able to handle the duplicity and shady antics in that place.'

'Do you think David will be elected?'

'Streeter certainly thinks so. Incidentally, he asked me, ever so discreetly, if I'd be amenable to helping Dave's campaign, writing speeches. Briefings and the like—'

'You aren't—'

John laughed.

'No way. Dave may be comfortable glad-handing, but can you picture me doing the same? I wouldn't last five minutes. That reminds me, I need to sit down with Fred about my contract. Shouldn't be any problems there, he always gave me a free hand when I was involved with him. It's almost eight, time for the both of us to get moving.'

*

Two weeks later, on a frosty, dark morning, John walked up the stairs to Fred's office, on the second floor of a modern building, its windows looking out at St Paul's Cathedral. Pressing the security buzzer, he noticed the plaque with the title *The Swiftian* attached to the wall next to the door, and chuckled at the reference; pure Fred, he thought. A shrill noise heralded the door being unlocked. He pushed against the door and walked into the small front office, where a young blonde woman wearing a low-cut sweater and a broad smile greeted him, saying,

'Ooh! You must be Mr Grimes. Fred's told me to—'

'Sorry,' John said, blushing involuntarily, 'no, I'm John Duncan. Nice to—'

'Come on, Johnny boy, in here!' shouted Fred, who had emerged from the main office. 'Samantha, this is our latest recruit. John, Sam here does everything for me. Don't let that bimbo appearance fool you, she's a star. Ain't that right, dear?'

Samantha, in two minds apparently, said,

'Fred, don't call me a bimbo. I've got six GCSEs. Mr Duncan—'

'John, please.'

She smiled at him and said,

'Yes. Fred's a real dinosaur, but he can't fool me. His wife came in yesterday and gave him what for. Made me laugh, honest it did. Fancy a cup of tea?'

'OK, Samantha, that'd be great. Thanks.'

She stood and walked slowly toward the small kitchen area, Fred watching her very closely, obviously full of admiration.

'Let's get you settled,' said the old lecher. 'By the way, I should have asked, I take it you've got your own laptop with you?'

'Nothing's changed then, Fred, I see. Yes, of course, but it's a new one. I went out and bought it yesterday. Call it a donation to the cause.'

'Cause? That sounds almost... noble, Johnny boy. What we're about can't really be described as noble. We'll be in the gutter with the scumbags known as the governing classes, but at least we can claim to be... Well, you know what I mean. Expose the tossers, chicanery—'

'Yes, yes, I know, Fred, it's a calling. You said there was a backer. Anyone I'm allowed to know about?'

Seeing Fred's head moving horizontally, he said,

'No, but I had to ask, not that it would influence anything we write of course. Getting down to business, when do you think there'll be an election? Have you heard anything?'

'May. For definite.'

John sat back in his chair, looking sceptical.

'The polls are ambiguous. What do you think?'

'How do you think your buddy will go? I hear the Benfleet association is excited by him after twenty years of that cretin Moore. I hear the guy was more than indignant at getting the heave-ho. Very angry, I heard. Swore to an associate of mine he'd get even.'

Taken aback, John said,

'Dave's very keen, and the chairman—'

'Streeter. He asked you to get on his team, didn't he? Waste of your talent. I assume, because you're here, that you declined?'

John laughed.

'I should have known. You're as well connected as ever. On those manifestos—'

'Fuck them. It's just gone eleven, time to visit the hostelry. You can meet a couple of my trusties.'

He put on his beloved scruffy green velvet jacket, handed John his rather more conservative one, and shouted to Samantha,

'We're off to gain some intelligence, my girl. If the PM calls, tell him we've gone to matins.'

John's next two hours were spent in a small pub, situated down a narrow cul-de-sac, talking with Fred and two of his latest protégés, young men who looked no older than nineteen.

'John, this is Greg, and Alistair, both Oxford men, but I don't hold that against them, solely because they're both admirers of the great man. In fact, John, you could benefit from re-reading Swift, very relevant, as always. These guys will be based in Westminster, lurking around the so-called "corridors of power". I'd thought of despatching Alistair over to Brussels, because of his facility with the language, but—'

'Why Brussels, Fred?' asked John as he picked up his whisky.

'Well now, John, I reckon this election will be influenced by the European issue. I know politics isn't your pet subject, but as I've mentioned before, the Lib Dems are promising a referendum on membership, so I fully expect – I'd put a bet on it if I was a gambling man – that both the other parties will find a way, a policy, to deflect the public away from the issue.'

'That's a stretch, Fred. Do you actually think the Lib Dems have the remotest chance of being anything other than a protest vote? They're all Jesus Christ sandals, beards and vegetarianism.'

Fred looked at his two young recruits, smiled, and responded,

'That's very ungallant of you. Some of those Lib Dem women... Don't you worry about the political side of things, Johnny boy. What really, really absorbs my thoughts these days is this proposition: suppose, just suppose, that all the parties commit to some form of a plebiscite, no doubt rigged to the advantage of the status quo position, to assuage the plebs? If they do insert something like that, my view is that it would have all the attributes of a ticking time bomb, a Pandora's box being opened.'

John, laughing at Fred's typically eccentric use of metaphor, said, shaking his head,

'Yes, I'm aware the Lib Dems have adopted the referendum idea, but are you thinking the Tory and Labour parties are fearful of them? They're a fringe party, Fred, on a good day. I can't envisage the scenario you're proposing coming to anything—'

'Point taken, John, but, as I've said, I want you to dig into the money side of their policies, when they're disclosed,' he paused, his eyes glittering, 'and now that I think of it, maybe you could run your critical eye over the EU's finances too. I hear their accounts haven't been signed off for years. Auditors are a damn nuisance. I know that from my own… Anyway, you get my drift. Come on now, troops, back to the shit-stirring factory!'

*

David, on his release from hospital, had gone back to work at his office near Lincoln's Inn just over a week after the assault. As a prospective candidate for the House of Commons, his leisure time rapidly diminished, to the point where his friends very rarely saw him. Anita, despite complaining to anyone willing, or unwilling, to listen, had her own, equally all-encompassing agenda: progression in her quest to rise up the Foreign Office ladder. As soon as David was given the all-clear, she dragged him over to Brussels, where they managed to locate a suitable flat within strolling distance of the Berlaymont building, the heart of the European Union bureaucracy.

One evening in early February, John took a call from David.

'Hi, Dave, this is a good surprise. How's it all going?'

'We've got it, John. Anita had her heart set on the flat. Very expensive, but, hey, she says it's worth the money, being so close to the action.'

'Oh, yes, you're talking about the place in Brussels. What about the upcoming election chances—'

'No worries there, John, it's a safe seat, and I think I'm making a good impression on the streets. Everybody's pleased to speak with me.'

'No, Dave, I meant, what do your bosses think will be the result, at the national level?'

'Piece of cake, John. Five more years of Brown? No chance. Oliver told me you'd turned down the offer—'

'Yes, Dave, sorry,' John cut in, sensing the disappointment in his friend's voice, 'but I can't commit—'

'No worries,' said David, unconvincingly, 'what with you toiling for the old soak, and Marilyn being up the… pregnant. Congratulations by the way.'

'How did you know about it, Dave? We've been keeping it quiet because of Marilyn's history.'

'She confided in Anita. Made her laugh. Poor Marilyn, Anita said she'd suspected, and had to prise the news out of her. She's too sensitive, worrying that Anita would be upset after the… the… You know, John.'

'Yes, she's very fond of Anita, always has been,' John said. 'Fancy meeting up anytime soon?'

'Busy all this week, John, but, yes, I'll keep a slot for you, say, next Tuesday. OK?'

John, surprised at David's careless, offhand manner, said,

'Yes, Dave. Call me for the when and where. I'm free most evenings. Bye.'

Turning to Marilyn, who was marking papers for her English A level students, he said,

'You didn't say you'd told Anita.'

'Oh, yes, John. She called me out of the blue yesterday, keen as mustard to give me her latest news from Brussels, earth-shattering she described it as being. You know how hyperbolic she can be. Anyway I was tired, after a day with the first years, and she asked me if I was "pregnant or something", so I told her.'

'How did she react?'

'In her time-honoured way. She said, "good for you," and then waxed lyrical about this place in Brussels, and her great new boss there, by the name of Jerome Barton. It was odd, almost bizarre. She was deadpan about me being... I suppose she had to find out sometime. I'm glad it's off my chest, I had been worrying about telling her. You know, John, on the surface the two of them seem to have put the tragedy behind them, but do you—'

'They're burying themselves in work, a sure sign of displacing their grief. I've never seen Dave so enthusiastic before. Politics used to bore him, but now, he's single-minded about getting elected. None of our business, but living apart five nights out of seven, not what I'd call the recipe for a good marriage.'

'One of my colleagues announced today he's standing in the election, for the Liberal Democrats, in Temperley. He was droning on this morning, saying the party was the only one democratic enough to support the idea of a vote on EU membership, and—'

'Not you as well. Bad enough that I have to endure Fred's... What's brought this up?'

'Well, John, I was thinking, after speaking with Anita, with her fully signed up at the Foreign Office, working in Brussels, how would she react if the Tories copy the Lib Dems and support a referendum too? She's a diehard Europhile, always has been. Can you imagine how much pressure she'd apply to David? Has he any solid views on the issue?'

'I've never heard him talk about it. At university neither of us were involved with any of the political clubs. Dave laughed at the enthusiasts. Nerds, he called them.'

Chapter Twenty-Five

Marilyn gave up work after the Easter break; she had intended to carry on as long as possible, but her doctor advised that she leave earlier because of her abnormally high blood pressure, a fact which disturbed John, to the extent that even Fred picked up on it.

'Feeling under the weather again, John?' he asked one morning after he saw him slumped over in his chair. 'Burning the candle at both ends? I'll have to speak to that wife of yours.'

'Sorry, Fred, these documents are a pain in the arse. Full of platitudes, wish lists and jargon. On the face of it, whichever party wins, an earthly paradise is bound to be achieved.'

'Christ, John, nobody in this office finds that conclusion surprising! Get real! This paper's outlook is to assume they'll say anything to get the voters' support, so I want you to translate what you call the jargon into plain English, and then to opine on whether any of it is achievable… But, look, Johnny boy, get yourself home to Marion… Sorry, Marilyn, and try to relax! Women pop out sprogs every day of the week… It's a piece of cake. Go on, piss off and come back when you can think straight.'

'OK, Fred, thanks. I'll likely be back in the morning.'

He packed his laptop, put on his jacket and left the office. Marilyn's finishing work early for maternity leave was increasingly playing on his mind. High blood pressure was not an uncommon issue, but John couldn't help but think about Marilyn's first pregnancy. Had the miscarriage been a result of her fiancé's violent death? Or had there been a more physical cause, a thought which had been nagging away at him.

When he got home, an hour later because of delays on the underground, Marilyn was out. Walking into the kitchen, he spotted a note beside the kettle. He unfolded it, and read her neat, precise handwriting.

'In case you're back before me, I'm at the doctor's. Don't worry, just a routine check-up. Should be back by five. Love you. x.'

John sat on a chair, ran his hand over his chin, thinking,

She was only at the doctor's a couple of days ago... Why has she—

He stood, went to the front door, took his jacket and left for the surgery, two Tube stops away. Fifteen anxious minutes later, he rushed into the reception, to see his wife emerging from one of the consulting rooms, saying,

'Thank you, doctor, yes I will. Bye for now.'

Turning for the exit she saw John, standing, and said,

'Hello, John, what are you—'

'Marilyn... Is everything OK?'

She blushed as waiting patients looked up from their various reading materials, having overheard John's obviously worried tone, and said,

'This is a pleasant surprise. Shall we go for dinner? I meant to go to the supermarket, but—'

He moved forward, took her arm, and marched her out into the cold early evening air and said, his voice displaying his continuing anxiety,

'What's the matter? You were here only a—'

'John, I appreciate your rushing over. I should have told you this morning, but, honestly, it slipped my mind. In fact, I've been less than frank. Doctor Griffiths insisted I visit him on a regular basis, because... because of my history. There's nothing to worry about. The pregnancy is going along normally, apart from the blood pressure. His only concern is that I avoid stressful situations.'

Noticing John's sceptical, concerned expression, she went on,

'So we'll have to give skiing a miss, and seeing too much of Anita... or David. That reminds me, John, one of my fellow educators was disturbed – her word – by David knocking on her door the other night. She said he droned on about the election, but when she asked for his view on Europe, he clammed up, or rather his minders ushered him away. Melanie – that's my colleague – said it was bizarre. They took hold of his arms, in a mock friendly way, and off they went.'

'He's a virgin candidate, and I expect the party takes care to avoid any negative soundbites. Frankly, I'm amazed that Dave would submit himself to being muzzled. You know him as well as me by now. Verbal incontinence is one of his more loveable traits.'

'Talking of Anita,' Marilyn said with a coy smile, 'she must be well settled now over in Brussels. The last time we spoke, she told me, after asking about my health, that, in her words, she was "having to deal with stupid, unreliable workmen". It seems the apartment had a few problems with the plumbing and something else – it escapes me for the moment – and—'

John smiled at her and said,

'Did you ask your doctor about these memory lapses?'

'No, I can't remember. Where are you taking your wife for dinner? Oh no, I've forgotten my purse too... Maybe I should...'

It was nearly midnight when their landline rang, John sprawled out on the settee, Marilyn having gone to bed two hours previously. He stood, rested a magazine he'd been reading onto the coffee table, and picked up the handset.

'Hello, who's calling?'

'Hi, John, Dave here. We never got around to organising that drink. I think we could do with a catch-up. Here I am, sat in my study, by myself. Anita's just off the blower. She's got a committee meeting she can't get out of, so this weekend's another solitary one. A pisser, again. Anyway, how are you getting along? Is Marilyn OK? Anita said she finished working early because of—'

John, disturbed by his friend's depressed-sounding voice, something he hadn't heard before, said,

'Yes, Dave, only three months to go. She's fine, apart from the blood pressure, but—'

'But what?'

'Oh nothing. OK then, let's have a session. Can't do tomorrow, is Wednesday OK? I'll be in the office. It's around the corner from St Paul's and I've been getting acquainted with a few boozers. Come along at one, and we can wander down—'

'Wednesday's fine by me. See you, John, and give Marilyn my regards. Bye.'

He replaced the handset and walked into the bedroom.

'Was that the phone, John?' asked his sleepy-sounding wife.

'Yes, sorry if it woke you. Dave, asking if we could meet for a catch-up as he put it. He seemed brassed off, I think because of Anita—'

Marilyn sat up in the bed, rubbed her eyes and said,

'Because of her erratic schedule – weekend meetings. Yes, she told me she's too busy to be able to spend every weekend in London. I can bet David's a bit miffed with it, but Anita seemed to regard it as nothing significant. Has David talked it through with her?'

'He didn't say he had, but I'll ask him if—'

'No, no, John, you know how open David is. If you ask him, he's almost certain to mention it to her, and… If he does raise the subject, fair enough, but please don't you—'

'Yes, you're probably right. Come on, move over, I'm tired.'

*

John got to *The Swiftian*'s poky office early the next morning, despite having spent a restless, sleep-deprived night. At eight Samantha came in, and surprised to see John poring over his laptop, said,

'You're an early bird, John. Trying to impress Fred?'

'An impossible task, Sam. No, I need to catch up on a few emails and suchlike, so I… Fancy a coffee?'

'I'll make them.'

'No, my turn. The dinosaur's not here to lecture us on gender roles.'

As he brought two mugs into reception, the phone rang.

'Goodness, someone's keen,' said Samantha as she lifted the handset. 'Has Fred forgotten to pay the rent, do you think? It's for you, John. A man, sounds worried.'

John took the proffered handset.

'Hello, John Duncan speak—'

'It's Dave. John, is it OK if I come around to your office? I need to ask you a favour.'

'You sound agitated, Dave. What's up?'

'Can I see you now?'

'Yes, I'm free until lunchtime. I've got a meeting in the City at three, so, yes. Where are you anyway?'

'I'll be over in twenty minutes. Thanks, John.'

'Who was that, if you don't mind me asking? I think I've heard the voice before.'

'When have you… Has he phoned here recently?'

Samantha leant forward in her chair, cupped her chin in her hand, and after a few seconds replied,

'Yes I think he has. Oh, I remember now, he spoke to Fred. Something about the election, I think. Is he a friend, or a contact? I can add the number to our database if you want. The boss insists I make a note of all incomings. Anyone would think he's a bit, you know, paranoid, that's the word, I think.'

'Yes, Sam, that's the word alright. Fred can be really paranoid at times. He likes to think of himself as some kind of secret agent—'

'Oh, does that make me Miss Moneypenny?'

John, despite worrying over David's urgent-sounding tone, laughed,

'Definitely, Sam, but he isn't exactly James Bond. Listen, I'm going to nip out. I forgot to buy the papers on my way in and there's—'

'I can get them if you like.'

'No thanks, Sam. I need the fresh air. Be back in a tick.'

He donned his jacket and went out, down the stairs and out to the street, now awash with people on their way to work. He entered a newsagent, and grabbed all the national dailies, most with headlines on various aspects of the upcoming general election. Just as he finished paying, he spotted David through the glass door, walking briskly in the direction of his office. He left the shop hurriedly and shouted out,

'Dave, over here! Hold on, it's not a sprint.'

David wheeled around. His face was ashen, and he muttered,

'John, it's Anita…'

'Not out here, Dave, let's get out of the cold. This way.'

'Good morning,' said Samantha, staring wide-eyed at David. 'Can I get you two a drink?'

'I'm OK, Sam, but maybe Dave here—'

'Can I have a hot drink please?' said David with a weak smile. 'Yes please, err, Samantha, can I have a tea, two sugars?'

'Coming right up. Oh, John, Fred called while you were out. He's not coming in today. An urgent appointment, he said.'

'Thanks, Sam. We'll be in my office for... Can you fend off the usual calls, unless it's my wife of course.'

'Right, John.'

'Sit down, Dave,' said John surveying his friend's face anxiously. 'What's up? You mentioned Anita. She hasn't been—'

'Involved in an accident? No, nothing like that. She's not coming home this weekend, in fact, I'm not sure anymore that our marriage—'

'What? Seriously? You've only been married—'

'John, she's accused me of having an affair, screwing one of the girls in the office, Eva, a PA for the senior partner. I've no clue why she'd think anything like that. I don't think she's even met Eva. Why is she doing this? You know I wasn't over the moon about her spending so much time in Brussels, but, no, I went along with it, to make her happy. That's what makes for a solid marriage, isn't it? Sharing and compromising for the other party? I'm beginning to think she's drifting away from me. Have you met her new boss? Jerome, can't remember the last name. She's always on about how he's assisted her career progression. I trust her, John, but he crops up in her conversation too often for my liking...'

'Dave, if her boss was female, would you harbour these suspicions? No, you would not. From what I've learnt about the Foreign Office, well, they're a close-knit, secretive bunch, so if I were you I'd dismiss—'

David looked disconsolately at John and said,

'Yes, I know what you're saying is logical, but why, why would she accuse me, out of thin air, of being unfaithful? And the way she said it, really weird. No anger, as you'd expect, especially from a girl like her, but no, just a casual, throwaway statement.'

'Casual? How?'

'We were discussing my folks' fortieth wedding anniversary, and she said I could take Eva as her proxy, because I was probably sleeping with her anyway. As I said, no anger, or any interest.'

'You know Anita better than me, but I thought from the first time I met her that she's, well, not what you'd call the most sensitive individual where other people's feelings are concerned. She throws out comments sometimes before she's thought them through. Are you sure she wasn't trying to wind you up? After all, you were asking her to go to a family function on a weekend when she thought she had to be at work. Possible?'

'It wasn't just any old family meal, John. My folks have never taken to her, and turning up might have made a good impression with them, but no, her bloody FO work had to come first! From the way she tells it, all they fucking do is attend endless meetings, discussion groups, seminars. I knew she was ambitious, and what with losing the baby... It's taken over her life. Nothing's allowed to get in the way.'

As John listened, disheartened by David's uncharacteristic mood, an idea occurred to him.

'Why don't you and Anita come around one evening for dinner?'

David stroked his chin, as if he were contemplating the suggestion, but suddenly, his face lightening, he replied,

'No, I've got a better idea, John. The party's got a big shindig, at the constituency office, next Saturday night, and as it happens, Anita's got the weekend off from Brussels – Easter break. Not many of those Eurocrats are religious, but they love their holidays. Should be a good night, and as their candidate, I'm allowed to bring two guests. What do you say?'

John was speechless for a moment. David's instant change of mood shook him, but he responded positively.

'I'll have to ask Marilyn, but I'd guess she'd love it. She's not been out much since she stopped work, so, what the hell. Provisionally, Dave, yes.'

'Thanks for listening, John. As always, my own father confessor. I'd better get back to the office. You'd think the partners'd be pleased, you know, to have an MP on their books. I assured them I could still do occasional work after I'm elected, but they're tight-lipped about it all. Give me a call once you've squared with Marilyn. Bye, mate.'

With these words, David stood, and oddly, shook his friend's hand and exited the room, omitting to say goodbye to Samantha as he walked briskly past her desk.

'He didn't look happy… if you don't mind me saying, John.'

'No, of course not, Sam. Dave's an old friend, and one thing I know about him is that he'll bounce right back, just as soon as his wife smiles at him.'

Chapter Twenty-Six

John spent the rest of the day at his desk, with only a few interruptions, and he pondered whether his initial acceptance of David's offer for Marilyn and him to attend a gathering of his potential constituents had been precipitate. He was well aware of his wife's aversion to crowds, and her being pregnant further cooled his thoughts on whether to attend, but he also knew she'd been restless at home since going on maternity leave. By four o'clock he'd been to his short meeting in the City and finished most of his tasks for the day. Taking his jacket and briefcase, he walked out to reception, telling Samantha he'd be working from home the following day. Outside, the weather was turning cool and rain was in the air as he strolled along to the Tube station. In the concourse he stopped, fumbled for his wallet, and just as he was extracting his season ticket, a familiar voice boomed out over the bustling crowd of commuters.

'Oi! Johnny boy, where the hell are you sloping off to?'

He wheeled round, startled by the sound of Fred, and saw him marching up, his arm entwined with a young, glamorous-looking woman who giggled quietly as he whispered something in her ear.

'Hi, Fred,' John replied, feeling slightly nervous, 'we were expecting you in the office today. Sam told me you had to—'

'Yes, John,' Fred replied, still in a loud voice, 'yes, I had to get into something tasty.'

He winked at the young woman, who giggled again as she squeezed his forearm.

'Oh, Freddie, you're just too—'

'Well, John, I can see you need to get off to the little woman,' he continued. 'You wouldn't think it, would you, err...'

'Janine.'

'Yes, Janine, this chap here, he's one of my former pupils. Taught him everything he knows and now, well, he's been busy on the domestic front too!'

Irritated, John said,

'Fred, I'll be at home tomorrow, but don't worry, I'll be back in the day after.'

'Right you are, my boy, and remember, always keep the wife onside. You might think you can fool them, but let me tell you, it's not possible. They've got an extra sense.'

John ignored him and went down the escalator, for once unimpressed by Fred's dinosaur tendencies, wondering how he'd managed to pick up the young woman. He descended to the platform, which was heaving with people. Once on the train, he stood pressed against the door, annoyed with himself that he'd left going home until the rush hour. Suddenly, a screeching sound deafened everyone on board, and the train came to a juddering stop. The lights in the carriage went out, and immediately several passengers began screaming. A few seconds later an obviously agitated voice could be heard.

'Apologies for the unscheduled stop. We will be up and running as soon as possible.'

Standing at the door, John thought he saw human movement in the tunnel. A man briefly shone a torch into the carriage then moved away toward the back of the train.

'Did you see that?' asked a terrified-looking middle-aged woman squashed up against him, so close he could smell the whisky-flavoured breath.

'Yes, probably the guard checking to see why the train's stopped,' John said. 'Don't worry, it's not a terrorist inci—'

The train began to edge forward jerkily, and then the lights returned. The woman, her face showing signs of fear, said,

'Oh, thank God. My husband was trapped when those animals blew up...'

John put his hand on her shoulder and replied,

'It's OK, we'll all be home soon.'

Marilyn was sitting in her armchair reading a magazine when he got in.

'I take it you managed to avoid the trouble on—'

'What? Oh, yes, I was held up for a few minutes. The train stopped and out went the lights. False alarm.'

'No, John, there's been a serious incident on the Tube. Two men tried to set off a device of some kind, but were overpowered by members of the public, just outside Westminster station. I was worried you might have been caught up in it until I realised you don't take that route home—'

She began to cry. John sat on the arm of the chair, put his hands in hers and said,

'I'm home now, so stop this. I'd have to be very unlucky to be injured. More than eight million to one, I'd say.'

'Sorry, John, maybe it's the hormones, but recently I've been having very dark thoughts, and—'

'Listen, Marilyn, I was speaking to Dave earlier, and he was laying off his worries big time. The way he was talking, I suspect he and Anita are at loggerheads, but out of the blue, he invited us to some big party on Saturday. I didn't accept. I told him I'd have to consult you. What do you think? Might be interesting.'

'The way I feel now, well, yes, let's go. I'm getting really fed up sitting around. It's depressing how you can fall into the daytime TV trap. Where is this event?'

'At his constituency office.'

'Oh, I thought you said it was a party. Do you mean it will be full of political people, talking about the election? Sounds dull, John.'

'Right, I'll tell him we won't—'

'No, no, we'll go. Even the dullest of events has at least one interesting person who can speak, and besides, I could ask a few pertinent questions if I get hold of... About education policy for instance.'

John smiled.

'Still at work then, I see. Teaching is a calling, not a job—'

'Don't mock, John, that is a factual statement, despite the adverse press the profession gets in ignorant quarters.'

*

Saturday came around quickly and both John and Marilyn were fully occupied with family matters, he assisting his brother with their mother's messy estate planning problems, and Marilyn, despite her blood pressure, helping her mother and the new, very nervous parish priest in planning the church fete.

They left for the party, which was to take place, not, as David had previously indicated, at the constituency office, but at a hotel near the town hall. Getting out of a taxi (John, concerned by his wife's health, insisted on this mode of transport) they were greeted by a middle-aged man dressed formally in an evening suit.

'Good evening, sir, and madam,' intoned the man, who appeared to know who John was. 'Very glad you could make it this evening. Mr Murray advised me that you are a very busy man, so, on behalf of the party, may I welcome you to our modest gathering, and on—'

John, trying to extract his hand from the man's grip, said,

'Thank you, we're only too glad to be here for David. This is my wife, Marilyn.'

The verbose man assumed a curious expression, and without saying any more indicated with his arm for them to enter the building.

'Who is he?' said Marilyn, as they ascended the stairs. 'He seemed ready to chat until you mentioned my name. Funny little man.'

'Never seen him before, dear, but he's very well dressed – for a bouncer.'

They walked into the crowded reception hallway, following the direction arrows. Marilyn, eyeballing Anita with an old, overly dressed woman, who seemed to be talking with a fair degree of animation, said,

'Look, John, over there. Let's go and rescue her.'

John smiled at the comment, and taking her arm, they strolled casually through the crowd. Anita, seeing them making their way toward her, patted the woman's arm and said,

'Oh look, Mrs… Err… Here are two of my oldest friends, Mr and Mrs Duncan, John and Marilyn.'

'Pleased to meet you,' said the woman, blatantly staring at Marilyn's bump. 'Not long to go now, I see.'

'No, that's correct,' said Marilyn, glancing at Anita.

'Can I get you two a refreshment?' the woman asked.

'Two soft drinks would be lovely, thanks,' said John. 'A good turnout this evening.'

'Oh, indeed yes, Mr Duncan, especially after the announcement of the election. The committee is very pleased to have Mr Murray as its candidate. He's going to do us proud.'

'Yes, he probably will,' said John. 'One thing about Dave—'

'Dave?'

'Oh, sorry, that's what I call him. We've been friends since we were toddlers.'

'Right, John,' said Anita, clearly anxious to move away from the woman, 'let me introduce you to some of the committee members. Dave's been waxing lyrical about you to all of them. They're very impressed with City types. Talk to you later, Mrs…'

'Godwin,' barked the woman, and under her breath, 'Yes, later, if you've got the time.'

'This way, you two. Oh, careful with that rail,' said Anita, guiding Marilyn away from the staircase banister as she marched over to the throng of admirers surrounding her husband. 'Dave,' she shouted, 'look who's turned up!'

The people around David turned, surprised by Anita's sharp-sounding exclamation, and as she advanced with Marilyn and John in her wake, made a pathway for them.

'Hi, guys,' David said with a broad smile, 'glad to see you. Listen up, people, these are two of my best friends.'

The crowd around him looked at John and Marilyn. David, sensing the awkwardness, carried on, 'John here was at uni with me. He used to be a hotshot in the City, but now he's a journo. Where is it you work now, John?'

'I'm at *The Swiftian*,' John said, but seeing the frozen, almost shocked faces in front of him, carried on, 'I'm their economics and finance correspondent.'

'Don't worry, folks,' said David, who'd also noticed the expressions, 'John's non-political. All he cares about is cricket, and now, given Marilyn's condition, being a dad.'

John, embarrassed and annoyed simultaneously at his friend's artlessness, said,

'Dave, can I have a quick word?'

'OK, John. Excuse us, folks. John wants my view on Yorkshire's chances for the championship this season.'

As the four of them walked toward the relative quiet of the lounge bar, David said,

'What's up, John? You've got that irritated look on your face again. The last time I saw it, Marilyn, he'd lost a fiver.'

'As thoughtless as usual, Dave,' said John. 'You sound like the perfect candidate. What was old Moore's majority? Over 10,000, wasn't it? With your unique ability with words, you'll just about scrape home.'

'Don't give up on the day job, mate. Stick to boring old numbers. That's the call for dinner. Come on, this way to the food.'

They walked along and into the large hall, which doubled as a banqueting and ballroom venue. Over the course of the next two hours, John and Marilyn sat, ate, and listened, he bored, she paying close attention to several speakers, the last of whom, David, made a very positive address, encouraging the audience to 'get moving on the campaign trail' and praising the leader for his efforts at 'modernising' the Conservative Party. At ten-thirty, they made their excuses, Marilyn looking weary, and got a taxi home.

'What did you make of all that, John? David spoke quite well, for a novice.'

'Preaching to the converted is normally an easy task, but yes, he came across as a plausible guy. He sounded, well, almost sincere.'

'Oh dear, the typical journalist. I think Cameron will walk it, after that dour Brown—'

'Fred's got the notion that Clegg and the sandals brigade

will do well. He reckons the referendum promise could win him votes—'

'Yes, maybe, and did you spot the one issue David omitted?'

'Yes, dear, I did, but then Anita, working in Brussels, may have stymied his bringing it up. If she believes in anything other than herself, it's the European thing.'

'Harsh, John, very harsh.'

'If the polls move toward Clegg's gang, just wait for the Tories' reaction. More than half of them are anti-Europe. On the quiet, naturally.'

Chapter Twenty-Seven

Gordon Brown's decision to call the election, having been anticipated for so long, excited David; as the candidate for the sitting party in a safe seat, he was expecting a smooth transition, from small-time solicitor dealing with conveyancing into the multi-faceted world of national politics. John, because of his doubts as to David's staying power (he got bored easily), wondered if the life of a newly elected backbench MP, not exactly thrilling, and taking orders from senior party officials, would quickly dim his boyish enthusiasm. Aside from this, John was also concerned for his friend's marriage; Anita was, on a good day, prickly, and very alive to perceived slights, either to herself or David. Ironic, given her public displays of near contempt for him.

Then there was the possibility which Fred had continually touched on: the public's cooling toward Britain's membership. What if the Tories, sensing this, made some kind of move, however oblique and surrounded with caveats, to assuage the public mood? How would Anita react?

John decided to quiz David about the issue. He'd not heard his friend expressing any strong opinion on Europe, but he felt that, as a new MP, he would have no option but to stand by whatever policy the Tories adopted.

A week before the election, in spite of being very engaged with *The Swiftian*'s continuing critique of all the major parties' economic policies, he rang David at home. To his surprise, because it was a Wednesday, Anita came on the line.

'Oh, hi, Anita, good to hear you. Time off? Is the main man about?'

'I do get home on occasion, John. No, he's out, walking the streets of Benfleet. They're most probably heartily sick of his childish, perennially grinning face by now, but he's under orders. What do you want?'

'Just called for a chat, Anita, to ask how you both are coping, what with all… Can you tell him I rang?' John said quickly, anxious to escape from a possibly cantankerous dialogue, judging by her acerbic remarks.

'What do you mean… How's Marilyn?' she asked, but before John could respond, she went on, 'Tell her I was asking after her. I phoned last week, left a message in fact, but obviously she was too wrapped up in… Bye, John.'

'Who was that?' said Marilyn, returning from the kitchen. 'Anyone I should know about?'

'Anita. I was looking to speak with Dave, about the election, and she answered. Very offhand. Par for the course, I suppose. By the way, she asked after you. Did she leave a message last week? I can't recall seeing it on the list.'

'No, John, she didn't.'

They were watching the late-night national news when the landline rang out.

'Hello, Dave, long time no speak. How's it goi—'

'Why did you call, John? Anita was livid.'

'What? I was only calling to ask you how the campaign was going. If she objects, Dave, I'll butt out. Is she worried you might not win?'

'No, she's not. Never mind what she does or doesn't think. John, I… we… don't appreciate our marriage being judged… Marilyn's always been a tiny bit jealous if you ask me—'

John, angered by this sudden animosity, retorted,

'Stop right there, Dave, you're talking out of your arse now. Neither of us are "judging" you and Anita. I told you, the call was simply, and only, to ask how things were going. If you can't be civil, perhaps it's best you put the phone down and reflect on what you've said. You aren't speaking to one of those cretins we had to listen to the other night. Bye.'

Visibly angry, he sat down beside Marilyn, shook his head in disbelief and said,

'That's it, Marilyn. He's just accused us of being critical of him and Anita. Apparently, we're sitting in judgement of their marriage. What the hell's come over him? Listen, don't strain yourself trying to speak with her. They're far too busy with their own petty little lives now.'

'I'm sorry, John,' Marilyn said softly as she stroked his arm, 'they're under pressure, I think, so—'

'You've no cause to be sorry, Marilyn. In fact, the more I think about his stupid, thoughtless accusation… He's the last person I'd have marked out as being capable of turning on his friends. Well, in the words of the poet, "Fuck him."'

Marilyn, smiling, said,

'Which poet was that?'

'Can't remember.'

She began to laugh.

'What's so funny? Dave was out of order.'

'Yes, I agree, but can you imagine the scenario? He comes in, and gets both barrels from Anita, so he calls and passes on the shrapnel to you. I can picture his little red schoolboy face as she berated him.'

*

John, still smarting from the altercation with David, got into *The Swiftian* late the next day, not having slept well. Samantha greeted him, saying, as cheerfully as ever,

'Morning, John. Fred's in your office, very excited too. He rushed past me and even declined a coffee.'

'Morning, Sam,' John said quietly, 'no drink for me either.'

He walked into the small room to see Fred, furiously typing on his laptop. Noticing John, he waved him to a seat opposite and said,

'Big news, Johnny boy. I hear the Tories are havering over this referendum idea... You know Cleggy boy's promised to give the people a say—'

'Yes, you've mentioned it, Fred, several times. It'll never happen.'

'A week or so ago I'd have concurred, John, but my sources, deep in Central Office, are getting edgy about the marginals, the ones Clegg and co are targeting, almost all of them Tory ones currently. I'd lay odds they'll make some kind of move, perhaps a statement, to fend off the Lib Dems.'

'Still not convinced, Fred. It's probably a rumour to wrong-foot Labour. Gordon "I agree with Nick" wouldn't countenance a plebiscite after the furore of the Lisbon Treaty fiasco. The very idea, giving people a say, it's laughable.'

'You know, John, you're still young, but you're getting to be far too cynical. I don't approve. Oh, by the way, I heard in passing that your best friend's seat is one of the Lib Dem targets. Have you spoken to him recently? If not, maybe you could pump him for—'

'No, Fred, I can't see myself speaking to Dave in the foreseeable—'

'I get it,' said Fred with a sly, knowing look, 'a parting of the political ways. I knew, deep down, that you were a closet socialist… After all, your good lady being a teacher, they're all about saving the world from the depredations of capitalism. And eating meat.'

'Drop it, Fred. I'm not in the mood.'

'Yes, I got that, John. Speaking of the fair Marilyn, everything going to plan? Sylvia and me didn't ever talk about sprogs, probably a good thing. I've a plethora of talents, John, as you know, but I wouldn't test my patience with a kid of our own.'

'A couple of weeks now, Fred,' John replied, his mood improving at the prospect. 'She can't wait. The only cloud on the horizon is her mother. Believe it or not, Fred, the mother-in-law's main, perhaps her only, concern from what I've heard, is whether junior is going to be christened.'

'And?'

'Marilyn, despite her placid nature, doesn't take to being pressured. She's a Catholic, but she won't let her mother dictate to her.'

Fred, possibly thinking he'd ventured into dangerous territory, changed the subject.

'Ah yes, religion. Too intellectual for a hack like me. If there actually is a god who made the world… he must have a morbid sense of humour. Politics, now, that's the area where you can see the devious workings of mankind. Take this leak, about the Tories and a referendum commitment, it fits perfectly into what I said, doesn't it? Can you see such a thing really being allowed to happen? Even if all three main parties "commit" to one, the vast machinery of what somebody termed the "big state" will be brought into play.'

He stopped, then, looking mischievously at John, carried on, 'And that, my friend, is where your relationship with David Murray could be useful.'

'How do you work that out?'

'Think about it, John. Let's assume, for the sake of argument, that the Tories do put a public vote on Europe on their to-do list, and that they win the election. Mr Murray will have campaigned on that basis, and—'

'I'm not following—'

'Let me finish my scenario, John. Where does his wife work? And live most of the time?'

'Wait, are you saying—'

'No, I'm theorising. Mr Murray and his wife serve as a perfect microcosm, the textbook conflict. He's the politician in favour of a vote, she's in the Foreign Office, home of the EU fanatics. Those gangsters would move heaven and earth, shoot their mothers, to prevent Britain leaving. It'd make for a few lively dinner table conversations.'

'Fred, you've not lost your ability to dream up conspiracies. Committing to a policy in party manifestos doesn't mean it will translate into action, and vice versa. The Iraq fiasco being an example few could better. If the Conservatives win a majority, they'll pay lip service to the idea, set up a committee to kick the notion into the long grass and hey presto! No, Fred, Dave may loyally follow party policy, but you said it yourself, Anita's employers will be actively engaged in sabotaging any move toward fantasy land, I mean this country leaving the EU, but they'll do it on the quiet, through diplomacy. The only scenario in which a plebiscite of any kind took place would be if the polls showed massive, definitive proof of public support for staying in. Even then, officials would frame the question to favour a yes vote.'

'My, my, John,' said Fred, sitting back in his chair, 'for a man who's always professed a dislike of political debate, you've obviously been giving the current situation a deal of thought. I'm thinking you should be the political correspondent for the paper—'

'No way, Fred. I only agreed to work for you on a part-time, freelance basis. Leave politics to the slimeballs in Westminster—'

'Now, now, Johnny boy, but mark my words, if it comes to a referendum, there'll be many an argument in families across the country, including, I suspect, in the Murray household… Right, OK, I won't mention it again. Are you busy with anything today? I should have told you earlier, that piece you wrote for last week's edition, the one concerning the lack of transparency in the EU budget—'

'Yes, what about it?'

'Raised a few eyebrows.'

'As if that will make any difference. No one's interested in deficits. They'll merely adjust members' contributions to make up the shortfall.'

'Right, I've got a few calls to make, appointments and so on, but are you up for a lunchtime session? Don't give me that look. You can have a soft drink. I'm paying.'

John, as always, succumbing to Fred's easy charm, said,

'Nothing urgent, and yes, I think I'll join you. Could do with a relaxant just now. Sorry if I was a tad morose when I came in.'

'No worries, my boy,' Fred replied, patting John's back too heartily as he walked past him. 'Twelve-thirty then. I'll get young Samantha to join us.'

For the rest of the morning John's mind kept harking back to the unpleasant talk with his oldest and closest friend. In spite of Marilyn's advice to keep his counsel, he bristled at the distinctly cold tone David had adopted, and that fatuous, childish accusation: judging! The word came back to John time and time again as he sat, vainly trying to concentrate on the article he'd started two days previously.

'Time to be off, John,' said an enthusiastic-sounding Samantha, who'd popped her blonde head around his door. 'Fred's just left. Told me to remind you that you're on the bell. I think that means you're buying the first round.'

She giggled as she donned her raincoat.

'Wait, Sam, we can walk down together, that umbrella's big enough for both of us. I forgot my coat this morning.'

They walked, slowly because of Samantha's very high heels, along the narrow, cobbled lane to the pub. John pulled open the door, and as he waved her in, a youngish blonde woman coming toward the exit looked directly, and he thought coldly, at him. He had a vague sense that he'd seen her before, and that she recognised him too. She pushed past him, saying a cursory 'thanks' under her breath.

'You made it then!' bellowed the man himself. 'I took the initiative, Johnny boy. As you see the glasses are all set up, including your lime and soda water. Jimbo here was getting agitated, but I told him you'd be here to settle the tab.'

'Could I have a malt please, Jim? Oh, and I'll take the lime juice too,' said John, as he gazed at Fred's two companions, both of whom were dressed in three-piece suits straight from the seventies.

'Oh, my sincere apologies,' said Fred, his face, red and puffy, displaying the effects, John surmised, of two or three beverages, 'this is John Duncan. He used to be one of your gang of kleptomaniacs, but gave it up for the shining light, the beacon if you will, of investigative journalism, and he... Yes, John, this is Mark Duggan and David Johnson. They work down in Canary Wharf. I was going to send you off to speak with them, but they informed me they'd be down this neck of the woods for… but, anyway, chaps, what do we think about how this election will go?'

'Mr McTaggart,' countered a clearly uncomfortable-looking Duggan, glancing nervously at his colleague, 'governments come and go, but the finance and service sectors always manage to cope with variations in policy—'

'But this one's more significant, don't you think?'

'No, I can't see why you'd think that,' said Duggan.

'The elephant in the room's getting impatient, my friends,' Fred replied, 'very impatient.'

'Don't follow you, Mr McTaggart,' said Johnson, with what John considered a sarcastic tone.

'The Europe issue, my boy. A referendum may be—'

'Not a cat's chance in hell. Membership is permanent, settled,' said Duggan. 'No sane government would jeopardise our place in the EU. Most of the electorate are ignorant of its benefits,' and added, with a sneer, 'Ask the great unwashed? Seriously?'

Fred smiled and, winking at John said, 'Yes, you're most likely spot on there, my friend. Fancy another?'

'No, we have to be off, got a date with the Old Lady around the corner. Interest rates may be on the move, but you didn't hear that from me.'

'Bye, lads, nice to have met you, all the best,' Fred shouted over the noise as they hurried out, then winking again at John said,

'A right pair of arseholes, John. You looked as though you knew them.'

'No, but I recognise the mindset.'

Samantha, having been silent during the exchange, said,

'That woman was looking daggers at you, John—'

'What woman?'

'When you held the door open for her. If looks could kill.'
Fred laughed and blurted out,

'One of his exes, Sam. John's a boring married guy now, but back in the day—'

'Shut up, Fred. I suppose you'd like—'

'Yes, as you're offering.'

Chapter Twenty-Eight

Once he'd got over the shock of being adopted as the Conservative candidate for Benfleet, David Murray had been swept up in a tide of events, dragooned into attending meetings and functions which would have tested the nerves, and probably the patience, of a saint. His overt bonhomie shielded a shy, almost timid personality, and John, notwithstanding the recent spat with his friend, was concerned that he might find it difficult to cope with the stress of having to juggle his parliamentary duties with his personal life. Until he had been approached, to his initial astonishment, by one of the partners in his law firm, he hadn't given any thought to a career in politics. Cricket, rugby and having a good time were his only leisure interests, though it could be said, by those closest to him, that they had been downgraded since his marriage. Anita disliked sport; 'sweaty men chasing balls around a field, with even sweatier, boozed-up men watching them,' was her considered view on the subject. According to Marilyn, her reaction when David informed her about the possibility of his entering politics was typically blunt. She told him that, as far as she was concerned, a political career was 'one step above being a criminal, but without the need for intellect. Backbench MPs are cannon fodder, Dave. Just make sure to duck when the flak starts up.'

John was simultaneously amused and worried by David's response.

'Anita, if the party can use my talents, whatever they are, I'll do my bit. An MP's job is to serve the country after all.'

In the final month leading up to the election, John hadn't seen much of David, but the evening before polling day, Marilyn, slouched wearily in front of the television, took a call on her mobile: Anita.

'Hi! How's David's campaign been going? I hear—'

A few moments later she carried on, 'Oh, that's good news. When do you start? Tomorrow? Really? But does that mean you won't—'

She closed the call.

'John, that was—'

'Anita, yes, I gathered that.'

'It was odd. I was about to ask her about... She cut me off, to inform me it's been confirmed, finally. She's been selected for that gold-plated job at last, telling me robustly that she – yes, John, she – had to jump through several hoops to secure it, and here's the strange bit: the job requires her to be permanently in Brussels for the next six months, starting tomorrow, so she'll miss David's declaration. A real disappointment! What job is so important, so vital, that a single day off for her husband's big day isn't possible? Poor David! He'll be so upset, not only about her missing the big night, but, in the longer term...'

John smirked.

'I know that look, John. What are you thinking?'

'I'm certain he'll be disappointed, yes, but maybe just a tad relieved too. She won't have to play the devoted, adoring wife, walking around the count holding hands with him. You know how she hates being seen as an object of curiosity.'

'John, if I wasn't so close – wait, I'll qualify that – if I hadn't been so close to her over the years, I'd say she's being deliberately callous to him. Anita, like God, works in mysterious ways. Never mind, it's up to them how they… Will you be going along to his count? Come to think of it, John, you could utilise your press badge – pass, I mean – to get in there at the death, maybe get a few quotes. Why don't you give David a call? I've an inkling he'd appreciate a friendly, I mean a genuinely friendly, face tomorrow night.'

'Why? After that juvenile rant last time we spoke—'

'John, be the bigger man. I'll bet David's regretting his outburst and being David, can't find a way to apologise—'

'Yes, yes, OK,' he said, with a pained look. 'I'll pick up the phone now, if that stops you going on!'

He pressed David's number on the speed dial, saying to Marilyn as he waited for a response, 'I'll have to be careful, if Anita… Oh, hello, Dave, it's me. How's it looking?'

A pause, and then,

'Sounds positive. Marilyn was suggesting to me that maybe I should make an appearance tomorrow night, moral support and all that. What do you say?'

Another, longer pause.

'OK then, I'll pop along just after ten. Marilyn? No, her blood pressure couldn't stand the strain, but she'll be there in spirit. Bye, Dave, and good luck, not that you need it in Benfleet. Even a tosser like you couldn't manage to lose there… And the same to you!'

'Did you have to be so—'

'Banter, Marilyn. He fell over himself saying how much he regretted having a go at me. Funny, his voice sounded, well, as if he was going to burst out crying… I should have known.

Dave's a soft touch. I hope he manages to stand up for himself in that nest of vipers.'

'You didn't mention about using your press—'

'Damn! Forgot that. Maybe I should run it past that chairman, what's his name—'

'Streeter.'

'That's it. I've got his number somewhere. Did I tell you, Marilyn, when I called him to give Dave a personal reference, the guy asked if I knew of any "personal, intimate issues" Dave may have had. "Any sexual peccadillos" was the phrase, I think. What a question. Sneaky. A thoroughgoing creep. If he was really concerned, he should have asked Dave straight up. Anyway, I'll contact him in the morning. I'll say I'm going in a personal capacity. Fred's reputation would more than likely ensure me being barred from the count.'

'So, you boys have made up. Good...'

She pulled herself up and said, with a sigh,

'I'm feeling a bit queasy again, John. Would you mind passing me that bucket? I'd have thought this would have passed by now.'

*

In *The Swiftian*'s office the next morning there was an air of excitement. It was general election day, and Fred was in an abnormally high state of agitation, barking out instructions to his two unfortunate young assistants, who seemed to be permanently on their phones. John walked in late, after ten o'clock. He'd insisted on taking Marilyn to the surgery, and in spite of her doctor's assurances to him, remained in a very nervous, brittle state of mind.

'Morning, John,' said a calm Samantha, sitting nonchalantly at her desk. 'How's your wife doing?'

'OK, I think. What's all the commotion about, Sam?'

'Fred's trying to set up interviews wi—'

Fred, on hearing John's voice, came into the reception and said, looking and sounding harassed,

'So glad you could spare the time, John. Listen, I know you haven't been up to speed on the election work we've been occupied with over the past three weeks, but would you mind doing the honours down at Labour headquarters, from about nine onwards? Old Craig's called off again. "Indisposed," he claims. Too many shots more like, but—'

'Fred, can't help you there. I've made arrangements with an old friend—'

Fred's eyes lit up, and brusquely cutting John off, said,

'Oh yes, I get it! You're going down to the count in Benfleet, David Murray's... Yes, that's right, and maybe you'll get a headliner, what with all the kerfuffle over that unfortunate interview, or rather, confrontation.'

'Not with you, Fred.'

'No? Then you haven't heard the latest. Your pal's turned a safe seat into a marginal. Not his fault in reality, given the Lib Dem surge nationally, but he got himself into a tangle when he was asked out in the street about his views on this referendum issue. The poor guy thought he was talking to someone he assumed to be a constituent, and I hear he huffed and puffed so much that his minder stepped in and shoved the "constituent" away. The Lib Dem candidate, a real greaser, rictus grin on full beam, commented on it via social media.'

'Yes, I heard a story similar to that, but, verbal gymnastics don't necessarily mean... You're right, I'm making an appearance to support Dave. He invited me after I—'

Fred jumped in, winking at him. 'You're going there to lend support to your oldest and best buddy! Very noble. But don't celebrate too robustly. I'll expect a nice little exposé of that Lib Dem cretin, especially if he causes an upset. Hey ho!'

John grimaced and went into his office, fired up his laptop, and checked for emails. At the top of the unread messages he was surprised to see the sender's name: Anita. The text, short, blunt and without any subtlety said,

'John, my husband expects you at the count this evening. Thank you, Anita Murray.'

He read it a second time, and without bothering to reply, decided to forward the note to Marilyn. Five minutes later his machine pinged.

'John, I'll bet that made you laugh. She's far too busy to be there for him, so you get the nod. Have you contacted that man – what's his name… oh yes, Streeter – about going?'

'No, not yet, been talking, sorry, listening, to Fred. You can imagine how hyped up he is today. He wanted me to stand outside Labour's headquarters tonight—'

'You aren't?'

'No, I've had my orders from Anita. Fred was more than OK with it. Listen, Marilyn, with all the action taking place after ten, I might as well pop home after lunch. I should have asked, how are you now? No more dashes to the toilet?'

'I'm fine, dear, feeling much better, and my blood pressure's down from the stratosphere.'

'Good. I'll be back by three at the latest. Today's very momentous. Fred's treating all his minions to lunch and… No, I'll be abstaining, given my probable late night amongst the Tory faithful.'

Ending the call, John sent off a reply to Anita, in the same clipped manner:

'Yes, I'm going to the count, John Duncan.'

*

When he arrived home, Marilyn ran to the door before John had managed to extract his key. She opened it, and to his surprise, flung her arms around his neck.

'Hi, John, you escaped from Fred's clutches then,' she said quietly, and whispered, 'Mother's turned up. I wasn't exp—'

'No worries, but I forgot to tell you,' he said, taking off his jacket, 'she phoned me – yes I know, unusual – to ask me if I'd like her to spend a few days at ours, because I'm so "busy" at the moment...'

He kissed her, walked into the living room and greeted his mother-in-law in the same fashion.

'Hello, John,' she said, blushing slightly, 'I hope you don't mind, but I'm so worried about Marilyn being here alone, and I'm sure you feel the same, so I—'

'Yes, and thanks again for... well, just for being here. Did Marilyn advise you of her latest readings? Blood pressure's down, and—'

'Oh, no, she hasn't, but I had similar problems when I was expecting her, and Marilyn had the same thing before...'

She stopped abruptly, going crimson, with a tear escaping from her left eye, which she quickly brushed away as Marilyn came in and asked,

'Tea everyone?' Spotting her mother's discomfort, she said, 'Are you OK, Mum? I told you, I'm fine, so stop the waterworks.'

Trying to appear calmer she replied,

'This one will be my first grandchild. I suppose you young ones will know the sex. I don't hold with—'

'No, Mother, we didn't ask, and what's more, we don't care.'

Chapter Twenty-Nine

The three spent a relaxed afternoon, despite Marilyn's mother's latent anxieties over Marilyn's pregnancy. She explained, at some length, the arrangements Father Delany was making, naturally with her help, for the celebrations to mark his fifty years as a priest. As she spoke, John could see many of his wife's characteristics in her; the enthusiasm, the serious-minded commitment to the subject at hand, were traits he recognised and admired in Marilyn.

His mind began to drift away; he thought back to when he'd learnt of her tragic first pregnancy, and ever since had been in awe at the way she had overcome it. Try as he might, he couldn't get his head around the horror of losing a child; Marilyn, he'd come to appreciate very quickly, took life very seriously, and the event must have left a scar. Knowing this, John, sitting in the living room, listening to his wife and mother-in-law animatedly discussing Father Delany's shindig, felt a lump in his throat, and he sensed his eyes beginning to cloud over.

Not given to abstract, speculative musings, John nonetheless began to contrast the reactions of his wife and her friend to their similar misfortunes. Despite their overtly differing personalities, they had managed to overcome and, on the surface, get their lives back to what could be described as normal. He was very aware that Marilyn's loss was always with her, and knew it would never fully be accepted, but typically she was getting on with her life. Anita remained an enigma to him, however, as she was to Marilyn. She had confided one evening, when discussing the likely posting to Brussels, that Anita's hyperactivity was more than just a determination to progress, and this thought worried John, as he knew David was a stranger to confrontation in emotional matters.

His reverie was interrupted by Marilyn.

'John, would you mind—'

'Yes... I'll make another pot of tea,' he mumbled, and jumped up from his chair. In the kitchen, his emotions began to calm down, but that thought – Marilyn's quiet, understated stoicism in the face of life's vicissitudes – came back to him again. He poured out three cups from the pot, put them on the tea tray they'd bought in Rome, and walked carefully back into the living room, but nearly stumbled at the sound of the landline ringing out.

'Careful, John,' Marilyn said, 'that's a new carpet. I know you're not enamoured with it, but, it's OK, put the thing down while I answer the phone.'

'Hi there, Anita. Yes, he's here, and... OK, OK, patience! I'll pass him over.'

John, irritated, took the handset.

'I got your message, John. I want you to be there by seven. David's agent wants as many people as possible to be photographed with him.'

'Are you in Brussels then?'

'What's that got to do with anything? Will you be at the count by seven? Yes or no, John?'

Suppressing a desire to fire back a sarcastic comment at Anita's hectoring, arrogant tone, he said merely,

'I've already let Dave know I'll be there tonight, so you can rest easy, Anita. Bye.'

'That was a bit sharp, John,' said Marilyn. 'Why was she calling? I expect she's been phoning round all his pals to beef up David's nerves. I'm still not convinced about his ability to cope with the demands of being an MP.'

'Yes, she was asking, no, demanding, I be there by seven,' said John, still very angry. 'That's a non-starter. The fucking cheek of it... Oh, I'm sorry, but—'

'So you should be, John,' said Marilyn, trying to hide her amusement at her mother's shocked face. 'Mother, the last time he swore was when I told him I was expecting. Say you're sorry, John.'

Visibly embarrassed, he said,

'Apologies, Jane. Marilyn's right. I'd better keep it together when... when I'm in the labour ward.'

He cleared up the crockery, still unnerved by his *faux pas*, and made his escape to the kitchen.

'Can I escort you home, Jane?' he said on returning, slightly more confident.

'John, I told you, Mother's staying here for a few days and—'

'No, Marilyn, until the baby arrives.'

'Pardon my forgetfulness. It's nearly seven, so I'll go and get my battle dress on for this evening's happenings. It'll take me at least an hour to get over there.'

No sooner had he left for the bedroom than Jane said, almost under her breath,

'John's very nervous, dear. I'm not one to interfere, but... but, is he aware of your little disappointment, you know what I'm—'

'Of course he is, Mother. Our marriage hasn't any secrets, and before you ask me, he's no saint – who is? – but as you'd expect, knowing... Well, he'd be a strange person if he didn't feel overprotective, and he's a kind, decent man—'

'Yes, very like Grant. Oh, he was a lovely man, dear, such a shame, being killed in that hit and run.'

Marilyn bit her lip in frustration at her mother's clumsy, unnecessary comment, saying tersely,

'If you say so, Mother. I've made up your bed, and John can get the portable television rigged up in the room. Sorry, but you'll have to watch those awful daytime programmes by yourself.'

Ten minutes later, John came into the now distinctly chilly atmosphere in the living room, and, sensing the unspoken tension, said,

'Right, I'm all set, girls. Any message for the candidate? Dave, I mean.'

'Tell him we wish him all the best, John,' said Marilyn, who continued, a wry smile on her face, 'but don't go so far as to greet him with a kiss, might make Anita jealous.'

'Marilyn, if I tried to do that, Dave would have a coronary. Touchy-feely's not his style. See you then.'

*

The journey over to Benfleet town hall, where the count and declaration were taking place, took John almost two hours, mainly because someone had decided to walk through a tunnel, delaying all trains until he was arrested. As he walked hurriedly toward the building, he checked his watch: ten-thirty. He took out his mobile to check for any messages, and was surprised to see two calls, which he had missed because he'd put the thing on silent. Both of them from a number he recognised: Anita's.

He stopped at the entrance and dialled her number, intent on telling her what she could do with her phone. No answer. Probably just as well, he thought, and returning the mobile to his inside pocket, marched into the hall. Before he got to the main entrance, a burly, middle-aged man with a shaved head and dressed in a three-piece suit raised his left hand in a gesture indicating he wished John to halt.

'Your security pass, sir.'

'I don't have one unfortunately, but if you ring Mr Streeter on that phone of yours, I'm sure he can vouch for me.'

'Name?' barked the man, coldly, and unsmiling.

'Duncan, John Duncan.'

'Is that Duncan John, or John Duncan?'

'I'll try to make it simple for you. My name is John Duncan. I'm a close friend of David Murray.'

'Who?'

Trying very hard not to laugh, John said,

'The Conservative candidate.'

The bouncer stared at John suspiciously for a couple of seconds and then spoke into his mobile,

'A geezer… Yeah, Duncan something… Says he's a mate of David Murray… Dunno. Right.'

He waved John forward, opened the door and said,

'OK, go through.'

John strode past and into a large, high-ceilinged hall which echoed with his footsteps. He looked around for an indication of where the main event was happening; hearing the sounds coming from the first floor, he assumed the best course would be to ascend the winding staircase. When he reached the landing, he noticed an arrow on the wall pointing to a large set of double doors, with a young, dark-haired woman, no more than twenty, he thought, sitting next to them reading a magazine. John walked up and asked her,

'Is the count taking place in there?'

'Yes,' came the reply. 'Have you got a pass?'

'No, but your colleague downstairs gave me the nod, after he'd spoken with—'

'Go on in,' the woman said, without looking up from her reading. 'The refreshment area is second on the left.'

John pushed through the heavy doors and surveyed the vast room – a mass of humanity rushing about in every direction, some carrying bundles of papers which looked like voting slips, and others standing, observing the proceedings. Recalling the woman's mention of the refreshment area, he turned, and despite the throng and the noise, spotted his friend, standing in the midst of a group of men, nodding his head. David, almost simultaneously, eyeballed him, and left his band of admirers, or more likely, his minders, and strode forward holding out his hand.

'Hi, John! You managed to evade the security team then. Anita said you'd be here by seven, but better late than never.' Turning to a guy who seemed to be in charge of his 'team' he said, too loudly,

'John's my best mate, we go back to primary school days. Used to be a star in the City, but gave it up to be a writer. He works for old Fred McTaggart's rag now, what's its name again… Oh yes, *The Swiftian*.'

As he shook David's sweaty hand, John noticed the pained expressions on the faces of the minders. One of them whipped out his mobile, turned away from the two friends, and muttered something inaudible, then came over and said,

'Yes, Mr Duncan, our chairman, Mr Streeter, is anxious to have a word. Can you follow me please?'

David's face fell, and he said quietly,

'Better go and see him, John. He's been badgering me all week to get you to come here. Between you and me, or *entre nous* as Anita has taken to saying, Streeter may have an ulterior motive in—'

'This way, Mr Duncan,' the minder repeated, looking agitated.

'Right, well, Dave, if I don't see you before the declaration, best of luck.'

The minder barged his way through the crowd of people standing about, John walking behind him. They reached the bar, where a group of half a dozen or so men, dressed as if they were expecting a summons from the Palace, were huddled closely together, speaking softly, all of them with very taciturn faces. John moved forward as the minder whispered into the ear of a man holding a half-empty spirit glass. The man, ruddy-complexioned from possibly one too many shots, smiled benignly at John and said,

'At last. Mr Duncan, pleased to see you could make it.'

'Hello, Mr Streeter. Are you expecting a good result this evening? I've not had a chance to quiz Dave on it yet and—'

Streeter frowned momentarily, but he recovered, saying,

'Err yes, he's very nervous, on edge you might say, but tell me, Mr Duncan, aside from being his good friend, why did you come along this evening? I understand you're a journalist, and—'

John, realising that David's slip had probably been communicated, and recalling Fred's less than positive comments on Streeter, replied somewhat tersely,

'Don't worry, Mr Streeter, I'm off duty tonight. There'll be no unattributable quotes, not in *The Swiftian's* pages certainly, but I can't vouch for my distinguished colleagues in the press.' Pausing for a few seconds, and noting Streeter's frozen look, he went on,

'It's unlikely there would be any national interest in this constituency's vote. It's a safe seat, I believe, and with the

best slant on things, none of the candidates is a "personality",
so—'

'Mr Duncan, I appreciate your frankness, but this race could
be a close-run thing. The Lib Dems have been door-stepping
what seems like every home over the last two weeks, and Clegg's
advocacy of a referendum may have caught on. Quite worrying.
My business would be badly affected if we ever did pull out.'

'Can't see any of that coming to pass. The Lib Dems are
fantasising.'

Streeter smiled, and said,

'Can I buy you a drink, Mr Duncan?'

'Thank you, a whisky if you will, and it's John.'

'Yes, John it is then. Tell me, if you don't mind my asking,
what made you leave the City? Was it the crash?'

'No, I'd had enough of the fourteen-hour days. It was
ruining my personal life, and I envied Dave his lifestyle. You
know, many people who know us reckon he was the typical
City hotshot, with his natural exuberance, but deep down, the
guy's a very serious-minded individual. He'll take his new job
as a… well, almost as a calling.'

'Yes, David told me you'd changed jobs, or should I say,
career. I take it you maintain good relations with your erstwhile
colleagues. You write on finance matters, on a freelance basis,
don't you?'

John, correctly guessing where this line of questioning was
leading said, half-jokingly,

'Yes, I keep my eye on the markets. Good fun, if you haven't
got a stake in them. Would you like any pointers?'

Streeter blanched.

'Oh. You've misunderstood me, sir. I was merely trying to
make conversation. I beg your pardon.'

He pushed past him and made his way toward the count.
John, irritated but not offended by the man's clumsy attempt

at seeking out a few tips, smiled and made his way out of the bar. Walking into the crowd directly in front of the raised area where the results would be announced, he spied an old sparring partner from his days in the world of finance – a middle-aged, overweight man, dressed in the old uniform once favoured by City types, the regulation three-piece suit, floral tie and striped shirt. Seeing John, he shouted out, startling people near him,

'What the hell are you doing here, turncoat?'

Tempted as he was to reply in kind, John said,

'I could ask you the same question, Justin. Have you got an interest in the result here? Could it be a financial one perhaps?'

Justin Stevens was a legend in City circles, not for his acumen with money, but for his uncanny ability to lose it, betting on hopeless cases. The joke amongst his more competent colleagues was that he couldn't be sacked because 'he knew people'. He grimaced and said, 'Returning a favour, old boy. Ollie Streeter and I are old friends, from school, don't you know.'

'Very noble of you I'm sure, Stevens, but this is a safe seat. Why would it need your valuable input?'

'Safe, you say? You're behind the times, Duncan. Those damn Liberals and their promise on Europe, can't let that happen.'

John turned away from Stevens, baffled as to why anyone with an ounce of common sense would have allowed David's campaign to be 'assisted' by such a man. He moved on to where the votes were piled onto tables, and surveyed the bundles of papers; even a layman could make out that David's pile was only just bigger than the Lib Dem candidate's. Streeter's caution was justified; an upset might be on the cards. He returned to the bar, confident that the result was some time off, but halfway there the tannoy blared out over the hall.

'Ladies and gentlemen, the declaration will be made in approximately five minutes, five minutes.'

The crowds began to push their way toward the podium, and less than two minutes later, the five hopefuls walked, with sombre expressions, onto the stage. John, seeing his friend's face, normally so open and honest, couldn't guess whether he had triumphed. As they stood together, the crowd became silent, a few individuals coughing the only sound, and after what seemed an eternity, a small white-haired woman whom John presumed, from her self-important expression, was the returning officer, walked slowly up to the microphone and, in a ponderous, affected voice read out the candidate's votes. David had won, by a majority of just over 1,000. The woman announced, with the utmost gravity, that David had been duly elected. John stared at David's expressionless face. He didn't seem to have taken it in, and when the presiding officer invited him forward to speak, the candidate standing next to him had to nudge him out of his apparent trance. David made a short, unimpressive address, and scurried off the platform, shepherded away from the crowd by a trio of heavy-set minders.

Knowing he wouldn't get anywhere near David, John sidled out of the hall and into the street, hailed a cab and went home. It was one-thirty in the morning. Marilyn and her mother were fast asleep, so he poured a whisky and sat down, resisting the temptation to switch on the television to check the election results, but thinking, yet again, whether David's new situation would affect his marriage. Anita's reaction to his winning played on John's mind; he had a strong feeling that she was ambivalent over his new-found, and, to John if not to her, surprising interest in politics.

He finished the whisky and went upstairs and into their bedroom, to find Marilyn and her mother lying in the marital bed, which made him smile. His wife being an only child, he appreciated how much Marilyn meant to her mother, and his mind returned to his earlier thoughts. After the miscarriage, the fear of history repeating must be playing heavily on her, and John, with similar anxieties, was glad for her to be close. The light from the hallway allowed him to look around, and on his bedside John saw a note, leaning against the lamp. He tiptoed forward, took the paper and left the room, his mother-in-law's gentle, subdued breathing the only sound. Downstairs, John, wide awake despite the long day, poured another drink before reading the note. Written in Marilyn's neat, precise hand, was the startling message, from Fred.

'John, can you come over and extricate me from this hellhole? Bored stiff, old boy.'

Below this Marilyn had written,

'John, can you go over to St Thomas's? Fred's been involved in some sort of bother, an accident, I think.'

Chapter Thirty

Late as it was, he called a cab for the twenty-minute drive to the hospital. Marilyn's cryptic message troubled him. If his old mentor had been in an accident, surely he would have called Sylvia. Agitated, he began to suspect that the word accident was a euphemism for something else. John had a strong feeling that, whatever had occurred, Fred calling him meant that his hospitalisation wasn't the result of an innocent event. He couldn't recall where Fred had planned to be the previous evening, but he knew the man would have been involved in covering the election results, and people's reactions which, if 'newsworthy' in his eyes, would appear in *The Swiftian*'s coverage. The taxi drew up at the hospital's accident and emergency door. After paying the driver, John walked into the reception, and shoving through the ragtag collection of drunks, staff, and a few people who actually looked in need of medical attention, asked one of the staff at the desk,

'Hi, I believe you have a Fred McTaggart here?'

With a bored, indifferent look, a grey-haired woman, dressed in a smock, took off her glasses and replied,

'Are you a relative?'

John hesitated, anticipating difficulty, but said,

'Well, no, but he left a message for me to—'

'He left a message? Wait a moment. McTaggart, you said?'

Before he could respond, the woman, putting her hand over her mouth, muttered something to a colleague, and then,

'He's in the third, no, the fourth cubicle on the right. Drunk, by the way he talks.'

Relieved, John turned away and walked briskly, less worried now. He got to the cubicle, and hesitantly pulled at the curtain.

'About time too! Where've you been? I called your place nearly four hours since!'

'And good evening to you too,' said John, irritably, but seeing the gash on Fred's bare left arm, 'What the hell's happened? That looks like a kni—'

'A couple of cocky midgets tried it on as I was leaving the pub on my way to Conservative headquarters. Tried to relieve me of my valuables... my wallet, I mean, Johnny boy, but they got a big surprise. You're right about the cut though. It's probably been done by a knife, but I can't remember seeing the thing. Look at my jacket over there, on that chair, ruined. Had it since my salad days in Carnaby Street. Fuck! It all happened so quickly, and the two scampered off like rats leaving the *Titanic* when I clobbered the main man – or boy to be more accurate – with my briefcase, right in his ugly gob! The bastards called me, bravely, after they'd made their escape, a Tory git. Me, John, a Tory!'

A nurse walked into the cubicle and interrupted Fred's monologue by saying,

'Reception informed me you were a friend of our guest here, Mr...'

'Duncan. Yes, he called my home and requested my presence here. How is he?'

'The doctor's stitched the wound and considers he should be kept in overnight for—'

'Don't be silly, nurse, I'm fine, nothing a few—'

The nurse frowned.

'If you insist, Mr—'

'I do. My colleague's volunteered to let me bunk up at his quarters for the night,' Fred replied decisively, 'and his wife's a wonderful, gourmet cook.'

'Very well, after you get dressed, make your way to reception to sign yourself out, and to collect the medication.'

'Thank you, nurse. John, toss over my garments and let's move out.'

'Don't you want to let Sylvia know—'

'She'd only worry, and then lecture me about frequenting... I'll let her know tomorrow... Maybe.'

'OK. You can have the spare room for tonight, Fred,' John said, and then, remembering about his mother-in-law as the taxi hurtled through the quiet streets, 'Oh, no, Marilyn's mother is with us at the moment—'

'Don't worry, I'll kip on any surface you care to let me use. Oh yes, she's a looker, isn't she?'

'What do... I meant to say, we can adjust the sleeping arrangements. I've got two camp beds from my student festival-going days, so we can use the living room for tonight. I'm curious though, why haven't you called—'

'Don't be nosy, young John, gets you into bother if you're not careful, best to be circumspect.'

They went into the house. John pulled out the two beds from the cupboard below the stairs and set them up in the living room while Fred sat reading one of John's magazines, *The Spectator*.

'Didn't know you took this rag, John.'

'I don't, just picked it up the other day. Which one of these—'

'No preference, old boy.'

*

The two men were woken by the sound of the kettle whistling.

'Coffee, anyone?' said Marilyn, looking down at them with a quizzical expression. 'I could ask how… Never mind, you're here now. How are you feeling, Fred?'

He raised himself up slowly from the bed and replied,

'Marion… Sorry, Marilyn, I appreciate I'm being a nuisance, but John here insisted, demanded in fact, I come here to recuperate after my altercation. Good man, your husband. I'll have some coffee, with a spot of God's water, to soothe my nerves, you understand.'

She smiled at him, shook her head and said,

'Coffee yes, whisky no, Fred.'

'Can't fault a man for trying.'

Half an hour later the three were sitting at the dining room table consuming breakfast when Marilyn's mother wandered into the kitchen. She stopped, and gazed suspiciously at Fred, who smiled broadly at her and declared,

'Marilyn, your mother is even prettier than you. Good morning, madam. My moniker is Fred, of the McTaggart clan.'

Mother-in-law blushed, walked nervously forward and took the outstretched hand.

'Pleased to meet you, I'm sure. How are you? That's a nasty-looking bandage. Serious?'

'Only a scratch, my dear, and it's all the better for seeing two beautiful ladies in the one room.'

Marilyn, slightly embarrassed by this exchange said,

'Is there anything you two need from the shops? Mother and I are popping out to—'

'We are?'

'Yes, we are. Best to get there before the crowds.'

'See you girls later then,' replied Fred, with a wink to mother-in-law as they left the room.

'What really happened last night, Fred? Can you remember anything about the two punters who attacked you?'

'Simple attempt at mugging, John. They'd obviously been eyeing me up in the pub, thinking it would be a piece of cake, given my distinguished, not to say elegant, appearance.'

'But why didn't you get on to the police? I've heard of several, maybe apocryphal reports of thuggery because of the election, and—'

'What? Good imagination, John. But wait, how did the circus turn out? This must be the most interesting general election since Thatcher whacked old Kinnockio where it hurts back in '87. That was a good one, John. The Welsh Windbag looked gutted. I couldn't stop laughing for days. Switch on the tube and let's enjoy the oh-so-humble politicians, telling us what they're going to do for the country, i.e. fuck all.'

John took the remote, sat back next to Fred, and for the next two hours they watched the results being analysed *ad nauseam* by the 'expert' commentators.

'Well, who'd have thought it?' Fred declared with a grimace. 'There'll be a coalition, for sure, with the veggie sandal-wearers calling the tune. That reminds me, how did Dave get on? I haven't seen Benfleet's numbers yet.'

'Oh, he got in, but the majority was down to just over 1,000.'

'That'll energise their marriage,' Fred commented, grinning. 'That wife of his, I'm told, on the best authority, that she's been earmarked as a high flyer in the Foreign Office. Her stint in Brussels has been noticed, by those who matter, which means she'll be up that ladder soon.'

'Your presumption is correct, Fred,' John said, taken aback by the mention of Anita, 'but I see your point. Dave's election material didn't refer to the EU directly, but—'

'Yes, Johnny boy, it's amazing how nearly everyone posted to Brussels, be they civil servants, business people, or even us journos, turn into glove puppets for the project, like, what's that phrase about how... Oh yes, Stockholm Syndrome. Ever been there, John? I have. Nothing of note there... apart from those girls in ABBA.'

'I think we should head off for the office. We must have a pile of messages to deal with. The next issue's due out by midnight. With what's his name, Clive, *hors de combat,* can you write up *The Swiftian*'s leader by six?'

John sighed.

'Really? I'd planned to finish off the article on the EU budget at home today. OK, Fred, I'll knock something off and email the piece over to you. Are you clearing off now?'

'Better make the effort. Can't believe I let myself be cornered like that last night. The more I think about it, John... Yes it's starting to come back to me. When I left the office, I did notice a few young men staggering around. At the time I dismissed them as election night bevvy merchants, but I think I saw the same group later in the pub. Odd, I call that. Was I being followed, and if so, why? I never buy strangers a drink.'

'Yes, Fred,' John replied, with a smile, 'maybe the guys were trailing you for a reason. Perhaps one of your exposés caused someone with a grudge... Wait, perhaps I should come in with you—'

'You mean as my bodyguard? Stop taking the piss, John. I was probably in the right place at the right time, from their point of view, that is. Call that taxi.'

Chapter Thirty-One

John got into the office late the next morning but before he'd managed to plug in his laptop his direct line rang.

His mother-in-law.

'John dear, it's coming! The baby's coming!'

Trying to suppress his anxiety, John said,

'Calm down. Where are you?'

'Marilyn's been taken into the labour... At the London.'

'I'll be there in twenty minutes.'

He grabbed his jacket, left the office, rushed along to the Tube and managed to get on a very crowded, humid train, hoping he'd make it before the child arrived, and, not for the first time, wondering if the birth would proceed without any problems. Marilyn's blood pressure came into his head. The journey, a mere fifteen minutes, seemed to be taking an age, and he kept checking his watch. He jumped out of the train, ran up the escalator and crossed the car-clogged street to the hospital entrance. Breathless, he rushed past reception, following the signs for the maternity unit; he knew the place fairly well, having visited with Marilyn on a couple of occasions.

'Hi, I'm John Duncan. I believe my wife is here already, and—'

'Her name?'

John, ignoring the stupidity of the question, replied,

'Marilyn... Marilyn Duncan. Where is she?'

'Doctor is assessing her at the moment. Take a seat.'

He obeyed, and, still out of breath, walked over to a row of very cheap-looking plastic seats, sat on the only one available, next to a bored-looking man reading a magazine, flicking through the pages, clearly not as anxious as himself.

'This waiting's a bugger, isn't it, mate?' Magazine man commented after tossing the reading material onto a table, 'I've been here for six hours now, and the missus hasn't popped yet. You look grim. Your first?'

'Yes.'

'Doesn't get any better, mate.'

'Mr Duncan?' shouted a nurse, emerging from behind a screen. 'Mr Duncan?'

John held up his hand, stood, and walked sheepishly forward as a row of heads looked up.

'That's me.'

'This way please,' said the nurse, who immediately wheeled around, John following her past the screen and toward the labour ward.

'How is she?' he asked the nurse as they continued walking.

'The doctor will explain matters.'

Suddenly, John remembered: his mother-in-law.

'Is my wife's mother with her?'

'I can't say, Mr Duncan, but please, hurry along.'

They moved along the corridor and the nurse motioned him into a small room, where a white-coated man was seated, writing. On John's entering, the doctor raised his head and indicated, by a nod of his head, for John to sit. Putting down his pen officiously, he said,

'Good day to you, Mr Duncan. I'm glad you got here in time—'

John blanched at the man's words and replied, losing his cool,

'In time? What the fuck do you mean by that? How's my wife?'

The doctor, without changing his expression, said,

'Calm yourself, Mr Duncan. Mrs Duncan, because of the position of the baby, will require a section. I trust you know what that means—'

'Of course I do! Can I see her?'

'Ah, um, well, I'm afraid not. At the present time she's unconscious, which is why, as I've said, it's fortuitous that you're here. I... we... need your permission to carry out the procedure. Time is of the essence. Your wife came here very distressed, as was the baby, so the sooner we have your approval, the better.'

Reeling from the doctor's words, John, holding back tears, could only say,

'Will she be OK, doctor? Tell me.'

'Mr Duncan,' said the doctor, pushing forward the paperwork and offering the pen, 'I have to be blunt. Given your wife's condition, and the baby's for that matter, we have to proceed with some urgency. Not ideal, given that she's only thirty-six weeks. Your wife is a young woman, and apart from her blood pressure, a healthy one. Can you approve us carrying out the operation? She's ready for theatre.'

John, feeling himself shaking, said,

'Where do I sign?'

He signed, gave the pen to the doctor, who said, returning the form to him,

'No, you have to sign, there, below the date.'

John, dazed, took the form again and signed, this time in the correct space.

'Now, if you could return to the waiting room, Mr Duncan. I'll come and advise you of the outcome. I understand your anxiety, but please, try not to worry.'

John left the room and walked slowly back to the waiting area, his thoughts dominated by the awful possibility. What if she didn't make it? Then his mother-in-law's disappearance occurred to him. Where was she? He walked, numb, back to the main entrance, and asked an officious-looking man behind a large desk.

'Excuse me, can you tell me where my mother-in-law is?'

The man stared back at him.

'Oh, it's you again,' he said, with a grin, 'can't keep you away. Do you mean Mrs Duncan's mother?'

'Funnily enough, yes, I do. Is she here?'

'No, Mr Duncan,' he said, looking uneasy on clocking John's angry expression, 'the lady had a nasty turn, just after your wife was taken into the labour ward. She was taken to A&E for monitoring. If you want to check on her, the department is along that corridor.'

John turned, and made his way to the emergency department. He asked the nurse at the entrance where Mrs O'Brien was.

'Oh, are you a relative?'

'I'm her son-in-law, John Duncan.'

'I see. This way please.'

She led him along to a cubicle, pulled back the curtain and said, 'Hello, Mrs O'Brien, your son-in-law's here.'

John looked askance at the woman lying on the bed, unable to speak. His eyes clouded over again. She looked drained, and somehow, much older than her sixty years.

'How's Marilyn?' she said, with some effort. 'Is the baby here yet?'

'No, she's going to theatre in a few minutes. What happened to you?'

'Oh, I'm sorry to be a nuisance. After I phoned you, I took a nasty turn. I've been having dizzy spells for a while now, but... I think I passed out. How's Marilyn?'

She stopped short, and appeared to lose consciousness.

A nurse came into the cubicle and said, 'Can you leave please? Mrs O'Brien needs—'

'OK.'

John walked back to the maternity unit, his head spinning, with a vague sense of guilt beginning to trouble him. He recalled Marilyn saying that her mother's health was a worry, and assumed that the pregnancy must have been a source of tension, but for the moment he steeled himself to put that thought aside; Marilyn's health was paramount. He sat down, and for the next hour fidgeted, stood, walked around the room, and began to think the worst. *How long does the procedure take? When will that damn medic come and tell me everything's alright?* His mobile rang: Fred.

'Johnny boy, I hear you had to run off to the hospital... I thought—'

'Yes, Fred, she's gone into theatre for a section. Marilyn's having the baby, right now, and for Christ's sake stop calling me Johnny boy!' His raised voice prompted a passing ambulanceman to say,

'Keep it down, my friend, people are anxious enough.'

Duly admonished, he said,

'Yeah, sorry.'

'Right, John, try to stay cool... Well, all the best for the little one. Call me when you've got the good news. Talk later.'

John ended the call, strode back into the waiting room and sat down again. He noticed the man he'd been speaking with earlier wandering in, a gloomy look on his face. Unsure whether to ask him, John muttered,

'Hello, still waiting?'

'No, mate. It's another girl. That makes three. Just brilliant.'

He didn't sound overjoyed, and left the building. A further twenty minutes passed, and John was starting to think the worst when the doctor he'd seen came into the waiting room.

'Mr Duncan, your wife, and your son, would like to see you. This way please.'

John raised himself from his chair, and walked, still anxious, behind the doctor. He was shown into a private room which seemed very warm, stuffy, and saw Marilyn lying on the bed, dozing. Beside her bed, their son was lying, also sleeping. He walked up to the cot, and stared at the boy, wrapped up in a bundle of white garments, his face bright red.

'What shall we call him, John?'

He wheeled round and said,

'Are you OK, Marilyn? The doctor said… He gave me the impre—'

'On cloud nine,' she said, in a whisper. 'Thank God I got it right, this time. He's beautiful, isn't he? Can we call him John? Where's my mother? She was getting very agitated when I had to sit down in that charity shop she's always going to and…'

She closed her eyes abruptly. John, panicking, rushed out and grabbed a passing nurse, who, after checking Marilyn's pulse, said,

'She's very tired, Mr Duncan, so her body's telling her to sleep. Go and have a cup of tea, you look like you need it.'

'How is she, really?'

'Very weak, but otherwise, well, give her a few days and—'

'Thank you, and the boy?'

'He's small, only five pounds, but otherwise healthy.'

John, slightly less anxious now, left the room and thought he'd better go and tell her mother the good news. After informing a very pleased new grandmother, John left the hospital and began walking along the street, his mind swamped with that mixture of numbness and exhilaration which affects almost every first-time father. Realising he'd gone past the Tube station, he hailed a taxi and went home. As he opened the door, the landline rang out, but stopped before he got to it. The answerphone kicked in: Anita.

'Hi, guys! You've no doubt heard the great news. My wonderful husband's now an MP. I'm coming over the Channel at the weekend to celebrate with him. I take it you two will want to join us. Will give you the details after I've congratulated Dave, and there's only one way to do that, nudge, nudge! Toodle pip. Oh, by the way, how's my best friend's pregnancy going? Hope all's OK.'

John smiled, but decided not to return the call; he was tired, hungry, and his only thoughts were for his wife and son. He ordered a pizza, which arrived half an hour later. Unable to concentrate his thoughts, he called his mother, but she was out. He sat in front of the television and absentmindedly ate the indifferent pizza. As he was putting the empty box in the bin, the phone rang again. He rushed over, terrified, thinking again that something might be wrong.

'Hello,' he said tentatively.

'Just heard, Johnny boy… sorry, John. The Duncan dynasty continues! Fancy wetting the boy's head?'

'How did you find out?'

'Sources, John, sources.'

'No, Fred, not tonight. I'm going over to see Marilyn and the boy.'

'Understood, dear boy. Give your lovely wife my regards.'

'Thanks. I'll be in touch, maybe tomorrow. I think Marilyn will be kept in for a couple of days.'

He put the phone down and went to the bathroom, took a shower, and as he was shaving, saw hot, stinging tears running down his face. Fully half an hour later, he got dressed, formally, the full works, as if he was going for an interview. Checking his watch, he was baffled; it was five to seven. Where had the time gone? He left and hurried over to the hospital, like a child rushing to meet Santa Claus.

Chapter Thirty-Two

Marilyn and her son, John junior, were released two days later, and John was advised to make sure she took things easily for the foreseeable, as the operation had been, in the doctor's somewhat vague words, 'a complicated procedure'. When they arrived home, her mother, who had been waiting there since her own departure from hospital, embraced Marilyn and the child, who promptly burst into screams.

'You should have told me those dizzy spells were getting more frequent, Mother. If I'd known—'

'Stop fussing, my dear, it was only because I was worried about you, after the last time—'

'Your mother's alright, Marilyn,' said John, cutting his mother-in-law off. 'You need to get your strength back, and fussing over any of us won't help. Can you get that please, Jane?'

'Hello, who is this… Oh yes, Anita. How are you? It must be a good few months since we spoke. Yes, she's home now. Poor dear, she had a really difficult time, Oh, I'll hand you over to John.'

'Hello, Anita. No, I was preoccupied with Marilyn. This

Saturday? I'm unsure whether Marilyn will be up to it quite frankly. What? Already? He's only just been elected.'

John put the phone down, turned to the two women and said, running his hand over his chin, 'I should have mentioned it earlier, Marilyn. Anita left a message, asking, no, demanding we attend a celebration this weekend.'

'Celebration?'

'His election to the House of Commons, and now she tells me Dave's going to be a PPS to the Minister of Culture.'

'PPS?' said Jane, perplexed.

'Basically, he'll be a bag carrier for the minister. It's a junior position, but getting noticed so early is very unusual, I believe. Anita's actually condescending to drag herself away from Brussels to lay on some kind of event for him. There'll no doubt be something for her in—'

'Now, John, try to look at it simply as an invitation. David's done well, and it'll please him that Anita recognises that. When did you say this event's going to happen?'

'Saturday, two days away. We're not going.'

Marilyn knitted her brows and said,

'No, I'm not attending, but you really should. He'll like you to be there. I know how fond he is of you. And don't use me as an excuse, Mother and I will cope. Men are hopeless with infants in any case, as you proved at the ante-natal classes, John.'

'Right, I'll speak to Dave, that's if I manage to get through to him.'

*

Feeling he'd left Fred in the lurch by not being in attendance at such a frenetic time for the paper, John went into *The Swiftian's* office the following morning, aware that Marilyn wasn't alone at home to deal with the baby. He arrived at eight, and was surprised to see young Samantha already busily typing at her keyboard.

'Congratulations, John!' she said as she jumped up, ran around her desk and embraced him. 'Fred told me last night, but he was disappointed when you said you couldn't make the celebration in the pub. He was here until gone nine last night, writing up a few notes on the election. He went on and on about the… what did he call it? Oh yes, a hung parliament. He tried to explain the meaning to me, but it might as well have been in Latin. If these politicians really wanted to do good for the country, they'd find a way and put it first. I think that's the gist of what he said. Fancy a coffee? I'm parched, finishing off Fred's notes. His scribbling's getting worse. Oh, sorry, John, I should have asked, how are Marilyn and the baby doing? Have you got a name for him yet?'

'Thanks, Sam,' said John, impressed by the girl's enthusiasm, 'yes I'd love one, and thanks, both mother and child are doing well. His name's John.'

'John?' Samantha said, her brows furrowing and then, 'Oh, he's having the same name as you then. That's nice.'

She walked over to the sink and switched on the kettle, and John, about to go into his office, stopped when the outside line rang.

'I'll get it, Sam.'

He picked up the handset and said,

'Good morning, caller, you have reached the offices of *The Swiftian*, home of the stories no one else dare print.'

'Hello, John, it's Dave here.'

John suppressed his mirth and said,

'Yes, Dave, I thought I recognised the voice. Sorry I wasn't able to speak with you the other night. Congratulations on your win, and I hear you've already started your climb up the greasy pole.'

'What? Oh, you mean… Yes, I've been marked out by the whips' office as a potential future minister. Might have been even better if we didn't have to cosy up to the Lib Dem crew.'

'Dave, before you go any further, Marilyn won't be able to make it Saturday, doctor's orders, but she's insisted I turn up. What time does it start? And where?'

'Congrats, and all that palaver on the boy's arrival. You said turn up? Not with you, John.'

'Anita spoke to me yesterday—'

He stopped, thinking he might have put his foot in it. David was silent, until he said,

'That's typical Anita, trying to surprise me. What is she planning?'

'Dave, I thought you were aware, sorry if I've upset the apple cart here.'

'No worries, John. I'll keep schtum and let her "surprise" me. She's some girl, don't you think?'

John hesitated.

'Yes, Dave, she certainly is. Unique. I won't mention I've told you when I arrive on the night.'

'John, can I ask you something?'

Intrigued by David's tentative voice, he said, 'Fire away.'

'Well, Mr Streeter was asking whether your paper would consider doing a profile… on me, as Benfleet's new MP.'

'He's the party chairman in Benfleet, isn't he. Yes, I remember him. He buttonholed me on election night, asking me about the financial outlook, and… I got the impression he was after some advice.'

'Really? He's got a haulage business, does a lot of work between here and Europe, I think, but going back to that profile idea, he mentioned to me in passing that a candid piece and maybe an interview would keep me in the public eye, especially as I've taken on the PPS role. What do you think?'

'Dave, although I write for old Fred's rag, technically I'm freelance, but I'd still have to run the idea past him. Any article, interview, or whatever you want to call it would certainly be candid.'

'I know anything you wrote about me would be honest and fair, John, and anyway, there's no skeletons in my cupboard. Will you do it?'

'Provisionally yes, assuming Fred likes the idea. We can discuss the project this Saturday, assuming of course that Anita lets me know where the "surprise" gig is happening.'

David laughed, and then added,

'Mr Streeter said that he'd like you to let him have sight of the piece before it goes public. Fair enough, I think. He's been the driving force behind my campaign.'

'No, Dave, it's a golden rule of Fred's, one that I agree with. You said you wanted a candid piece. If that's the case, editing by an interested, one could say biased, individual, is out of the question.'

'But, John, you'd have to be happy with any changes Streeter might like. I can't see the problem.'

Noting his friend's downbeat tone, John replied,

'Listen, Dave, I'll give your suggestion some thought, and we can discuss it later, maybe at this mysterious shindig. Tell you what, I'll write up some words prior to any final decision on the idea. Dave, we'll have to curtail this, my mobile's ringing. See you.'

'That was naughty, John,' said Samantha with a grin, 'your friend's done really well, getting elected. Is he the one who went to university with you?'

'Yes, Dave Murray, and I'll admit I was, frankly, amazed when he told me he'd taken up politics, but then, he's full of surprises. He used to be the man about town, always playing the field, and then, suddenly, he tells me he's met this girl,

Anita, and hey ho, a month later he gets engaged. Oddly enough, that's how I met Marilyn. She and Anita are old friends from school, and she invited her to the wedding.'

'Yes, you've told me this before, John.'

'Sorry, it must be parenthood kicking in. What time did you say will Fred be back?'

'I didn't, he's due here by five, unless he gets waylaid again, or as he put it, he gets laid on the way. He's quite vulgar at times. No wonder his wife—'

'Yes, quite,' John said, 'he never gives up on those old jokes. I think I'll pop out for a sandwich before I get stuck into—'

Samantha stood up and said, 'No, John, I'll go. The usual, is it?'

'Thanks, yes, and get a couple of cakes to go with the cheese ploughman's. I'll hold the fort.'

She took her jacket, lifted her handbag and left the office.

John started up his laptop, took a quick look at the newspaper headlines, and had opened his article, intending to get to work on the troublesome conclusion when his mobile rang.

'Hello, John, you've been blabbing to Dave. The Yorkshire mafia in full operation.'

'What's up, Anita? Did I spoil your surprise?'

'Yes, John, you did, but I've put it off. Can't make it this weekend. As I hadn't invited anyone, there's no damage done, but now Dave's aware, he'll most likely, knowing him... He's such a child at times. John, you'll not mind soothing his ego.'

'What?'

'Invite him round to yours for a meal... invite a couple of your friends, except that old lecher who thinks he's a journalist, Frank or whatever he's called. It's the least you can do. In the circumstances. The sooner you speak to him the better.'

'Does Dave know you're not coming over this weekend?'

'Err, now that you mention it, no. Just a moment, John, my other line's ringing.'

John heard her speaking with a raised voice to someone for a couple of minutes, finally saying to the unfortunate individual, 'Just fucking do it!'

'I have to go, John. Do me a favour, for once, tell Dave about my no show this weekend. I'd do it, but I have to dash for a very annoying meeting, and in any case, he gets too clingy. Bye.'

John put the phone on his desk, sat back and sighed loudly.

'Everything OK, John?' Samantha said as she walked breezily into his office and deposited a bag onto the desk. 'Couldn't get the ploughman's, so I picked up cheese and pickle.'

When he didn't respond, staring at his laptop, she said,

'Earth to Mr Duncan.'

'Right... Hi, Sam, thanks for the sandwich. You were saying?'

'What's up? You look like you've had bad news. Is it your—'

'No, no, sorry. Dave's wife called, just after you left. She asked, no, demanded that I entertain him this weekend. That party she was organising, it's off, because she's busy.'

Samantha shook her head.

'She's a funny one. From what you say, they're chalk and cheese. It's more common than you might think.'

'What do you mean, Sam?'

'My mum's forever telling everyone me and Jim are so different. He loves football and beer and I hate sport, but we've been together for two years now.'

The two sat and ate their sandwiches, Samantha talking excitedly about her upcoming weekend break to New York.

'Jim wouldn't let me down like your friend's wife, John. Relationships without trust don't always last, you know.'

Chapter Thirty-Three

John managed to finish his pressing items by four, and in spite of his desire to speak to Fred, decided to go home. He'd called Marilyn, but she didn't answer either the mobile or the landline, and, wondering why, he said to Samantha as he walked out of his office,

'I'm off home now, Sam, tell Fred I'll catch up with him in the morning.'

He arrived home an hour later, and, opening the front door, called out,

'Marilyn?'

No answer.

He walked into the living room, noticing that the baby carriage, normally positioned at the door, was gone. Assuming Marilyn and her mother were out for some fresh air, he made himself a coffee and sat down, switched on the television, scrolled absentmindedly through the channels, but jumped up when he heard the front door being opened and the sound of his son expressing, very loudly, his displeasure. Marilyn came into the room, looking gaunt, and said,

'Oh, hello, John. We didn't expect you home so early. We took John junior out for a breath of fresh air, but he's... Well, you heard, he's not happy. I hope nothing's wrong with him.'

She sat down and wiped her brow.

'All babies have these little tantrums, dear,' her mother said as she walked in, cuddling the baby, who was still trying to scream the house down, 'but you're doing far too much! Tell her, John. Perhaps you should be at home for a few days. Marilyn told me you can make your own hours—'

'You're right, Jane,' John, sensing the veiled rebuke, said, 'I'll stay here for the rest of the week. You look a tad weary too, if you don't mind—'

'John dear, I'm fine, it's your wife you need to concern yourself with. Here, take John. I'll make us all a nice cup of tea.'

When she'd gone into the kitchen, John, anxious, asked Marilyn,

'Listen, tell me straight, are you alright? Remember what the doctor told us. You have to be careful. You're recovering from surgery, and major surgery at that.'

Marilyn stroked his cheek, and said,

'John, it's alright. I got too enthusiastic, we were out for too long and now I'm just a little overtired. Won't do it again. Promise.'

She inclined her head to the boy and continued, smiling,

'My, you've got the magic touch with our son. He's sleeping. Can you put him down in the cot please? He won't be out for long, the boy's always eating.'

He walked over to the cot and very gingerly put the boy down. His eyes flickered briefly then closed.

'Had a busy day phone-wise. Anita and Dave called me, within fifteen minutes of each other, and I've well and truly put both my feet in it.'

Marilyn laughed.

'Both your feet? Strange expression. What did they say?'

'Remember Anita's plan to throw a gig to celebrate Dave's election win? Well, the man himself called me today, asking whether I could write something, basically a hymn of praise, and unfortunately I let it slip about the party. He knew nothing about it, but after we'd discussed the merits of an article, he seemed OK.'

'John, really!'

'I know, I know! But shortly after, Anita called. She'd spoken to Dave, and I expected her usual tantrum, but no, she was all sweetness and light, which—'

'She wanted a favour.'

'How did you… Yes, she's too busy in Brussels to make time for a party, despite her previous comment about organising the thing, and she's bailed. And so… Anita asked me to invite Dave over at the weekend, as a consolation prize you might say. The oddest thing about the conversation was that, although she said she'd spoken with him, she asked me to tell Dave the party's been cancelled. Why would I have to tell him if she'd already… Sometimes that woman… Oh, I can't make her out at all.'

'I don't think she's aware herself. I think that job – whatever it involves, she's very evasive on the subject – isn't helping either. Did you agree to follow her orders? Perhaps a dinner party with one or two friends might lessen poor Dave's disappointment at Anita's… Yes. I'll ask Geoff and Mary.'

'Mary from school, you mean? Who's Geoff?

'Yes, Geoff's her partner. He's in the Met, a detective sergeant, I think. He was a colleague of Grant's… Could make for an interesting evening. Mary's forever regaling us with the more intimate aspects of his career.'

'All very fine, Marilyn, but are you sure you'll—'

'John, we can get those caterers we used for my mother's birthday, they do small events like this.'

'With you, me, Dave and your two friends, that makes five. Can I ask old Fred along? He's quite the raconteur. Should we organise a babysitter?'

'No, Mother will do the honours. You know, it's a bit awkward. She insists on doing everything bar feeding John junior.'

'OK, if you speak with Mary, I'll deal with Dave, and Fred. Funny thing though, Anita told me not to invite "Frank".'

'Frank?'

'Fred.'

*

John spent the rest of the week working from home, and despite his son's healthy lungs, he was able to concentrate on a project he'd been contemplating since leaving university: his first novel. He had a firm hold of the plot, and was working on a synopsis when, late on Friday afternoon, his mobile rang.

'Long time no speak, Johnny boy. Where've you been the last few days? Still haven't wet the boy's head with your mentor, have you?'

Realising he had omitted to invite Fred, John said,

'Right, yes, sorry, Fred, I've been at home helping out, so to speak, but listen, we're organising a little soirée to celebrate Dave's recent success, and Marilyn would love you to come along. What do you think? Can you spare the time?'

After a long pause John said,

'Fred?'

'Consulting my bulging diary, old boy. Yes, I think I could grace you and your lovely wife. Saturday, you say? What time?'

'Seven, Fred, and no need to bring a bottle.'

'Of course I'll be bringing a bottle, my boy. I may be a rough diamond, but I know the social graces. Besides, I know your taste in wine: vino collapso. Thank the lovely Marilyn for her kind offer. I'll turn up for duty at seven sharp. Oh, and I've got a bone to pick with you. I hear you're writing the new MP's biog for old Streeter. He'll want it to be more like a hagiography, with himself as Dave's éminence grise.'

'I haven't agreed yet, Fred. Dave's asked if I'd consider it, but if you have a problem with the idea, I'll decline, and besides, I don't do whitewash jobs.'

'You don't need my permission, John, you're a free agent, but remember... I value your sceptical financial eye, old boy. Never mind, we can chinwag on this later. Looking forward to meeting your MP friend. Bye, John. Till Saturday evening then.'

John chuckled at his old friend's cynicism, a quality Fred would describe as realism, and recalled how, when he'd first encountered him, at a Labour conference seven years previously, he had been unceremoniously ejected from the main hall after he'd called out to the stage, saying in his distinctive, stentorian voice,

'On with the revolution comrades! Down with class traitors!'

Fred confessed later that he'd made this particular scene because he'd been barred from the lounge area after criticising the 'exorbitant' prices in the lounge.

'These socialist types, milking the punters naïve enough to believe in their po-faced sanctimony. Farcical and sinister at the same time.'

This reminiscence caused John to lose his train of thought, and smiling again at his friend's sometime juvenile sense of humour, he switched off the laptop and walked into the living room to see his mother-in-law changing his son's nappy.

'Where's Marilyn?'

'She went for a little nap, John. Told me she was tired, but if you ask me, the girl's run down.' He didn't answer and walked back out toward the bedroom, where Marilyn was getting dressed.

'Are you well, Marilyn? Your mother said you should—'

'Don't listen to her. I'm getting just a little fed up with her mollycoddling. It's bordering on interference, and but for the fact that's she besotted with the little man, I'd send her packing.'

John, shocked by the outburst said,

'It's only natural, Marilyn. Try not to get stressed by her, but, no, I—'

'Not you as well, John. Don't stand there like a guilty schoolboy. What is it?'

'I was going to ask whether you feel you're up for this thing tomorrow evening.'

'Yes, I am. Mary and Geoff have said they'll be here. I take it Dave and what's his name, Fred, yes, Fred, are coming too?'

'Both of them, yes.'

'Good,' Marilyn said, walking out of the room, 'I'm going to feed our son now, and then if you could take him out for a spot of fresh air, I'll confirm with the caterers – three courses. That leaves you with the onerous task of getting the wine and liqueurs.'

John smiled.

'Yes, what?'

'Fred was telling me he's bringing a bottle too. It seems my skills in that department are negligible.'

'He, of all people, said that? Remember the vinegar he brought over when you said you'd work with him?'

She began to laugh and continued,

'You were ill for days afterwards. He must have a lead-lined stomach.'

As instructed, John took his son out for a walk, enjoying the relative freedom of strolling along to the park ten minutes from their home. Feeling warm in the late afternoon sunshine, he stopped at a booth, bought a soft drink and sat on a bench overlooking a boating lake. John junior woke and began to exercise his opera singer's lungs once again. John threw the empty plastic bottle into an adjacent bin, picked up the boy, red-faced and fierce-looking, and started to rock him gently. An old, white-haired woman came up to them, gazed lovingly at the child and said,

'If you don't mind me saying, son, your little one needs changing.'

John stared at the woman, who was, in his view, standing too close. When she attempted to touch the baby, he pulled back abruptly and said, his voice displaying irritation,

'You're probably right. I'll get him back to his mother before he deafens everyone. Thanks.'

Walking home at a brisk pace, John wondered why he had been so short, aggressive almost, with the woman; she hadn't posed any threat. Then it clicked; he was the boy's dad, his protector. Not being of a philosophic bent, he nonetheless pondered on his upsurge of paternal feeling. This musing was interrupted when he heard a familiar voice calling out from behind.

'John! John! Hold on there.'

He halted and turned his head toward the voice. Father Delany was marching up, red-faced and out of breath. He said,

'There he is! The very epitome of the doting dad. Hello, John, let me have sight of the boy.'

'Evening, Father. Jane was telling us the other day about the church fete, and mentioned—'

'A roaring success, my boy, but let me see the little man. Yes, he's a sturdy chap, isn't he?'

Looking at the child, and pulling that gormless, grinning face which adults, usually men, think will impress a child he said,

'Would you mind telling Marilyn I'll pop in to see her tomorrow? She asked me to visit, maybe to discuss christening arrangements, but I had two funerals yesterday and a parish meeting all day today. Just escaped actually. Good to see you. I'm so happy Marilyn's been blessed. She'll be a wonderful mother. Goodbye, John.'

He held out his hand. John could see the emotion in the man's eyes and said,

'I will, Father. Bye for now.'

He arrived home, took John junior out of the pram and went into the living room with him. Marilyn, sitting on the settee next to her mother and looking more relaxed, said,

'Oh, you two were a long time. He'll need his nappy changing by the smell. Give him over, John.'

'No, Marilyn, I'll see to it.'

'OK, Mother. John, I've sorted the catering people. They'll have the food here by six-thirty and—'

'I met Father Delany as I was crossing the high street, Marilyn. He told me to say he'll pop in tomorrow, about arrangements for—'

Marilyn, blushing slightly, said, after her mother had left the room,

'Yes, Mother gave him chapter and verse on my "difficulties" and invited him to come in to see me, I mean, us. She's expecting John to be christened as soon as. Look, can we discuss this later? In fact, I'll call him tonight to postpone his visit tomorrow. We've enough on our plate with this soirée.'

'If you want the lad christened, well, it's fine by me. I've no strong feelings either way. I suppose your mother's got dinner organised then?'

'Yes, it's in the oven. What I was saying earlier, about you being a long time, she was concerned dinner would be spoiled.'

'Actually, I'm really hungry now. One thing about Jane, she's a great cook, unlike you.'

'How dare you, John,' Marilyn said as she picked up a cushion and tossed it at him, 'my spag bol's the best in London, give or take. Oh, that reminds me, tomorrow's main course is meat-based, roast beef. I suppose Fred's not a vegetarian. If he is, we can give him some nice carrots and peas.'

'Fred, a vegetarian?'

'Thought not.'

Chapter Thirty-Four

Marilyn's mother, having given herself the role of nanny for the day, whisked young John, complete with all his possible requirements, off to her sister's in Edmonton, which left Marilyn, simultaneously relieved and anxious, to prepare for the dinner party. By four, she had finished all the necessaries, including setting out the cutlery on the dining room table.

'John, you did remember to advise David and Fred when we were sitting down?'

'Yes, Marilyn, stop worrying, those two guys can eat for England. Wait, there's the doorbell. Can't be the caterers so soon. I wonder...'

He walked to the hallway and opened the door, to be confronted by David.

'Not late am I, John?' he said. 'Anita told me to make sure I arrived on time, so, here I am.'

'No, Dave, you're early, very early in fact. We're not eating until seven.'

David scratched his head and replied, looking perplexed,

'Oh, I must have misheard Anita. Should I go away and come back in a couple of hours?'

'No, don't be silly, Dave, no need. Come on in. We can watch the football results and have a chat.'

The two men walked into the living room. Marilyn shouted from the kitchen, 'Who was that, John?'

'You'll never guess,' said John, winking at a still mortified David, 'it's one of those damn politicos asking for our vote. No one told the clown the election's happened—'

Marilyn, sounding irritated, said as she came into the living room,

'What are you muttering about... Hello, David. You're early. Did John give you the wrong time? Typical of him.'

She kissed David on his cheek.

'Never mind. It's good to see you, and congratulations. John, make the man a coffee. I'm nipping out to the off licence, for the gin you omitted to purchase.'

She took her handbag and left them together. John sat down, took the remote and switched on the television.

'Dave, just to warn you, Marilyn suggested we invite Fred, you know, Fred McTaggart, along tonight. He's promised to be on his best behaviour... No politics, so he'll be quiet, hard as that may be to take in.'

Looking unconvinced, David said,

'I think I've met him before, John. He's quite the character. The typical hack reporter. Did you say you're working with him, on and off?'

'Some freelance work, yes. Wake up, I've told you this before! I'll get us those coffees.'

Marilyn returned twenty minutes later with the gin and said,

'John, has my mother been in touch?'

'No, do you want me to phone?'

'No, I expect young John's OK.'

'Of course he is, dear.'

'I haven't met the little man yet, John. He's not here then?'

'Marilyn's mother's got him for the day, probably showing him off to all her friends and relations.'

'You two are lucky. Sometimes I think Anita's...'

John, picking up on the emotion in David's voice, said nervously,

'Fancy a dram, Dave? I know it's not in the rule book, but, hey, who gives a toss.'

'Thanks, John, I'd love one.'

*

Six-fifteen, the doorbell rang. Before John could raise himself from the settee, he heard Marilyn saying,

'Good, I was starting to worry. Follow me please.'

'That's the food arrived safely. Don't know about you two, but I'm starving.'

'You got caterers in then?' said David.

'Marilyn wanted to cook, but I insisted she take it easy. That's probably Mary and Geoff at the door now. She's a colleague of Marilyn's. Her husband's in the police, which leaves us one short of a full house. Fred should be here any minute. He's always hungry when he's invited to one of these things.'

Mary and Geoff were ushered into the living room by a flustered-looking Marilyn, who did the introductions. John was struck by Geoff's taciturn, solemn expression, thinking the man was there on sufferance; Mary, in contrast, appeared to be a lively character, clearly at ease in company. David, more relaxed after downing two whiskies and a long discussion with John, said, in response to Mary's enquiry,

'Yes, my wife's something of a rising star in the Diplomatic Service. She's based in Brussels, but gets home most weekends if I'm lucky... No, I meant—'

He means he's a hopeless cook, folks,' John said.

Everyone, except Geoff, laughed.

'We're eating at seven sharp, people,' said Marilyn, 'that's if John's partner in crime arrives.'

'If he's late, maybe Geoff here could caution him,' said Dave, immediately adding, 'Oops, poor joke. Sorry, Geoff, you're probably off duty.'

'No problem,' said Geoff, maintaining his expressionless look.

On the stroke of seven, Fred vigorously pressed the doorbell.

'Hello, everyone,' he said strolling into the dining room, 'told you I'd be punctual, Johnny boy. As promised, here's the bottle. Let me see now, Dave and I have met, I think, but—'

'This is Mary, and her husband, Geoff,' John said. 'Mary's a colleague of Marilyn's.'

'Oh, really? What do you teach, Maisy?'

'English, err, Fred.'

'I see,' he said, and spotting Marilyn bringing in two containers of vegetables added, 'Something wicked this way comes!'

'Oh, very funny, Fred. If that's your best effort, you'd—'

'*Mea maxima culpa*, my dear Marilyn, I'll behave.'

Everyone sat around the table and began the meal. Marilyn, having been on edge all day over the possibility of the caterers' food not matching her expectations, was notably relaxed, her guests commenting favourably on it, Mary in particular, saying she would keep them in mind should she and Geoff entertain over Christmas.

Despite the pleasant atmosphere, John was concerned by Fred's manner; he appeared to be preoccupied by something, but as time wore on, and the wine flowed, he became more at ease. As Marilyn was serving up the dessert, the doorbell rang.

'Who can that be? John, go and chase away whoever it is. Mother's staying the night at her sister's so...'

'Just a minute, folks,' said John as he made his way to the hallway, getting annoyed by the continuing noise from the bell, 'someone's going to get an ear-bashing.'

'You should have allowed me to deal with the bell-ringer, Marilyn,' Fred commented, 'John's no use with confrontation.'

Chapter Thirty-Five

A hushed, familiar voice could be heard as John closed the door, and then, more audibly, he said,

'We weren't aware you'd be coming, but not to worry, come on in and join the others.'

Following him into the dining room came Anita, holding a large briefcase. David, startled, got up from his chair, walked over and embraced her.

'Didn't you get my text, Dave? No?' she barked. 'Sorry, Marilyn, but I couldn't let his celebration go past without me, though I had a hell of a trek to get here, with that damn Eurostar delayed again.'

Marilyn, as taken aback as David, muttered, running her hand over her chin,

'Yes, unfortunate, but if you're in need of sustenance—'

'In need of… Once an English teacher… I had a sandwich on the train but I expect I'll survive—'

'There's plenty of food left over, thanks to my reliably careless caterers, would you believe. Sit at the table while I nip into the kitchen. Take Anita's coat, David.'

'How are things in the evil empire, Mrs Murray?' Fred

asked her, with a wink to John, who frowned.

'Where's the baby, John?' said Anita, pointedly ignoring the facetious enquiry.

'She's with Marilyn's mother, being shown off to all and sundry.'

'I'm not "all and sundry", John. Oh well, that lets me off the hook. I bought the child a gift, but left it in the flat, mainly because I was rushing to the station.'

'You look a trifle stressed, Anita,' John said. 'Would you like a drink of some kind?'

'I see,' Anita said, glancing at the several bottles arrayed on a side table, 'Marilyn's back on mother's ruin again. Get me a double... please, John. I hope you haven't been encouraging my husband to imbibe over the odds. He's suspiciously quiet.'

'No, Dave's a responsible public servant now. Like you, Anita, working for the benefit of us all—'

'Is that you trying to be witty, John?'

'Obviously not, my dear lady,' Fred broke in, 'but if—'

'Dear lady? Oh please! Are you tonight's cabaret, err... Fred, isn't it?'

Fred smiled and continued, 'We are lucky in this country to have so many people willing to work on our behalf, the envy of less happy lands indeed.'

John looked over to him, fully aware of his friend's intentions.

'Envy of less happy lands,' Anita said, her face displaying a curious expression, 'that's right. Do you mind if I sit next to you?'

'No indeed,' Fred replied, standing to adjust her chair, 'I'd be honoured.'

Another curious look.

'Well, it's the only vacant place... Mine I presume, Marilyn?'

'Yes, Anita, hope you like it,' Marilyn said as she deposited a plate on the table.

'Ah, good old English roast beef,' Anita said, with a barely disguised grimace. 'That's what they call us over in Brussels, *Les Rosbifs*. They're a funny crowd.'

'And that's their polite description for us, I'd wager.'

John ran his finger across his throat at Fred, who laughed, and told the room,

'Poor old John's worried I might lower the tone with my tabloid cynicism. Very sorry, Marilyn, I'll be a good boy.'

She said, with a wry smile,

'I expect nothing less from you, Fred. John tells me you're the best raconteur in London. Do you have any gossip that's not political?'

'In reality, Marilyn, all gossip is political, whether it's in the personal arena, or amongst our friends in Westminster, or indeed Brussels these days.'

'These days?' said Anita. 'Please, explain.'

'Certainly, my dear—'

'I'm not your "dear".'

Fred smiled benignly and said,

'I apologise most humbly for my rather formal language, but don't fret, we chauvinists are a diminishing species. What I was alluding to is the gulf, which has always been there of course, but is now becoming more public in this blessed plot, between the rulers and the ruled. The pretence, the myth, that in Lincoln's memorable words, "government of the people by the people", is how this country is run. Well, the mask is slipping.'

John, losing his patience, and his cool, at this display of Fred's childish sense of mischief, said,

'We're not going to indulge in political debate tonight, Fred. It's a party for Dave here.'

'Quite right, John, time for my second *mea culpa* of the evening. Despite my innate scepticism, as I've just been—'

'Fred!'

'Despite it, David, my sincere best wishes to you in your new career. I know Johnny boy vouched for you with old Streeter, and he's a man – John, I mean – I'd trust with my life, or my wife for that matter... Though whether I'd trust her... Anyway, Marilyn, I'm thirsty, after all that humble pie... Would you be so kind?'

She took over a half-finished bottle of red.

Geoff, until this point silent, apart from the usual pleasantries, said,

'Whatever one's politics, I think we can agree that Marilyn's done wonders this evening—'

'Yes,' said Anita, 'and the caterers weren't bad either. Good choice, Marilyn.'

Geoff continued, and raising his glass said,

'Here's to our hostess!'

Everyone echoed his toast, and before they'd sat down, Anita said,

'And another clinking of glasses, folks, for the man of the hour, Benfleet's new, stellar member, Dave Murray!'

Marilyn, beginning to look and feel apprehensive, went into the kitchen to get the coffee and drinks. John followed her.

'Why on earth did she feel the need to surprise us, turning up like that without forewarning us, John? It's almost as if she wanted to... wanted to disrupt David's evening, embarrassing him in the process.'

'It could have been worse, Marilyn. Fred's aware she's based with the Foreign Office in Brussels. I wouldn't be surprised if he's plotting to insert a piece on EU diplomatic initiatives shortly, quoting anonymous sources, one of them here. Did you see how his eyes lit up when Anita came in?'

Fortunately for the Duncans' nerves, the rest of the evening passed amicably, with most of the conversation homing in on family matters, including the provision of day care for toddlers (Mary and Geoff had two-year-old twin girls). Obviously bored, Anita and David left the party, quoting her need to be up 'at the crack of dawn' for an urgent appointment in Whitehall. As they were leaving, Anita asked Marilyn if John junior was going to be christened. 'I expect you'll want me as a godparent. Dave is happy to do the honours too.'

'Err… Yes, Anita, of course, I'd love you both to be… I haven't spoken with Father Delany yet, so the date isn't set—'

'Date? Surely it'll be on a weekend? I'm free the Sunday after next, so tell old Delany to get moving and book it. He's an easy-going one at the best of times. Likes his post-prandials.'

Marilyn smiled as she noticed John's pained face and replied,

'Anita, as it's you, I'll request that the priest is aware of your crowded schedule.'

'Yes, Marilyn, you do that. David, stop loitering there like the proverbial rabbit in the headlights. Have you called that taxi?'

'Yes, dear.'

'Goodnight, everyone,' Anita said, and glaring maliciously at a recumbent Fred continued, 'and, Marilyn, be sure to avoid inviting hacks for your next soirée.'

'Goodnight, my dears,' Fred shouted back, raising his half-empty glass in mock salute, 'and don't do anything to upset the apple cart, Dave.'

Chapter Thirty-Six

John junior was baptised in accordance with Marilyn's firm Catholic faith, Anita and Dave acting as the child's godparents. David shed a few tears as the priest uttered the solemn words during the service. Later, at a reception for the family and guests, he said quietly to John while his wife was cosying up to an unusually nervous Father Delany,

'John, how does Anita seem to you?'

'As exuberant as usual, Dave. Why do you ask?'

'You know what I'm getting at… don't you?'

'I do, Dave, but in my eyes, Anita's displaying her usual, self-assertive persona.'

'Outwardly, yes, but I'm worried, have been for ages to be honest, that all this… this obsession with her career—'

'Dave, whether you can believe this or not, well, now that I'm a parent, I can comprehend how shattering it must have been to lose a child. We've both been impressed, or in the vernacular, gobsmacked, at the bravery you've shown, you and Anita, since it happened, and…'

John felt a lump in his throat, but went on, '… you two agreeing to be godparents today… John junior's a lucky boy.'

He put his arm round David's shoulder, shook his friend's hand and said,

'Tell you what, mate, let's pop around the corner to the Duke of Wellington. The girls won't notice.'

The girls did notice. Anita said as they tiptoed out,

'What a pair of cry-babies. You know, Marilyn, all men are children really, Dave especially.'

*

Over the course of the next three years the two couples gradually became more distant, each, in their own worlds, fully occupied. John, initially sceptical about working with Fred at *The Swiftian*, became virtually a full-time journalist, and Marilyn doted over their son, surprising herself with the realisation that she didn't miss her former profession.

David, seen by many in the political world as a rising star, had made an unfortunate decision, in his wife's eyes if not for his career, to advocate forcefully his party's commitment to a vote on Britain's membership of the EU. On a rare visit to their home, both Marilyn and John picked up on a coldness between Anita and David; her perennial, affected disdain for him seemed to have developed into something close to animosity. Marilyn confided to John that perhaps the lack of what she termed a 'family life' was the underlying cause.

'Many couples have happy contented relationships, without producing, for one reason or another, offspring, Marilyn. No, I suspect the problem lies elsewhere.'

'She hid her despair when that poor child was stillborn, John, but I know her. It's most likely been playing on her mind ever since.'

'Yes, I understand what you're saying, and being apart five days out of every seven would be a strain on any permanent relationship, but there's more to it. For instance, you and me have divergent views on several issues, religion for one, but we each respect the other's opinions without ever getting into a spat.'

'What are you rattling on about? Religion? We've never had a discussion on—'

'No, we haven't, but listen, think about their situation. He's a politician now, you could say in government, part of a regime which is possibly going to allow a vote on Europe. Now, consider Anita. She's still in Brussels and, according to sources close to *The Swiftian*'s proprietor, is seconded to a team of officials tasked with downplaying any advantages Britain's leaving the club might be advanced by the anti-EU brigade. "Getting the retaliation in first," as the old rugby phrase goes.'

'You're saying tittle-tattle about what may or may not materialise in the outside world is affecting their marriage? A long shot, I'd say. To think that Anita is anything other than a small cog in a very large machine is, despite what she'd have you believe, for the birds. She's a linguist, a translator for goodness' sake, not a policy maker. Besides, I've not heard her express any definite opinion on the EU issue.'

'Marilyn, Fred's convinced, from his sources, that the unit she's part of was set up with Whitehall's covert assistance, in anticipation of a possible campaign. The official view is that Britain shouldn't leave, and therefore—'

'Pie in the sky stuff, typical Fred gossip. I can picture him, sitting in one of those sleazy boozers in Westminster, huddled up with some junior, probably disaffected civil servant and being fed nonsense. Have you ever considered the possibility that he might just have his own agenda, more than just gossip and speculation?'

'He's made no secret of it. He loathes the EU, but then, his views on politics in general can be... can be summed up by the name he gave the paper. He told me once the only man he'd like to speak with from the past would be Dean Swift.'

'Anyway, John, leaving aside your theory, our two friends are both unhappy, whatever the cause, and it breaks my... it breaks my heart to see poor Anita like this. Underneath her sardonic, cruel exterior, there's a wounded, tortured soul looking for redemption.'

John put his arms around his tearful wife, impressed again by her altruistic nature. Suddenly, the sound of John junior brought them back to reality.

'His naps are getting shorter,' Marilyn said, wiping a tear from her cheek. 'Can you go in and pick him up. He'll be hungry now.'

*

John went into *The Swiftian*'s office the next morning, his discussion with Marilyn playing on his mind. Her continuing worry of their friends' marital situation disturbed him, and as he sat staring at his emails, the thought occurred: perhaps David's concern over his wife's erratic behaviour, which he'd outlined over several drinks in the pub a few weeks after he'd been elected, was a reflection of his own sense of loss. John knew that neither he nor Marilyn were in a position to help, a realisation that depressed him.

Scrolling down his list of messages, most of them either cold calls, advertisements or political announcements, he was shaken out of his reverie by the entrance of Fred, holding a pile of documents and newspapers.

'Top of the morning to you, Johnny boy,' he bawled. 'My, my, you look like you've lost that fiver I lent you. Don't fret, you can keep it!'

John looked up, and in spite of his depression, said,

'No, Fred, just a bit under the weather. You're full of the joys. What's with all those—'

'Big news, John, very big news: it's on!'

'You can't mean another bloody election. This Tory-Lib Dem agreement—'

'No, it's official: Cameron's announced, talking to that bunch of gasbags, the 1922 lot, that there's going to be a referendum. Didn't say when, but he can't renege the way the Brown crew did.'

John, shocked and incredulous, said,

'Was this from your mole in Central Office, or just the usual pub gossip, Fred?'

'Can't tell you, John. You should know that, but listen, the story's set to be front-page news, and, in spite of sceptics like you, poo-pooing the idea, well, I—'

'Even if a vote is allowed to happen, you've overlooked one flaw in your enthusiasm for it. What, precisely, will be the question? If you ask me, it'll be framed to ensure the correct result: the authorities here will devise a form of words, maybe after consulting with their co-conspirators in Brussels and—'

'I'd never have guessed, John,' Fred interrupted, 'my protégé's seen the light at last. Eureka! But before we get engrossed in how *The Swiftian*'s going to react, you appear a tad depressed. Anything old Fred can advise you on? Is your namesake keeping you up at night?'

'No, Fred, nothing like that. Between you and me, we've been concerned about our friends' marriage. Marilyn's brooding over it, but we can't see how—'

Samantha walked in and said,

'Sorry, I didn't know you guys were in conference. Coffee all round?' Fred looked at her admiringly and replied,

'You get more beautiful every day, my dear. Yes please.'

When she'd left the room he said, quietly,

'John, you're right, you can't do anything, and, take it from one who's been through the living hell known as divorce, keep out of it. Marriage is difficult at the best of times, and in this particular case, probably doomed. I'm presuming here, but I think you're referring to the Murrays, Dave and Anita?'

'Yes, Fred, and now, if this story of yours is genuine… OK, yes, but if it is, then, I've got the same opinion as you. Her close involvement with the Brussels machine doesn't exactly fit well with his position as part of a government contemplating a vote on Europe, does it?'

'John, that work you were doing on EU finances a while ago, it was a forensic, yet passionate critique of the whole corrupt regime, very impressive. Would you care to update it? I think I'm correct in saying nothing's changed, but now there could be considerable mileage in revisiting the issue.'

John shook his head and started to laugh.

'See, my boy? Old Fred can lighten the darkest mood with his natural, God-given charisma.'

'No, Fred, I was pondering—'

'Careful, John, you might hurt yourself. Oh, go on then, enlighten me.'

'I was thinking, what will the official *Swiftian* line be when, or rather if, a vote is sanctioned?'

Fred sat down facing John across his desk, cupped his chin in his palms and said, using his most solemn tone,

'We're both experienced, rational, dispassionate journalists, John, so we shall examine carefully all the evidence, the pros and the cons, and then… advocate leaving the den of thieves and shysters.'

John sat back in his chair and burst into laughter.

'Age hasn't had any effect on you, has it, Fred?'

'When you've been around this circus they call the political world as long as I have, John, it's crystal clear, even for the dimmest mind to comprehend, that it is stuffed with ne'er-do-wells – charlatans, secondhand car salesmen and imbeciles. The only fun in our game is exposing their inadequacies and scams.'

'OK then, Fred,' John said, his mood much improved by Fred's seemingly permanent sense of the absurd, 'I'll dig up the article and have a look at it. This time I think I'll go over to the lion's den for some in-depth research. Will our coffers take the strain?'

'The coffers aren't overflowing, but this new situation has the possibility to rectify it. Our proprietor, *entre nous*, is not what you'd call a Europhile, so I expect she'll continue our funding. I'm going to meet with her next week in fact. Come to think of it, John, it could be advantageous if you accompanied me. I'll speak to her this afternoon. How does next Thursday at the Savoy, twelve-thirty, sound? Keep it in your diary, my boy.'

For the rest of the day John went over his original work and article, now almost three years old, and when Samantha came into his office to ask him about his movements, he said,

'I'm calling it a day, Sam. Is there anything specific you wanted to ask me?'

'I was only going to ask… Never mind… If you don't mind me saying, John, you're looking tired. Are you sure you should be here?'

'Lack of sleep, Sam. That boy of ours just loves late-night TV. I think I'll go home to give Marilyn a break. See you tomorrow.'

He arrived home an hour later, thanks to a malfunction on the Tube, and walked in to see Marilyn talking on the landline, holding young John in her arm.

'OK, OK, Mother, yes I expect we'll be able to come, I've told you before. If John junior has his nap at the normal time, we should be over at the fete by three, it doesn't get going until then anyhow. That's John in from work now, so I'll hang up. Speak later, Mother. What? Yes, he's fine too. Bye.'

'Was that conversation about the church thing this Saturday? Sorry, Marilyn, I forgot. She called me at work this morning. I should have passed on her message.'

'Mother didn't mention she'd spoken with you, but anyway, I told her we'll be there whenever, John—'

'Yes, I caught that bit. Shall we order a takeaway?'

'Good idea. Pepperoni for me. I'm starving, this guy never stops.'

Chapter Thirty-Seven

John and Fred's lunch date with the proprietor, an elderly lady, Mrs Ingram, was postponed when she called Fred to inform him that she'd had a fall at home.

'The old girl's just too careless, John,' Fred told him. 'I spoke with her last night, and she agreed with your suggestion.'

'Suggestion? Go on then, tell me.'

'Well, it could well be easier if you waltzed over to Brussels and ingratiated yourself with all those bureaucrats. She knows an MEP sympathetic to the cause—'

'The cause is it now, Fred?'

'Call it what you like, my boy. As far as I'm concerned, the more we can glean the better. I'm confident you feel the same. Oh, I've just had, can you credit it, another brilliant thought: that Murray woman, Anita. She's a potential—'

'Before you get any ideas, she's bound by the Official Secrets Act.'

'How long have you been in journalism, John? Whenever anything contentious, divisive or debatable crops up there's the possibility of "sources" letting slip juicy pieces of information, but I shouldn't have to tell you, should I? Knowing the woman on a personal basis, no one outside this office would think anything of you and her having a catch-up over a dinner or two. Yes, it's perfect!'

'Listen, Fred, I think you're making two very large assumptions. First, that Anita is privy to anything remotely significant, and second, that she'd divulge, wittingly, confidential information. You may not appreciate it, but I know, from both her husband and her conversations with Marilyn, that she lives for the job. Keep this to yourself, Fred... No, I mean it. Some time ago she had a miscarriage, and I believe this job's become very important to her now, so the idea that she'd jeopardise it, well, to me it's far-fetched.'

'Very logical, my boy, but others have risked much more than their jobs in pursuit of this or that object... Normally sex of one kind or another. Part of any human's make-up since the Garden of Eden. It's up to you, and I admire your loyalty to your friends. Don't pull that face, I do, honestly. Have you spoken with the lovely Marilyn about the possibility of a short stay in Brussels? I'd say you could take her and the boy over for a city break... But, on reflection, what's remotely interesting in the city? That statue of the boy pissing in the square is all I can think of. Very symbolic.'

'Actually, Fred,' John said, chuckling at the statue reference, 'that won't fly. This boy of ours, he's almost the sole topic of conversation at home, and I don't think Marilyn would like us to disrupt his routine.'

'Well, go home and discuss it with her. I can organise accommodation over there, thanks to my contacts with... never mind who, but it will be near the Berlaymont building. I spent a few weeks over there when the Lisbon Treaty was being devised. There's plenty of waterholes near it too.'

'I still can't see her agreeing to the prospect, but I will enquire.'

John told his wife that he would be spending a few days away on the assignment, and in spite of his concern, mentioned Fred's suggestion that they go as a family.

'Sounds like he's trying to give you cover, John.'

'Cover?'

'Don't come the naïve cub reporter now. We go there, stay in a self-catering place for a week or so, and masquerade as tourists. Fred's such a romantic. What's that Hitchcock film again?'

'No idea, Marilyn, and thanks for the vote of confidence. No worries, I'll go over myself.'

'When?'

'He's organising the accommodation as we speak.'

'Oh dear.'

'No, he promised me it'll have hot and cold running—'

'Whisky?'

'Very good. He suggested I make contact with Anita while I'm there, but I'm not keen.'

'Why? I think she'd appreciate a friendly face. I'd guess she must be lonely at times, especially after working hours, so, yes, be the Good Samaritan. She loves to think of herself as a discriminating foodie. Dinner might be an education for you.'

'I've got your permission then.'

'To go to Brussels? No, that's your job. To socialise with Anita. It might be a good idea to let David know when you will be going, so that he can advise her. She hasn't been home for the last two weekends, pressure of work apparently. Poor David... John, get him to come over for dinner tomorrow.'

'OK. I haven't spoken with him for, let me think, over a month. Last time I saw him he looked drained, presumably because of his long hours. He said the minister's not the most caring of taskmasters, but he's brought it on himself—'

'How?'

'You'd think he might have taken leave of absence from his job at the law firm after he was elected, but he told me Anita insisted, insisted – you can hear her saying it, can't you? – that he shows his face at least once a week there. She's a devious one at times, Marilyn.'

'How do you make that out, John? It's called being prudent.'

'Yes, I can see how you'd argue that. His seat in the Commons isn't the safe Tory one it was, and of course, prior to his conversion to… politics, he was ambitious enough to think he might ultimately be made a partner.'

'Really? I've always thought of David as being content to work away in the conveyancing field. Ambition isn't one of his obvious qualities.'

'As I was saying, Anita's the driving force behind him now. If it was in her gift, he'd be Prime Minister by the time he was forty, but he's not the ruthless type, that's her province.'

'Oh goodness, and you're going to socialise with her!'

'You've known her far longer than me, am I being unfair?'

'Yes, she's definitely single-minded, but you can't argue that she's not a hundred per cent behind David. She sees her influence, encouragement, in furthering his career – careers, I should say – as being positive. He may be the most easy-going chap going, but I'm sure he appreciates that support. Opposites do work. Look at you and me. I'm the laid-back rational academic, you're the cynical tabloid writer. We rub along nicely. Why shouldn't they?'

'Right then, the cynical hack's going to contact his dull, boring friend. I'll call his constituency secretary to arrange a meet.'

'You do that, John.'

Pre-empting John's call, David phoned him at *The Swiftian* the next afternoon.

'Hi, John, how about we have a jar or two tomorrow? I've got a favour to ask.'

'No problem, Dave. What kind of favour?'

'Not on the phone, John. Tomorrow, twelve at the Red Lion?'

'OK, Dave.'

'I'm meeting up with Dave tomorrow, Marilyn,' he announced when he got home. 'A little, well, mysterious.'

'What?'

'He said he wants me to do him a favour but wouldn't elaborate.'

'It isn't concerning the profile that Streeter wanted you to write a while back?'

'Streeter? Oh, I'd forgotten about that ages ago. You know I decided against doing it. No matter how I played it, most people would have viewed the piece as a free advertisement for Dave. In any case, he's doing well without my assistance.'

'Good decision. Even Anita thought the idea was naïve. Stupid, she called it. Did I tell you she berated him, Streeter, for reason or reasons unknown, at a private function for local party members after the election? It created quite a stir, but they're so enamoured with David that the thing was hushed up.

'Where are you meeting… Why don't you ask him over for lunch instead? I'd like to see him too. Call him.'

John dialled Dave's personal mobile. He'd been around politicians long enough to avoid contacting them on their official devices. He answered after only two rings.

'Hi, Dave, Marilyn wants to you to come over for lunch tomorrow. She still doesn't trust us to visit the pub and maintain decorum. How about it?'

A hesitation.

'Dave, are you there?'

'OK, John, what time? I have to be back in the committee rooms by three.'

'Let's say twelve. Marilyn's keen to see you.'

'Keen to… Right, John, I'll come over, and… Thanks.'

'He'll be over by twelve. He sounded, if anything, more – what's the word? – guarded, than yesterday. Might be an interesting lunch. Oh, he said he has to be back in Westminster by three.'

*

David arrived on time, carrying a heavy-looking briefcase. He appeared in a happy frame of mind, and played with John junior, who took to him immediately, the two lying on the living room carpet, the boy screaming with delight as 'Uncle Dave' did various animal impressions.

'You'll get him all hyped up, David,' said Marilyn as she placed the food on the dining room table. 'If he doesn't go down tonight, I'll be calling you.'

They sat around the table, and David, talking animatedly about his 'exciting, busy' life as an MP, appeared his usual self, at least to John. Marilyn remained unconvinced, waiting for him to bring up the 'favour' David had mentioned.

'Is Anita home this weekend, David?' she asked, while passing over the salad bowl. 'I'd like to have a chat with her about—'

'No, she's not,' David said, sharply, his face suddenly taking on a depressed look, 'this will be the second, no, the third weekend she's been tied up. I think they're taking advantage of her good nature. You know, Marilyn, I've got this feeling… that the job's getting to be an obsession with her, and what's worse, her bosses know it too.'

John, awkward at this outburst, and attempting to deflect David's thoughts, said,

'Dave, I'll be spending some time over there in the next few weeks, doing some legwork for *The Swiftian*. All this referendum speculation means—'

'Can you speak with Anita, John? I'd appreciate your opinion.'

'My opinion? On what, Dave?'

He sat back, sighed noisily, and blurted out in a despairing voice,

'On whether our marriage has got a fucking future, John! Sorry, Marilyn, but I'm at my wits' end, trying to juggle the two jobs, and her being away so much. I was happy enough to give up the legal work, but she demanded I kept it on. You know me, John. I'd never have made it up to partner. All those public-school types keep those jobs for their mates, or their feckless kids.'

John stood, walked into the kitchen and came back with two glasses of whisky.

'Take this, and then tell me what this favour entails. If it's about your marriage worries, forget it. We can't get...'

David grabbed the glass, consumed the alcohol in one gulp, then said, slowly, apparently calmer,

'No, that's my problem, shouldn't have said. Maybe I'm getting things out of proportion. We're both up to our necks in work... Anyway, listen, John, this favour. I already knew from someone, a party official, that you were going over there to dig up dirt for Fred's rag. It's his style after all, and I've been pressured into asking... no, wrong word, pleading with you, not to rock the boat.'

Visibly shocked, John stuttered,

'You can't be asking me to... to, in effect, tow the approved line? Tell me, Dave, what is it?'

'I... I don't know. All I do know is that government circles are nervous, nervous enough to fear adverse stories popping up, disturbing the status quo.'

'To put your mind at rest, if not those of your friends in the bubble, Dave, I'm researching material to update an old piece I wrote nearly three years ago – to wit, the EU finances and the continuing lack of a set of fully audited accounts. There'll be no exposés of scandal, well, not the kind your mates are worried about. I'm disappointed in you, Dave. How long have we known each other? I can't quite understand why you're so worried about me going over. Is there something I might come across which would justify official "nervousness"? Frankly, if people, here and in Brussels, can casually dismiss questions over umpteen years of dodgy accounting, then for the life of me I can't think of anything that would... cause them any problem.'

'Yes, John, you're probably right. Sorry, forget I mentioned it. I'll go back and tell the minister—'

'The minister?'

David sniggered, and said,

'He's not the sharpest. His permanent secretary was nodding his head sagely when he asked me to contact you. Puppet and string come to mind.'

'Dave, tell him my visit to investigate corruption is a front for me, to enable a liaison with my mistress—'

'David! You'll tell them no such thing!'

'There you have it, Dave, the Catholic conscience kicking in. I was joking, Marilyn, but... your face.'

Both men laughed. Marilyn, her face a picture of disapproval, said,

'Right, I'll be asking Anita to keep tabs on you.'

Chapter Thirty-Eight

When John picked up his hotel reservation and Eurostar tickets at *The Swiftian*, he asked Samantha,

'Is our leader due in today? I left a message on his mobile last night.'

'Yes, he's got a date with some guy by the name of Streeter. Ten o'clock he's written in the diary—'

'Oliver Streeter?' John said, stunned.

'I think so, John. What's the matter?'

'Do you know which of them organised the meeting?'

'Actually, John, I do. The guy phoned yesterday. He sounded, well, annoyed about something, and when I told him Fred wasn't available – true this time, John – he instructed me to let him know.'

'So, Fred called him back last night then?'

'Must have, he put the appointment in the diary after I'd gone home. Is he someone important?'

'Not really, Sam,' John said, wondering if Streeter was going to buttonhole Fred about the issue David had mentioned, 'though to hear him speak you might get that impression. He's Dave's local party chairman and seems bent on pushing his career upwards. When Dave was running for parliament, Streeter asked me to write a profile on him, but he won, even without my input, so why he wants to talk to Fred…'

'You'd better get a move on, your train leaves in an hour. Fred told me to get first-class tickets. I had to ask him twice, but he said it was all covered, whatever he meant by that. The hotel's four-star too.'

'Right, Sam, thanks. I'll call in every day. Oh, how long am I booked in for?'

'A week. Have a good trip, Mr Mystery.'

John gave Samantha a kiss on the cheek, picked up his things and left the office, still mulling over Streeter's motive in asking to speak with Fred. David's tentative suggestion that he shouldn't 'rock the boat' came back to him, and during the three-hour trip John's thoughts centred on the conundrum. After checking in at his hotel, very close to the Berlaymont, he dialled *The Swiftian*'s office. Samantha answered.

'Hello, John. Did you get across alright?'

'Yes thanks. Good choice of hotel, Sam. Is the old rogue still at his desk?'

'Yes, he's on the outside line at the moment. Do you want to hang on? He's been talking for half an hour already, so he shouldn't—'

'No, could you ask him to return my call?'

'Will do, John. Bye for—'

'Oh, Sam, did Streeter make an appearance?'

'Yeah, he came in. Funny-looking bloke. When he got here, Fred, surprise, surprise, hadn't made it in, and the guy sat opposite me. Made me feel uncomfortable, John, creepy, his hands were all over me – not literally of course. I would have improved his face if he'd tried.'

John smiled at the description.

'After Fred got in, they were only in his office for ten minutes, but I could hear his – Streeter's – voice raised a couple of times. He was complaining about having to deal with idiots, and someone called David – couldn't pick up the last name – but when they came out, he was looking happier. Fred took him for a "refreshment" and when he came back told me to block any calls from him in future. "The guy's a slimeball," was Fred's comment.'

John, unnerved by the possible reference to David, said,

'That's great, Sam, a perfect description. I've met him too. See you later.'

He put the phone down, took out his laptop and emailed Fred, guessing that the man would forget Samantha's message as soon as she gave it to him. He made a cup of coffee and sat down to read, as best he could, the complimentary French language newspaper. Half an hour passed until he heard the ping signalling an incoming message. It read,

'Johnny boy, congrats on making it into enemy territory unobserved (*Fred's been down at the pub*, John surmised from the prose). What can I do you for? Your message didn't specify.'

Annoyed, John dialled *The Swiftian*, and to his surprise, the man himself answered.

'Well then, it's the special agent. Didn't you get my email?'

'What did Streeter want from you, Fred? I hear the name David came up in—'

A long silence, until,

'John, he wanted to know *The Swiftian*'s intentions on—'

'Intentions?'

'We've made it into the bigtime, John.'

Impatient, and irritated by Fred's vague responses, he said,

'What the fuck are you gibbering on about, Fred?'

'Ah... Now I've got you interested, my boy! Streeter said, in sonorous tones worthy of Mr Micawber – good book that

– yes, but anyhow, he said that people, "important" people, he said, are concerned about how certain sections of the press are going to treat this referendum con.'

'Nonsense, Fred. Those "important" people already know the attitudes of the press, pro and contra—'

'You're missing my point, John. He was referring, without actually saying it, to publications like our own esteemed journal. We might have a small circulation, but we also have an intelligent readership, opinion formers and so on. He's an odd one though. Took him to the pub, and I got the impression he'd love to shut us down. Kept his hands in his pockets, tells you a lot... But anyway, he gave me his opinion of most of the parliamentary party, the Tories, I mean. It was a rare moment of veracity. They'd be unemployable in any other occupation, he said. When I asked him to give me a few juicy examples, he became coy, as if he'd said too much.'

'Sam told me he overheard him shouting off about someone named David. David who?'

'Can't recall that, John, he was wittering on in general terms, I think, throwing names all over the place, including yours. Doesn't like you, my boy.'

'Really? Did he happen to mention anything about Dave?'

'Dave? Oh, yes! No, I can't remember if... But he asked about the contacts I have in the City. He's a sly one, John. He dropped a few names. I hadn't a clue who any of them were though. I suggested he ask you—'

'He already has.'

'Really? Never mind him, did Sam get you fixed up?'

'Yes, she did, thanks, Fred. Before I go in like a bull in a china shop, is there anyone you'd like me to hunt down? We should have discussed this already, but I'm here now—'

'Yes, there are a few bods you might consider interviewing. I'll email the names to you in the morning. You have a nice, sober evening now. Oh, and apropos Streeter, he mentioned Murray's wife. Seemed quite taken by her. Strange that, I heard he prefers his vice versa—'

'Most people are, Fred, one way or another. What do you... Oh, really?'

It was nearly eight, and John, not having risked eating any of the bland offerings on the Eurostar, was hungry. He looked briefly through the freebie magazines on a desk, but not finding a restaurant enticing enough for him to venture out of the hotel, he left his room and took the lift down to the hotel's eaterie on the ground floor. At its entrance, the *maître d'*, dressed in a bright blue and white uniform, greeted him with a broad, doubtless sincere smile: '*Bonsoir, Monsieur Duncan. Vous avez faim?*'

John glared at the man, wondering why, if he was aware of his nationality, he'd addressed him in French, and replied,

'Yes, I am.'

'Follow me to a table, sir, *à côté de la fenêtre*, sorry, by the window?'

'OK,' John said as he trailed after the fleet-footed man. 'Can you get me a drink? Beer please.'

'*Mais bien sûr, monsieur.*'

John ate the unimpressive main course, fillet of beef, without enthusiasm, and mused again on what was behind Streeter's visit to *The Swiftian*. Fred's dismissive opinion of the man was in one sense accurate, but he felt there was more to the visit than the fishing expedition Fred had written it off as being. Why would anyone seriously consider that *The Swiftian*'s influence on events be anything other than marginal? Streeter's enquiries about Fred's contacts (the idea made John smile) in the world of high finance came back to him. Yes, his motive was financial, not political. He tried to recall what line of business Streeter was in, but it wouldn't come. *I'll ask*

Dave next time we speak, he thought, *and I'll tell him about his 'admiration' of Anita.* He laughed at how she'd respond to the unsolicited admiration. His meal finished, he rose from his table and wandered out of the restaurant toward the lobby when his mobile rang.

'Hello, Anita, this is a pleasant surprise. You're a good detective.'

'What? Oh, yes. I called *The Swiftian* after Marilyn couldn't give me the hotel's name. Your paper must be in the money, booking you in there… Or, more likely, on the take. If you like, you can stand me dinner… Their restaurant's five-star.'

'You're too late, Anita, I've already eaten, just leaving it in fact. We could do lunch, or dinner tomorrow if you'd grace me with your company.'

'Are you trying to be… No can do, John, two meetings in the diary, the second a working dinner with… a high-ranking official. Can't put it off, even for you.'

'Well, I'm here for the week—'

'Doing what exactly?'

'Some research, financial, very dry, but Fred asked me to—'

'Very dry? Fred? That's seriously droll, John. Oh well, seeing as you won't elaborate, I'll just have to squeeze it out of Dave later. How's Marilyn? She was a bit short with me earlier. Always was a moody girl.'

'She's just fine, Anita. If there's nothing else, you've reminded me. I'm going to call her after this—'

'Christ, you're getting to be as poodle-like as Dave! Call me on Thursday about a get-together. I might be available then. Bye now.'

John, annoyed by her offhand, sarcastic tone, checked his watch: nine-thirty, eight-thirty in London. Should he chance calling his wife, possibly disturbing the boy? After the conversation with Anita, he was anxious to speak with Marilyn, but decided it best to refrain. He made a mental note to call before breakfast.

Chapter Thirty-Nine

John's sleep was disturbed by loud, wailing sounds coming from the streets twelve floors below his room. He struggled out of his bed, stubbing his toe painfully on a bedside table as he struggled to locate his watch, and walked gingerly over to the window. Below him, on the busy road, he could make out several emergency vehicles – ambulances, police cars and a single fire engine – all with their lurid, unearthly lights flashing. The combined noise from these vehicles continued, though all of them were stationary, but he was unable to ascertain the cause of their mass arrival. Feeling weary, he shuffled over to the door, switched on the bedroom light and sat at the small table next to the full-length window.

He noticed that his laptop, which he'd set to charge up six hours previously, was at a hundred per cent, and he decided, while the noise continued, to check for any emails. One appeared, from David, timed at ten past midnight, British time. It read,

'Sorry to bother you at this hour, John, but I thought you should be aware. Mr Streeter visited your boss today. Don't be angry, but when I advised him that you weren't digging up anything adverse on the EU, other than the accounts thing you mentioned, he was seriously put out, so I expect he went over to persuade old Fred to lean on you. As if! I'm not sure why he's so anxious, unless he knows something I don't. Take care. David Murray MP.'

John's first reaction to this was disbelief; David wasn't the most discreet of individuals, but even he should have realised that sending messages on his official, government laptop wasn't the wisest of moves. John wasn't a technology expert, but he knew that all communications by anyone involved in the machinery of government were subject to scrutiny and, potentially, hacking. These thoughts were brought to an abrupt end by urgent, persistent knocking at his door. When he opened it, a nervous-looking man, dressed in the hotel livery, said, in heavily accented English,

'Very sorry for disturbing, *monsieur*, there has been an incident outside the hotel, and I've come to tell you, and everyone on this floor, that the matter has been resolved. Would *monsieur* like a warm drink?'

John, wrong-footed by the interruption, said, 'No thank you, and I appreciate your telling me about the trouble outside. Was it simply an accident?'

'I believe so, *monsieur*, two *voitures*… *pardon*, two vehicles crashed, right at the hotel's entrance.'

'Goodnight, or what's left of it, to you, and thanks again.'

He closed the door, walked back to the desk and began typing a bland, cool reply to his friend's email, sending it to David's personal address, stressing that he didn't appreciate messages when he was on holiday. The more he considered David's email, the more unsettled he became, so he got dressed, intending to go out for a walk to gather his thoughts. When he got down to the reception lobby, there were dozens of people milling about – agitated, frightened guests, hotel staff, and men in uniforms. A few, heavily armed, he noted, were standing at various points both inside and outside the lobby. Accident? John, who'd witnessed the confusion and terror of the July 2005 incidents in London at first hand, knew that something major had occurred, or more likely, given the lack of any obvious damage, been prevented. He pushed past the throng of people, walked to the exit and out to the street, moving away from the confused scene. Ten minutes later he strolled into a bar and ordered a beer.

'Is this place open all night?' he asked a waiter, who seemed preoccupied by the continued wailing of sirens in the distance.

'Yes, *monsieur*. Do you know what happened?'

'I was going to ask you the same question.'

The waiter frowned and said, gesticulating angrily as he wiped a table,

'Many demonstrations over there, at the Berlaymont. Foreigners coming into our city, living off our taxes, chasing our young women, and making trouble for the police, setting off explosions. *Sauvages!* It shouldn't be allowed here.'

'Do you think this situation is anything to do with—'

'They're criminals, only want money, houses. Take, take, give nothing back.'

The man was obviously seething, and John said only,

'I see. Thanks for the beer. I think I'll go back to my hotel, things are quieter over there now. Goodnight, or rather good morning.'

When he got back, most of the emergency vehicles had left, leaving only a couple of police cars parked outside the reception. Walking into the lobby, a policeman, carrying a serious rifle, wearing a stab vest and an ill-fitting baseball cap, held up his arm in front of John.

'Papers, *monsieur!*'

'My passport's up in my room, sorry.'

'Hands up!'

John stared, incredulous, at the fierce-looking gendarme, who shoved him roughly against a wall.

'What the fuck? Do I look like a terrorist?'

Ignoring John's protest, the policeman moved forward and padded down his body. Finding nothing, he said,

'Go for your passport and return here, now!'

Shaken, and very angry, John went to the lift and pressed the button for the twelfth floor. In his room, he went to the window and peered down; there was a burnt-out van, partially obscured by refuse bins. He took his passport and returned to the lobby. His favourite policeman was nowhere to be seen, so he walked over to reception and said,

'I was asked to bring my documents by one of your friendly gendarmes—'

'Don't worry, *monsieur*,' responded the young female receptionist, who looked very tense despite the forced smile, 'the incident's been resolved now. The hotel's very sorry for the disturbance to you and other guests. Would you like a coffee, or perhaps something stronger?'

'No thank you. Do you know what happened? I noticed a van next door, looked as if it had been on fire.'

'It was a false alarm, *monsieur*. These days the security forces are on twenty-four-hour alert. I believe, as you say, there was an accident just outside, and when the fire was noticed, well—'

'I understand. Thank you again.'

He went back to his room, opened the laptop and sent a message to Marilyn, assuming the 'incident' would be on the breakfast news back home. He checked his watch: five-thirty. Hopefully John junior, and therefore Marilyn, would be in the land of nod. From experience with their sleep-averse boy, however, John knew that she would often take him into the living room and watch television, usually one of the twenty-four-hour news channels.

The email sent, he lay down on the bed, but soon realised sleep was not an option. He raised himself up and turned on the television, scrolled down the seemingly endless list of channels and settled on a local French language news channel. A very excited young female reporter, dressed as if she was going to a cocktail party, was standing directly in front of the hotel, intoning about the incident. From his scratchy knowledge of the language, he made out that the authorities had assured the public that it was not terrorist-related. The standard 'nothing to see here, move along now' reaction of most police forces, John thought. He scrolled down the channel list again until he came to one which was showing *Casablanca*. The film had just started. He sat back on the bed.

John was startled by the sound of insistent knocking. Disoriented, and realising he'd fallen asleep, he went to the door.

'Good morning, *monsieur*. Would you like to come down to reception?'

Confused, John said, rubbing his right eye, 'What? Why?'

'A security issue, *monsieur*. Very sorry, but the police need to check everyone staying at the hotel. Please, *monsieur*, bring your passport. Please.'

'What? I've already shown it to reception!'

'Apologies, *monsieur*, but the police—'

'OK, OK, I'll be down in a minute.'

John shut the door, went to his briefcase and took hold of the passport. At reception, a number of guests, clearly and vociferously as annoyed as John, were standing in line while a uniformed officer inspected their documents, giving each person a suspicious look. He took his place behind an elderly couple, and when he arrived in front of the gendarme, handed over the passport, which was given back almost immediately. John walked off toward the restaurant; it was nearly seven and he was hungry.

'John! Over here!'

Startled, he wheeled round in the direction of the familiar voice.

'You were miles away, John,' said Anita. 'I didn't know you were coming over this week. Are you staying here?'

'Yes,' John replied, puzzled at her forgetfulness, 'for the week. I'm doing some... This is a bolt from the blue... Are you meeting someone?'

Anita came forward and kissed his cheek.

'I popped in for a coffee. Do you want to join me? John, you look a trifle, well, dishevelled.'

'There was a spot of bother here overnight, I thought you might have heard—'

'I did. It was some old drunk crashing a furniture van into a car around the corner. As usual in these enlightened times, Armageddon descended on the street. Bloody inconvenient. I'd made plans for... Anyhow, let's go in and you can fill me in on all the sleaze back home.'

John ordered a full cooked breakfast, which he consumed eagerly while Anita sipped her coffee. She informed him that 'Dave's been too busy running around for his boss to manage a visit, but, typical man, he seems to think I can just drop everything I'm doing here to minister to his needs in London.'

'You're being harsh on him, Anita. Remember I told you, he asked me to look you up and take you out to dinner.'

'No offence, John, you aren't my type.'

John laughed.

'You aren't mine either. Another coffee?'

'Yes. How are your wife and son? Is Marilyn still playing the doting mother?'

Before he could reply, she said abruptly, blushing,

'Forget the coffee, John, I have to dash. Maybe dinner later this week?'

Without waiting for a reply, she grabbed her handbag, stood and rushed out of the restaurant. John, astonished, watched as she walked briskly to the reception desk, tapped a tall, dark-haired man on the shoulder and when he turned, embraced him. The two of them walked over to the lift and a few seconds later got in.

John got up, walked out and went toward the same lift, thinking the worst. Back in his room, the scene he'd just witnessed depressing him, he opened his email box to discover a message from Marilyn.

'Are you safe, John? Please let me know, please!'

He picked up his mobile and called her, feeling guilty that he hadn't done so already.

'Hello, John! I've been worried sick. Mother rang here at four this morning – you know how she can't sleep – and told me she saw a report about a terrorist bomb at your hotel. Thank goodness you're there in one piece. You aren't hurt? Oh, I couldn't stand it if—'

'Marilyn, calm down. I'm fine. It was a false alarm, a van crashed and hit a car. That's all… I ran into…'

He stopped, thinking it wasn't the right time to mention Anita's appearance and mysterious assignation.

'How's the boy?'

'He's sleeping now, but my mother calling woke him. Did you manage to get any rest? Have you eaten?'

'Yes, I've just had my breakfast. Pretty good it was too after all the excitement. Funny, after a shock, I always feel hungry… Oh, and I bumped into Anita—'

He bit his tongue.

'Where?'

'Well, I'd gone out for some fresh air. When I came back for breakfast there she was, in the lobby, on her way to work—'

'What time was this?'

'Early, the restaurant had only just opened.'

'How did she look to you? Last time I saw her she looked strained, in spite of her usual bluster.'

'Look? OK, I think. Actually, we didn't speak for more than a few minutes, and she had to rush off for another of her meetings. They're all important, vital, don't you know.'

'Now, now, John. Anyway, what are you up to for the rest of the day?'

'I'm waiting on Fred to ping over a list of contacts he says I need to track down, but naturally it hasn't materialised yet. I'll take a stroll around the sights this morning, dodging the war zone of course—'

'That's not funny, John, at all!'

'No, sorry. On the Anita front, we arranged to meet up for dinner, the date and time to be confirmed of course. She asked after you, by the way.'

'Of course she did, John. Can you hear him? That's your son now. Better go before he really starts up the full *fortissimo*. Call me tonight. Mother's decided to stay over for a couple of nights, as I obviously can't manage without you. Bye, love.'

John, feeling depressed after hearing his wife's ill-disguised, worried-sounding voice, went down to the lobby to pick up one of the sightseeing maps. Browsing, his attention was drawn to raised voices outside the tourist information office: a foreign male voice, possibly eastern European, and a female voice familiar to him. Looking up he saw the man Anita had greeted earlier holding her arm, attempting to persuade her to follow him back into reception. She was having none of it, and John heard her say, loudly,

'Piss off, Marco, we're finished now!'

Instinctively, he stood behind a pillar and observed the scene. Anita threw what appeared to be a small package at the man and stormed out of the building. The man stood for a second, shook his head, then walked forward, picked up the package, walked slowly back to the lift and vanished.

Chapter Forty

John left the hotel and made for the Grand Place, using the tourist map he'd picked up. Strolling along, he tried to make sense of what he'd witnessed. Anita raising her voice, at a man she clearly knew fairly well, and that phrase, 'we're finished', troubled him. Did it indicate that she had been having some kind of liaison, an affair? The anger in her voice when she'd uttered those words could be interpreted as *prima facie* evidence of... John couldn't bring himself to believe it; that she would have been so open, to have behaved like that in full public view, knowing he was close enough to have heard, and perhaps seen, the altercation.

He arrived at the corner of a street which led directly into the Grand Place, possibly the only famous landmark of the city. The large expanse of the square was beginning to be crowded by people, most of whom appeared to be office workers, judging by the formal attire, many of them carrying bags, briefcases, and some clutching newspapers. A large clock tolled the hour; it was eight, and in spite of recently finishing a coffee, he felt thirsty. Sitting down at a pavement café, a small man with an apron around his waist rushed up to the table.

'Can I have a latte please?'

'*Bien sûr, monsieur*,' replied the waiter, who retreated just as quickly as he'd arrived, coming back with the drink on a large tray.

'Anything to *mang… pardon…* to eat?'

'No thanks, getting warm now.'

The waiter marched off without replying. John, having spotted the complimentary papers lying on a large table, went over and picked up *Le Figaro* and returned to his seat.

His basic French was able to pick up the main story of the hour, the apprehension of opinion formers in Paris about the potential danger of the Front National. John sighed and turned to its financial section, which featured a long article on the prospects for the euro currency and the perils of fiscal indiscipline in southern Europe, a topic which brought John out of his ruminations on Anita's behaviour. He despatched the coffee, shouted, '*Au revoir, merci*,' to the harassed-looking waiter, who waved back at him, and began walking back to the hotel, hoping that Fred, as he'd solemnly promised, had sent over the list of people he wanted John to grill. Walking into the lobby, he saw the man who'd been with Anita coming out, pulling a large suitcase on wheels. He got into what appeared to be a private car, a limousine, with a uniformed driver assisting him with the suitcase. The car sped off into the now busy street. John, intrigued by this, decided to try his luck at reception.

'Excuse me, can you tell me where the gentleman who's just left was going? I was booked to interview him, but I've mislaid his mobile num—'

'We can't divulge such information, *monsieur*, certainly not to private investigators.'

'No, of course not.'

Walking away toward the lift, a grey-haired man, scruffily dressed and smelling of tobacco, tapped him on the shoulder and said under his breath,

'A word in your ear, my friend, the man you asked the concierge about… Be careful. If you'll pardon my… He's not a guy to mess with…'

John, taken aback, said,

'Careful? What do you mean by that? And who are you anyway?'

The man smiled, shook his head, walked off to the exit and merged into the crowds outside.

Back in his room John checked his laptop, but Fred's promised list hadn't arrived. Annoyed, he dialled *The Swiftian*. Samantha answered.

'Hello, John. No, he's not turned in yet, but that just might be because he was at a function with his wife down in Canterbury, something to do with one of her charities. I only know this from the note he left on my desk after I'd gone home. Why don't you call him?'

'Yes, I'll do that, Sam.'

'OK, John, and I'll jog him along when, or more likely if, he shows his face. Bye for now.'

Fred didn't respond to John's call, so he decided to go along to the Berlaymont and listen to the parliamentary session, which he'd learnt from the information desk in the hotel would be taking place all day. Approaching the massive, ugly building, a prime example, John thought as he surveyed the monolith, of modern architectural bankruptcy, he was accosted by a small group of demonstrators, who for reasons not immediately clear blocked his path. He managed to sidestep them, waving away a young man who thrust a leaflet in his face, and moving toward the entrance, past the flags of the twenty-eight member states, he saw Anita, accompanied by a tall well-dressed man, not Marco, walking quickly about twenty yards in front of him. She looked flustered, and just as they made it to the door, she turned, seemingly looking for someone, and, spotting John, gave him an unconvincing, forced smile, nodding her head in recognition. As he was about to reach the entrance, his mobile rang: Fred.

'Listen, John, I'm on my way into the office. I should be there in just over an hour and I'll send over the details you require. Had a bit of a disastrous evening, I can tell you, my boy. Can you credit it? Two masked yobbos tried to mug us on the way from the station. Didn't get any cash, but they swiped my briefcase, which, as luck would have it, didn't contain my laptop, but Sylvia was terribly shaken. You know, that's twice now I've been done over. Me, a law-abiding, inoffensive chap.'

'Are you both OK, Fred?' asked John. 'You don't think there was another motive for you being attacked?'

'John, no, I don't consider there was anything other than greed behind either incident. You should stop reading all these conspiracy novels, my boy. Who'd want to damage me, and what possible reason, other than simple robbery, could there be? I'm not exactly Deep Throat, am I? Besides, they tried, and failed, I can tell you, to swipe old Sylvia's bag.'

'No, Fred, you're not the typical secret agent,' said John, smiling at his friend's comment. 'Take care. I'll get moving on things once you send over those contacts. I'm about to take a peek at the session in the parliament now. Talk later.'

Walking into the reception and up to the security barriers, John was uneasy at what Fred had described; not many members of the public are mugged, assaulted, more than once. He noted that on both occasions Fred's assailants were young, and wearing masks. Was it possible both incidents were more than simple muggings? Targeted assaults often had non-mercenary motives, and why would he be singled out? *The Swiftian*, as an admittedly satirical, and, to its enemies a trouble-making, publication, could not, given its small circulation, be seen as a threat to the status quo, the establishment, however that vague term was defined. No, too far-fetched, he concluded.

John sat in the public gallery for an hour, listening half-heartedly to a debate on fishery policy, but he couldn't shake the notion that the assaults on Fred might not be simple muggings. The thought lingered, and as he sat, bored witless by the interminable mumbling of the MEPs, it loomed ever larger in his mind. Over the years Fred had made a habit of, as he put it, 'defenestrating' various public figures, and doubtless had run up a series of enemies, some of whom had foolishly attempted revenge through the courts, but latterly, at *The Swiftian*, he had concentrated on issues rather than individuals' peccadillos, a fact which John considered made the idea of Fred being targeted a less than probable theory.

His meandering thoughts were brought to a halt when a young man stood up two rows in front of him. Waving an anarchist banner which he'd somehow managed to conceal from the security detail, he shouted out in a language John didn't recognise. People near him looked around, and the MEPs, probably thinking the man had malign intentions, quickly made for the exits. Two very timid-looking officials approached him and after a few seconds of discussion he was escorted out, still shouting. John, thinking the incident as entertaining as it was frightening, followed the rest of the audience out and walked back to the hotel. Fred, true to his word, had sent over the list of potential contacts.

*

Six days later John was in Brussels Midi station, walking to the Eurostar, when he was hailed from behind by Anita.

'John, going home, I presume? Would you like some company? I've made this trip too many times already, but I need to keep my eye on Dave.'

John, taken aback by her dishevelled appearance, said,

'Hi, Anita. Yes, of course. The train looks to be quiet, judging by the lack of passengers on the platform. Here, let me lift that suitcase for you. Looks heavy.'

'Thanks, John. Yeah, I'm taking a few days off. Can't really afford to, but Dave's got some big, important function at the weekend, so… Have you finished your hatchet job here then?'

'You could say that, Anita, but, as the phrase goes, I couldn't possibly confirm—'

'Oh very witty, Sherlock. Frankly speaking, this place, and that crew of hustlers in the Berlaymont, are really the pits. What the hell made them choose this dump for the "capital of Europe"? You've no doubt observed, John, that for all the bustle, the appearance of action, the decisions are taken miles, sorry, kilometres away from here. Behind closed doors.'

'Good grief, Anita, you sound… sceptical.'

'No, not sceptical, just frustrated. I was posted here, don't misunderstand me, to advance the cause, Britain's cause, but the machinations, the double-dealing… Oh, fuck it, John, it's just gone twelve, so come on, I'll let you buy me a drink. This table's unreserved. Waiter!'

She sat, wearily, at the table, and took out her laptop. The waiter arrived.

'Two large whiskies please,' said John. 'Are you hungry, Anita?'

'Not for their food, but don't let me stop you.'

He sat beside her and said,

'What's this function Dave's dragging you along to?'

'A drinks reception at his department. Should be a hoot, John. Can you picture it? A host of tenth-rate artists, mainly writers, I suspect, droning on about the indifference of the hoi polloi to their wonderful creations, and the parsimony of officialdom. In plain English, the absence of funding for their unreadable creations.'

John laughed, and said,

'You know, Anita, that could have been Dave speaking. He's not—'

'Yes,' she said, smiling at him, and tapping his arm went on, 'he was anxious to get on, and took the job at the culture ministry to further that climb up the pole. I think he's starting to get bored by it all now though. Has he spoken to you about it, John?'

'Actually, no. The last time we talked he was asking me to take you to dinner, but with one thing or another, we didn't get a chance.'

'Don't feel guilty, John. Maybe you and Marilyn can come around to ours on Sunday. We could give you the rundown on Saturday's gig.'

'OK, I'll ask Marilyn. I expect she'll jump at the chance to get out of the house—'

'Jump at the chance? She's not imprisoned, John. Knowing her cantankerous, interfering old bat of a mother, I'd bet she'd jump at the chance to babysit. I used to feel sorry for poor Marilyn, always respectful to her, tending to her every whim. A selfish, embittered old dear. Don't quote me, John.'

'No, don't worry, my lips are sealed. I only meant getting out, away from her circle of new mothers, will be—'

'What? Marilyn loves being a mother. Made for it, I think. Give that waiter a shout, John. I'm still thirsty. God, this trip's a real bore.'

Chapter Forty-One

When John got home, the place was empty. He'd told Marilyn to expect him by six, thinking he'd catch the afternoon train, but finishing up earlier, he'd boarded the midday one. He went into the living room, as usual very tidy despite the best efforts of John junior, picked up his unopened mail (Marilyn made a point of not opening letters addressed to him), and saw a large, brown A4 envelope with his name and address handwritten in bold capitals. Carefully opening it, he pulled out a photograph. It was a picture of David, bleary-eyed, with his hand around the waist of a young blonde woman, who appeared happy with the attention being shown. It seemed to have been taken in a nightclub, and besides David and the girl, several other people were obviously enjoying themselves. John didn't recognise any of the males in the picture, many of whom, like David, were paying their respects to other young women. He assumed the photograph had been sent to him for a reason, and probably not a benign one. The sender appeared to know he was a close, personal friend of David, so that would seem to rule out blackmail as the motive. Baffled, John went into the kitchen to make a coffee, and as he was coming back with a mug, the front door opened, accompanied by his son's unmistakeable bellowing.

'Hello, dear, you're home early. I've been out with this one at the park. He loves chasing after the geese.'

She moved forward and embraced him.

'You've been drinking, John. Not in the house, I hope.'

'No. I finished earlier than expected, and decided to get back to my loving family. I bumped into Anita at the station and she bought me, correction, I bought her a couple of drinks and—'

'You had to keep her company. Is it a state visit then? By Anita, I mean.'

'Funny. Dave's got some reception on Saturday and she's condescended to accompany him. He'll be happy she's going, he hates these official duties.'

'No one twisted his arm, John,' she said, and frowning at the parcel lying on the coffee table, 'You shouldn't have bought him that trinket. The house is full of toys and such like, and he only really plays with his scooter now anyway.'

'Anita invited us to theirs, Sunday night.'

'Oh yes… What did you say?'

'I told her I'd have to ask you.'

'What? You make me sound like the proverbial harridan, bossing you about. I'll call her tonight. Do you want to go?'

'I'd like to have a catch-up with Dave, so—'

'Right. I'll accept her kind invitation. Hope she's improved her culinary skills, though I doubt it.'

*

John made an early start the following day, getting into *The Swiftian*'s office by seven-thirty. By nine he had run through all his post, and when Samantha breezed in he said, holding up a large brown envelope similar to the one he'd come across at home,

'This letter, Sam, looks like it was hand-delivered. Do you recall how it got here?'

She came forward, peered at it and said, while removing her jacket,

'Oh, that, yes, I came in yesterday and there it was, lying on the floor next to the post. I put it on your tray. Funny, Fred teased me about it. He said it was an assig… assig—'

'Assignation.'

'Yes,' she said, blushing, 'he said it was from one of your harems. He's so cheeky sometimes.'

'Not quite, Sam. It only had a photograph inside. Nothing else.'

'Oh, a photograph? Who'd send you a picture?'

'Haven't got a clue. It's a photo of Dave, at a party by the look of it.'

Interrupting their dialogue, in walked Fred, carrying a large briefcase, and dropping it noisily on the floor he said,

'Good morning, my children. Shouldn't you both be toiling, rather than gossiping? Oh, I see you've been outed, Johnny boy.

Moving closer to him, he inspected the photograph and continued, 'Who's the lucky man? Wait, that's your mate David Murray, the rising star, though if too many copies of that orgy get out, he might just fall quicker than he rose.'

John, clearly rattled, said,

'Fred, can we talk in private. No offence, Samantha, but—'

'None taken, John. What I don't hear, I can't repeat.'

'No, Sam, I wasn't saying I don't—'

Exchanging glances with her, Fred broke in,

'She's pulling your leg, John. Come into my lair and advise me of your findings in the Tower of Babel. Yes, Samantha my girl, two coffees would go down a treat.'

'Bad night at home, John? You look knackered.'

'Everything's fine on that front. No, before we get to the Brussels excursion, it's that photo. Sam told me it was hand-delivered. There was only the photo in the envelope.'

Fred rubbed his chin vigorously and said,

'John, I'm aware you and Mr Murray go back a long way, and I expect you think you know the man intimately, in the platonic sense that is, but that picture has obviously unsettled you, and—'

'Fred, I got the same photograph at home. Similar envelope, with no text, just the damn photo.'

'Very, very intriguing, I agree, but why would the blackmailer send it twice? Better check with your mother. Maybe she's got a copy too—'

'Christ, this isn't funny. It's potentially serious, Fred.'

'Yes, John, it is. In my experience, I'd say you, or more likely Mr Murray, can look forward to receiving a further communication, of the written variety, with a request of some sort. On the face of it, though, my reaction to seeing it would be: so what? A man is dancing, albeit, closely, with a young woman, probably at a party. Not what you'd consider debauchery, but then, all politicians, no matter how lily white, have enemies, often arising from jealousy. Now that I think of it, your bosom buddy wasn't the Benfleet association's preferred candidate. Remember that old codger who buttonholed me in the Admiral just before the election? He was bemoaning how national party bosses routinely overruled local associations, and… Yes, Benfleet's original choice to replace that cretin Moore was the feisty woman who paraded herself as the local choice. An "ordinary woman" I think was her pitch.'

'I thought Dave was the only candidate after old Moore got the boot.'

'John, maybe it's plain, old-fashioned spite, the woman scorned, and suchlike cobblers that's the genesis of those photographs.'

'I hope your theory's borne out, Fred. Let's get down to this EU budget piece. Have you cast your eyes over it yet?'

*

Two hours later, they broke for an early lunch. Fred, in a jovial mood, led both John and Samantha to the Admiral, where over a long, semi-liquid lunch, he expounded his prognosis on the state of the country. John, after initially agreeing with his boss's conclusion over the photographs, was becoming dubious. Were they a warning, a threat, rather than a prank?

'Fred, I think I'll nip over to Benfleet and have a word with Dave. He's doing a surgery this afternoon and—'

'You haven't told him yet?' Fred responded after putting down his glass, looking surprised. 'Assuming of course he hasn't received his own personal copy, unsigned naturally. Tell him old Fred was very impressed with his dance companion. Big—'

'Fred!' shouted Samantha, in mock indignation. 'You're a dinosaur!'

'Compliments are always welcome, Samantha, whatever the source!'

John arrived at David's surgery at four, half an hour before it was scheduled to begin. He walked into the hallway and asked a middle-aged, stern-looking woman sitting behind a table,

'Is Mr Murray here?'

'Surgery is in half an hour.'

'Yes, I believe so. Can you tell him Mr Duncan would appreciate a quick word?'

The woman stood, and without responding, opened a door and disappeared, returning a few moments later followed by David, who held out his hand on seeing John.

'Good to see you, mate,' he said. 'Anita tells me you and Marilyn are coming around on Sunday. Great. Bring the little guy too. She won't mind.'

Noticing his friend's serious expression, he went on,

'Something up, John? Come on into my den.'

They walked through the door and David ushered John, who was thinking of how best to drop the bombshell, into his cramped-looking office.

'Well, John, how can I be of assistance? I've been using that phrase quite a lot recen—'

'Dave, have you received any odd mail in the last few days?'

David laughed and sat back in his chair.

'Odd mail he says! By the sackload, John, the bloody sackload. Why do you ask?'

'When I got back from Brussels, I discovered a handwritten envelope, containing only a photograph, at home. Nothing else, just the picture, of you, Dave, partying at a nightclub. With a very attractive young woman.'

David's face became red, and he looked uncomfortable, fidgeting in his chair.

'Have you got the photo on you?'

John took it from his pocket and passed it over the desk. David picked it up, and began to smile.

'Oh, this was a bunch of us at Dino's, celebrating Eva's birthday. That's her, next to me,' but he continued, his face darkening, 'but why would anyone send it to you?'

'Maybe because I'm known to you?'

'But that makes no sense, John!'

'I agree, but another copy was sent, or rather left, in my office, which... which might indicate that—'

'That whoever sent them wanted me to be embarrassed, exposed? But it was an innocent party. I'll give you, we had a few drinks, but I'd never cheat on Anita. I love her, John, and even if I didn't, she'd kill me if there was anything to it. I'm not the most intellectual person, but I am an honest one. What do you think I should do?'

'Ignore it.'

'Really? And what about *The Swiftian*? I assume it was deposited there in the hope, the expectation, that the paper would feature it. Another example of Tory sleaze. Right up Fred's street, isn't it?'

'Dave, we won't be using it. You can rest assured on that, but in your position, I'd make some discreet enquiries—'

'Like what?'

'This girl, Eva, you said, does she have a boyfriend, for example? Think outside the box, Dave, eliminate the possibilities. Oh, and one other thing, Fred mentioned that Benfleet had a sitting prospective candidate before you were parachuted in. Another possibility, I'd say.'

'Thanks, John, will do. And I'd appreciate your not raising the subject on Sunday. Has Marilyn seen it?'

'No, but you know her, Dave. Your marriage is your affair, sorry, wrong word, your business. The last thing she'd do is hurt her friend. No, you have to get to the bottom of this. Whoever sent these isn't… doesn't have your best interests at heart. Wait, I've just had an idea, was this thing an organised event?'

'How do you mean?'

'Was the venue specifically booked for a private party? If so, who booked it? Was there a guest list—'

'Hold on a minute… You're racing away.'

'Dave, these are the things you should be looking at.'

'Yes, thinking back now, on the day in question, John, I was in my office, packing up my briefcase to head off back to the house when I got an email, informing me of the party. I'd no previous knowledge of it. I didn't even know it was Eva's birthday. She's a part-time employee of the constituency party, the daughter of one of Mr Streeter's fellow committee members. Maybe I'll toddle along to the nightclub and make some enquiries—'

'No, Dave, not one of your better ideas—'

'Why not, John?'

'You're an MP, Dave, and you walk into the nightclub, presumably to ask questions about a party, attended by yourself and, as the photograph makes clear, several young women. It's an open invitation to any number of people – the manager, staff and so on – to go to the more intellectual members of the press and drop you in the *merde*.'

David frowned, rubbing his chin.

'See what you mean, John... Would you...'

'Go and do a Sherlock Holmes? I'll think about it, Dave. I'd better make a move, Marilyn's expecting me back. Her mother's coming around for dinner, to see the boy really, but... She means well. I'll call you tonight, after I've spoken with Marilyn.'

On the journey home, John, normally keen to follow up this type of mystery, was concerned about getting too involved in what appeared to be some kind of sting. Loyalty to his friend inclined him to do what David had asked, but he was apprehensive. What if his explanation, and his statement about hardly knowing the girl were... were untrue? His gut feeling was that the photograph hadn't been taken innocently, but the reference to Streeter John thought significant in some way. He determined to consult Marilyn on the issue. When he arrived home, his mother-in-law was already there, busying herself upstairs with her grandson's bathtime. He wandered into the kitchen, put his arms around Marilyn's waist and said,

'Hi there, I've got a thorny problem for you to ponder—'

'Is this concerning that stupid photograph again?'

Puzzled, John said,

'How did you know about it? I don't—'

'No,' Marilyn said, with a wry smile, 'you omitted to mention it, but I saw it lying on the kitchen table, you know, before you hid it in your coat. What's the issue with it anyway? David went to a party and danced with a pretty girl. So what?'

'I wasn't trying to be secretive, but I agree. Nothing in the photograph itself is, or could be, viewed as untoward, but the fact that someone took it on him or herself to send it to me—'

'Could it be a stupid practical joke? One of those disreputable associates of yours from the world of journalism?'

'Good try. A copy was sent, I mean handed in, at *The Swiftian* as well.'

Taking off her oven gloves, Marilyn said,

'Let me look at it again, John.'

They walked into the living room. John took the picture from his briefcase, handed it over and looked intently at her face as she gazed, frowning, at the now crumpled photograph.

'John,' she said after a few seconds, 'that girl David's holding, how well does he know her?'

'He said hardly at all. It seems she works part-time in his constituency office, and the occasion was her birthday party apparently.'

'Apparently?' Marilyn, raising her eyebrows, replied. 'What exactly does that mean?'

'Dave said he wasn't aware a party had been organised until the last minute and he went along out of—'

'A sense of duty? Really, John, you don't believe that, do you?'

'I'm not following, Marilyn.'

'No, I can see that. Look, in my experience, men invited to something like this invariably accept, whether they're married or not, in fact the married ones are often more likely... Just look at the picture again. All those young, mostly attractive, women, and then cast your eye over the males. None of them look as though they've turned up out of a "sense of duty", do they? I expect David toddled along for a bit of innocent – I assume – flirtation, nothing more.'

Her face creasing into a coy smile, she said,

'John, do you think he'll tell Anita about this?'

'Not sure, dear, but he'll have to, and soon. Going back to my problem, or more accurately, dilemma, Dave asked if I'd make some discreet enquiries—'

'What do you mean?'

'To locate the source, the photographer, to ascertain why—'

'No, no, no! Let him do his own digging. I can't believe he had the gall to ask you!'

'Because, as a public figure, any questions he might ask would attract attention.'

'That's his problem, John, not yours. If he's so worried, which is odd in itself, if he is innocent, let him hire a private detective.'

Chapter Forty-Two

John's dilemma was intensified two days later when he received a call at *The Swiftian*. He had gone in early on the Saturday morning, hoping to finish off a short piece on the never-ending saga of the Greek financial crisis. Ten minutes after he'd let himself in and dealt with the temperamental alarm, the landline rang out. Rushing over to the phone, he knocked it off the desk, but managed to grab the thing before it hit the floor. He picked up the receiver and said,

'Hello, who is this?'

'Keep your eye on Mr Murray,' rasped a gruff, male voice, sounding out of breath, 'he's not what he seems. The straightforward, honest-as-the-day-is-long man... Yeah, right! Dino's isn't his only haunt after dark.'

'What do—'

John heard the phone being put down. Shaken by the man's voice as much as by what had been said, he looked up at the wall clock – seven-thirty – and considered who could have known he was in the office. Only Marilyn was aware. He stood, walked over to the window and peered out at the street, at this hour almost deserted. After a few moments, still wondering who had called, he went back to his desk and packed up his laptop, his thoughts now miles away from Greece, put on his jacket and walked over to the alarm, which he managed to reset at the third attempt thanks to his nervous, agitated state. All the way home the words said in that weird phone call kept whirring around in his head. Who made it? How had this person known he was in the office?

'Hello, John,' his wife said, looking surprised, 'back already? Did you forget something?'

'No, I didn't, I'd just arrived when I got a very strange call.'
'Oh?'

'Yes, a man, who made an accusation about Dave, saying he's not what he seems—'

'What?'

'Marilyn, did you tell anyone I was going into the office today?'

'No, why would I? You only decided late last night to go in this morning, and I haven't… Are you implying—'

'No, I'm not, but what I'm baffled by is how this anonymous guy – he had a very odd voice too – could possibly have known I would have been at *The Swiftian* so early, and on a Saturday too. I can't make sense of it.'

'This has shaken you up, John. Here, take John junior while I make you… us a strong coffee.'

As Marilyn was making their drinks, John put his son on the floor and began to help him with his clumsy efforts at building a house with the plastic bricks lying around. Disturbing this, his mobile rang, making him jump. Picking it up off the settee, he said,

'Hello? Who—'

The line went dead.

'Who was that?' said Marilyn, coming in from the kitchen. 'My mother said she'd call this morning, but not this early. Well, John?'

'No idea, the caller didn't speak. Wrong number, I suppose.'

'Yes, it would have been, John, a coincidence, no more than that. Put John in his highchair while you have that coffee. Your coming back early is fortuitous though, you can babysit him while I pop out to the shops. Meant to go yesterday but… John, are you listening?'

'Marilyn, do you think I should call the—'

'No, you most certainly shouldn't. Changing the subject, I hope tomorrow night's purely a social occasion, no office talk, just a pleasant evening. Oh, by the way, my mother's coming over for the weekend to babysit, which means we could stroll around to the local tonight for a break. What do you think? John, for goodness' sake, answer me!'

'Yes, sounds good. I'll walk along to the high street with you and take him to the park again.'

*

They arrived at David and Anita's the following evening at seven.

'Hi there,' said the hostess, taking off her apron, 'everyone fit to tuck in?'

'Yes, thanks,' said Marilyn as she took off her coat. 'Hope you don't mind, but we brought two bottles, one of each.'

'No problemo,' Anita responded tartly. 'Dave, use those glasses on the coffee table.'

The meal passed quietly, Anita, unusually restrained, not contributing much to the admittedly mundane conversation, with David apparently relaxed, telling everyone slightly risqué stories about his experiences as a junior minister.

'Dave, for God's sake, give it a rest,' Anita said, starting to look agitated, 'not everyone's so enamoured with the minutiae of Westminster plotting as you seem to be, and for the love of Christ don't bring up last night's debacle.' Putting her hand on David's arm she continued, 'Tell me, Marilyn, I'll bet John here doesn't bore you out of your pants with puerile gossip, secrets he comes across.'

'I'm sorry, Anita,' John said, 'my lips are sealed with regard to such matters. Journalists and their sources are akin to doctors and patients.'

'Oh, so you admit, John,' Anita shot back, her eyes glittering, 'your little rag does have stories that actually interest the public?'

John, inwardly bristling at her rudeness, hid it by saying, 'We do indeed, and one or two of them would make you sit up and notice—'

'Come on then, my friend, shock me.'

'No, Anita, you're teasing now, but I'm sure you've seen and heard things in Brussels which the press is unaware of, it's a secretive place. I failed completely to learn anything I didn't already know. A wasted trip.'

'Stop it, John,' said David, frowning, 'you know well enough she can't speak about anything in her job, just like you, so leave it.'

'You see, Marilyn,' said Anita, grinning at her friend, 'that's my loving husband all over. Always defending me, such dedication, love. Some people would sneer at his puppylike, slavish loyalty to me, but I can't blame him, can I, darling?'

She leant over and kissed him lingeringly on the lips. David blushed crimson, and when Anita sat back, smiling, he glanced at John, who, as their eyes met, thought he saw something odd in his friend's expression, as if he suspected John was aware of…

For the rest of the evening, with the two couples becoming more animated as the wine flowed, John paid close attention to David's body language. He was half-convinced that his friend was hiding something, and when Anita made a casual reference to what she termed the 'loose moral climate' amongst the political classes in Brussels, he spotted David blushing again. Marilyn, noticing this, said,

'It's getting too warm in here, John, go and get us some water. Poor David's melting. I'm sorry, David, we have the same problem at home. Whenever my mother's there she's always turning the heat up. She thinks John junior's in constant danger of frostbite.'

David laughed nervously and said,

'Yes, I'd like a glass of water. I'll give you a hand with the glasses, John.'

He followed John into the kitchen, and as he put four glasses on a tray said quietly to him,

'Is something up, John? You look worried. It's not that stupid business about the anonymous call you mentioned on the phone last night, or that photo, is it? I asked around at the constituency office after you left, discreetly of course, but everyone seems to think I'm doing a good job.'

John turned and looked him straight in the face, and with a very stern look said,

'Dave, just give it to me straight, are you sure that call was just a stupid, malicious one, made because of... of jealousy—'

'John, you know it was—'

'So there's nothing meaningful behind it?'

A hesitation. David swallowed hard and replied,

'No, John, I don't think so. Why are you cross-examining me? You sound like one of those arsehole interviewers on television.'

'Good, let's get these drinks to our other halves before they suspect we've eloped.'

David laughed nervously.

'What were you two conspirators plotting in there?' said Anita, smiling. 'If it's about that rumour—'

John exchanged glances with Marilyn, who shook her head. Anita picked this up and continued, clearly enjoying their discomfort,

'Don't go jumping the gun. It's not been confirmed yet, but once it is, we'll all be going out for a celebratory bash.'

David, relieved, said,

'You know neither of these two would blab, Anita, so—'

'I know, Dave. OK, guys, listen, I'm in line for a new job, after my work on... The details are confidential, but I can say I'll be a bigger, much bigger fish in the pond. A special assignment is all I can safely divulge... but there's a febrile—'

'So, you're coming back to London, Anita? David will—'

'No, Marilyn, still at the heart of things, in Brussels. We'll have our work cut out, with this talk of a referendum.'

The phone rang. John, nearest to it, picked it up.

'Is that his bookie?' said Anita. 'I think we'd better call it a night. Dave's dragging me to his parents' in Leeds tomorrow. Haven't seen them in ages, thank goodness, but some duties are inescapable, aren't they, Marilyn? That was a short call, John. Bad news?'

'No, wrong number.'

David helped Marilyn with her coat, and as she was embracing Anita, he said quietly to John,

'I've got a free morning on Tuesday. Can we have a meet in the morning, at your office, say around ten and—'

'You see, Marilyn, those two are definitely up to something. Look at their schoolboy guilty faces. Well? Spit it out.'

'Dave was asking if I can get my hands on Test match tickets, for Lord's.'

'That's right, Anita, I'd promised John I could acquire a

couple through "channels" but no joy, so he's going to use his… his old contacts in the City.'

'Of course he is, Dave. We'd better keep our eyes on these two, Marilyn. If I didn't know Dave better, I'd say they're off to… Anyway, lovely evening, guys, except for the dessert. Don't much like that recipe you gave me, Marilyn. Bye.'

Chapter Forty-Three

John was taking a shower before going to bed when Marilyn shouted through from the bedroom,

'John, a man just called asking if you could give him a ring, first thing Monday, he said. I've got his number. A Mr Streeter, the name's familiar.'

Pulling a T-shirt over his chest, John walked into the bedroom and said,

'It's a bit late to be calling someone's private number, it's after ten now. How did he sound to you?'

'Abrupt I'd describe his voice, and his manner too. Oh, I remember, isn't he the party bigwig in David's constituency?'

'That's him,' said John, wondering why the man felt it necessary to call so late on a Sunday night and not explain the reason. Arrogant was the word for it, to assume he'd obey the instruction, but once the irritation wore off, he began to think it might have something to do with David, and that led him back to the anonymous call, and more significantly, the photographs. He took David's word as gospel, but the hesitant denial of any wrongdoing came back to him.

'Can I have that number, Marilyn, please?'

'I've written it down on the pad downstairs.'

'Good, this won't take long.'

'You aren't thinking of calling him back now?'

'He's got a nerve to disturb us at this time of night, but… Maybe… I'm going to return the favour. It'll bug me if I don't find out what he wanted.'

He went downstairs, Marilyn following him, and into the lounge. At the phone John picked up the pad and waved Marilyn to the drinks cabinet, making a motion with his hand to indicate he'd prefer a stronger liquid than coffee. He dialled the number.

'Hello, who on earth is calling?' a female, agitated voice answered. 'Don't you realise it's nearly midnight?'

'Sorry to bother you, Mrs Streeter, but your husband has just called me, so I thought I'd return the call, thinking it must be important for him to call so late. Do you know what—'

'He's gone out… Mr…'

'Duncan.'

'I'm sorry, but it's none of your business. An urgent family matter. Are you sure he called your number? He's been busy talking to several people by phone this evening. If he did call you, it would have been by mistake. Goodnight.'

'Well?' Marilyn asked as she handed him a whisky, which he gulped down. 'Oh dear, this is serious, isn't it?'

'His wife answered, quite annoyed, flustered too. He's gone out, a family matter, she said. Why she felt the need to say that I don't know, but she told me he's been "busy" all evening making calls. Do you think he might have received that photo, got into a panic, given that the girl is the daughter of one of his business associates, added to the fact that he personally engineered Dave's adoption?'

'What did Anita call you and David earlier? Conspirators? The truth is probably more prosaic, and innocent, John. Did

I hear David right? Asking to speak with you on Tuesday? Anything I should be aware of?'

'He didn't go into specifics, couldn't with the acuteness of Anita's radar scanners, but it's odds on he wants to talk privately about that photo.'

'John, tread carefully with this. I know you'll tell me Dave's as pure as the driven snow, but politics has a way of changing people. He wouldn't be the first, or the last, to be corrupted by the pursuit of power and influence. Make sure you know what you're getting into, and don't compromise yourself, if—'

'Where's all this come from, Marilyn? Dave's only human, but I can't imagine him being dragged into anything sleazy. Being cynical, he doesn't have the required dishonesty, or the brass neck. He genuinely believes, unlike the more sceptical among us, that being in the House of Commons is for the purpose of improving the country's situation, people's lives.'

'I'm serious, John, be very careful. There's more to this than meets the eye, and that man… Streeter.'

'Yes, Marilyn, point taken. Let's forget all this and try to get some shut-eye before the guy next door decides to start singing again.'

*

As requested, the following morning John, before he started work, called the number Streeter had left.

'Good morning, Streeter Associates, can I be of assistance?'

'Mr Streeter please. Tell him it's John Duncan, returning his call.'

'I'm afraid he is in conference. If you leave your number, I shall advise him of your call.'

'He's got my number, thank you.'

'What's up with you, my hangdog friend?' Fred shouted as he took off his coat. 'Where's that girl? It's gone nine!'

'She's got the day off, Fred. I'm on reception duties today. What's your schedule?'

'Hitting the keys until eleven; lunch with Proctor, the member for South Mimms; afternoon kowtowing to our tight-fisted proprietor. You?'

'I've just told you! Reception, but I'm looking into a personal matter—'

'On company time?'

'Very funny, Fred. When I say personal, it might, just might, evolve into something we could use—'

'Ah yes, Dave... Don't try that innocent look with me, Johnny boy,' Fred responded, and winking, continued, 'Westminster's a village, old son, a very small village.'

'What have you heard?'

'Heard... and seen, John. Heard and seen.'

'Less of the cryptic, Fred, doesn't suit you. Well, spill!'

'OK... Heard first. The word is that young Dave has taken to partying, big style. Nothing wrong with that. Our public-spirited MPs need to unload, to relax at times from their onerous endeavours on our behalf and... With the wife out of the picture on weeknights—'

'And seen? You said seen, too.'

'Yes, I did. Your friend turned up at one of my lesser-known centres of knowledge—'

'Which one, Fred?'

'The Red Lion.'

'And... Come on, you were saying?'

'The place was packed, and he arrived, his shirt hanging out of his trousers, with a gorgeous filly. Both had been imbibing before they arrived, and consequently mine host turfed them out.'

'Fred, Dave likes to go out with Anita, his wife, partying as you termed it, because she's in Brussels most weeks.'

'His wife? No, you forget, John, I've met the woman. One of those types you wouldn't turn your back on, in both senses of the phrase. No, the girl was blonde, and rather voluptuous with it. Eve, I think I heard him saying.'

John leant back, speechless, an action which caused Fred, smiling, to say,

'Christ, you look... almost surprised, John. Didn't take you for a judgemental cove. I'll say this though: when I said I'd heard, I assumed it was the usual malicious gossip, which often originates through jealousy and, being charitable... No, seriously, I can be at times. Most MPs socialise with their staff, especially if they're young, lively and suitably humble.

'The best way to find out is to ask the man himself. You've known him for yonks, which normally means you can tell if he tries to pull the wool, so to speak. I've got an idea—'

'Oh dear—'

'I'll invite him for an intimate chat tomorrow, about this rumoured boost for the arts his boss is keen on. You contact him and get him to the Admiral for twelve, agreed?'

'OK, I was due to see him tomorrow anyway.'

'Good, we can compare notes afterwards.'

*

John sat listlessly at his desk until three, wondering if he should, despite Marilyn's warning, attempt to discover the source of the rumours about David. Going to the nightclub, asking questions about the 'private party' was fraught with unwelcome possibilities. He considered how else he might glean any reliable evidence. Fred's typically throwaway description of seeing David with a blonde, whom John assumed to be Eva, his part-time PA from his constituency office, suggested that he may have been less than discreet. Like Fred, John knew how febrile the current atmosphere was in political circles; it was possible to recruit enemies without having offended anyone.

Alone in the office, and having written a few hundred words for the editorial, he closed up his laptop and was about to go off home when his mobile rang.

'Good afternoon, could I trouble you to let me speak with Mr Duncan?'

John recognised the lugubrious, self-important voice: Streeter.

'Speaking. I believe you wanted to speak with me urgently. Now listen, I don't appreciate being disturbed late on a—'

'Mr Duncan, we can't discuss what I... Can you come around to my office? I'm in Bond Street.'

'What? Now?'

'If you don't mind, the matter is—'

John, his journalist's natural curiosity aroused, replied,

'Give me half an hour.'

At Streeter's premises, on the third floor above a furniture showroom full of customers, he was ushered into a small office, stacked high with filing cabinets.

'I'll get straight to the point, Mr Duncan,' Streeter said, irritably waving his secretary out of the room. 'You're very close to Murray, are you not?'

'Dave? Yes.'

'For the good of his career, and indeed his marriage, to that awful woman... can you give him some fraternal advice? I've harangued him, but he wouldn't listen.'

Thinking he knew what Streeter was alluding to, John said,

'Yes, I've heard some wild rumours, but he's already assured me they're nonsense. As it happens, I'm seeing Dave tomorrow, but—'

'Rumours?' Streeter, his face suddenly displaying a nervous look, said. 'What have you heard?'

'Just fatuous gossip, the kind many politicians are subject to, and a photograph showing him partying… No, I don't mean that kind of partying, just him, out dancing, with his PA, Eva, I think she's called.'

Streeter, looking more relaxed, said,

'Oh yes, young Eva… A lovely girl… Mr Duncan, the reason I wanted to run something past you is—'

Getting irritated, John said,

'What exactly? And why mention Dave's marital status?'

'Strictly *entre nous* you must understand, some of us in the party are concerned that Murray's stance relating to—'

'Right, Streeter, stop right there. Dave's political views are of no concern to me, and if, as I suspect, you want me to influence him, about anything, you can forget it. I'm leaving. This was a waste of my time, and I'm sure Dave will be less than impressed by your clumsy attempt to influence him… Goodbye.'

John, managing, just, to control his anger, left the building, intending to update his friend on Streeter's devious, underhand bid to use him to extract some kind of favour. What Streeter was 'concerned' about intrigued him, but he knew David would have an inkling; it was probably the old story. The party didn't like its MP to think for himself. On the train home, John pondered what the issue was. And the reference to his 'marital state'. A mystery, but he determined to grill David.

Marilyn was out with their son when he arrived home, so John took the opportunity to phone David, who answered after only two rings.

'Hi, John, I thought we were meeting up tomorrow. Have you discovered something?'

'No, but I've just been with Streeter.'

'What?' said David, sounding very surprised.

'He called the house the other night and left a message, and again at the office this afternoon, requesting my presence over at his place – Bond Street—'

David, obviously unsettled, said,

'Why, John?'

'In short, he's not happy with you. And—'

David let out a long sigh.

'The man's a control freak, John. He's forever banging on, pushing me, to "use my influence", a joke in itself, to get the idea of a referendum put on the back burner. I've told him, several times, that a junior in the culture ministry has nothing to—'

'Dave, he didn't mention the referendum, he said he, and his committee, were concerned about—'

'He's seen that photograph, hasn't he, John?'

'No idea, and I didn't give him the chance to elaborate, but he said something very leftfield, Dave.'

'What? Tell me.'

'He asked if I'd give you some "fraternal advice", for the sake of, I quote: "your career and your marriage". I understand why he might like to talk about your career, but your marriage? If I were you, Dave, I'd have it out with the guy.'

'I'm not sure that's a good idea, John, and now that I think of it, I wouldn't be surprised if he's behind that photo, and I wonder if he's planning, no, plotting, on using it to—'

'Make you toe the line?'

'Exactly. Which is why finding out who took the fucking thing has to be sniffed out.'

'Oh, on that subject, I'm taking Marilyn to Dino's on Friday, Dave. As it's for our anniversary, I'll be asking the *maître d'* if he knows a decent snapper to take our picture. It's worth a try, don't you think?'

'Thanks, John, this is a big thing for me. I'm sure Anita doesn't think I'm a philanderer, but if she eyeballs that photo before I establish the background, I'll be up shit creek, with the paddle halfway down my throat.'

'Just an idea, Dave, outlandish, I know: why don't you, in fact why haven't you, mentioned this to Anita? Better for you to come clean rather than some random stranger dropping you in it. Once she calms down, she'll appreciate the honesty.'

'I should have, in fact, maybe I'll call her after this conversation. She's not due back until Saturday.'

'OK, Dave, I'll have to dash. Let me know if anything turns up before we meet. And, as I've said, if I were you, I'd be very circumspect. If Streeter asks you whether we've been talking – I doubt if we will – tell him… tell him no.'

'What? Oh, right, got you. Bye.'

Chapter Forty-Four

John's mobile rang. He sat up in bed, peered at his wife, and reached over to his bedside table, eventually locating the phone.

'Hello,' he said quietly, as he hauled himself out of the bed and walked to the door, 'who is this?'

'John, don't sugarcoat it. How long have you known about Dave screwing this tart?'

Carefully shutting the bedroom door behind him, John said,

'Anita, what are you talking about?'

'You expect me to believe you? I'm not a fool. Don't you try to protect him!'

'Listen, Anita, it's very late, and you're upset, but you need to speak to Dave—'

'So, you're admitting you've known about it for... How long?'

'No, I'm not. Speak to him.'

'He told me about a photo of him and... He denied it meant... But he would, he's a man!'

John, half asleep, trying to make sense of this, said,

'Anita, did he tell you it was only a birthday party for the girl? Eva, I think she's called.'

'I don't give a shit what her name is. The clown phoned me tonight and tried to make out it was just an innocent party! Birthday my arse. Bold as brass!'

'You've just said he denied it… Did he call you tonight or did you call him?'

'What? I've just told you! He called me and confessed to canoodling with that bimbo! Very inconvenient, I was having dinner with Marco… Told me straight out, yes, he'd been snapped "dancing". Believe that and… With… Eva!'

'She's his PA at the constituency office, Anita, and it was a birthday party for her.'

'Oh, yes, yes, of course it was, that was his excuse. He's obviously pulled the wool over your eyes, but not mine, John, not mine. The bastard's going to pay for humiliating me!'

'This isn't the time to chew the fat over what's nothing more than speculation. You must know, Anita, that the circles Dave moves in since he got into… They're full of chancers, opportunists, and green-eyed losers. Before you lay into him, think on this: he's denied it to you, and me as it happens—'

'So he bares his soul to you first. Did he ask your advice as to how he could break the news to me?'

'No, it wasn't like that. I approached him after I got two photos, hand-delivered, at home and the office. He was baffled, and worried that someone, for some unknown reason, has got it in for him. I also got an anonymous phone call bad-mouthing him.'

'If Dave's so pure, so innocent, why would anyone go to the trouble—'

'Are you serious, Anita? Because whoever's behind this is probably jealous that he was elevated so quickly. He was a surprise choice as the Tory candidate after all, probably why that creep of a chairman, Streeter, is so anxious. He asked me to see him as a matter of fact and—'

'What?' Anita said, her voice raised again, this time sounding nervous. 'You've spoken with him? Why?'

John, surprised by the sudden change in her tone, said,

'Because he asked me to have a word with Dave. His apparent concern was over his political stance on... Have you met the guy, Anita? Struck me as just a tiny bit sleazy, arrogant, and supercilious with it... Anita?'

She was silent for a moment, then replied, sounding emotional,

'Just the once... Oh, and again at Dave's adoption meeting. We didn't really speak. He was too busy pushing him around the room, doing the introductions. Not many of the crowd there seemed to know who Dave was. His wife's a sour-faced bitch though. Gave me the impression she wasn't pleased with her old man.'

'I'm tired, Anita, so perhaps we can leave things for now. Goodnight.'

Tiptoeing back to the bedroom, John thought he heard his son stirring in his room. He detoured there and saw him standing up in the cot, and as he moved forward, held up his arms. John lifted him, went over to the armchair Marilyn used when nursing the boy and sat down, trying to think again what was behind those damn photos.

*

'Wake up, John!'

He opened his eyes and stared up at Marilyn, who was holding their son.

'Didn't you hear him?'

'What time is it? I was supposed to be going in to see Fred this morning.'

'Couldn't you sleep?'

'Anita called last night, very agitated over those photos. Dave told her about them and she thought it… Well, she was ranting on about—'

'Yes, I can imagine…' She smiled down at him. 'Is David still in one piece?'

'I told her to sort it with him, and eventually I think she agreed, because she calmed down, very quickly now that I think of it, after I mentioned Streeter's call, so yes, I expect they'll… God, how can he put up with these eruptions?'

'Come on downstairs and have a coffee. Do you actually have to see old Fred this morning? Go in later, we can take John out for a family stroll.'

John stood, stretched his arms in the air, and followed them down to the kitchen.

*

They were sitting around the kitchen table, with young John watching the portable television while depositing most of his breakfast on the floor, when the landline rang.

'Watch him, John, I'll answer it,' Marilyn said, as she stood and marched into the living room. 'OK, don't worry, no, it's no problem. See you then.'

She returned and said,

'That was David. He's coming over for a chat with you. He sounded uneasy, upset almost. I hope—'

John could see she was worried, and said, trying to lighten the mood,

'At least the poor bugger's alive, dear. I guess Anita's given him a stay of execution.'

Marilyn smiled wanly and said,

'I suppose it's possible she's accepted David's assurance about the photos, but, as I've told you, she's the type who bears grudges, and acts on them. Always.'

John called Fred's mobile and left a message, saying he'd be in after lunch. Half an hour later he returned the call.

'What's up, John? I was hoping we could run through a couple of things before we go to press. I assume you've completed your analysis of Osborne's budget, which, by the way—'

'I'll try to get in by three, Fred, but I've got some personal business to sort. It can't really wait.'

'Personal business? Ah yes, your mate Murray's nocturnal excursions. For a common or garden solicitor, he's become quite the dilletante since he got into the House of Horrors.'

'How did you—'

'Try to keep up, John, we've already discussed his shenanigans... And the photograph, gold dust, and if I weren't so fond of you, it'd be all over our front page. But I thought we were going to grill him—'

'He's due here any minute, Fred. I've got a distinct notion he wants to ask me for help of some kind. He told his wife about it, but unfortunately she didn't respond too kindly.'

'Oh yes, John, poor bloke. He's married to the fearsome Anita in the FO dirty tricks crew, based over in Brussels. To paraphrase the Iron Duke, I don't know what she does to her enemies, but by Christ, I bet she terrifies her husband!'

John winced at the reference; he'd endured many of Fred's monologues on Wellington. Suddenly, an idea came to him.

'Fred, I got a shock the other day. Old Streeter called me over the weekend and asked for a personal chat, which turned out to be all about Dave—'

'Isn't he the agent in Benfleet?'

'No, the local party chairman.'

'That's right, I've heard he's got some exotic proclivities. What did he want?'

'Well, he affected concern for Dave, saying there were rumours flying around, and he suggested I give him some "fraternal advice". But it's just struck me: the girl in the photo, the one he's dancing with, is the daughter of a local party member. Strange, that she got the job... I think I'll ask Dave when he gets here. Oh, that's probably him now. See you later, Fred.'

Marilyn opened the door and said,

'Hi, David, come in. Would you like a drink? I'm making tea for John and myself.'

'No thanks, Marilyn, I've not got much time. Is John in the—'

'Dave,' said John coming to the door, 'are you OK? It's alright, Marilyn's aware. Let's go in there and talk.'

'John, she's blown a gasket. I tried to reason with her, but no, I'm Don Juan apparently. Just wouldn't listen, and now she's cancelled coming home this weekend. What can I do to repair this, John? That photo's going to mean the break-up of—'

'Remember I said we're going to Dino's tonight, Dave, so perhaps if you hold fire. Don't do, or just as important say, anything to make matters even worse. One thing that's occurred to me just now: this girl, Eva, how much do you know about her?'

'Next to nothing, John. I was sifting through some papers at the office, when Mr Streeter came in and introduced her. He'd noticed I was snowed under with all the paperwork – you've no clue as to how much – and told me she could help me with it on a part-time basis, as a volunteer. That's about it really. Why do you ask? She's a lovely girl, very willing, and despite the fact we hardly knew each other, invited me to that party. She even told me she was impressed with how I manage to cram in all my work so efficiently. Yes, I can't recall how I managed before Mr Streeter recruited her.'

John, scratching his head, said,

'I've asked you this before, Dave, but are you certain there aren't any other skeletons... No, bad choice of words. You haven't done, or said, anything which someone could use to their advantage? Political opponents, for example? Or, perhaps more likely, your friends in the party?'

David frowned and looking directly at his friend said,

'Honestly, John, no, I've been working my butt off trying to make myself known outside the culture ministry. It's such a tedious place, and I'd love to be transferred out, but—'

'No fun listening to the luvvies' moans, I suppose?'

'Exactly, John. Some of those self-important twats... God, it's soul destroying. You'd think I'd shot their mothers, the way they drone on about funding.'

John smiled at the comment, thinking of the occasion he'd been unfortunate enough to have interviewed a certain pillar of the acting profession concerning tax breaks.

'Have you got anything on today, Dave?'

'Yes, a reception tonight on the Terrace, a delegation from Brussels funnily enough, discussing some concert tours from... Forget now, but I'm looking forward to a couple of hours' worth of bullshit. Why do you ask?'

'Well, I told Fred I'd be in after lunch, but let's pop into the Admiral after Marilyn serves up. He might have a few ideas on your enemies—'

'Enemies? I don't think I have—'

'None you're aware of, that's obvious, Dave. How about it?'

'What are you two boys plotting?' Marilyn, walking into the room, said. 'I can always tell, David. He starts to talk like one of those newsreaders.

'Is spag bol OK… God, I hate that abbreviation, but—'

'Sounds great, Marilyn. John's invited me over to a meeting with Fred after we eat. Thanks.'

Marilyn's eyebrows raised at the comment.

'A meeting with Fred? Better fill your stomachs. Alright, boys, sit down and I'll bring it in.'

Chapter Forty-Five

Fred was sitting at a table near the door, talking quietly to a young, dark-haired woman who was busily writing on a notepad.

'Nothing changes then, John,' David commented as they walked up to the table.

Seeing their approach, Fred stood and said,

'*Buongiorno*, boys. What can I get you?'

'Make the most of this, Dave,' said John, 'it must be a full moon. Two pints of best bitter, Fred.'

'Barman, you heard the gentleman. Well, lads, can I introduce you to a fast-rising star in the journalistic firmament, Kate McTaggart. She—'

'McTaggart?' said John. 'Let me see, the name sounds exceedingly familiar. Where have—'

'My niece, John. Just down from Glasgow University. She desires a career in my noble profession, so naturally, being a pillar of—'

'Wisdom?' David said, chuckling.

Fred turned to his obviously apprehensive niece and said,

'You see what we're up against, my dear Kate. Wit on a level we poor journos can only hope to aspire to.'

'Pleased to meet you,' said David, holding out his hand.

'Likewise,' she replied. 'If you don't mind me saying, I think I recognise you.'

'He's a junior minister in the culture ministry,' said John, 'and I'm John Duncan. I work with your uncle at *The Swiftian*.'

'John, I was pondering—'

'Fred does a lot of pondering, Kate,' said John, winking at her, 'invariably in famous think tanks like this one.'

'As I said, Kate, such wit. John, I'd appreciate it if you could spend a day or two with her in the office. You've nothing specific on at the moment, have you?'

'Well, no, Fred,' he replied, feeling slightly wrong-footed, 'but I was going to finish—'

'*Molto bene*, my boy! How are things in the House of Horrors, David? I hear the referendum's a done deal between Laurel and Hardy.'

'Laurel and Hardy?' said Kate, puzzled

'Cameron and Clegg, dear.'

'Oh, yes.'

'I hear someone's got it in for you, David,' drawled Fred, 'an occupational hazard, I'm afraid. Any ideas as to who the culprit is? I was surprised when I heard. I don't think the culture ministry is a hotbed of intrigue. If you want my take on it, I'd say look closer to home—'

David, appearing stung, said, 'What do you mean by that? Home?'

'Err...' Fred stuttered for a moment at David's aggressive reaction, 'well, and this is only a theory, I've no concrete evidence to back it up, but I would assume that, and don't be offended, as you emerged from nowhere to be the Tory candidate, perhaps a few noses were out of joint.'

'I was selected in a fairly open process, Fred, and I was grilled about my personal life by the committee. They gave me a unanimous vote of confidence at the time, and again, at the AGM.'

'If you're sure about them, David, then I'd recommend you review your actions in political matters. Decisions. Policies you've been party to. The culture ministry may be uncontroversial, but these tread-the-boards wankers are a precious bunch, and bear grudges for the most trivial, to normal people that is, reasons. The phrase culture vultures comes to mind. Yes, I like that one.'

John groaned, and said,

'That was bad, Fred, even for you. I think we can leave Dave here to go back over his less than tempestuous sojourn at the culture vulture ministry. Any ideas, mate?'

'Nothing comes to mind, but I take your point, Fred. The last spending round was a disappointing one for quite a few bigwigs in the arts community. If you don't mind, I'll make my way over to the House before my soirée tonight. Bye.'

He walked toward the door, stopped, and returning to the other three, said quietly to John,

'John, are you going out to that place, Dino's, with Marilyn tonight?'

'Yes, Dave, haven't forgotten.'

'What's that, John?' Fred interrupted. 'Nightclubbing? Didn't think your other half was a great socialiser.'

'That's right, Fred, you didn't think. Yes, Dave, Marilyn actually booked a table. We were lucky, there's a private party in there tonight, so it should be lively, if not informative—'

'Informative, Johnny boy? Are you on a mission, a story?'

David blanched.

'No, Fred,' John replied, 'Dave recommended the place, and as Marilyn's not been out recently, I thought—'

Fred, eyeing up the two men, said, his face creasing into a knowing smile,

'Oh, I believe you. Take note now, Kate, lesson one for the aspiring journalist. When someone tells you – I'm referring to politicians – why they're doing something, treat what they say with a dose of scepticism. My rule of thumb is this: the action normally involves some form of advantage for the person doing it.'

'You'll hear a lot of this from your uncle, Kate,' John said, 'but I'd agree that, yes, scepticism is an essential prerequisite, but an open mind is too. Take poor Dave, for instance. I've known the guy for ages, and as his friend, would naturally give him the benefit of the doubt, but as a journalist, curiosity to dig into the allegation would trump—'

'Aha! Now I get it,' Fred broke in, 'you think you'll be able to delve into how that photo was taken without Dave noticing.'

'Photo?' said Kate.

'Yes, John received two photographs of Dave, taken at this nightclub, dancing with his young personal assistant, and now John's taking the missus there for a "romantic" evening. Classic John! Two birds, one stone.'

'Actually, Fred, it's not a clandestine visit. Dave asked me to eye up the place.'

'Fred,' Kate said, 'you told me *The Swiftian*'s a satirical, no-holds-barred paper, chasing up stories the mainstream press—'

'Don't fret, my dear, we don't normally dig for the salacious. We haven't enough staff, or the time… I'm joking, Kate. No, there's enough chicanery going on in the political world, and we'd only highlight the sexual element if it influenced policy. I'm talking blackmail. It's almost two, I need to be off as well. John can you give Kate the guided tour?'

They dispersed, and John and Kate made their way to the office, meeting Samantha at the door.

'Hello,' she said, 'you must be Kate. Pleased to meet you. Do you guys fancy a coffee?'

'Good idea, Sam. We'll be next door all afternoon. Fred instructed me to apprise Kate as to how we go about our work.'

'Could I sit with Samantha for a while, John? I'd like to get—'

'OK, Kate. Gives me a chance to run through the spam.'

*

Half an hour later John's internal phone rang.

'John, sorry to disturb you—'

'No problem, Kate. What is it?'

'I'm doing the phone while Sam's out at the chemist. I've got an angry-sounding gentleman on the line, demanding to speak to you—'

'Not that bookie again?'

'No,' she replied, laughing nervously, 'a Mr Streeter. He says you've got some information for him.'

'Don't worry, Kate, the guy's a fu... a clown, but put him through.'

'What do you want, Streeter?'

'Have you had that word with Murray yet? He's got a constituency surgery tomorrow.'

'Yes, I have.'

'And?'

'Private discussions between friends are just that, private, but I will say this: I don't think Dave has done anything that might embarrass you or your association.'

'What? But is he going to support the government line on—'

'This conversation is over. In fact, it never took place. Goodbye.'

John slammed the receiver down, loudly enough for it to be heard in the reception area. Kate opened his door hesitantly and said,

'He didn't sound too happy, and he was rude with it. Do you mind me asking—'

'He's not one of our contacts, sources, but… Well, as you're on the team now, Kate, he wanted me to "have a word" with Dave because… Actually, I don't know why, probably not that photo, he didn't mention it. The thing's strange. Streeter was instrumental in getting Dave selected, and now he appears to be nervous, referring to "rumours" about him. Having spoken with Dave, I'm more inclined now to dig into Streeter's background, his business activities too.'

'I see. I hope you didn't mind my asking—'

'Of course not, Kate. By the way, I'm not sure how much Fred's told you about me. I'm more relaxed writing about financial matters. Your uncle's the cat's whiskers when it comes to investigative journalism. He's fearless, a dangerous trait sometimes, but I'd recommend you hang on his every word. You're doubtless familiar with his bluster, but take it from me, the man's a phenomenon. Fifteen years ago, when none of the more illustrious of his peers would touch it, Fred chased after the truth behind that fiasco in the Middle East, and the cabal of liars who profited from it.'

'Yes, I remember that. Didn't he get beaten up one night shortly after he published a story?'

'Battle scars he calls them. He tries to disguise it, but sometimes his speech is affected by the bang on his head. That sounds like Sam now.'

Kate went back into the reception area.

*

John and Marilyn entered Dino's just after eight and were ushered to a table near the door. Halfway through their meal, Marilyn said,

'Look, John, over there, that photographer. Do you think the girl who's getting married, or more likely her bridesmaid, has hired him?'

John peered over at the young, casually dressed man, who was walking around the large table where ten young women, most of them half-cut, were sitting. He was taking several pictures of the party, who posed in various attitudes, their inhibitions diluted by the alcohol. When he turned to face the bride, he spotted John gazing at him, and after handing over his card to the lucky girl, came directly over.

'Evening, squire,' he said breezily, 'you look like you're out celebrating. Would you like me to capture the special occasion? Your missus looks spectacular in that outfit by the way.'

Affecting a guilty pose, John said, in a tremulous voice,

'Err… What do you think, dear? This snapper's offered to catch us in flagrante. For your information, David Bailey, my wife's safely in bed at home, so, *entre nous*, keep it to yourself—'

'Oh, Humphrey darling, I've always wanted a picture of us together… Please!'

John, amused by Marilyn's eager impression of the secret mistress, laughed and said,

'OK then, but don't flash it around the office. You've no clue how jealous the old bag can be. Right, mate, do us a couple, but—'

'I'm very discreet. We get plenty of guys in here with their bits on the side, and you'd be amazed at how many suspicious wives hire me to… I shouldn't say any more.'

'I follow you, my friend, but my line of work's not too far removed from yours. I've split up more than a few happy couples in my time, and between you and me, I could use a decent photographer. I'm shit at taking "discreet" snaps. Nearly got my lights punched out once. Maybe you and me could do business.'

'Sorry, mate, but I'm in hock… I meant to say, contracted to the proprietor. She really wouldn't like me to leave, not just at the moment, until I—'

John, realising what the man meant, said,

'Pity, but anyway, how much for the two of us? The pictures, I mean.'

Before the man could answer, a middle-aged, grey-haired woman, dressed incongruously in a black suit with a bright orange blouse, came over and barked,

'Richard, get a move on! Those girls want some more pictures.'

John couldn't place it, but he was certain he'd heard the voice before.

*

They got home just before midnight. Marilyn went to check on her mother and son, both of whom were sound asleep in his bedroom.

'Do you fancy a nightcap, John?' she said on returning to the living room. 'You're very quiet.'

'Marilyn, that woman at the restaurant, it's been bugging me, I've heard her voice before, but I can't place it. Very annoying.'

'Mrs Valerie Streeter.'

'What? How do you—'

'Over the door: the licensee, Mrs Streeter.'

Chapter Forty-Six

Anxious to tell David what he thought he'd learnt at Dino's, John left a message on his mobile, leaving no doubt about the importance of speaking to him.

'Morning, John,' said David, cheerfully, 'you sounded agitated. What can I do you for?'

'Come around to *The Swiftian*, now, if you can. Fred's out at the moment.'

'Is he... Oh, yes, I'm with you now. It's about last night at—'

'Dave, just come over.'

An hour later, he rang the bell and hurriedly climbed the stairs, Samantha letting him in.

'Coffee?'

'No thanks.'

'You took your time, Dave.'

'I'm here now, John. I suppose from your tone you've got something concrete.'

'Maybe.'

'John, I'm really busy, I didn't trek over here for a maybe.'

'I met the guy who, I'd lay odds, took that photograph,

Dave. He more or less admitted that he takes pictures on instructions from the proprietor—'

David frowned, scratching his chin. 'Why would the proprietor—'

'By the name of Streeter, Dave. Mrs Valerie Streeter. If you assume she told the guy to photograph you, I'd say it's not a stretch to link it to your constituency chairman.'

David, having listened intently as John explained, sat back, his mouth open.

'Where does this leave me, John? If you're suggesting he's out to get me for some reason, well, I can't understand it. He was the guy, remember, who pushed me into it in the first place, him and Anita, that is, so why? What should I do?'

After a few moments of silence, the two men staring at each other, David took out his mobile.

'Who are you calling, Dave?'

'Streeter.'

'Is that wise? Or prudent?'

'Not with you, John.'

'If our suspicions are correct and he's, for whatever reason, undermining you anonymously, you should use similar tactics. Make enquiries, on the quiet; avoid his mates on that committee. You said yourself they're as thick as thieves. And this Eva girl, how close are the two of you?'

'Jesus Christ, I've told you already, John! She's my assistant, nothing more.'

'Do you think she might be involved in this? She's the daughter of one of—'

David's eyes narrowed, and, looking directly at John, he said,

'No, I can't see she'd have anything to do with... Anita commented somewhat cruelly in passing when they met.

"Thick as shit" was her opinion of the girl. Unfair, she's very accommodating.'

'Dave, I wouldn't describe her like that in front of Anita. Another thing: I always got the impression she was – is, how shall I define it? – well, ambivalent concerning your entrance into politics, but now you're saying she encouraged you?'

'I don't see what you're getting at, John. In fact, it was Anita who introduced me to Streeter, at a New Year's party.'

The dialogue was interrupted by Samantha, who burst into the room, her eyes watery.

'John, John! It's Fred! He's been—'

'What on earth's the matter, Sam? Come over here and sit down.'

'That was his wife. She's in A&E. He's been attacked again.'

'Which hospital, Sam?'

'St Thomas's.'

'Listen, Dave, let's hold fire for the moment. Sam and I are shutting up shop and heading over there.'

'OK, John,' said David, as shocked as the other two, 'let me know how—'

'Yes, but come on now, Sam, never mind the post.'

*

When they got to the hospital, John, holding an emotional Sam by the arm marched up to the reception desk and asked for Mr McTaggart.

'He's being assessed just now, Mr—'

'John,' said Samantha, 'isn't that Fred's wife over there? Look.'

Turning, he spotted her, and still holding Samantha's hand, walked over.

'Hello, Sylvia, what happened?'

'He was walking along the street, in broad daylight. Two men attacked him. Why, John, why? This isn't the first time either. Who the hell's after him? And why? The doctor's just warned me... Fred might not—'

'Do the police have any theory as to who's responsible? When he left the office, he was going to meet a source, on a story... Samantha, who was the contact?'

'He was very tight-lipped this morning, John,' Samantha, holding back sobs, replied. 'The last thing he said, just as he was leaving, was... Let me think, oh yes, something about breaking a corruption thing, a cover-up, I think. He looked, you know, anxious to see—'

Trying to suppress his irritation at her vague answer, he said,

'He didn't give you any indication of where he was going?'

'No, but he said the man, or woman, I suppose, was very influential in political circles. Oh, I'm not sure now, but he was very excited, you know how he is sometimes, John.'

Two men approached.

'Which one of you is Mrs McTaggart?'

Sylvia looked up at them and said in a tremulous voice,

'Me. I suppose you're the police?'

'Yes, madam, I'm DS Mitchell and this is DC Griffiths. Do you have any idea as to how your husband came to be in the vicinity?'

'No, officer, I don't,' she said, and glaring at them, continued, 'have you caught the bastards yet?'

'We're not sure of the exact circumstances at this time, Mrs McTaggart and—'

'Circumstances?' Sylvia shot back at the policeman, her eyes on fire with rage. 'What the... He was attacked, walking along the street, minding his own business! You haven't got hold of them, have you, and here you are, asking me, about "circumstances"!'

John put his hand on her shoulder and said,

'Officer, I'm… we're colleagues of Fred… Mr McTaggart. I believe he was going to interview someone, but unfortunately, he omitted to inform Samantha who, or where he was going. That's all we know.'

'Interview? Who?'

John, tempted as he was, bit his tongue and said,

'He's a journalist, and I assume was going to speak to one of his sources—'

'A journalist? Had he any enemies, people he'd annoyed?'

'Plenty of them, but I can't think of anyone who'd resort to thuggish violence to stop him, but he was assaulted a while ago, on election night as a matter of fact. Fred shrugged it off as a simple drunken incident, but I'm beginning to think it's more sinister.'

'I see,' said DS Mitchell, scratching his balding head, 'it doesn't appear to have been a simple robbery. His wallet and his briefcase were found on his person at the scene.'

'Makes my point, I think,' said John.

A doctor, holding a clipboard, approached hurriedly, and walking up to Sylvia said,

'Mrs McTaggart, your husband wants to speak with you.'

'How is he? For the love of Christ, man, tell me!'

The doctor smiled, patted her arm and replied,

'He's one tough cookie. We thought initially his head wound might have been serious, but the X-rays are clear. This way please.'

She followed him through a door.

Samantha burst into tears and said,

'Oh, John, thank goodness! Poor Fred.'

John took her arm and said,

'Bear up, Sam, let's go for a coffee while Sylvia gives poor old Fred a piece of her mind.'

Chapter Forty-Seven

Leaving the hospital with Samantha and Sylvia, John mulled over the possible reasons why Fred may have been singled out, targeted, by persons unknown. Had the great man stumbled across a story, an exposé, which could have resulted in him becoming an inconvenience? That seemed a plausible theory in light of his secretive, cryptic comments to Samantha when he'd rushed out of the office.

Next morning, still with a feeling of shock at Fred's assault, and unable to rationalise a motive for the attack, he turned his attention to Streeter's connections, and his eagerness in pushing a hitherto apathetic David into politics; John was becoming increasingly suspicious that the man was less than honest. In short, he was convinced that the man had an agenda, unknown to David, which he was determined to uncover.

As an experienced journalist, and having spent nearly ten years in the City, he was only too well aware of human frailty, but this situation was different, because it was personal. He was about to be shocked to his core.

*

Sitting at his desk, reading and deleting the mass of emails which had piled up since he'd last been in the office, he was disturbed by Samantha, who came in, still tearful, and announced,

'John, Mrs Murray's here, she looks upset.'

He went into reception, and unaccountably, a feeling of dread descended on him.

'Hello, John, I need to apprise you of—'

'Of what? This really isn't a good time, Anita, I—'

She grabbed his arm roughly, and said,

'I heard, John. How is he? Anyway, I've come to tell you something, concerning him indirectly, and I don't expect you to judge me. I know you're a rational, calm man.'

'Anita, what on earth are—'

She looked very much on edge, possibly in fear of something, and despite his continuing worry over Fred, he could see she was in trouble of some sort.

'Sam, can you make us some coffee please? I think Anita and I are due a—'

'Yes, John, I'll be two minutes.'

He took Anita by the arm into his office, closed the door and ushered her to the chair opposite his desk. He stared intently at her as she removed her jacket and put it over the back of the chair. It was obvious to him that she was on the verge of tears. For what seemed like an age, the two sat, John continuing to gaze at her, Anita fidgeting with a stapler on his desk, trying to avoid direct eye contact.

John knew he was about to be told something momentous, but despite his apprehension over what that might be, he said,

'Why are you here, Anita? I understood you were in Brussels until the weekend.'

'John,' she said, her voice still with a nervous, almost desperate tone, 'were you even a tiny bit surprised when Dave got the nod for Benfleet, just before the election?'

Taken aback by this, he replied, 'Well… yes, Dave never evinced any interest in politics, ever since I've—'

She held up her hand to interrupt him and said,

'Stop, I have to… When Dave came into the labour ward, with those bright optimistic eyes of his glittering at the prospect of… of meeting his son… Oh Christ! Why did it have to be… so cruel! When these things happen, the world always feels for the poor mother, but I'll say this, John: the look on Dave's face when that oaf of a doctor informed him… That look's haunted me ever since. I don't think it will ever go away.'

John, very uncomfortable at seeing her like this, and beginning to well up himself, stood, walked around the desk and embraced her. She sobbed for a few seconds, then, wiping her eyes, motioned him back to his chair.

'Dave, well, you know what he's like, he tried to act like the strong, resolute guy, comforting me, telling me everything's alright, but I could tell, deep down, he was feeling those sensations, the ones I felt: desolation, emptiness, being cheated. On the surface, most people wouldn't have picked up on it, but I knew. He needed something, a challenge if you will, and for a long time I couldn't think of what—'

John, fighting back tears now, stuttered,

'Yes, Anita, we were both worried about Dave. He seemed to have gotten over—'

'A few weeks later, I was speaking with an old acquaintance at a drinks reception, when a middle-aged guy sauntered up to me and asked if he could have a quiet word. I thought "another sleazeball" but considered it might be a good laugh to disabuse the perv… Anyway, he knew who I was and got straight to the point.'

'"Is your husband interested in politics?" he asked me, but before I could respond, he outlined his "problem": his constituency needed a fresh face, and he assured me that some friends of his had been impressed by Dave's legal skills. Very funny, John, Dave and legal skills aren't that close. Then it struck me. Giving him an interest, a hobby if you like, might, just might, help lift him out of the slough of despond.'

She stopped, and wiped her eyes again, then,

'I have to confess, I played a trick on Dave. I arranged for us to dine out at an Italian place in said constituency, Benfleet, oh, you know the name…'

'Yes, Anita, carry on.'

'The restaurant was very quiet until, after we'd finished the dessert and were about to leave, in came four suited dudes, including the one who'd buttonholed me, and came over to our table.

'"Pleased to meet you again, Mrs Murray," said perv number one, staring at my cleavage, "and this must be Mr Murray."

'Dave stood and shook their hands as they introduced themselves. To cut a long story short, they set out their position, talking like secret agents, even though the place was virtually empty. Dave was gobsmacked. Basically, they wanted him as a prospective candidate, and he agreed, somewhat reluctantly, to go to the selection meeting the following Monday. One of the men looked less than happy. You know him, John: Streeter. The meeting was sparsely attended, the atmosphere similar to a funeral, but most of the zombies there seemed less than keen on Dave, and because no decision was possible, lack of a quorum, I think, the gathering finished. A day later, I was having a spot of lunch prior to going into work, when the doorbell rang. I was startled when I opened the door: Streeter. He lifted his trilby and said, "Good morning, Mrs Murray. May I have a quiet word?"

'"Dave's at the office, sorry."

"'A word with your good self, Mrs Murray… If you don't mind.'

"'OK, but I have to be off shortly.'

'When he got to the living room he said,

"'Mrs Murray, your husband's nomination is touch and go. How keen are you to support his selection?'

"'Of course I support Dave, why wouldn't I?'

"'I have a fair degree of influence over my fellow members… I could possibly swing it… If you could show me some—'

'The look on his pasty, ugly face told me, John. I could have killed the slimy bastard there and then, but I managed, despite myself, to maintain my customary good manners. I thought, go along with… I mean, lead him by the nose. Christ, it was big enough, with a rather unattractive feature, a mole… Ugh.'

"'Well, Mr Streeter,' I said, "I'm desperate for Dave to succeed, so perhaps we might come to an arrangement. You scratch my back, and I'll scratch…" You should have seen his oily mug, John. He was over the moon, convinced I was amenable. Thinking how long I could string him along for, I said,

"'I'll need a guarantee, Mr Streeter. Until then…'

"'I quite understand, Mrs Murray. I'll be in touch,' he said, with his sweaty face gleaming. "Oh, and by the way, how is Marco these days?"

'He restored the absurd trilby on his shiny head and left. Walked off with a limp, if you follow me.'

John smiled at her comment, and said,

'He wouldn't be the first to try that particular form of… of, well, what would you call it?'

'Dirty old bugger. The very idea of his hands… And his flabby attempt to blackmail me, mentioning Marco. Strange as it may seem, Dave won the nomination easily after that conversation, probably assisted by Don Juan, which is why I have to tell Dave about it.'

'Why tell him? Nothing untoward happened, you've done nothing wrong, and should old Streeter attempt to blackmail you, well, you can deny the whole thing. Remember, the guy's married, and I'm certain he wouldn't like his missus to be made aware. Besides, this occurred over three years ago, so why do you want to dig it up now? He's a busted flush. Forget it, Anita. I can't see why... Water under the bridge.'

'I wish I could forget it, but there's more. Streeter knew Marco from when he was giving evidence to a sub-committee working on EU transport policy. He, Marco, called my office in Brussels out of the blue and introduced himself, saying that he needed to have a "private meeting" with me concerning Dave's opinion on Europe. As you'd expect, John, I was curious, and not a little worried, but I agreed to go to his room – stupid, I know. When I got there, he... he tried to... to, well... You can imagine, but he chose the wrong woman, and now the two of them are using that "assignation" to pressure me to get Dave to resign his seat.'

'I'm confused, Anita. What reason does this Marco have—'

'He's in bed with Streeter's firm, something dodgy, and I think it's what your friend had cottoned on to, and why he was targeted. Now that I've found out their clandestine link, he and Streeter have threatened to tell Dave about my "meeting" in that hotel room, and probably that I... with Streeter to get Dave's nomination. A fucking mess, and I don't know—'

'Call their bluff. I know for a fact Dave trusts you, and you can counter the threat by letting him know Streeter's machinations. But, aside from the ludicrous, clumsy attempt to pressure you, why does he want rid of Dave?'

'His stance on this referendum nonsense. Dave's supporting the party line. It only struck me recently that Streeter never had any intention of insisting on me sleeping with him, no, it was all about blackmail, getting me to influence him in the direction Streeter wanted.'

'Oh, right,' John said, sitting back in his chair. 'I get it now! Streeter's got significant ties with Europe. He mentioned his business has a lot of work there, so I expect he might be nervous about—'

'Yes, and his friend Marco too. I tell you, John, my eyes have been opened these last couple of years – endless, pointless meetings, all of us pretending to be doing important things. In reality, the whole show, the edifice, is a massive fraud.'

'Can I make a suggestion, Anita?'

She looked directly at him and said, with a wan smile,

'That's why I came here, John.'

'Tell Dave what you've just outlined to me. We both know he'll take you at your word, and leave him to deal with those two-faced cowards in Benfleet. It's clear now: that photo was designed to pressure him into resigning, and because it failed, they're trying to get you to—'

She stood and put on her jacket.

'OK, John, I'll tell him tonight. Can you let Marilyn know about this? I may have to come over to yours after I—'

'You're always welcome at ours, but I'm sure it won't come to that. Trust Dave. I'll get a cab for you.'

'No. I'll walk to the Tube. Thanks, John.'

She embraced him, kissed his cheek and walked slowly out of the building. John, sorely tempted, resisted the urge to call David, but instead he phoned Marilyn.

'Hello there, what's the matter? Is Fred OK?'

'I've been speaking with Anita. She came to the office and told me a very nasty story, concerning Dave's constituency chairman. He's a piece of work.'

'A nasty… What do you mean?'

'Some really loathsome goings-on. They want Dave out, and Anita's being pressured, blackmailed, to make him give it up.'

'John, by the sound of your voice you're upset about something… More than what you've just said. What is it?'

'Oh, nothing earth shattering, but Anita's been shaken by it, she looked very distressed, so don't be surprised if she phones, or if we get a visit this evening.'

Chapter Forty-Eight

As he was packing up to go home, his mind buzzing with Anita's startling revelations, the office phone rang.

'Hello, *The Swiftian*. Who's—'

'John, it's me.'

'Hello, Dave. Have you spoken to Anita this afternoon?'

'Actually, John, no, but I'm a bit concerned. She left a message on my laptop, something about having to tell me something urgently. For a moment I thought she meant she might be... But the language she used made me wonder if there's some kind of problem. Why did you ask if I'd talked with her?'

'Ask?'

'If I'd spoken to her. Wait, have you been talking with her today?'

'Err... Yes. She came to the office this afternoon.'

'Why?'

John, becoming very uncomfortable, said,

'She asked for some advice, Dave. I think you'll need to speak to her yourself—'

David's normally placid mood changed abruptly.

'John, you're not a fucking priest in the confessional! Tell me, what's up?'

'It's between you and her Dave. Honestly, it's best the two of you sit down and—'

'Thanks for nothing, John. Did she say she was going home? Can you divulge that, or is that top secret too?'

'Just talk with her, Dave.'

'Oh, you can be sure of that. I've been summoned over to Streeter's place first, something can't wait until tomorrow apparently—'

'Dave, speak with Anita before you go to meet him. I mean it, before you see him.'

'What the... Bye, John.'

Disturbed by his two fraught, and in David's case acrimonious, conversations, John climbed the stairs to the flat. Marilyn was out, having typically left a note saying she was at the shops. He sat down wearily after pouring a glass of whisky. David's mention of going to a meeting with Streeter stuck in his mind. Why the need for an immediate dialogue, and at the man's house rather than at the constituency office?

Increasingly concerned, he dialled Anita's mobile, without response, then toyed with the idea of calling David back. Maybe his friend could be persuaded to delay the Streeter conversation, to give Anita the chance to speak with him. He sat back, depressed, in the armchair, with a feeling of helplessness overcoming him.

'John, can you help with these bags, or better still, our son!'

He stood, moved to the hallway, to be greeted by John junior, red-faced and smiling, with his arms outstretched to his father.

'You look tired again, John, or should that be worried. I know that face. Come on, let's get some food inside you, and you can regale me with all the sordid details re—'

'I'm fine, but those two, they really need to sort things out between them. Secrets always reveal themselves in the end.'

Looking at him with a curious, puzzled expression, she said,

'OK, take laughing boy here into the lounge and keep him occupied while I make something to eat.'

'Right, John, those two are seriously disturbing you, aren't they? Tell me, what's so significant that—'

A frenzied knocking on their door prematurely put an end to their *tête à tête*.

'Goodness, John, who can that be, hammering away like that? Better check, it might be poor Miss Stevens downstairs again. Go on, see who it is.'

Getting slowly up from his chair, he left the room and went to the front door. The person on the other side of the door stopped the hammering, and he stood, listening. Maybe it was a prankster, and he turned back, feeling tired, but before he'd reached the lounge a familiar voice cried out.

'I know you're there, John, let me in! It's important.'

He went back to the door and opened it to discover Anita. She had a terrified, wild look, and seemed in a confused state, pushing past him and into the lounge.

'This is a surprise, Anita,' Marilyn said, apprehensively, given the frenzied look on her friend's face. 'I take it this isn't a social ca—'

'He's dead!'

'What? Who?'

'I killed him.'

Speechless for a few seconds, Marilyn responded,

'What? How did this happen?'

When Anita, staring wide-eyed at the window behind Marilyn, didn't answer, she grabbed her by the shoulders, shouting,

'Is he at home?'

She turned her head to Marilyn, beginning to shiver.

'I... I'm not...'

'Well, you must know where this "killing" occurred! Anita, are you listening?'

'He's in the living room... I... I'm not... I...'

John, dazed, and concerned by what he perceived to be Anita's mental state, gently took her by the arm.

'We're going there, now... I said now, Anita! Tell the police, Marilyn, quickly!'

Twenty minutes later, having taken the front door key from her, they entered the house. He switched on the hallway light and made his way hurriedly into the living room. After fumbling against the doorway, he found the light switch. Looking around the large, overly furnished lounge, he couldn't see David. Walking behind the sofa, John spotted a briefcase lying, opened, next to the drinks cabinet, with various official-looking papers strewn across the carpet.

Only now realising Anita wasn't in the room, he called out, very confused,

'He's not in here, Anita. I'll check upstairs, perhaps he's in the bedroom.'

She came into the lounge and sat on one of the armchairs, saying nothing.

'You told me you'd killed him! What the hell's been going on between you two?'

Silence.

'Well? You obviously haven't killed him, have you? I'll call his mobile, just to make—'

'No!' she screamed at him as she lunged for the phone in his hand. 'You can't... I should never have listened to you earlier! Why did he... I was never going to—'

John, convinced now that his friend was alive, looked at her and, taking her limp, cold hand, said in a low, calm voice,

'You're coming back to our place, you're in no fit state to—'

The loud wailing of a police vehicle startled both of them. It stopped directly in front of the house. Two burly, taciturn officers emerged. They ran up to the front door.

John shouted,

'Sorry, guys, it appears to be a wasted trip. We've just checked in the house. My friend isn't in. A misunderstanding and—'

'Was it you made the call?' the older officer barked at John. 'Something about a dead body at this residence?'

'Err, no, my wife did, after Mrs Murray turned up at our place in a very disturbed state, as you can see, but as I said, a miscommunication. She got a message about a death and thought it concerned her husband. I think she's suffering from a nervous collapse, working too hard in a stressful job—'

John stopped, wondering how he'd managed to cook up this version of events, and gazed at the two officers.

The policemen looked at each other, and then Anita, who sat, impassive, her lips moving silently. The second one said, after scratching his head,

'A mix-up? Sure it wasn't a practical joke? We've got enough on our plate without nutters and attention seekers wasting our time. Maybe we should take a look inside, just to be sure.'

John sat Anita in the study, and said,

'I'll show them round, don't worry.'

The three men proceeded to walk around the house. In the bedroom John said, quietly,

'I think this hinges on a domestic disturbance,' and he went on, 'I suspect they've been having problems recently. That briefcase on the floor there, and those papers, well... Anita's always been highly strung.'

Not looking convinced, the senior policeman responded,

'OK, sir, but we'll need to follow up. What's the guy's moniker, David something—'

'David Murray. I'll give you his office and mobile numbers.'

'Fine. Thanks. Tell the lady she's damn lucky we're not taking this any further.'

'Will do, and thanks.'

John took a silent, brooding Anita to his flat. Climbing the stairs, he eyeballed his wife peering out from behind the curtain. Anita followed him to the front door, which Marilyn had opened, and the two walked quietly into the house.

'Would you like a cup of tea, Anita?' she asked, trying to appear unconcerned. 'You're looking tired.'

'Yes please, and I'm sorry... I can't think—'

She burst into hysterical sobs, covering her face with her hands. Marilyn moved forward, clearly upset, and was about to embrace Anita, who pulled back, saying in a surprisingly determined voice,

'Listen, John, after I called on you today, I went back to the flat. Dave wasn't home, in fact he still hasn't come back. I recalled he mentioned something about a meeting with that... that pervert, so I decided to pre-empt any trouble, to stop him telling Dave... by going over to his house. When I got there, I saw the front door was open to the four winds... But I ventured in, thinking they'd already started. I shouted out, but there was no answer. I went into the lounge, but from behind me, someone shouted out, a garbled, angry voice... And I... Then I panicked and ran, out of the house, into the street, and then to the Tube. When I... I...'

She fainted, crashing off her seat and onto the floor. Marilyn kneeled over her and shouted at John,

'Quick, don't just stand there, help me put her on the sofa. We should let her sleep it off, she smells strongly of whisky.'

They lifted her, and laid her carefully on the sofa. She began to move awkwardly, and seemed to be settling, until the sound of John's mobile brought her round. She sat upright, her eyes wide, with a terrified look, and blurted out,

'I've killed Streeter... I'm sure he...'

With those words, she lay back and went to sleep.

'Who is it, John?' said Marilyn, as she moved Anita's arms to her side.

'Dave. He's on his way over here. He sounded distracted. Is she OK lying there? Maybe we should take her to casualty.'

'No, let her sleep for the time being. I presume David wants to speak with her. What's all the secrecy for, John?'

'The short version is that Streeter wants Dave out, and he's been using some underhand tactics to effect it. That photo being one of his efforts. It was a set-up.'

'Set-up?'

'The girl, Eva whatever, I'm sure she was in on the scheme, getting Dave blotto, and then the picture.'

'Is that all? Surely—'

'Anita has her own problem too. When Dave was mooted as the candidate, his campaign was floundering until Streeter made his move. He visited her and made the suggestion that if Anita was willing to sleep with him, Dave would sail through—'

'Anita's got her fair share of faults, but—'

'I know, the idea's way out there, and she told me she never contemplated... But she played a dangerous game, leading him on, but Streeter's motive revolved around blackmail, not sex... A lever to get rid of Dave for political, or more accurately, business reasons should he become troublesome. These bastards really are the pits—'

The doorbell rang. John opened the door. David barged past him and into the lounge, and seeing Anita on the sofa, said, with a voice near to breaking,

'What's happened? Is she… OK?'

'Yes, David,' Marilyn said, patting his shoulder, 'she's overtired, I think. Let her rest for the moment.'

'Christ, she's really done it now… I've just been over at Streeter's place, John. When I got there the front door was open, but I went in, and there he was, lying on the floor groaning, with blood running from his nose and mouth. I phoned for the ambulance, and his wife came in, but I don't think she eyeballed me, then I legged it to our place. Anita wasn't in. So, I've… The thing is, John… I found her handbag, Anita's, on the floor at Streeter's, in the hallway, open. She must have been there. Why?'

'Sit down, David,' said Marilyn, 'I'll put the kettle on.'

The two men sat. David, looking anxiously at Anita, said,

'John, why do you think she went over to see him? Was it to meet me? She knew I had a meeting scheduled—'

'Let's wait for Anita to enlighten us, Dave. She would have had a good reason. Was he badly hurt, do you think?'

'Probably not, John, but why would she have whacked him?'

'That's an assumption, Dave. Here's the tea.'

Chapter Forty-Nine

Anita woke ten minutes after her husband arrived. She slowly raised herself from the sofa, and surveying the other three, smiled weakly at David, who jumped up from his chair, ran over and hugged her.

'Thank Christ you're OK, Anita!' he said, stroking her hair. 'Why did you go over to Streeter's place? I didn't—'

'I don't think you should be talking about that just now, David,' said Marilyn, 'can't you see she's not a hundred per cent?'

'No, it's fine, Marilyn,' Anita said, almost in a whisper, 'I'm a bit clearer now, but could you get me a drink, soft, that is.'

Marilyn, shaking her head, and frowning at David, went into the kitchen.

'Dave, where were you? I wanted to see you before you spoke with… I had something to tell… no, to confess, about him and me—'

'Marilyn's right, love, you're not up to—'

'Dave, he propositioned me, when you were chasing after that useless Benfleet constituency. He made a deal, or thought he had: if I slept with him, he'd ensure you'd—'

David, stunned, said,

'You aren't serious, Anita!'

'I am. But believe me, Dave, I had no intention to carry it through, and I thought he'd given up, but now, after that photo... That's it... He's trying to destroy our marriage and your prospects, because of—'

She lay back on the sofa, covering her face with her hands, sobbing, a picture of misery. David, equally miserable, took her hand and said,

'Anita, I know you were there earlier today... No, don't look at me like that. I found your handbag, and brought it back here. No one spotted me, so you're in the clear. The bastard got what he deserved, and he can stick his constituency up his fat... I'm fed up with all the bullshit that goes with being an "honourable member". The very description's a sick joke.'

She sat up and put her arms around his shoulders, kissing his cheek.

'Wait, wait! I'm not finished. That photo, Anita. I should have known better than to go to a "party" with Eva. She's a sly one, but I was always trusting with people, and—'

'That's enough for now, David, let her rest,' said Marilyn.

*

Anita seemed to recover quickly, and the next morning she and David went back home. Over the course of the week, however, she became increasingly agitated.

'Dave, I'm going to the police.'

Knowing what she was referring to, David affected ignorance.

'Why?'

'I need to tell them what happened over at Streeter's place that night. Don't even try to talk me out of it. This needs closure, Dave. I mean it.'

'Before you even think about that, I've got a surgery at the office today, and if I see him, well—'

'OK,' she said, 'I'm going into work this morning, to resign.'

'You're kidding me! After all that hard work, the sacrifices you've made. It's not—'

'Fair? Maybe not, but recently I've had the distinct impression I'm being patronised, humoured by the suits, pompous self-satisfied windbags, telling each other how enlightened they are, promoting a woman. And as you've found out since you were foolish enough to take me on, I don't like the feeling. Dave, do not try to argue. The decision's made, so I can start looking around for a real job, well away from the piranhas. And anyway, Brussels sucks.'

David arrived at his constituency office at ten.

'Morning, Stella,' he greeted the surly volunteer at reception, and noticing her troubled look, said, 'something the matter?'

'Mr Streeter has resigned from the committee. Unfortunately, I opened his letter by mistake, didn't see the "P&C" on the envelope. It seems his wife's health has got much worse, so he's taking her on a cruise.'

David, hiding his satisfaction at this turn of events, said,

'Oh dear, I wasn't aware Mrs Streeter was poorly, but I'm sure he's done the honourable thing, Stella.'

'That's right, Mr Murray, honourable, you chose the right word. Such a polite man too. We'll miss him.'

David went into his office and called Anita, without response, and before he could think, his first constituent came in.

An hour later, as he was listening to an old man, very angry at having been ignored by the council over his housing benefit, the phone rang.

'Hello, David Murray.'

'Good morning, sir, Sergeant McMillan here. We've got your wife at the station, in a state of some distress. Can you come down and collect her?'

Shocked, David ran his free hand through his hair and said,

'Why is she with you? What's happened? Is she… Has she been in an acci—'

'Yes, sir, she's fine, physically, but she turned up here an hour ago, claiming to have assaulted a guy called Streeter. Initially we took her seriously, and we checked with this Streeter bloke. He told us she was mistaken, because although your wife insisted, very strongly, that she attacked him last Tuesday, he said that he was out that evening. Odd, though, the officer I sent along said he had an angry-looking nose. His wife confirmed his story. If you don't mind me saying, Mr Murray, I think you should take your wife to her doctor. She seems unwell.'

'I'll be with you in a few minutes, sergeant, thank you for your concern. My wife has been under a serious amount of strain recently, and I'll take note of your suggestion.'

He took Anita home. She was visibly shaken, and apologised, saying,

'I'm sorry, Dave, but I had to make a clean breast of it, no matter what that creep has told you—'

'I didn't speak with him, Anita. He's left the committee, officially because his wife is ill, and they've decided to go off on a cruise, over Niagara Falls with a bit of luck. The police haven't had any reports of incidents near their house, so you can rest easy, he won't be raising the issue. Scared the missus might hear of his repulsive behaviour toward you. I almost wish he had been at the office. I might—'

'No, Dave, you wouldn't have, but I feel cheated.'

'I'm not with you.'

'I committed a crime, and should be held accountable.'

'Come off it, Anita, he got what he deserved, and in theory, you could argue that you were the victim of a crime – his attempt at blackmail.'

'Oh, very clever, almost devious, a very political response, Dave. It's a serious matter, of right and wrong, and—'

'If you're so worried, go and see old Father what's-his-name for confession. In his shoes, I'd tell you to say three Hail Marys or whatever you Catholics do to absolve yourselves.'

She smiled.

*

John and Marilyn were surprised a week later by an invitation to a dinner party from their friends. Following Anita's visit to the police station, David had called John and told him the sequence of events, which he passed on to Marilyn.

'Thank goodness, John. That will be a weight off her shoulders, but giving up that career... I hope she knows what she's doing. Anita's a very active, "has to be busy" kind of person. I'll get Mother to babysit, although John junior might be getting too much of a handful these days.'

They turned up at seven, and were greeted warmly by Anita. Both of them were impressed by her mood; she appeared to be back to her old, confident self.

'Just the four of us, Dave?' said John, surveying the dining table, laid out for six, as he took the offered glass from his relieved-looking friend.

'Two more, a surprise, to me as well. Anita insisted on them coming along. She wants to have a chat with—'

'Oh yes, who, Dave?'

David, grinning, said,

'Two people, both by the surname of McTaggart.'

'Why on earth… Wait, you a "chat", with Fred? That can only mean—'

'John, you know Fred's a born again Eurosceptic, and talking to an insider was too much for him to resist—'

'I thought Anita's opinion of him was less than complimentary but… She's bound by the Official Secrets Act, Dave. She can't divulge—'

'Yes, John, but she fully intends to let slip a few interesting leads for the old soak to sniff after. Nothing criminal, she assures me, only the misinformation side of things.'

'I'd warn her not to—'

The doorbell rang. David went to the hall, and in came Fred, carrying two bottles, with his niece behind him.

'Good evening, my friends! Where's mine hostess? I must donate these bottles of Chateau Ayrshire to her. The very finest gibbering juice. Helped young Rabbie with his seduction technique back in the day, although I read somewhere that on occasion he drank so much of it himself that he couldn't rise—'

'Now, now, Fred,' said Marilyn, kissing his cheek. 'Have you recovered fully after that—'

'Yes, my dear.'

'I hope you're going to behave. I see that glint in your eye.'

'Being in the company of three beautiful women, it's no wonder, my dear Marion.'

Over dinner, the conversation flowed easily, with hardly any mention of politics – odd, given the proximity of the election – until Anita stood, holding her glass, and said,

'Friends, a toast to my husband, the soon-to-be ex-MP for Benfleet!'

'This is news to me, Dave,' said a very surprised-looking Fred. 'Had enough of the shit factory, my friend? Oh, *entre nous*, that old lecher Streeter's got the heave-ho. To the relief of many a young chap in the corridors of—'

Anita sat down, suddenly very agitated and said, obviously surprised,

'What did you say, Fred? Young men?'

'Yes, my dear Anita. Behind that respectable, stuffy exterior, he harbours the tastes which were extolled in many an ancient Greek ode—'

'Are you saying he's gay?' said Anita, her face ashen, which Fred picked up on.

'Yes, but in more common parlance, he's a wanker, possibly literally if his advances are unsuccessful. And—'

'That's enough, Fred,' said John, also having noticed Anita's reaction, 'we aren't at *The Swiftian*, trading lurid gossip.'

'My apologies, dear lady. I'm getting too long in the tooth to be shocked by anything these cretins get up to, but, as we all know, power corrupts, eats the soul, so we should all be glad we don't have any – power, I mean.'

Anita, recovered, and laughing at his monologue, nodded her head vigorously and said,

'Dave tells me he and his bitch of a wife have fled on a world cruise, but to hell with him. Fred darling, do you know of anyone who might appreciate the unexpurgated musings of a former insider?'

'Anita, I—'

'Oh shut up, Dave,' she barked, 'get that bottle of malt. Is that to your taste, Fred?'

'Do I recognise the voice of a fellow "swivel-eyed loony"?'

'No, Fred, you don't. They're all resident in Brussels, and sections of the FO,' Anita said with a sarcastic laugh. 'We all know what FO stands for, don't we? "Foreigners' Office."'

'That's funny,' Fred responded with a laugh, 'and more polite than the much more basic, but equally accurate—'

David, getting nervous, said tentatively,

'It's getting late, folks, after midnight now, so perhaps…'

'Yes, we have to rescue my mother too,' said an equally nervous Marilyn, and embracing Anita said, under her breath, 'are you OK?'

'Of course I am, Marilyn! You're not my nurse. And before you make the suggestion, I'm not going to see any trickcyclist either!'

'Thanks for coming, guys, and don't fret about the mess, Dave's got time on his hands now. I'm knackered, so if you can shift yourselves, I'll see you later. Night!'

Chapter Fifty

Two issues later, a long, detailed article surfaced in *The Swiftian*, quoting 'impeccable, but unnamed sources', laying out what the paper claimed to be the preparations being made for the forthcoming referendum on Britain's membership of the European Union. The paper quoted an 'authoritative figure, close to government' who asserted that officials in Brussels and Whitehall were said to be apoplectic following the passing of the bill to allow a vote. It had been assumed privately that the politicians' commitment to the idea was merely a bribe to a gullible electorate.

In spite of her husband's unease and concern, Anita admitted to him the day following the appearance of *The Swiftian* that she had, in her words, 'spilled the beans' on what she insisted was the determination of her erstwhile colleagues to ensure the 'correct' result.

Fred was ecstatic at the furore the article created, telling John not to concern himself over any repercussions: 'The circulation's gone through the roof, Johnny boy. The bastards don't like it up 'em. Tough!'

Unsurprisingly, the government, in a paroxysm of self-righteous shock, ordered an immediate inquiry to pinpoint the leak, an official telling the assembled press that 'no stone would be unturned, to root out the person responsible'. A day later, four heavies, posing as policemen, descended on *The Swiftian*'s office, using a warrant to sift through every filing cabinet in the place, without success it should be said. Both Fred and John, who'd taken down Anita's testimony, hadn't committed anything to paper, or their laptops, but had been questioned for hours, again fruitlessly from the authorities' viewpoint.

Suspicion fell on Anita after a colleague in the Brussels office pointed the finger, and she was taken in for interrogation, but the police, without any physical evidence, and faced with her outright denial of disclosing anything she said might be, in her words, 'against the national interest', released her the following day. David went to the police station where she was being interrogated and insisted on staying there until she came out.

'Hello, Dave,' she said as she walked defiantly along the corridor from the interview suite. 'I've a good mind to sue these cretins. I'm still, officially, a civil servant, and this is how they treat loyal staff!'

A burly man came up to them and said,

'Your passport will be returned once all our enquiries are completed, Mrs Murray. You may go now.'

'Where do they get these goons from, Dave?' she said, and with a sarcastic laugh, 'Sorry, Dave, that city break in Brussels will have to be cancelled – permanently.'

Still with her trademark cynicism she asked, rhetorically,

'You don't suppose I'll get a reference from my soon-to-be previous employer, do you?'

They went to John and Marilyn's for a prearranged dinner. Marilyn had berated her husband for what she termed his collaboration with Fred in putting Anita into the 'line of fire'.

'All this excitement over the vote, it's a smokescreen,' John said, dismissively. 'The thing will be rigged, doctored, to ensure we stay in the system. Just look at what Anita said they've been up to. They're masters of the dark arts.'

During the meal Anita hogged the conversation, telling the other three about her new idea: to start up a consultancy business, specialising in advising small firms in their dealings with the EU Commission's trade requirements.

'With my background, I'm bound to attract clients. The mountain of regulations surrounding cross-border transactions is mind-boggling—'

'Is that wise, Anita?' said John, with an anxious look at David.

'Are you questioning my judgement again? You should stick to writing those tedious articles and leave—'

'OK, OK, Anita,' said Marilyn, 'he means well, and you know he cares for you in that respect—'

'In what respect, Marilyn? I'm capable of making rational decisions. You, of all people, should know. No one pushes me around, intimidates me.'

Turning to John, she went on,

'That's one thing I do admire about that sexist dipso you work with: he's fearless, despite the physical intimidation—'

Startled, John said,

'Why did you bring Fred's altercations into the conversation... Wait, are you—'

'Oh for Christ's sake! You can't be that naïve, John. The man's a pain in the arse for too many significant people, although I never did understand why he irked them so much. For all his wonderfully bombastic rants about Europe, his journal wasn't exactly a bestseller, or influential. My old colleagues in Brussels were avid readers. "*Fou*" was how they described him. They used to laugh themselves silly at his hyperbolic language.'

'You're implying—'

'Saying, John. Despite the guy liking to think of himself as some kind of martyr to his Euroscepticism, the truth is more prosaic. I'll grant you, he and his wife – Sylvia, isn't it? – were victims of a simple mugging, but the other two incidents, well...'

'Your imagination's as vivid as ever, Anita,' said Marilyn. 'Fred's mouth is his worst enemy, shouting off his opinions in pubs the way he does. It's not really surprising that he could end up in fisticuffs, and I—'

'Think what you like, Marilyn,' Anita said, her voice slightly raised, 'but I—'

'But what?' said John.

Anita took her glass, drained it, and, looking solemn, said,

'Fred was on the point of uncovering some very unusual business deals being mooted over there, with a few individuals here, and in Brussels, more than anxious to keep their... less than conventional activities quiet.'

She continued, warming to her subject.

'Oh, what the hell! That's probably why he was done over, firstly as a warning, and the second time, well, he's lucky that he's got such a thick skull.

'I'll say this for him though: the reason he kept schtum, not telling you, John, about who he was going to see before the second mugging was...' she stopped, and after a few moments went on, 'because he was aware how dangerous these people were... are, and you have a family, John... There I go again, motormouth. For God's sake don't say anything to him, he'd only deny it anyway.'

*

Anita's typically confident assertion that his mentor had been targeted troubled John, to the extent that, despite her insistence on not bringing it up with him, he confronted Fred the next day.

'I'd book her for a psych exam, John, the woman's off the beam. Oh, I'm sorry, forget I said that, but she's definitely been taken in by those Le Carré fantasies—'

'What are you—'

'Yes, what I mean is … Why would any serious, rational person be perturbed, undermined, threatened, by the admittedly acerbic pieces we publish? When are we ever mentioned, let alone reviewed, by our illustrious peers in the print or broadcast media? Joe Public is largely blissfully unaware of *The Swiftian*'s existence. And the notion that I, a run-of-the-mill hack, would be the subject of one of those contracts you see in godawful films… Just crazy.'

'Don't try to belittle what happened, Fred. I think you should be circumspect in public.'

He smiled at John.

'Don't you concern yourself, Johnny boy. I'm packing heat from now on,' he said, patting John on the shoulder, and then, with his familiar full-throated laugh, 'and before you ask, there's no truth in the rumour that I'm on the government's Christmas card list. Stop worrying about me. Me, on a hit list! Don't be stupid.'

John, although amused, again, by his friend's childish attitude, said,

'Anita told us you were on the point of breaking a… Who was it you made an appointment with—'

'You don't want to know—'

'Yes, Fred, I do.'

His face taking on an uncharacteristically stern look, Fred replied,

'OK then, Johnny boy, I got a call, from a Belgian number, advising me to… to meet with a guy called Marco – I wasn't given his surname – but when I got to the meeting point, I had that rendezvous with a couple of… less than friendly members of the public.'

John, stunned at the reference to 'Marco', said,

'Fred, when I was on that fruitless gig in Brussels, I saw Anita talking to—'

'Yes, John, I know, Anita. She's a very surprising woman. I recall describing her as fearsome, to her enemies, most of them in official circles, I'd warrant. That's a suitable adjective, but for the rest of us, well, fearless is a better description.'

'As I was trying to say, I overheard, and saw, Anita having something of a discussion with a guy she referred to as "Marco" but she didn't mention him during our discussions with her when we were preparing that article, did she?'

'No, that's true, but what she did tell us confirmed my theory: Marco was merely a ruse, a bait, to get me to go along to meet my two friendly assailants. I couldn't resist it, John. I'd heard through one of my snouts – Christ, I'm talking like the Old Bill – one of my sources, I should say, that old Streeter and said Marco were trying to scam some euros out of… never mind. You know better than me, John, that if you know the right people over there, acquiring funds for any old piece of dodgy business is easier than Joe Public could ever imagine.'

Epilogue

As the 2015 general election approached, David stood by his intention to leave politics, and on a warm, sultry evening, Anita went with him to the Benfleet constituency office, to be met by the new chairman, Guy Wilson. The dialogue was short; Wilson made no attempt to persuade David to reconsider his decision. As they left the building and walked toward their car, they were accosted by a young woman David, blushing, recognised: Eva, Wilson's daughter.

'Hello again, Dave,' she said, wearing a broad grin, 'and hello, Anita. Left Brussels, I hear.'

'Come on, Dave, let's go, the air's not too fragrant around here.'

Unlocking the car, he said,

'Thanks, Anita, I was more than half expecting you to, well, react a bit more aggressively.'

'We all have our faults, Dave, no point in stirring up the past.'

*

Anita started up, as she'd outlined to her friends, a consultancy business, which struggled in its first few months, and David became increasingly concerned for her, as she seemed to be preoccupied by the effort of consolidating the firm's few clients. He noticed her getting more and more on edge, and began to consider there was something outside of work troubling her.

For her thirty-fourth birthday he surprised her by booking a city break to Venice, thinking the atmosphere of La Serenissima would act as a tonic. She appeared pleased, but on their first evening, sitting in a canalside bar, she said, her face serious, and slightly apprehensive, 'Dave, you think you know me, don't you?'

'Of course I know you, for nearly six years. The best six years of my life, obviously.'

'No, I mean, what I'm really like, the—'

'Oh, your personality. Yes, you're something else, babe. Nobody messes with my Anita.'

She frowned, and he thought he saw a tear, but she put her hand on his arm and said,

'Listen to me, I have to get this off my chest. Years ago, I did a terrible thing, a terrible, heartless thing, something that can never leave me.'

David, very worried, said, 'Come on, Anita, nothing's that bad, to make you like this—'

Looking genuinely frightened, something he hadn't seen previously, she went on,

'Dave, you know about Marilyn and her fiancé, Grant? Well, that night, the night he was killed, when he was supposed to be picking her up after he'd come off duty… he'd been with me.'

David, not following, said,

'With you? How? I don't understand. He was killed before he was due to meet Marilyn—'

'Yes, Dave, but the reason he died, the reason, was because of me. We'd been seeing each other, behind her back. She thought the sun shone out of his arse, more fool her as it turned out...'

David, shocked, said, 'You're saying you were going out with this...'

'Grant.'

'With this Grant, what a bastard! Two-timing his fiancée. Right, I can see why it would have upset you, but—'

'No, Dave. I knew they were engaged, and that she was expecting.'

'Then, why for the love of Christ were you—'

'Because... because when she snubbed me after an incident at university, I made a point of getting my own back. When I first met the guy, I wasn't aware Marilyn was involved with him until one night, when he'd gone to the gents, his mobile rang... which he'd left on the bar, and I saw Marilyn's picture on it.'

'God, Anita, why didn't you stop seeing him?'

'I wanted to pay her back.'

'For what?'

'I know, it's stupid, nasty and childish. The whole thing's been eating away at me ever since he died. I was too chicken to go to his funeral. I couldn't have looked Marilyn in the eye, and it was only when we were planning our wedding that I plucked up enough courage, after a good few shots, to invite her. And you know the worst, just about unbearable part of it, Dave? She thanked me – me! – for inviting her. "Thanks, Anita," she said, "sorry for blanking you all these years, it was unkind of me."'

David sat, unable to utter a word, and tears filled his eyes.

Noticing this, she said,

'Yes, I can see it. You hate me. Trouble is, Dave, I love you, so much, but if you want to—'

Stuttering, he said, 'If you're the person I think you are, you'll confess this to Marilyn.'

'I did, Dave, last Friday.'

'That must have been awkward, for her as well as you.'

'I, and most of our peers, at school and university, used to laugh at her, constantly ribbing her about that straight-as-a-die outlook of hers, but she never responded in kind.'

'So, how did she react? Have you lost your best friend now?'

'I blurted it out, quickly, assuming I'd be shown the door, but she just stood, looking at me and then, God, how can she... threw her arms around me.'

'What did she say, eventually?'

'It was strange, Dave, she spoke very calmly, you know the way she does, but her tone gave away... Well, as I said, strange.'

'Don't ever refer to it, or him, again, Anita. This is in our past, and as far as I'm concerned, is buried there. The subject is closed. I'm impressed, really, that you came to tell me... It was very brave of you.'

David, still reeling from the confession said, with a tremulous voice,

'The woman's a saint.'

'Yes, but she insisted that John should never know, so don't...'

'No.'

*

Marilyn had been startled when, a week previously, at just after nine on a rainy morning, the doorbell rang insistently. She switched off the television and went to open the door: Anita.

'Can I come in, Marilyn?' she asked, sounding anxious.

'Yes. Of course, come on in, you're soaking. It's inclement out there. Are you feeling alright? You look terrible, Anita. Has something happened? David?'

'No, he's OK, but, Marilyn… I need to. Christ! Have to… tell you something.'

Later that afternoon, Marilyn walked along to collect her son from school. Since Anita had unloaded her guilt and genuine, so it seemed to her, remorse, Marilyn had thought of nothing else. Determined as she was not to divulge Anita's tearful confession to anyone, her conscience began to weigh uncomfortably on her. She and John had always been completely frank and honest with each other, and now there was something which she had decided to conceal from him. Despite telling herself that it was for the best, she found the dilemma almost unbearable. Why should she withhold the confession? Anita had been more than a bitch to her in their school and college days. Then the thought occurred: observing at close quarters her friend's behaviour since they had reconciled at Anita's wedding, Marilyn came to the conclusion that the woman must have been in constant emotional turmoil, reasoning that although Anita might have hoped her burden of guilt would lighten with time, instead it had burgeoned to the point where it had brought her close to despair.

Standing at the school gate, one of the mothers said, 'Are you OK, Marilyn? Is something the matter?'

'No, I'm fine,' Marilyn said, only now noticing the tears running down her cheek, 'that boy, he's always passing on his germs.'

*

John remained ignorant of Anita's confession, but, late one evening a few days later, he said, after a bottle of red,

'Marilyn, has Anita had a personality transplant? She's been, well, almost civil recently.'

'Maybe she's finally maturing, seeing the good in people instead of her "the whole world's out to get me" attitude. I think she's come to terms with—'

'What?' John asked, surprised by his wife's phrase, 'come to terms.' 'Strange expression.'

'Realising that always looking for the worst in people gets… leads to unhappiness, anger, and makes you ill, emotionally.'

'There you go again, Marilyn, overlooking her sometimes cruel words and actions. Some might say you took the gospels literally: "let him without sin cast the first stone", I think the saying goes.'

'Yes, but you've omitted the second part: "go, and sin no more".'

'What do you mean… Are you referring to Anita? Sins? Tell me more.'

'No I wasn't. Nothing to tell.'

'Unusually cryptic, for you. Fancy opening that other bottle of red winking at us? I'm thirsty.' A wry smile appearing on his face, John leant forward and said,

'You don't suppose she'll be taking up holy orders anytime soon? Taking on good habits?'

Recovering composure with John's flippant, semi-inebriated remarks, she said,

'No, that's out of the question. Listen, John, keep this to yourself until it's… She's pregnant, against doctor's advice, I believe.'

'Good grief! So that's why she's… Dave's not—'

'Obviously not. I was stunned when she told me, but that's typical Anita. As determined as ever.'

'That explains something.'

'What?'

'Oh, Dave called me at work last Friday. Apparently he was surprised, sounded worried actually, when he got out of bed. She wasn't in the house. He asked if Anita had come to ours. Seems he's been concerned about her state of mind the last few weeks, so I told him what you'd said to me, you know, about that party the two of you were planning with old Delany.'